The Day I Wandered to the Ghost Town

A Mystery in Virginia

William C. O'Sullivan

Copyright © 2025 William C. O'Sullivan

First Edition- 2025

E-book ISBN-978-1-8380806-9-3

Paperback ISBN-978-1-9193224-0-7

Hardcover ISBN-978-1-9193224-1-4

www.williamosullivan.co.uk

Editors: Malory Wood & Judith Sophia

Editor: William C. O'Sullivan

Cover Illustration: Canva Pty Ltd

Cover Design, Interior Illustrations, & Interior Design: RH Publishing

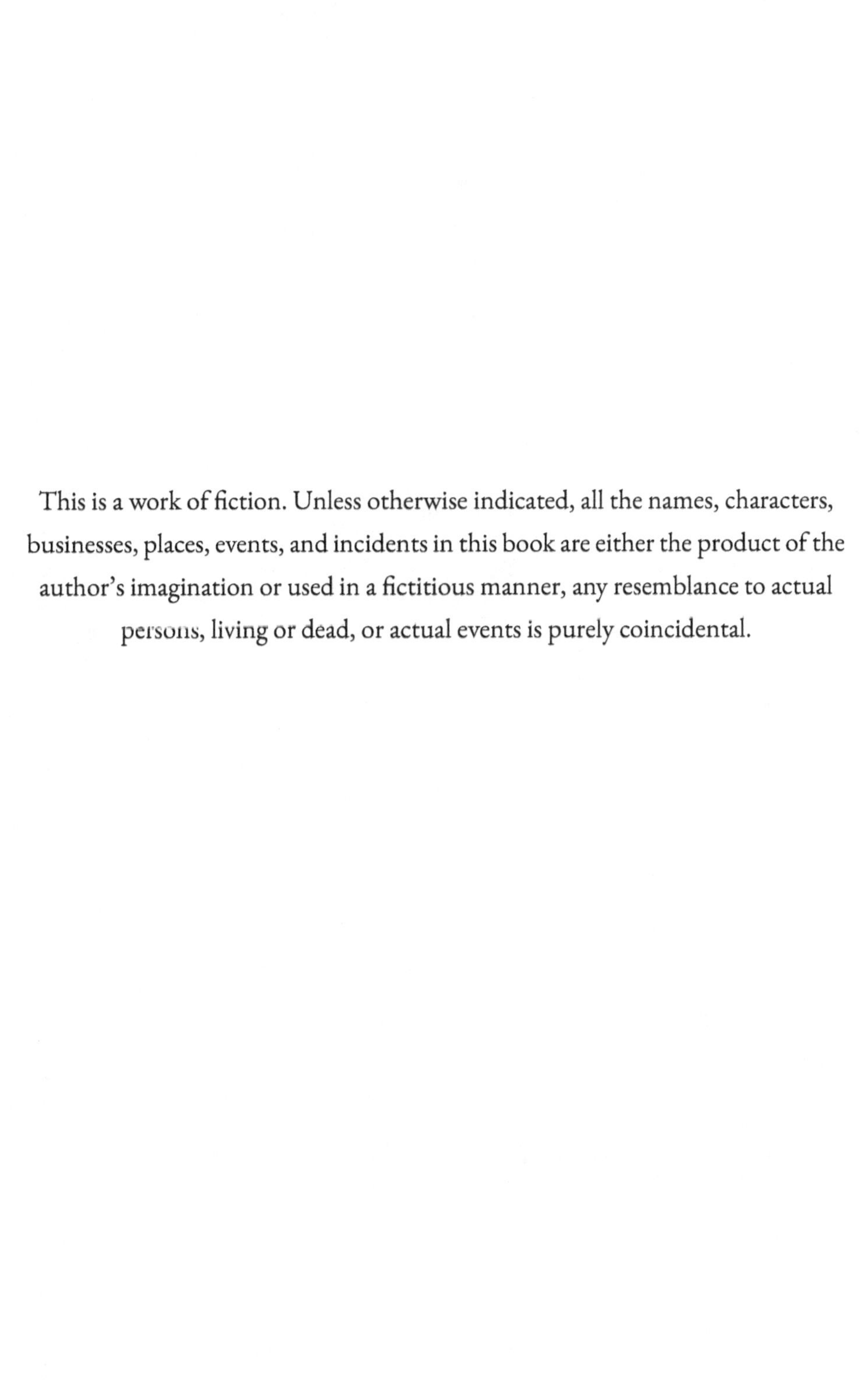

This is a work of fiction. Unless otherwise indicated, all the names, characters, businesses, places, events, and incidents in this book are either the product of the author's imagination or used in a fictitious manner, any resemblance to actual persons, living or dead, or actual events is purely coincidental.

Contents

"All that we see or seem is but a dream within a dream."

- Edgar Allan Poe

1

A Mysterious Encounter

A thunderclap split the August night sky over Blacksburg, Virginia, in 1971. Rain drummed against the dusty windows of the Iron Man Inn, the only bar still open on Main Street after midnight. Inside, the air hung thick with the bite of cigar smoke and stale beer.

Ebenezer O'Rourke pushed through the door, shaking off the rain from his coat. A journalist for *The Virginia Daily*, and a man long resigned to his solitude, he carried the weary look of someone who'd spent too many nights chasing headlines that led nowhere.

He took his usual seat at the bar and rapped twice on the counter. "Double whiskey on the rocks," he said, voice rough from smoke and exhaustion.

The bartender, polishing a glass with a rag that had seen better days, raised an eyebrow. "Rough day, I take it?"

Ebenezer gave a humorless chuckle. "You could say that. Deadlines, rewrites... and not a single happy story in the lot."

The whiskey came fast. He lifted the glass in a small salute, then downed it in one long swallow. The burn hit his throat, warm and sharp, grounding him.

On the counter beside him lay today's *Virginia Daily*. The headline blurred in the dim light, but one word caught his eye—*Missing*. He frowned, slid the paper closer, and began to read.

On the front page of the article, the headline read: *Ghost Towns in Virginia.*

Ebenezer frowned, scanning the words carefully, his brow creasing in thought. He scratched the side of his head, wondering what it would be like to explore one of those forgotten places himself. *Would I ever get the chance to cover a story like that?* he mused silently.

His eyes drifted to the byline. "Christian Painter," he muttered, a small smile forming. "He wrote this one. Figures—always chasing the strange stuff."

The bar door creaked open. Ebenezer turned toward the sound. An old man, easily in his seventies, stepped inside. He wore a weathered coat, a beaten cowboy hat, faded blue jeans, and black boots scuffed from years of wear. As he approached the counter, a musty smell drifted through the air—like an old coat that had not seen daylight in twenty years.

The man placed his hands on the bar. "Hey, waiter, can I get a beer? And make sure it's a cold one, thank you."

Ebenezer watched him, curious. "Evening, old timer," he said casually.

The old man turned, eyes shadowed beneath the brim of his hat. "Howdy," he replied in a low, gravelly voice.

Ebenezer leaned slightly toward him. "What is your name? I haven't seen you around this neighbourhood. Out of town, I am guessing?"

"My name's Grant," the old man said, tipping his hat slightly. "And no, I am not from this part of town. I am originally from Abingdon, Virginia."

Ebenezer smiled, setting his glass down and extending a hand. "Pleased to meet you, Grant. My name is Ebenezer. Born and raised right here in Blacksburg. What brings you to town?"

Grant cleared his throat before shaking Ebenezer's hand. His grip was firm, rough—like someone used to challenging work. "Just passing through," he said. "Figured I'd take in the sights, see what this place is all about."

Ebenezer nodded, amused. "Oh, I see. Not much to look at, but she's got her charm."

Grant's gaze shifted to the newspaper on the counter. He leaned closer, the dim light catching the lines around his eyes. "I have been to Damascus—near the Creeper Trail. Heard some stories about that place. Folks say it is haunted."

Ebenezer laughed, a sharp bark that made a few heads turn. "Really? You believe in all that?"

Grant did not smile. His eyes stayed fixed on Ebenezer, calm but serious. "It's true," he said quietly. "The article in that paper—every word of it. But it does not tell the full story."

Ebenezer leaned back on his stool, still chuckling. "And pigs will fly," he said, waving a dismissive hand.

Grant did not answer. He just stared into his beer, the corner of his mouth twitching—not a smile, not a frown.

Grant does not look impressed. His brow tightens, and he sets his drink down with a heavy clink. "This is not a joking matter, son. What I have seen and heard is something I never thought I would believe in—until that very day I heard noises in the town and felt an unusual energy." He leans forward, voice dropping. "What I'm about to say is this town is haunted. And whoever went to Damascus... they never came back alive, from what I have heard."

Ebenezer's face drains of colour. He fidgets with his sleeve, his nervousness betraying him. "So, Grant, if this is true—how come Christian and you got out alive? Why hasn't anyone reported the missing? And why hasn't anyone made more stories about this place?"

Grant exhales sharply and shakes his head, his gaze fixed somewhere far beyond the bar's walls. "Listen, young man, no one steps foot in that town anymore. No one should—not the police, not detectives, not anyone. I was lucky to escape. I was one step ahead, sensed something was not right." His voice lowers again, rough, and deliberate. "The town's full of dead people—but not corpses you would see in this reality. They look... freshly dead."

He pauses, the glass trembling slightly in his hand. "Christian went during the day. But if he had traveled through the night..." Grant's eyes flicker toward Ebenezer, a grim understanding passing between them. "The chances would've been very slim for him to come out alive."

Ebenezer rubs his forehead and shakes his head, disbelief and fear wrestling behind his eyes. He leans closer. "So, you have traveled there yourself? During the day—and managed to get out alive? Then how did you?"

Grant chuckles dryly, taking another slow sip of his drink. "That," he says, eyes narrowing, "is a story you might not want to hear."

Grant leans back slightly, his eyes narrowing as if replaying the memory. "Well, let me put it this way... I traveled during the day. The hauntings only happen at night. If I were you, I would stay clear of that town—day or night. You might feel something strange in the daylight, but when darkness falls..." He pauses, his voice lowering to a rasp. "Something deadly, something that does not want to be disturbed, lies waiting. It is like the whole place is alive—and angry."

Ebenezer smirks, though the unease in his eyes betrays his curiosity. "Okay, but how do you know something mysterious happens at night? Have you seen anything?"

Grant gives a short laugh and shakes his head. "You would not believe me if I told you. I felt something crawling through my veins even in the day. But from what I have heard things get worse after sundown. Like I said, strange things happen at night."

He reaches into his jacket pocket and pulls out a folded slip of paper, sliding it across the counter. "If you want to know more about Damascus, take my number. I am staying at the Blacksburg Motel. You can reach me through the reception desk if you need to talk."

Ebenezer takes out his small notebook and pen, jotting down the motel number. Then he offers both items to Grant so he can confirm the details. "Thank you, old timer. I will stay in touch. Next time, we can continue our chat about the ghost town of Damascus."

Grant finishes the last of his beer and sets the empty glass on the counter. "Thank you for the drink. How much do I owe you?"

The waiter glanced at Grant. "That'll be three dollars, please."

Grant handed over the bills, tipped his hat in thanks, and made his way toward the restrooms.

Ebenezer looked back down at the newspaper article, his brow furrowing as he muttered under his breath. "Hm. Why hasn't anyone ever reported the missing? It is strange... the police must know something, surely."

He reached for his wallet and handed the waiter a few bills. "Here you go, friend. Ten dollars—and keep the change."

The waiter smiled, pocketing the tip. "Thank you, sir. Hope you have a great evening."

"Same to you, friend. Oh, and I never caught your name," Ebenezer said with an easy smile.

"My name's Carl," the waiter replied.

Ebenezer nodded. "Well, Carl, it is a pleasure. And a word of advice—look for a better job. You are too sharp for this place."

Carl chuckled softly. "I will bear that in mind. Thank you."

Ebenezer rose from his seat and pushed through the bar's smoky air toward the exit. Just as he reached the door, a young woman stepped inside. She brushed past him, her gaze briefly meeting him before shifting toward Grant appearing from the men's room.

She wore a navy-blue coat and matching trousers, her black boots clicking lightly on the worn wooden floor. Her long brown hair framed a face both calm and alert, and her pearl-blue eyes swept the room with quiet authority. On the right side of her coat gleamed the small, unmistakable letters: **FBI**.

Ebenezer glanced back at the young woman with a faint smile before continuing his walk toward his apartment, just ten minutes away from the bar.

The woman stepped closer to Grant, studying him for a moment before speaking. "Hello, mister. How are you?"

Grant turned toward her, his expression cautious. "Hello, ma'am. What can I do for you?"

"I'm with the FBI," she said, her tone firm but kind. "I know who you are, and I need information about Damascus—and what happened there."

Grant raised an eyebrow. "Can I see your badge? Forgive me, but anyone can stitch an FBI patch onto a coat these days."

Without hesitation, she reached into her jacket and produced a badge. "Here you go. Agent Julia Hague. I've been looking for you, Mr. Grant. I understand you have knowledge about the ghost town of Damascus. I want you to gather as much information as you can for me."

Grant leaned back slightly, his voice calm but edged with warning. "Julia, that's not a pleasant story. And Damascus isn't a safe place to go poking around. What I've seen and heard there isn't something you investigate on a regular day. My advice—stay away from Damascus, or you'll regret it."

Julia narrowed her eyes slightly, catching the edge in Grant's tone. "Mr. Hennessey, our records show you went to Damascus unharmed. You've seen and heard things—strange things—that could help us. You have information we need about that town. So, I'm asking you to come with us to Damascus and help us solve this case. I have a feeling this isn't something the Bureau has ever dealt with before."

Grant's expression hardened. "So, it looks like you've been spying on me! How do you even know I went to Damascus?" he shouted, his voice rising.

Julia remained calm, her tone steady. "My team saw your car driving away from the area. Few vehicles have been seen leaving that town, Mr. Hennessey. We happened to be there at the time."

Grant hesitated, rubbing his jaw. "Let me think about it. I will get back to you."

Agent Julia studied him for a moment, slightly bewildered but keeping her composure. "All right," she said, handing him a small card. "Here is my contact number. Call me when you decide. And know this—your protection is guaranteed at all costs. I have five FBI agents assigned to this operation. You will be well cared for, so there is no need to feel pressured or nervous."

Grant gave a long sigh, nodding faintly. As he stepped out of the restroom and back into the dimly lit bar, he lifted his whiskey glass and drained it in one quick motion. "No problem," he muttered. "I'll call you. I'm staying at the Blacksburg Motel. I'll reach out once I'm at the reception—ask the clerk to connect me."

Agent Julia smiled. "Okay, I'll see you soon. For now, stay safe."

She stepped out of the bar, crossed the quiet street, and opened the door of her shiny blue 1970 Chevrolet Camaro. The engine rumbled to life, and within seconds she was gone, taillights fading into the dark Virginia night.

Meanwhile, Ebenezer continued his walk toward his apartment. The air had grown heavy, the sky thick with dark clouds that seemed to swallow the moonlight. He looked up and exhaled. "Beautiful," he murmured. "What a sight."

As he turned back toward the bar, he spotted Grant walking in the opposite direction, heading toward the motel. "Hey, Grant!" Ebenezer called out, jogging a few steps closer.

Grant turned and waved. "Ebenezer! Hey there. Remember—don't go to Damascus. Remember what I told you. You know where I'm staying, so ring me if you want to meet up. Have a good night!"

Ebenezer lifted his hand in return. "Sure thing! I'll call you. Good night!"

Grant disappeared inside the Blacksburg Motel while Ebenezer continued down the dimly lit street toward his apartment. Ten minutes later, he reached his building, keys jingling in his pocket. He unlocked the main door, climbed the narrow staircase, and found his apartment.

"Boy, oh boy," he sighed as he stepped inside. "What an evening. I think I need another drink."

He crossed the small living room, opened a cabinet, and pulled out a bottle of Scotch whiskey. In the kitchen, he reached into the freezer for two ice cubes, dropped them into a glass, and poured a generous measure of Scotch.

"Ahhhh... so refreshing." Ebenezer sank into the sofa, whiskey glass in hand. He reached for the remote and flicked on the television, searching for the evening news. The hum of the old set filled the room.

A red banner suddenly scrolled across the bottom of the screen: **Breaking News.**

Ebenezer straightened, eyes narrowing on the flickering image.

The broadcaster's voice cut in. "We're bringing you an update on the mysterious town of *Damascus*, Virginia—located near Creeper Trail. The FBI has issued a warning urging people to avoid the area. Reports of strange and unexplained incidents have surfaced, and even local police have been advised to stay clear. We have an eyewitness joining us live from a Virginia motel—please welcome Grant Hennessey from Abingdon, Virginia. Grant, thank you for speaking with us."

Grant cleared his throat. "Thank you."

The correspondent continued, "So, Grant, what can you tell us about Damascus?"

Grant nodded slightly before responding. "Well... this place has been abandoned for years. Nearly seven now. I came across a story about it—residents went missing, and strange things kept happening. Even the police won't go near it anymore; they're too spooked." He paused, lowering his voice. "The reporter who wrote that article, Christian Painter—he's been there himself, in broad daylight. He said he saw shadows moving through the empty houses as he walked past. He could feel something watching him. He swore it wasn't human... and honestly, I believe him."

"I went there myself," Grant continued, his voice trembling slightly. "And I felt... different around that place. There were signs everywhere— 'Do Not Enter,' 'Enter at Your Own Risk.' That alone tells you someone—maybe the police—has been posting warnings during the day, trying to keep folks from neighbouring towns away. So, my advice to the people of Blacksburg: please, don't go there. Stay away from Damascus. And stay away from Creeper Trail, too."

"Thank you, Grant Hennessey, for joining us live," the broadcaster said.

"My pleasure."

Ebenezer froze; his eyes locked on the screen. *Grant? The same man I met earlier.* His stomach tightened. The realization hit like a cold wind through the room.

He rose from the sofa, pacing. "Christian Painter," he muttered under his breath. "If anyone knows what's really going on, it's him."

Grabbing his apartment keys from the hook, Ebenezer snatched up his camera and slid it into the worn leather bag resting by the door. He hesitated for a moment—he didn't know exactly where Christian lived, only that his articles were published out of Abingdon. Still, that was a start.

He slung the bag over his shoulder and stepped into the night air, the hallway light flickering behind him. Outside, the chill of early spring brushed against his face as he approached his shiny red Ford Cortina parked beneath the streetlamp. Sliding into the driver's seat, he turned the key, the engine coughing before it roared to life.

Pulling the choke, he gripped the wheel, his reflection faint in the windshield. "Let's see what you've really found, Christian," he murmured. Then, with a low rumble, the car rolled into the darkness—toward Abingdon, and toward whatever waited in Damascus.

2

THE MEETING

As Ebenezer drives toward Christian's house, two ravens sweep past his car and settle on a nearby lamppost. The sight makes him uneasy. "That's not something you see every night," he mutters. "Two ravens, flying alongside a car in the dark..."

For a moment, confusion prickles at him, but he shakes it off and returns his focus to the road. Ebenezer travelled a few minutes as he knows where Christian lives. He has been there before on a few occasions.

So, the drive takes only a few minutes. Pulling over at the curb, he shifts the gear into park, lifts the handbrake, and removes the keys from the ignition. The car engine clicks as it cools in the autumn night. After a pause, he steps out, shutting the door behind him.

"Looks like I'm here," he says to himself, voice low but resolute. "Now I need to get some answers from Christian—and find out what exactly he saw in Damascus."

He walks up to the porch and presses the doorbell. The sound echoes like a church bell—deep, metallic, and unsettling. *Ding-dong.*

Moments later, the lock clicks, and the front door creaks open. Christian stands there, face half-lit by the warm glow of the hallway. "Good evening,

Ebenezer. It's nine o'clock," he says, raising an eyebrow. "What brings you here at this hour?"

"Sorry for coming so late," Ebenezer replies, his tone urgent but controlled. "I just need to know more about your trip to Damascus—what you saw while you were there."

"Ebenezer, come inside," Christian says, stepping aside to let him through.

They walk into the living room, where the soft amber light flickers against the walls. "Take a seat," Christian adds.

Ebenezer settles onto a worn leather couch, his eyes drifting around the room. The shelves are lined with trophies, medals, and framed photographs—achievements he never knew Christian had. *How had he never noticed this side of him before?*

"Would you like a drink?" Christian asks.

"Yeah, why not? Do you have whiskey?"

"Sure. Jack Daniel's or Johnnie Walker Black Label?"

"Black Label, please." Ebenezer offers a small grin.

Christian disappears briefly into the kitchen. Moments later, the faint clink of ice echoes from the other room, followed by the familiar *glug* of poured liquor. He returns carrying two glasses, amber liquid swirling over ice. "Here we go—whiskey on the rocks."

"Thanks," Ebenezer replies, accepting the glass.

Christian sits across from him, expression thoughtful. "So," he says slowly, "you want to know about Damascus? And I suppose Creeper Trail, too?"

Ebenezer looks up, his gaze sharp now, the weight of his questions pressing between them.

"Actually," Ebenezer said, leaning forward slightly, "I'd love to know what you experienced in Damascus—what you *saw* while you were there."

Christian took a slow sip of whiskey before replying. "I must say, the town looked completely isolated. The roads were cracked, the houses rotting away... and the worst part—there were bodies scattered everywhere." He paused, his voice lowering. "Some were decomposed beyond recognition. Even the trees looked as if they were dying."

Ebenezer stiffened in his seat. The words hit him harder than he expected. He pictured the deserted streets, the smell of decay drifting through the air. His grip on the glass tightened.

Christian continued, his eyes unfocused as though recalling a nightmare. "I was petrified when I saw them. Then I noticed something—a shadow moving between the homes. It wasn't natural. It seemed to glide, slow and deliberate, like it was *searching*."

Ebenezer said nothing, his pulse quickening. The ticking of a nearby clock filled the silence.

"I followed it," Christian went on, "because I couldn't just leave without answers. I was investigating, after all. The shadow led me toward an abandoned saloon at the end of the street. I stopped for just a second, and—poof—it vanished. When I looked up, two ravens were perched on the hotel roof, staring straight down at me. That's something you don't see often."

Ebenezer nodded slowly, setting his glass on the table. "You said two ravens?" His tone sharpened. "That's odd—I saw the same thing before coming here." He frowned, thinking. "And this shadow you followed—what did it look like? Did it have a shape? Could you describe it?"

Christian swigged another sip of whiskey. "Yes, I can describe it to you. It looked strange—unnatural. It didn't resemble a human shadow at all. It was tall, uneven, like it was made of smoke trying to hold a shape. Definitely... *unhuman*."

"So, you're saying this shadow was last seen heading toward the abandoned saloon bar?" Ebenezer asked, leaning forward. "That could mean it *wanted* you to follow it inside."

Christian hesitated, the glass halfway to his lips. "Perhaps," he murmured.

Ebenezer pressed on. "Did you go inside the bar?"

Christian shook his head. "No, I didn't," he said quickly. "I should have, but something about it felt wrong." "Instead, I kept walking through town, looking for signs—anything that might explain what happened. Then I noticed bloodstains leading up to a small white house. The door was slightly open."

He paused, his expression darkening. "When I went inside, I saw them—bodies everywhere. Men, women... lying still, eyes open. No stab wounds. No gunshots. Just—fresh corpses. It looked like they'd only died moments before."

Ebenezer's face tightened. "Fresh? As in, recently dead?"

Christian nodded. "Yes. I thought it was just that house, but when I went to another, it was the same blood on the porch, bodies inside, untouched, no signs of struggle. Whoever—or whatever—did this left no trace. The air was heavy, like the town itself was holding its breath."

Ebenezer ran a hand through his hair, trying to make sense of it.

Christian got to his feet and began pacing the room. "It doesn't make sense. Blood everywhere, yet the bodies don't decay. Whoever's behind it... isn't human. That's my belief—but maybe I'm wrong." He stopped by the window, staring out as if replaying it all. "I remember wondering why the police hadn't arrived. But then I saw a patrol car by the sidewalk—doors flung open, windows shattered. And inside..." He swallowed. "The officers were dead too. Same thing—no wounds, no rot. Like it had all just happened."

Ebenezer sat quietly for a moment, letting Christian's words sink in. "So, that means the police must have already known something was happening there," he said slowly. "But they never reported back because they couldn't—they were killed." He leaned forward, concern tightening his voice. "Did you see any more police cars, Christian?"

Christian nodded, his hand trembling slightly as he set down his glass. "Yes... I saw dozens," he said, his tone hushed. "Parked along the streets, some with their doors open, lights still flashing. It surprised me even more. Whatever did this—it's intelligent, deliberate, or something far from human. To take out that many officers without a trace?" He shook his head. "Ebenezer, I'm telling you, this was the strangest discovery of my entire career as a journalist."

He paused, glancing toward the dim window as though the memory might still be lurking there. "Anyway, about the shadow..." His voice lowered. "I have this feeling that it's connected to all of it—that's why the officers never made it back. They didn't report in, and no one ever filed them missing. Maybe the department knows more than they're admitting... maybe they're hiding it."

Ebenezer blinked in surprise. "That's... unsettling," he murmured. He rubbed the back of his neck, trying to make sense of it all. "There's something else I wanted to ask you."

He hesitated before continuing. "When I got back to my apartment that night, I turned on the television. There was a live interview—some guy named Grant. I'd just met him at my local bar earlier that day." Ebenezer frowned. "The news reporters were questioning him, and he mentioned *you*. Your name came up. He said he'd read your article about the ghost towns in Virginia."

Christian looked startled. "Grant mentioned *me?*"

Ebenezer nodded, finishing the last of his whiskey. "He did. Either he's read your work... or he's more involved in this story than he's letting on."

Christian frowned, clearly puzzled. "I've never met the guy," he said, rubbing his temple. "But I'm guessing he believes what I wrote about Damascus."

Ebenezer leaned forward suddenly, an idea sparking behind his eyes. "Then we'd better go to the police station ourselves," he said. "Find out why they've kept this whole thing quiet—and why none of it's been reported on the news. Come on, Christian, we can't sit here doing nothing." Ebenezer felt more confident as he wanted to get to the bottom of the situation.

Christian hesitated, worry etched across his face. "Are you sure you want to go there?"

Ebenezer gave a wry half-smile. "We're journalists, remember? This is what we do."

Christian nodded slowly, conviction replacing his fear. "All right," he said, pushing himself off the sofa. "Let's find out what's really going on—at least there are two of us this time."

He set down his half-finished glass of whiskey, the amber liquid trembling slightly as he released it. Then he went to change, trading his pajamas for jeans and a thick wool coat.

Minutes later, both men stepped into the chilly night air. The streets were quiet, heavy with mist. They made their way toward Ebenezer's car parked along the curb.

"Hop in!" Ebenezer called across the roof of the car, his breath fogging in the cool air.

Christian opened the passenger door, casting one last glance back toward the dimly lit house before sliding into his seat. Ebenezer climbed in behind the wheel, the engine rumbling to life as the headlights cut through the darkness ahead.

The car roared to life, its engine breaking the stillness of the night as they pulled out onto the narrow road. The short drive to the police station took no more than five minutes, yet it felt much longer to Christian. The air inside the car was thick with tension, every passing streetlight flickering across his uneasy expression.

He wanted to publish the story—every haunting detail of it—but dread gnawed at him. What if it cost him his career? His freedom? Or worse, his life? There were truths men in power didn't want unearthed, and Christian feared he was about to dig too deep.

3

A New Partner in Crime

E benezer and Christian finally pulled up in front of the police station.

"Okay, here we are. Let's go inside," Ebenezer said, pushing his door open.

Inside, the reception area smelled faintly of coffee and old paper. A woman sat behind the desk, phone pressed to her ear, her tone clipped and businesslike. When she noticed the two men, she raised a polite finger, silently asking them to wait.

She ended the call a moment later and offered a courteous smile. "Good evening, gentlemen. How can I help you?"

Christian stepped forward. "We'd like to speak with your head detective, please."

"Of course," the woman replied. "But is it urgent? If not, I'll have to ask you to make an appointment."

"Yes, it's very important. We must speak with him right away," Christian said firmly.

"And who might you gentlemen be?" the receptionist asked, her tone polite but cautious.

Ebenezer sighed before replying, "My name's Ebenezer O'Rourke, and this is

Christian Painter. We're both with the *Virginia Daily*. We'd like to speak with the detective in charge of your department."

The receptionist nodded and picked up the phone. "Detective Marshall, I have two reporters from the *Virginia Daily* here to see you."

Ebenezer and Christian waited, watching her expression as she listened to the reply on the other end. A moment later, she hung up the receiver.

"Detective Marshall said he'll see you both in his office. Go straight down the corridor and turn left—you'll see his name on the door."

"Thank you, beautiful lady," Christian said with a grin.

Ebenezer rolled his eyes. "Come on, Christian. Let's go."

But Christian wasn't done. He shot the receptionist a playful wink. "A pretty woman like you working in a police station? You could be a model who looks like that."

The receptionist's smile stiffened. "Sorry, you're not my type—but I appreciate the compliment."

Ebenezer chuckled, shaking his head as they walked away.

"Ha-ha! Come on, Casanova. Let's meet Detective Marshall."

Christian looked slightly dejected but followed Ebenezer down the corridor toward the detective's office.

A sharp knock sounded at the door.

"Come in!" Detective Marshall called out.

Ebenezer and Christian stepped inside. It was the first time they had seen the man in person. Detective Marshall was tall—around six-foot-three—with grey hair, hazel eyes, and a neatly trimmed beard to match. He wore a navy blazer bearing the gold Blacksburg crest above the heart, with two gold stripes at the cuffs, a crisp white shirt, and a black tie beneath an officer's hat.

"Hello, gentlemen," he said, his voice calm but commanding. "The receptionist told me you wanted to see me urgently. What can I do for you?"

Ebenezer met the detective's gaze. "Detective Marshall, we're from the *Virginia Daily*. We'd like to talk about the disappearance of officers from your department."

Marshall exhaled slowly, studying them. "Isn't that my job to be asking *you* questions?" His tone softened a little. "But very well—since you work for the paper, I'll speak."

Ebenezer continued, his expression firm. "We believe you haven't told anyone about these disappearances. We'd like to know why this has been kept a secret from the town."

Detective Marshall's jaw tightened. His hazel eyes darkened as he leaned back in his chair, the air in the office suddenly heavier.

"Gentlemen," Detective Marshall began, his tone grave. "I felt it wasn't right to publicize the disappearance—especially after what I've seen and heard."

Christian leaned forward. "I know exactly what you mean, Detective. There were no bodies—no trace of them at all. Only blood."

Detective Marshall rubbed his grey beard and lowered his eyes, speaking with quiet emotion. "This is a mystery to me as much as it is to anyone. My men vanished without a sound, without a clue. If I'd shared this with the town, panic would've spread like wildfire. And worse, curiosity. People would've gone searching for that place. More lives could have been lost." He looked back up at them, his expression weary. "Keeping this quiet was the only way to protect them."

Christian's jaw tightened. "It's too late for that, Detective. I already published the story in the *Virginia Daily*. But I left out certain details—things too disturbing, too unbelievable to print."

Ebenezer finally spoke up, his tone measured. "Christian says he saw a shadow moving from door to door in every house—and then it vanished inside that old bar in Damascus."

Christian nodded firmly. "That's right. Whatever it was, it didn't move like a person. It sounded—and looked—completely unnatural."

Ebenezer smirked slightly. "So, you think there's some kind of spirit or ghost behind all this?"

Detective Marshall's expression faltered. His hands began to tremble, and he clasped them together to steady himself. "I've thought the same thing more times than I care to admit," he said quietly. "I want to return to that town and investigate—but I won't risk taking my officers this time. I'll go alone, armed, and I'll find out what's really happening there."

Ebenezer leaned forward, studying him. "One more question, Detective. What made you decide to travel all the way to Damascus? It's over a hundred and sixty kilometers from Blacksburg—a two-hour drive."

Detective Marshall sighed, his voice low and deliberate. "I know the police department in Damascus well. One of their officers reached out to me for help—several of his men vanished after visiting the Virginia Creeper Trail. I couldn't ignore that. So, I went."

Christian looked at Ebenezer, keeping his composure throughout the interview. "Ebenezer, let's go with Detective Marshall and uncover what's really happening. If we solve this mystery, we could make a name for ourselves—maybe even write about it!"

Ebenezer frowned, his voice steady but laced with worry. "I'm not thinking about fame or writing an article, Christian. I'm more concerned about what happened to those officers and the people of Damascus. Maybe they weren't *missing* at all—perhaps they were trapped inside those abandoned buildings or homes. That could be why no one's seen or heard from them."

Christian nodded thoughtfully. "You might be right. I didn't go inside many homes or buildings when I was there."

Detective Marshall listened quietly, absorbing every word. A flicker of determination crossed his face as his thoughts shifted. Finally, he spoke. "You know what, gentlemen? I've changed my mind. I'm going back to Damascus to find out what happened to my team—but on one condition. We do this discreetly. The FBI mustn't know we're going. I can't stand their interference. Agreed?"

Ebenezer and Christian exchanged a glance and answered together, "Agreed, Detective."

"Good," Marshall said firmly. "Let's go find my men—and discover what really happened to the Damascus Police Department."

The three men left the office, stepping out into the pale afternoon light. Their footsteps echoed down the hallway as they walked toward the unknown, bound by purpose, fear, and a chilling sense that something in Damascus was waiting for them.

The three men stepped out of the police station, the night air cool against their faces. Detective Marshall pointed toward his unmarked police car. "Okay, hop in. We'll go together," he said.

Ebenezer and Christian exchanged a quick look before walking toward the car. They climbed inside, the leather seats creaking beneath them. "Buckle up, gentlemen," Marshall said with a half-smile. "We're heading for Damascus."

The clock on the dashboard read **9:30 p.m.** as Marshall started the engine. He steered the car out of Blacksburg, the tires humming against the quiet road. "We'll drive through Radford, Wytheville, and Marion," he explained. "That's the quickest route to Damascus, near the Creeper Trail."

Christian gazed out the window, watching the dark Virginia countryside slip by under a heavy blanket of clouds. Ebenezer, restless, studied the dials and switches of Marshall's undercover vehicle. "We should stop somewhere later and grab something to eat," Ebenezer said.

"Sure thing," Marshall replied. "There's a diner near Marion that's open late."

By the time they reached the outskirts of Radford, the dashboard clock blinked **11:00 p.m.** The sky had grown darker, the moon struggling to pierce through thick clouds. Detective Marshall had been driving steadily for over an hour when something caught his eye.

"Look, gentlemen," he said, nodding toward the shoulder of the road.

Both Ebenezer and Christian leaned forward. "Oh my God," Ebenezer breathed. "Stop the car, Detective."

Detective Marshall eased the car to the roadside and cut the engine. The headlights illuminated a **dead deer** sprawled in the ditch, its body twisted unnaturally. Christian opened his door first and stepped into the cold night air, crouching beside the animal for a closer look.

"Goodness," Ebenezer murmured, crouching near the animal. "What could have caused this deer to be lying on the side of the road?"

"It could've died naturally," Christian suggested, though his tone lacked conviction.

Detective Marshall knelt beside the body, scanning the road and ditch for signs of a struggle. He returned to the car, opened the glove compartment, and pulled out a small first-aid kit. Slipping on a pair of rubber gloves, he crouched again and examined the deer more closely.

"This deer didn't die naturally," he said after a moment, his brow furrowed. "Look at it—no signs of sickness or decay. It looks perfectly healthy, yet it's dead. That's... not right. I've seen plenty of road kills across Virginia, but never one like this."

Christian frowned. "So, what are you suggesting, Detective? That this deer was killed in some unnatural—or maybe *non-human*—way?"

Ebenezer gave a nervous smirk. "You two have been watching too much television. It's just dead, that's all we know."

Detective Marshall stood, tugging the gloves off and tossing them back into the kit. He rubbed his forehead, troubled. "There's no point calling animal control—it's too late for that. Let's get back in the car."

The three men climbed inside, shutting the doors against the cold night air.

"I just can't shake the feeling that something else happened to that deer," Detective Marshall muttered, gripping the steering wheel. "My gut tells me this wasn't natural."

Christian nodded slowly, his eyes fixed on the dark road ahead. "I agree with you, Detective.

"I totally agree! This isn't normal—but we'll find answers, because that's what we journalists do. Isn't that right, Ebenezer?"

Ebenezer shakes his head, clearly uncertain. "Christian, I don't know what to think. What amazed me is that the deer looked fresh. No sign of blood, no smell—nothing. Still, I'll trust my instinct. It died naturally... unless we find evidence otherwise."

Detective Marshall starts the car and pulls back onto the road. "I'll drive another twenty-five minutes, then we can stop for a quick bite to eat. You mentioned you were hungry earlier, Ebenezer."

Christian gives a shaky laugh. "Sure, Detective. I *was* hungry, but after seeing that deer, I'm not sure I can look at meat the same way. What about you, Ebenezer? Feel like eating?"

Ebenezer exhales, his face pale. "I think I've lost my appetite after what we just saw. It made me feel sick."

Detective Marshall glances at Ebenezer through the rearview mirror. "I see things like this all the time—animals hit by cars or bikes. But nothing like that deer. Try not to dwell on it too much. We'll figure it out. It's as much a mystery to me as it is to you both."

Ten minutes later, an old red GMC C/K 2500 series truck sat parked near Bisset Park. As the three men continued toward Radford—about twenty-two kilometers from Blacksburg—Detective Marshall glanced to his right as they crossed the Lee Highway Bridge, the dark ribbon of the New River glimmering below.

He drove to the end of the highway, turned left onto Berkley Williams Drive, and steered toward the park. The evening light was fading fast.

Ebenezer frowned and exchanged a look with Christian. "Detective, why are we heading toward the park?"

"Exactly!" Christian added. "Why the park?"

"Look, gentlemen," Detective Marshall said, pointing ahead. "See that abandoned truck? Looks like a GMC C/K 2500 series. Let's get out and look around."

Both men hesitated, confused but obedient.

"Okay, Detective," said Christian, opening the door. "But it's just an old truck in the middle of a park. Someone left it there and went to a nearby shop or something."

Ebenezer squinted toward the vehicle. "How could you tell the model from this distance, Detective?"

"Because I own one," Detective Marshall said, keeping his eyes on the distant vehicle. "It's back in my garage at home. And tell me, Christian—why would anyone leave their truck out here in the middle of the park, nowhere near the main lot? Doesn't add up."

He slowed the patrol car, turned onto the gravel path, and eased to a stop near the old red GMC. The engine hummed quietly before he set the brake. "Something's off. Let's take a look."

Detective Marshall reached into the glove compartment, retrieved his flashlight, and stepped out into the cool evening air. The park was still—too still. "Okay, gentlemen," he said, nodding toward the shadows. "Let's spread out and check the area."

Ebenezer and Christian climbed out, their shoes crunching on the gravel.

"Hello!" Detective Marshall called, his voice echoing through the trees. No answer. Only the distant sound of water from the river.

He swept his flashlight beam over the vehicle—windows rolled up, no movement inside. He touched the hood. "Still warm," he muttered. "Whoever owns this truck was here not long ago."

"Maybe they went for a walk," Christian suggested, glancing around uneasily.

"Maybe," Detective Marshall said. "But people don't leave their engines warm, and keys go missing without reason. Let's keep looking—there might be something nearby."

They fanned out slowly, the flashlight cutting through the dark.

Then Ebenezer stopped short. "Look, Detective!" he shouted, pointing toward the line of trees about two hundred yards away.

Detective Marshall and Christian turned. Under the faint wash of moonlight, a man's body lay crumpled beside a tree, motionless.

The three men sprinted toward the motionless figure.

"Check if he's breathing, Detective!" Ebenezer shouted.

Detective Marshall knelt beside the man, checking for signs of life—airway, pulse, breath. His face tightened. "No breathing... no pulse," he said quietly, though his tone carried a stubborn edge of hope. "Let's get him into the car. There's a hospital in Radford—we'll try to get him there fast."

He knew, deep down, that the man was already gone. Still, something in him refused to give up. Maybe there were answers waiting in that hospital—records, someone who might identify the victim, something to explain what had happened here.

Together, the three men lifted the cold, limp body and carried it to the car. They laid him gently across the back seat before climbing in, Detective Marshall behind the wheel.

"Good Lord," Detective Marshall muttered, glancing in the rearview mirror. "He's ice-cold... and turning blue."

Ebenezer's voice cracked. "Hurry, Detective—drive faster! Maybe we can still save him!"

"I'm doing the best I can," Detective Marshall replied, accelerating onto the main road. "If there's even a chance this man isn't gone, I'm not wasting it."

Christian leaned forward. "Do you have a road map?"

"Right here." Detective Marshall grabbed the folded map from the glove box and handed it to him while keeping one hand on the wheel.

"Let's find the nearest hospital," Christian said, unfolding it under the faint glow of the dashboard light. "Ebenezer, help me look. Two pairs of eyes are better than one."

The two men bent over the map as the car sped toward Radford, the night outside pressing close around them.

"Found it!" Ebenezer exclaimed. "Detective, you need to turn around—head to the opposite side of Berkley Williams Drive, then take New River Drive."

"Well done, Ebenezer," said Detective Marshall, following the directions.

As they approached New River Drive, the faint glow of the Radford Theatre appeared on the right-hand side. "Where to next, Christian?" Marshall asked, keeping his eyes on the road.

Christian ran his finger down the map. "Take a right onto Tyler Avenue. According to the grid, the hospital's a little over nine kilometers away."

"Then we'll be there in about fifteen minutes," said Detective Marshall. He pressed harder on the accelerator. The engine groaned as the speed climbed, making his passengers grip their seats. "Hold on tight, gentlemen."

In the back seat, the man's body shifted slightly. His skin had turned a pale shade of purple, drawing uneasy glances from both passengers.

Ebenezer turned to the window, his voice uneasy. "That's strange. Two ravens just flew past the car. That's the second time I've seen them tonight."

"It's just birds," Christian said flatly.

"But you don't see ravens flying this late," Ebenezer muttered. "Usually, they're out in the morning—or near sunset."

Detective Marshall shot him a glance in the rearview mirror. "Gentlemen, enough about birds. We've got an unconscious man in the car, and you're talking about ravens? Let's focus. The hospital's up ahead."

Ebenezer fell silent, staring out the window as the dark silhouettes of the ravens faded into the night. He couldn't shake the feeling that their appearance meant something—that maybe, just maybe, the birds were a warning.

4

An Unusual Finding

The three men finally arrived at Radford Hospital.

"Okay, here we are," said Detective Marshall. "Let's get this man inside and see if the doctors can figure out what's wrong with him."

He jumped out of the car and took hold of the unconscious man's head and shoulders while the others supported his legs.

"Goodness, he's heavy!" Christian grunted.

Ebenezer shouted toward the entrance. "Help! Can somebody help us?"

A door opened nearby, and a man in a white coat stepped out of the cleaning storage room. "Over here!" the doctor called. "Bring him this way!"

The doctor rushed to them, motioning toward a stretcher. "Quickly—let's get him up here!" He called for backup, and within moments, nurses and attendants appeared, moving with precision and urgency. The three men stood aside, watching in astonishment as the medical team surrounded the patient, their movements efficient and calm.

"Thank you," said the doctor. "We'll take it from here—but I advise you not to enter while we're examining him. We need to determine the cause of his condition first."

Detective Marshall exhaled, catching his breath after the effort. "Understood,

Doctor. Thank you."

The doctor gave a curt nod as the team wheeled the patient down the corridor. Over his shoulder, he called back, "My name's Doctor Arthur Fitzgerald. And who are you three—and where did you find this man?"

Detective Marshall straightened up and replied, "My name is Detective Colin Marshall, and these two men are Ebenezer O'Rourke and Christian Painter. I'm with the Blacksburg Police Department, and they are with the *Virginia Daily*. We found this man lying unconscious in Bisset Park and brought him here."

Doctor Fitzgerald placed a stack of paperwork on the reception desk and gave them a brief nod. "All right. We'll treat him and update you on his condition once we know more. In the meantime, take a seat—there's coffee by the corner."

"Thank you," Christian said.

Ebenezer wasted no time pouring himself a cup from the steaming pot. He glanced at the detective with a grin. "You know, Detective, you never told us your first name."

Marshall smirked faintly. "It's just my nature. I've never been much for first names. I prefer to keep it low-key."

"Why's that?" Christian asked, leaning back in his chair.

Marshall gave a dry chuckle. "Like I said, I just prefer being called Detective Marshall. Keeps things simple."

Ebenezer laughed between sips. "No problem, Officer! Christian, want me to pour you a cup?"

"Please do," Christian replied.

"Sure. How do you like your coffee? Silly question—I should know this since we work together. Two lumps of sugar and no milk, right?" said Ebenezer.

"Spot on!" Christian replied as Ebenezer handed him the cup. "Thanks. I needed this. Feels like it's been one long night."

The clock above the waiting room read a few minutes past midnight. The hospital corridors were silent, the only sounds the hum of fluorescent lights and the distant echo of footsteps. The three men sat in uneasy stillness; each lost in his own thoughts.

Ebenezer, despite the caffeine, drifted off in his chair, head tilted back. Christian sat forward with his hands pressed to his cheeks, replaying the night's events in his mind—the unconscious man, the eerie quiet of Bisset Park, and those two ravens circling the car. He couldn't shake the feeling that all of it was connected somehow, tied to the strange town they'd been heading toward.

Detective Marshall remained alert, quietly cleaning his handgun with a folded cloth. His face gave nothing away, but his mind wasn't still. He kept wondering whether this incident was just a coincidence—or the first real sign that something darker was unfolding in that ghost town.

5

STRANGE OCCURRENCES IN BLACKSBURG

Meanwhile, back in Blacksburg, Grant Hennessey brushed his teeth, washed his face, and stared at his reflection in the bathroom mirror. He muttered to himself, "Jesus Christ, Mary, and Joseph—Damascus sure did scare me while I was there. Anyway, I hope that young man takes my advice and never sets foot in that place."

Grant wiped his damp face with a flannel and made his way to bed in his room at the Blacksburg Hotel. He lay back, eyes fixed on the window, watching the night sky stretch dark and endless above the town. The moon hung low, half-hidden by slow-drifting clouds.

His eyelids began to grow heavy, and he drifted toward sleep—until a sudden gust of wind rattled through the open window. Grant's eyes snapped open. The curtains fluttered like restless hands.

He rose slowly, feet touching the cool floorboards, and stepped toward the window to shut it. But as he reached out, he froze.

Outside, perched on the narrow ledge, was a fox. Its eyes glowed in the moonlight, unblinking and unnervingly human. It opened its mouth—not in a snarl, but in a sound that curdled his blood. The scream that followed was high and sharp, the pitch of a terrified little girl.

"What the hell? That's odd. Why would a fox look straight at me and growl? That's something you don't see every day."

The fox stopped growling and began trotting along the side road, as though nothing had happened.

"Unbelievable," Grant muttered. "That was... surprising."

He pushed the window open wider, curiosity outweighing caution, and kept his eyes on the animal. The fox was still walking, tail low, when it suddenly turned back toward him. Its lips curled again, the same eerie snarl cutting through the night air.

"Good Lord, that fox has issues," Grant said under his breath.

He shut the window despite the heavy humidity. "Ah, I need some sleep."

As he turned from the window, something caught his eye—a lone man walking toward the hotel entrance. Grant watched for a moment, uncertain, then dismissed it. Another late traveler. He rubbed his eyes and headed for bed, eager to forget the strange encounter.

The man entered through the hotel's front doors and crossed the quiet lobby to the reception desk. The room was empty, lit only by a dim lamp behind the counter.

"Hello? Is anybody here?" he called out.

A few seconds later, a young woman appeared from the back office, smoothing her uniform. "Good evening, sir. How can I help you?"

"Good evening," the man replied, catching his breath. "My name is Jacob Dalton. I work for the *Virginia Daily*. I'm also the manager of the *Gazette*. Here let me show you, my badge."

Sandy Moore, the receptionist, leaned forward to inspect it.

"All right, Mr. Dalton," she said politely. "What can I do for you?"

"I understand you have a guest staying here—a man named Grant Hennessey. I need to speak with him, if that's possible."

"I'm sorry, sir," Sandy said evenly. "But I'm not allowed to give out guest information."

Jacob frowned, impatient. Without another word, he turned and started up the staircase, his voice echoing through the quiet hall. "Grant! I need to speak with you!"

Sandy stiffened. "Sir, you can't do that! I'll have to ask you to leave the premises at once."

Realizing he was making a scene, Jacob exhaled sharply, then walked back down the stairs and out through the front doors.

Sandy sighed and reached for the telephone. She dialed Grant's room number.

Upstairs, the phone rang. Grant stirred from a heavy sleep, blinked at the clock, and picked up the receiver.

"Hello, Grant speaking."

"Good evening, Mr. Hennessey. I'm sorry to disturb you," Sandy said, keeping her tone professional. "A man named Jacob Dalton from the *Virginia Daily* was here asking for you. I followed protocol and didn't disclose your room number."

"Thank you, Sandy. I appreciate that," Grant replied.

She hung up. Grant sat on the edge of the bed for a moment, rubbing his temples, his mind already racing.

"Why would someone from the *Virginia Daily* be looking for me?" he muttered. "What could they possibly want?"

He dressed quickly and decided to take the stairs instead of the elevator, his thoughts heavy with unease.

Outside, Jacob waited near the entrance, the cool night air settling over the quiet street. Footsteps echoed on the stairwell. Moments later, Grant appeared in the doorway, stepping into the dim light spilling from the hotel windows.

Jacob heard the approaching footsteps and turned toward the hotel entrance. A moment later, the door opened, and Grant stepped inside. The two men regarded each other briefly before Jacob spoke.

"Good evening, Grant. I'm sorry to bother you at this hour, but I've been hoping to speak with you. My name's Jacob Dalton—manager of the *Virginia Daily* here in Blacksburg. It's an honor to meet you."

Grant nodded politely. "Good evening, Mr. Dalton. The pleasure's mine. What can I do for you?"

Jacob hesitated. "Would you prefer to talk somewhere private, or is the lobby all right?"

"Let's find somewhere quiet," Grant said.

"Then perhaps the bar," Jacob suggested. "It should be empty at this time of night."

"Good idea."

They walked back through the front doors together. Behind the desk, Sandy looked up, her expression tightening before she masked it with a professional smile.

"Would you gentlemen care for something to drink?" she asked evenly. "We have an excellent selection—single-malt whiskey, draught beer, and a fine list of red and white wines."

"Sure," Grant said. "Can I have a draught beer, please?"

"Yes, sir. One beer is coming up." Sandy turned toward the taps, forcing a polite smile that didn't quite reach her eyes. "And for you, Mr. Dalton?"

"A glass of sparkling water would be perfect, thank you."

"Okay — one beer and one sparkling water," Sandy repeated, her tone briskly professional though a hint of irritation lingered beneath it.

"Thank you," Jacob replied.

The two men moved to a pair of lobby chairs near the quiet bar. The soft hum of the overhead fan filled the pause between them.

"So, Mr. Dalton," Grant began, "how can I help you?"

Jacob shook his head lightly. "Please — call me Jacob."

"All right, Jacob," Grant said, leaning back. "What can I do for you?"

Jacob folded his hands. "I wanted to talk about the statement you gave earlier today — the one to the media regarding the stories about Damascus."

Grant sighed and rubbed his temple. "Ah, so that's what this is about. I had a feeling Damascus would come up."

"Yes, Grant. I'm aware that one of my journalists actually visited Damascus. I assume you've read our article about the ghost town — is that right?"

"That's right," Grant said. "I read the article—and it's true."

Jacob cleared his throat and continued, "Have you, by any chance, met with Christian?"

Grant shook his head. "No, I haven't. But I did meet a journalist at the bar not far from here. His name was Ebenezer."

Jacob raised an eyebrow. "You met Ebenezer? What did you two talk about?"

Grant adjusted his shirt before answering. "I understand that journalists like you are just doing your jobs—publishing strange stories and all—but I warned Ebenezer not to visit Damascus because of what I've experienced there."

Jacob paused as Sandy approached with their drinks.

"Here we go, gentlemen—one beer and one sparkling water," she said, placing the glasses on the table.

Jacob nodded. "Thank you for the drinks."

"You're welcome," Sandy replied with a faint smile. "If you need anything else, just give me a shout."

"I will," Jacob said politely as she walked away to continue her work.

"Now," Jacob said, turning back to Grant, "where were we? Oh, yes—about Ebenezer. I'm glad you warned him not to go to Damascus, but I have a feeling he'll go anyway. He's the sort who'll chase a story no matter the risk—he wants to make a name for himself, whether he believes the tale or not."

Grant's expression tightened with worry. He lifted his glass and took a long drink of beer. Jacob followed with a small sip of sparkling water.

"I hope he never goes," Grant said quietly.

"There's only one way to find out," Jacob replied. "Let's go meet Ebenezer."

Grant nodded. "All right—let me finish my beer, and then we'll go."

Jacob agreed with a short nod.

"Let me pay for the drinks — I insist," Jacob said.

Grant took another sip of his beer and smiled. "Thank you, Jacob."

Jacob placed a ten-dollar bill on the table. Both men finished their drinks, thanked Sandy at the bar, and stepped out of the hotel into the cool Blacksburg evening.

The streets were quiet, their footsteps echoing faintly against the pavement. A light breeze drifted through the trees, carrying the scent of damp leaves. Both men shared the same silent hope — that they might still catch Ebenezer at home.

Neither of them knew that Ebenezer, along with Christian, had already decided to make the trip to Damascus that very evening.

"Ebenezer doesn't live too far," Jacob said after a moment. "We can walk to his place."

"That's not a problem at all," Grant replied. "I don't mind walking."

They continued down the dimly lit street for several minutes until Jacob pointed ahead. "That's where Ebenezer lives."

"Great," Grant said. "Let's hope he's still home."

They stopped at the small, weathered house and climbed the creaking front steps. Jacob pressed the doorbell. The shrill ring echoed through the house, startling them both.

"Ebenezer! It's Jacob — your boss! Can you open the door, please?" Jacob called out.

There was no answer. The silence that followed was heavy and unsettling. Grant glanced at Jacob uneasily.

"This doesn't sound good," Grant murmured. "I think Ebenezer ignored your advice and went to Damascus."

Jacob frowned. "He isn't supposed to make other arrangements. That job was never assigned to him."

Grant exhaled slowly. "I think we should both get some rest and figure this out in the morning."

Jacob nodded. "Fine. But I'll go back to my office and have a word with Christian first thing tomorrow."

He didn't yet know that Christian would not be coming to work the next day.

"Grant, it was a real pleasure meeting you," Jacob added, his tone softening. "I'll find out what's going on and update you tomorrow."

Grant nodded and extended his hand. "You know where to reach me. Have a good night."

Jacob shook his hand firmly. "See you tomorrow."

6

A Strange Death

Back at Radford Hospital, thirty-four minutes past eleven that night, Ebenezer lay snoring softly on the bed. Christian watched him with an uneasy expression while Detective Marshall paced the waiting room, his shoes clicking against the tile.

"Stop pacing, Detective! You're making me nervous," Christian hissed under his breath.

Detective Marshall stopped and exhaled. "I just want to know what happened to that man—and why his body suddenly turned purple. There were no cuts, no bruises. It's strange. I've handled plenty of cases, even decomposed corpses, but I swear I've never seen anything like this."

Christian frowned, unsettled by the detective's words. "The doctor and the medical team know what they're doing. I'm sure they'll give us some answers soon."

"I hope so, Christian," Detective Marshall murmured.

Christian rose and walked toward the operating-room doors, peering through the small window. Inside, Doctor Fitzgerald and his team worked steadily over the patient. The doctor glanced up, met Christian's eyes, and moved toward the door.

"Is there anything you need?" asked Doctor Fitzgerald.

Detective Marshall, who had been lingering nearby, hurried toward the operating room door.

"Doctor, have you found the cause of this man's condition?" Christian pressed, eyes fixed on the surgeon.

"Forgive me for peeking in," Detective Marshall added. "I was just curious how you and your team were doing."

Doctor Fitzgerald's expression tightened at the interruption.

"It's... strange, Detective," he admitted. "I've never seen a body like this before. The skin has changed color, but there are no marks, scratches, or bruises. He looks drained—fragile. I can't identify the cause, but what I can tell you is that he is no longer alive."

Detective Marshall scratched his head, grimacing. "Oh my... so you're saying there's nothing you can do?"

"I'm afraid not, Detective. And I'm sorry," Fitzgerald said solemnly. "This is something I face every day, but this—this is one of the strangest deaths I've ever witnessed. It feels as though something has drained his very energy... but don't quote me on that."

At that moment, Ebenezer stirred. He opened his eyes, stretched with a loud yawn, and noticed both Christian and Detective Marshall were no longer by his side.

"Detective? Christian?" Ebenezer called out.

Detective Marshall waved him over. "Hey—come here. We've got some bad news."

Ebenezer stepped closer, apprehensive. "What do you mean, bad news? Is he dead?"

Doctor Fitzgerald met Ebenezer's gaze with quiet sorrow. "I'm afraid so. I'm sorry, gentlemen. We'll conduct a post-mortem and notify the next of kin once we've confirmed the man's identity."

Doctor Fitzgerald frowned. "So, your gut feeling tells you this man didn't die naturally?" asked Detective Marshall.

"It appears that way," Fitzgerald replied. "I've examined many deceased patients, and usually the skin takes on a yellowish hue — the typical signs of death. But this one..." He hesitated, glancing back toward the operating table. "This body looks almost fresh, despite the purplish tint. The skin is unusually soft. It's unsettling."

He straightened, removing his gloves. "Don't worry, gentlemen. I'll keep you informed of any findings. My next step is to identify the family and notify them."

Detective Marshall reached into his coat pocket and pulled out a business card. "Here, Doctor. Take my card — it has my number. Please contact the department as soon as you learn anything new and update me directly when you reach the family."

Fitzgerald accepted the card with a nod. "Thank you, Detective. I'll keep in touch and share any developments."

He turned back to his team at the operating table, his tone grave. "Time of death — eleven forty-seven p.m., August 5th, 1971," he announced.

Detective Marshall ran both hands through his hair in frustration. "So first we find a deer dead on the road — fresh, no wounds — and now a man under the same circumstances. This is beyond coincidence. I'm starting to see a pattern here." He turned toward the others, urgency creeping into his voice. "Let's move. The deer was found not far from Radford, so I say we keep going and reach Damascus as soon as possible."

Ebenezer let out another heavy yawn. "Detective, I'm exhausted. Can't we figure this out in the morning?"

Christian nodded in agreement. "He's right, Detective. We've had a long day. Let's get some rest and continue the first thing tomorrow."

Detective Marshall exhaled sharply but relented. "Fine. You win. We'll check into a nearby hotel and leave at sunrise."

He turned back toward Doctor Fitzgerald. "Doctor, where's the best place to stay around here?"

Fitzgerald thought for a moment before replying. "Gentlemen, you should try the Radford Inn on Tyler Road — about five kilometers from the hospital."

"Perfect. We know where that is," said Detective Marshall, giving a quick nod.

Ebenezer rolled his eyes but followed as the three men exited through the hospital doors and stepped into the cool night air.

Detective Marshall started the police car and steered down Tyler Road toward the Radford Inn, the tires crunching softly against the gravel. The silence inside the car was heavy — the kind that comes after seeing something that doesn't make sense.

"I can't wait to see what the rooms look like," Ebenezer muttered.

"Tomorrow morning, we'll head to Damascus," Christian said quietly, staring out the car window. "Maybe we'll finally discover what's really happening."

Detective Marshall gave a small nod but said nothing. The hum of the engine filled the silence as they drove through the empty Virginia roads.

7

LOVE AT FIRST SIGHT IN RADFORD

Detective Marshall eased his police car into a narrow parking space in front of the Radford Inn. It was 12:01 a.m. The wind howled through the trees, carrying with it the first loose leaves of autumn. Far beyond the rooftops, a pale moon hung low and watchful.

"Here we go, gentlemen," Detective Marshall said, cutting the engine. "We're finally here."

The three men stepped out, stretching stiff legs after the long drive. The inn looked relatively modern, though the paint was peeling in places around the entrance door. Its neon sign buzzed faintly against the wind.

Inside, the lobby was quiet—too quiet. They approached the reception desk; no one stood behind it. Christian noticed the small brass bell at the corner and gave it a sharp tap.

"Hello?" he called, raising his voice. "Is anyone here?"

A door creaked open behind the counter. A woman stepped out, smoothing her uniform. Her name badge read **Jessica Steele**. She had long blonde hair, striking blue eyes, and skin that gleamed under the lobby's dim light.

"Good evening, gentlemen," she said with a professional smile. "Welcome to the Radford Inn. Do you have a reservation, or would you like to book a room tonight?"

Christian stood silent for a moment, caught by the sparkle in Jessica's blue eyes. When he finally spoke, his words stumbled.

"W-well... we'd like to book a room for the night, please," he managed. "My name's Christian, and these are Detective Marshall and my colleague, Ebenezer."

Jessica's smile widened. "Wonderful. It's a pleasure to meet you, gentlemen. I have just the rooms for the three of you."

Ebenezer and Detective Marshall exchanged amused glances, each grinning at Jessica as if struck by a sudden crush.

"Well now, young lady," Detective Marshall said, lowering his voice with mock formality, "has anyone ever told you how beautiful you are?"

Jessica laughed, her tone playfully seductive. "I hear that every time a man checks in—on duty or off. But it never gets old."

Ebenezer joined in. "I imagine this place stays fully booked—especially when guests know you're behind the desk."

Jessica tilted her head and smiled. "Thank you, sweet sugar."

Ebenezer flushed and touched his cheek. "Oh my god, I'm actually blushing!" he said, laughing at himself.

Detective Marshall cleared his throat pointedly, restoring a trace of authority. "All right, ma'am, what rooms do you have available for us tonight?"

Jessica turned to the reservation ledger.

"I happen to have three separate rooms available," Jessica said brightly. "You're in luck! Each of you will have your own set of keys. There's a fresh bath towel and shower in every room, along with a small minibar. You'll be on the third floor. Breakfast is served from seven to ten a.m. in the dining room just off the lobby, to the right."

"That's great! And how much will it cost, Miss Jessica Steele?" Christian asked.

Jessica glanced down at her name badge, smiling at the mention of her name. "For one night, the rate is a hundred and fifteen dollars."

Christian reached for his wallet, but Ebenezer caught his hand. "Let me—please. I insist on covering tonight for all of us."

Christian blinked in surprise. "Are you sure?"

"Of course," Ebenezer replied, calm and certain.

He handed the cash across the counter. Jessica accepted it with a courteous nod. "Thank you, gentlemen. I wish you all a pleasant stay at the Radford Inn." She placed three brass keys on the counter. "Your rooms are 310, 311, and 312—right next door to each other. If you need anything, simply dial 000 from your room phone, and I'll be happy to assist you."

Detective Marshall picked up the three keys and handed one each to Ebenezer and Christian. "Here you go. Let's get some rest—we've got a big day tomorrow."

Jessica tilted her head, curiosity flickering in her eyes. "What's happening tomorrow, Detective?"

"We're heading to Damascus first thing in the morning," Marshall replied.

Her smile faltered, replaced by unease. "Damascus? Why would you go there? Everyone knows that place is haunted. I wouldn't set foot there if I were you."

Detective Marshall gave a thin, dismissive smirk. "I need answers. Too many of my men disappeared in that town, and I intend to find out what happened—to them, and to the police department stationed there."

Jessica's brow furrowed. "Detective, I've heard the same stories. No one makes it back alive—especially after dark."

He nodded gravely. "We found a man unconscious in Bisset Park earlier. He was taken to the hospital, but he died soon after—from causes the doctors couldn't explain. We just came from there. And we've already seen strange things on the road... and we haven't even reached Damascus yet."

Christian stepped forward, his voice steady but heavy with conviction. "It's been a grim journey, but we have to stay strong. I was in Damascus during the day, and I saw something—a shadow moving from door to door. The last place it slipped into was a bar. That's where we'll start."

Ebenezer joined the conversation, his tone thoughtful. "I've never been one to believe in the supernatural, but it's strange—an entire team from the Blacksburg and Damascus police vanishing without a trace. And not just them; many residents disappeared too. Now the whole town feels... abandoned."

Jessica folded her arms, her expression tightening. "Just be careful out there. I don't want to read your names in the papers—or worse, see them on the front page of a Virginia tabloid."

Christian grinned. "Don't worry, we'll be fine. And when we come back, I'm taking you out to dinner."

"Hold your horses, Christian," Detective Marshall cut in dryly, while Ebenezer shot him a look of disbelief. Jessica laughed softly, a hint of color rising in her cheeks.

"Well," she said, smiling at Christian, "I appreciate your confidence—it takes courage to ask a woman out like that. I'd love to have dinner with you... but only if you come back alive. Promise me that."

Ebenezer frowned, shaking his head. "How the hell do you just ask a lady out in the middle of a murder investigation? You really are a Casanova, aren't you?"

Detective Marshall chuckled, pocketing his key. "All right, lover boy—and you too, Ebenezer—let's leave the lady in peace and get some rest. We've got a long day ahead."

Christian gently touched Jessica's hand. "Good night, beautiful lady. I'll see you in the morning."

Jessica's cheeks flushed, and she looked away for a moment. "Good night, Christian."

The three men ascended the stairs, heading toward their rooms.

"The hotel's pretty nice, don't you think?" Ebenezer remarked.

"It is," Christian agreed, a grin spreading across his face. "And even nicer that Jessica works here!"

As they walked down the corridor, a shadow flickered at the far end.

"Whoa... what was that?" Detective Marshall asked, narrowing his eyes.

Christian and Ebenezer exchanged glances, then turned to the detective. "What did you see?"

Scratching his head, Detective Marshall replied, "I just saw a moving shadow near the end of the corridor."

Christian's brow furrowed. "Are you sure?"

Ebenezer chuckled softly. "You're just tired. You probably imagined it. There's no shadow lurking here. Let's get to our rooms and rest."

Detective Marshall proceeded cautiously, moving slowly toward the corridor's end. He tensed as faint noises reached his ears, hand gripping his gun. Approaching the source, he discovered a chocolate Labrador resting quietly.

"Oh, it's just a dog," he muttered with a relieved laugh.

He unlocked his door, stepped inside, and closed it behind him.

Christian glanced at Ebenezer and whispered, "I believe the detective, one hundred percent. He's seen something because I've seen it too. Keep an open mind—don't let it all be your imagination."

Ebenezer chuckled softly. "Christian, get some sleep. We'll talk in the morning. Good night, and rest well."

Christian rolled his eyes and nodded. He opened the door but paused, still thinking about what Detective Marshall had witnessed.

"I don't think I'll sleep," he muttered to himself. "Hmm... maybe I'll wait an hour, sneak downstairs, and have a chat with Jessica. That sounds like a good idea."

He unbuttoned his shirt and trousers, removed his socks, boxers, and shoes, and headed to the bathroom. Entering the walk-in shower, he turned the hot and cold taps on. "Wow, this shower is amazing!"

He grabbed the complimentary shower gel and shampoo, applying the gel to his body. A shadow lingered near the shower, unnoticed by Christian. His eyes were closed as he lathered himself. When he opened them to reach for the shampoo, the shadow had edged closer—but as he turned, it vanished suddenly.

Christian sang quietly to himself while washing his hair, the tune of Johnny Cash's *"Ring of Fire"*

Five minutes later, Christian turned off the hot and cold taps and grabbed a towel to dry himself. "Exactly what I needed after a long, late evening," he muttered.

Luckily, he had packed extra clothes in his backpack. He slipped into a cream-colored shirt, navy blue jeans, socks, and brown shoes. "Maybe I'll sneak out early, since I'm already ready," he whispered to himself.

Carefully unlocking his door, Christian tiptoed down the corridor toward the stairs, aiming for the reception desk to see Jessica. When he reached the main floor, he saw her seated behind the desk, quietly attending to paperwork.

"Jessica? Jessica!" he whispered softly.

Jessica looked up, noticing Christian, now looking fresh and composed. "Hey, why aren't you asleep?"

"I had to see you," he said, a playful smile tugging at his lips. "I couldn't just stay in the hotel room knowing such a beautiful woman is here all alone. I wanted to keep you company."

Jessica laughed softly. "Aww, you're so sweet. Sure, you can keep me company."

"I just had a shower, and I'm feeling fresh and clean after my horrid evening," Christian said, brushing damp hair from his forehead.

"Oooooh, that is nice! I like a clean and fresh man," Jessica replied with a teasing smile.

Christian leaned slightly closer. "Oh, do you now? Well... I want to tell you something," he murmured.

Jessica hesitated for a moment, glancing around the hotel reception. They barely knew each other, and the office was technically a public space. Yet, there was something different about him—an unexpected honesty in his eyes that made her lean in. She allowed him to whisper in her left ear, their gazes locking in a moment of charged silence.

A sudden loud noise cut through the room, breaking the tension. Jessica jumped back. "What was that?" she asked, her voice a mix of curiosity and alarm.

Christian's brows furrowed. "Goodness, that was loud!" He scanned the reception area, alert.

From the stairwell, Ebenezer and Detective Marshall were already hurrying down. Their eyes widened at the scene before them.

"Did you hear that?" Detective Marshall asked sharply.

"That was a tremendous noise!" Ebenezer added, voice tight with concern.

Christian nodded toward them. "I think it came from the entrance."

Detective Marshall drew his handgun and opened the door, peering into the windy night. "I don't see anything out here," he said cautiously. "With this wind, maybe something fell."

Ebenezer's eyes narrowed as he looked around the empty entrance. "It still baffles me how the noise was so loud, sounded like something had dropped from the sky, and yet there's no trace of any debris!"

Both Detective Marshall and Ebenezer returned to the hotel lobby, quietly shutting the door behind them.

"Anyway," Ebenezer began, raising an eyebrow, "what brings you here at this hour, Christian?"

Christian grinned cheekily. "I just felt restless, so I thought I'd keep Jessica company."

Jessica smiled and pressed a quick kiss to his cheek. "You are such a gentleman," she said.

Ebenezer chuckled at her comment.

"Well, I hope he is," Christian muttered, shooting Ebenezer a playful frown.

"Of course I am a gentleman," he replied, gesturing toward Jessica with mock pride, "especially with a young and beautiful lady like this."

"Okay, lover boy," Detective Marshall interjected, his voice firm but amused, "I think we all need some rest. In the morning, we'll figure out what caused that noise. Something's off about this... all of it. And I intend to get to the bottom of it."

It was now 1:03 a.m. in Radford. Detective Marshall and Ebenezer climbed the stairs toward their rooms, leaving Christian behind in the reception area with Jessica.

"I'll stay with you and make sure you're safe, Miss Jessica Steele," Christian said warmly.

Jessica felt a wave of relief and comfort at his presence. She hugged him tightly. "I feel so protected with you. I haven't felt this safe in a long time. Thank you...

my prince."

Christian kissed her gently on the lips, then lifted his gaze to meet her shining blue eyes, holding the moment with quiet tenderness.

"I like you," Christian said softly.

Jessica hugged him again, a smile lighting her face. But then concern creased her brow.

"I don't want anything to happen to you when you go to Damascus," she admitted.

Christian held her gaze. "I'll be fine. And I'll come back for you. I need to figure out what's been happening over there."

Jessica's grip tightened slightly. "I know you'll be fine... and I know you'll come back for me."

The connection between them felt immediate, unspoken, and profound. Hand in hand, Christian led Jessica upstairs to his room. They knew time was fleeting, so they chose to spend the night together.

Alone, they shared a private, intimate moment. The closeness deepened their bond, and afterward, both felt a sense of contentment and connection.

"Christian... I've never felt anything like this before," Jessica whispered, pressing herself close to him.

Christian smiled, brushing a strand of hair from her face. "Neither have I."

Wrapped together in the warmth of the duvet, they held each other, hearts entwined and comforted by their newfound closeness.

"I love you," Jessica whispered.

Christian's eyes widened in surprise, happiness flooding his face. "I love you, too. I know I do. I feel something with you—it's a wonderful feeling." "I don't normally fall in love this way, just to let you know I, but something tells me this is fate, and I feel a sense of warm feeling with you." Said Jessica.

His heartbeat quickened.

"Feel my heartbeat," he said.

Jessica pressed her hand against his chest and smiled. "I love the feeling."

Together, they drifted slowly into sleep, comforted by their closeness.

It was now 1:14 a.m. in Radford. Outside, the wind howled, rattling the hotel windows. Detective Marshall, unable to sleep, rose and moved to his window, glancing at the darkened sky.

Suddenly, a black cat appeared, staring directly at him, ears flattened and tail twitching with a low, warning purr.

"Goodness... What's that cat's problem?" he muttered.

The cat continued its low growl, prompting Detective Marshall to sigh and step back from the window.

Meanwhile, Ebenezer switched off his lights, gazing at the night sky with quiet anticipation. "Tomorrow will be a big day," he murmured. "I need to make sure my camera batteries are ready to capture this ghost town."

He checked his camera bag and tested the camera. "Perfect. Works like a charm."

Setting it on the dressing table opposite the bed, Ebenezer yawned and prepared for a brief night's sleep.

Hours passed. By 7:21 a.m., all three men—and Jessica—had slept soundly for over five hours. Detective Marshall opened his eyes and checked his watch, ready to face the new day.

"Oh, mother of God! I better wake the others."

Detective Marshall swung his legs out of bed and headed for the bathroom. He brushed his teeth, washed his face with warm water and soap, and took a quick shower. Five minutes later, he stepped out, dried off with a towel, and dressed swiftly in his police uniform.

He made his way down the hall to Ebenezer's room. "Knock, knock... are you still sleeping?"

Ebenezer's eyes fluttered open as he glanced at his watch. "Oh God... it's half past seven already! I better get up. Hold on, Detective, I'm going to get ready... Give me ten minutes."

Detective Marshall rolled his eyes. "Okay, Ebenezer. I'll head back to my room. Once you're ready, meet me there. Got it?"

"Yes, sir!" Ebenezer called after him.

Next, Detective Marshall approached Christian and Jessica's room. "Knock, knock," he said cheerfully. "Hey, lovebirds, time to wake up. We've got a big day ahead of us!"

Christian and Jessica opened their eyes, exchanging a soft smile.

"Did you sleep well, beautiful?" Christian asked, his voice warm and teasing.

"It was amazing! I haven't felt like this in a long time, and you really took care of me," Jessica said softly.

"I'm glad to hear that. But now I must get up—I've got a big day ahead, and I need to solve this mystery."

Jessica's smile faltered, concern flickering across her face. "Please... look after yourself and make sure you all stay safe."

Christian kissed her gently and smiled. "We will be fine. I promise I'll come back for you."

Jessica's eyes glistened with a tear as she quickly put her arm around him. "I know you will. You are brave—and that's what I admire in a man."

Meanwhile, Ebenezer dressed quickly and closed his hotel room door behind him. He made his way to Detective Marshall's room.

"Detective, may I come in?"

"Come on in," the detective replied.

"Let's go meet Christian and begin our journey to Damascus," Ebenezer said. "Time to get to the bottom of this so-called ghost town. Let's see what we can uncover."

Detective Marshall raised an eyebrow and smirked. "Alright... here we go."

Christian continued kissing Jessica softly. "Yes, guys, I'm all set. Okay, beautiful, I have to go with the boys now—but I'll be back. I love you."

Jessica smiled, her hand lingering on his arm. "I love you too, handsome."

Christian kissed her one last time, then walked away to meet Ebenezer and Detective Marshall. Together, the three men headed toward the hotel exit, ready to face whatever awaited them in Damascus.

Jessica opened the door for the three men and waved goodbye.

Before leaving, Detective Marshall glanced at her. "Quick question—about the dog I saw last night. Is that yours?"

"Oh, yes! My Labrador. His name is Prince."

"Right. I saw him relaxing in the corner and wondered what that was. Next time, please make sure he's with you—I almost thought it was an intruder," the detective said.

"Sorry about that, Detective. I'll make sure," Jessica replied.

"Good. And thank you for your hospitality while we stayed at your hotel."

It was now 7:46 a.m. The three men climbed into the police car.

"Okay," said Detective Marshall. "It'll take about an hour and a half to get to Damascus. I want to understand what happened to my police force—and why this town has become isolated."

As he backed out of the parking spot, Ebenezer glanced up at the hotel. Two ravens perched ominously on the roof; their black eyes fixed on him.

"Look, guys! I keep seeing two ravens. It's like they're trying to tell us something," Ebenezer said, uneasy in his voice.

Christian and Detective Marshall followed his gaze. "Maybe, but we can't read their minds—and I'm pretty sure they can't talk," Christian replied with a small grin.

Detective Marshall guided the car onto the main road, and the trio began their early morning journey to Damascus.

8

AN UNFINISHED BUSINESS

Back in Blacksburg, Grant Hennessey woke with a start and glanced at his watch.

"Oh my... 7:51 in the morning! I better get moving," he muttered.

He swung his legs off the bed and headed to the bathroom. Standing in front of the mirror, he scratched at his beard and washed his face with soap and water. Just as he was drying off, a knock came at the door.

"Can you open the door, please?"

"Can you come back later? It's way too early," Grant snapped.

The knocking continued.

"Can you open the door, please?"

Grant sighed. "Fine, fine. I'm coming! Jesus, what sort of hour is this? I could be sleeping right now."

He opened the door to see Julia from the FBI standing there.

"Mr. Hennessey, you didn't call me, so I was wondering if you'd like to join us for an operation in Damascus," she said.

Grant yawned, rubbing his eyes. "Julia, I told you I'd call you about this."

Julia laughed lightly. "Well, some things can't wait. I need you on this mission—and I have more news for you."

Grant's interest piqued. "I remember walking into the bar and passing a man just before I approached you. You must've had a detailed discussion about Damascus."

Grant's expression darkened. "So, you've been spying on me? Is that what your team does—snoop on everyone?"

Julia chuckled again, stepping into the room and pacing back and forth.

"Well, Grant, we've been watching you, and we believe your new friend Ebenezer O'Rourke is already on his way to Damascus with a few companions. One of them seems to be working with Virginia Daily, and the other is Detective Marshall, someone I know well. I say we go there and find out what they plan to do."

Grant's eyes widened in surprise. "Son of a gun! I never thought Ebenezer would actually go. I warned him not to, but I suppose he's a journalist and will take the risk to get a story out of all this. Okay, Julia, I'll come along with you."

Julia's face lit up with a smile. "Thank you, Grant. I'll wait downstairs while you get ready. Then I'll drive you to Damascus so we can see what's really going on."

"Sure thing, Julia—but I must warn you... this ghost town isn't something to take lightly. We'll need to tread carefully."

Julia nodded confidently. "Don't worry. I have an experienced team—over ten years in the FBI. We're fully armed and prepared for whatever we might face."

Grant's expression hardened. "Look, Julia... what I've seen and heard there is hard to believe. This is something no human being has ever truly encountered. Weapons alone won't help—you'll need your mind more than what's in your hands."

Julia paused, clearly taken aback by Grant's words.

"So, you're saying we might be facing something no man or woman has ever encountered before?"

Grant laughed, a deep, resonant sound. "Hahaha... you really don't know, do you? You'll see for yourself soon enough. But when I finally come face to face with this... strange thing, I'll handle it myself."

Julia smiled. "Alright, Grant. Let's discuss more in the car. I'll be waiting downstairs." She turned and walked down the stairs as Grant closed the door behind her, shaking his head in anticipation.

The sun rose over Blacksburg, painting the sky clear and cloudless. Grant readied himself for the journey to Damascus. "I have to warn Ebenezer—he's walking straight into danger."

Stepping outside, he spotted Julia waiting with a team of five FBI agents. He scratched his head, impressed. "You've assembled quite a team, Miss Julia."

"Of course," Julia replied. "I need a team I can trust. Let me introduce them: Agent Mark Swanson, Agent Conrad O'Toole, Agent Jonny Ziegler, Agent Miguel Ventura, and finally, Agent Denzel Price."

Grant offered his hand to each. "Pleased to meet you, gentlemen."

"Agent Denzel, will you come with us in my car? He's worked alongside me for a long time," Julia asked.

Agent Denzel nodded. "Grant, don't worry about a thing. We'll protect you at all costs. Just help us solve this case, and we'll make sure you're rewarded."

"Don't worry about me, Agent Denzel. I know this area and have heard things. Just stay alert and keep your eyes open at all times."

Denzel felt a pang of unease but climbed into the car without another word. Julia started the engine, and they drove toward Damascus, with two other cars carrying the remaining four FBI agents following closely behind.

"So, Grant, tell me more about Damascus," Julia said, keeping her eyes on the road. "What you told me back at the hotel... it's not something I hear every day."

"All I can say is that you need to see it for yourself," Grant replied. "I never thought I'd witness anything like this. My advice—stay close together and show no fear. What you're about to face is beyond what anyone would expect. There's a reason this town was abandoned—something terrible happened there. I just hope we can solve this and all make it out alive."

Agent Denzel chuckled nervously. "So... you're saying there's a ghost out there? I'll believe it when I see it, thank you very much."

Grant smirked at Denzel. "Let's get to Damascus and see for ourselves, shall we?"

Julia drove steadily, her team following closely behind. They left Blacksburg, heading toward Radford, where Ebenezer, Detective Marshall, and Christian had stayed.

Meanwhile, Jacob woke with a start, quickly dressed, and prepared to head to work. His apartment was just a five-minute walk from the Virginia Daily office. Upon arrival, he was greeted warmly by the staff he managed—over twenty journalists.

"Good morning, everyone!" he called.

"Good morning, Jacob!" came the chorus of replies.

Taking a deep breath, Jacob made his way to Christian's office and knocked.

"Knock, knock—Christian?"

A colleague replied, "Christian isn't in today. Neither is Ebenezer. Neither of them reported to work."

Jacob's expression hardened. "Ah... I think I know where they're headed." Without hesitation, he left the office, determined to catch up with Grant.

As he walked, he noticed Grant and the FBI agents driving past, oblivious to his presence. Jacob entered the hotel, where a new receptionist—a woman in her early fifties—greeted him with a warm smile.

"Excuse me, can you help me?" he asked.

"How can I help you?"

Jacob looked at the receptionist, a hint of concern in his eyes. "Did you happen to see an old man checking out of the hotel?"

"Yes, I did. He just left with a young lady—she works for the FBI."

Jacob scratched his head, puzzled about why the FBI would be interested in Grant.

"Okay, thank you."

"No problem."

Jacob quickly left the hotel and walked briskly, planning to gather a few essential items from his office. Five minutes later, he arrived and hurriedly searched through his desk, taking his camera and a handgun. He left the office discreetly, locking the door behind him, muttering under his breath, "I think I know where Grant is headed... Damascus."

He called for a taxi to return home and retrieve his car so he could drive himself to the ghost town.

9

A WARNING

It was 8:26 in the morning. Ebenezer, Christian, and Detective Marshall were driving toward another town in Virginia—Dublin, a small community in Pulaski County.

"Where are we, Detective?" Ebenezer asked.

"We're in Dublin," the detective replied, "and we need to head toward Pulaski, then take Route 81 toward Draper. After that, we'll continue to Fort Chiswell. It's still a long drive before we reach Damascus."

Christian gazed out the car window, taking in the town's quiet streets and the clear blue sky. "Detective, we should probably stop for food somewhere halfway to Damascus," he suggested.

Ebenezer nodded in agreement with Christian. "I'm with you. Stopping for some food isn't a bad idea at all."

"Yes, guys," Detective Marshall replied, "we'll stop when we reach a town called Marion, about forty-six kilometres from Damascus."

Suddenly, a sheriff's car appeared in the left-hand lane as Detective Marshall continued driving. The sheriff noticed the police car from Blacksburg and quickly started his engine, following closely with a wailing siren.

"Guys, I need to pull over and see what the sheriff wants," Detective Marshall said.

The officer stepped out of his vehicle. He wore a dark grey shirt, black tie, black trousers, and a khaki cowboy hat. Medium-built and about one hundred ninety centimeters tall, he had long blonde hair, a beard, and piercing blue eyes. A patch stitched to his left shoulder read *Upper Dublin Police*.

Detective Marshall rolled down his window.

"Gentlemen, can you step out of the car, please?" the officer asked.

"That won't be necessary, Officer," Detective Marshall replied, glancing at the badge. It read: Alan Montgomery.

"Where are you three headed? You were driving pretty fast," Officer Montgomery asked.

"Can you see who I am? I'm from the Blacksburg Police Department," Officer Alan Montgomery said, laughing at Detective Marshall.

"So what?" Montgomery continued. "I have the authority to stop anyone passing through my town—even a police officer. I'll ask again: Where are you three headed?"

Detective Marshall frowned. "We're going to Damascus, to tell you the truth."

Montgomery glanced at Ebenezer and Christian. "And why are these two men with you?"

Ebenezer answered, "We're from *Virginia Daily*. We want to investigate the disappearance of our police officers in Blacksburg and find out what happened in the Damascus police department as well."

Montgomery laughed, a hint of disbelief in his voice. "You do realize that Damascus is isolated and dangerous! No one goes there anymore; it's a ghost town."

Christian joined in. "I've already been there, Officer. This will be my second visit, so I think I have an idea of what to expect."

Montgomery's expression turned concerned, defensive. "Look, gentlemen, I'd turn your car around and head back to Blacksburg. For your own safety, I strongly advise you to stay clear of Damascus. It's a no-go zone."

Detective Marshall shook his head firmly. "Officer Montgomery, I understand your concerns, but we need to discover why my men have vanished. We must find out who is responsible for these crimes. We're going to Damascus."

Montgomery reached for his gun. "Get out of the car and put your hands on your head where I can see them!"

Detective Marshall raised his hands in surprise. "This isn't necessary. Calm down. Put the gun down and let's talk like civilized adults."

"Quiet! Do as I say! Get out of the car now! Slowly... Now, you two as well!" Officer Montgomery shouted, visibly nervous.

Ebenezer and Christian stepped out of the car slowly, followed closely by Detective Marshall. The three men placed their hands behind their heads.

"Okay," Officer Alan Montgomery said, "I need you three to remain silent until I call my team and escort you to the Dublin Police Department for not heeding my advice."

Detective Marshall's hand moved swiftly to his gun at his side. He leveled it at Montgomery. "Listen carefully. You are pointing a gun at a detective. I could arrest you for that. I suggest you put your weapon down and hear me out. Get back in your car, drive back to your town, and act as if this conversation never happened. That is an order."

Montgomery reluctantly lowered his gun, acknowledging the detective's instructions.

"You'll regret this," he muttered. "I'm only trying to protect you three from danger. That's all!"

Christian laughed, raising his voice. "Will you ever shut up? Take your car back to your town and leave us be!"

Ebenezer glanced at Christian, a mix of surprise and pride on his face. "Christian, you really do surprise me. I never thought I'd hear you talk back to a police officer... but I'm impressed."

Christian shrugged. "Well, sometimes you have to let your frustration out. Today just had to be that day."

Detective Marshall rolled his eyes at both men. "Anyway, Officer, we're leaving now. I suggest you go back and grab a donut or something. That's what police are famous for, anyway."

Montgomery offered a sarcastic smile, returned to his car, started the engine, and drove off.

"Phew, that was close! How did you reach for your gun so quickly, Detective?" Ebenezer asked.

"Well," Marshall replied, "let's just say I have bags of experience. This officer was definitely a rookie."

"You are awesome, Detective!" Ebenezer said, shaking his head in admiration.

Christian muttered, "Jesus Christ... I need a beer after this. The first time anyone's pointed a gun at me."

The three men climbed back into their car and continued their journey toward Marion.

10

AN UNKNOWN CASE TO SOLVE

It was 8:47 in the morning in Blacksburg, and the sun shone brightly over the town. Grant glanced at the road ahead, feeling the weight of the journey before him—one that could change his life for better or worse. Agent Julia drove steadily, her eyes briefly flicking to a road sign on the left. Bold letters read: *You are now leaving Blacksburg.* Grant sighed.

"Julia," he began, "tell me—why put yourself and your team in so much danger?"

Agent Julia met his gaze. "You know our title and our job—we're the FBI. This is the most important case we're handling right now. With your help and information, I believe we can crack it. You've been there, you've experienced—or at least heard—things we don't even know about. So please, Grant, help us solve this unusual case. As Denzel says, your safety is guaranteed. I'll make sure my team protects you at all costs."

Grant nodded. "I appreciate that. But we must get there before Ebenezer. He has no idea what he's about to witness, and this is his first time. My first experience wasn't pleasant either, but I adapted as I went. We need to reach him before he steps into danger. Can you promise me that, Agent Julia?"

Julia smiled. "We'll do our best. Let me alert the team behind us and ask them to increase speed—safely." She clipped her walkie-talkie from her belt pocket and spoke into it. "Agent Mark, Agent Conrad, increase your speed as I'm about to accelerate. Over!"

"This is Agent Mark. Copy that, over!"

"This is Agent Conrad. No problem. Over to you, Agent Julia."

Mark and Conrad gradually increased their pace as Julia pressed down on the accelerator. Denzel rolled down his window, lit a cigarette, and inhaled deeply.

"You don't mind if I smoke, do you?" he asked with a smirk. Grant shot him a quick grin.

"Not at all. Go ahead."

Denzel reached into his coat pocket, grabbed a pack of cigarettes, and lit one. He offered it to Grant.

"Would you like a cigarette?"

Grant shook his head. "No, thank you. But I appreciate the offer."

Denzel turned his attention back to the road, exhaling smoke out the window. Grant folded his arms across his chest and stared at the rear window, realizing Blacksburg was now behind them. He let out a slow sigh, the weight of the journey ahead settling on him.

Agent Julia glanced into the rearview mirror and caught Grant's nervous expression. "Are you alright?"

"I'm nervous, to be honest," he admitted. "But I must stay positive. We need to reach Ebenezer."

Julia offered a reassuring smile. "Exactly. Stay calm. Take a short nap if you want."

Grant rested his head against the seat and closed his eyes, trying to steady his mind for the journey ahead.

11

LOVE IS STRONG WITH SOME HELP FROM A STRANGER

Back in Radford, Virginia, Jessica struggled to concentrate while working at the Radford Hotel. Worry weighed on her, and a sadness lingered behind her smile. She sat at her desk, tapping her fingernails against the desktop.

Her colleague, Marilyn Keywood, walked into the office. "Good morning, Jessica."

Jessica returned a small smile. "Good morning, Marilyn! How are you today?"

"I'm fine," Marilyn replied, "though I could really use a coffee. I had to rush to get up this morning—I thought I might be late!"

Jessica laughed softly, tucking a strand of hair behind her ear. "Even if you had been late, it wouldn't have mattered. I would've managed somehow."

Marilyn noticed immediately that Jessica wasn't herself. "Are you all right? You seem... different. Usually, you're full of life, but today you seem a bit down. What's on your mind?"

Jessica walked over and gave her friend a tight hug. "Oh, Marilyn... I met someone yesterday—a really kind and caring man. He's a guest here, and I think I've already fallen for him, even though I just met him last night!"

Marilyn's eyes lit up with excitement. "That's wonderful! Tell me more about him."

"Well," Jessica said, a shy smile forming, "he came with two other men. One seemed to be a police officer, and the other a colleague. They were all lovely, but... I felt an instant connection with Christian. There was something magical about him."

Marilyn's smile widened. "What's his name again?" Christian! Said Jessica. And what did he do to make you feel so happy? I know you pretty well, and from your stories, you don't always have the best luck with men... but something tells me this one made you feel special—like a queen. Am I right?" Said Marilyn.

"Yes!" Jessica replied, a dreamy smile spreading across her face. "He made me feel so special. He always noticed me, to really listen. I felt his warm presence around me, like he was there just for me. I've never felt like that before—until he walked through those doors. Suddenly, it felt like my life was about to change. I had shivers all over, but in the nicest way."

Marilyn's eyes sparkled with excitement. "That's wonderful, Jessica. Tell me... did you two...?"

Jessica's cheeks flushed crimson. "Yes, we did. And it was amazing. Christian made me feel incredible. It all happened so quickly, but I was happy—truly happy."

Marilyn leaned against the reception desk, curiosity and excitement mixed on her face. "So, when will you see him next?"

Jessica's expression softened, turning from smiles to worry. "That's just it... He's gone to Damascus with the two men he came here with, and I'm terrified for him. We both know Damascus is a no-go zone, and I can't shake the feeling he's in danger."

Marilyn's face mirrored her concern. "Hmmm... that does sound sudden. What does he do for a living?"

Jessica helped Marilyn organize the guest files, continuing, "He's a journalist, so he's chasing a story. That's why I'm worried. I can't help but think... What if this is the last time I see him? I almost feel like I should follow them!"

Marilyn paused, placing a gentle hand on Jessica's arm. "Really? But that would put you in danger too. I think it's better to stay here. I'm sure Christian knows what he's doing."

Jessica's eyes glistened with determination. "I love him, Marilyn, and I need to be there with him—to protect him. Come with me! Let's go together and bring them back somewhere safe."

Marilyn hesitated, her brow furrowed. Traveling all the way to Damascus was risky, but when she saw the seriousness in Jessica's eyes, her resolve softened. "I don't think it's a good idea to make a trip to Damascus... but if this is the man you love—which I don't need to guess, because I can see it—then okay. We'll go."

Jessica's face lit up in disbelief. "Are you sure?"

"Yeah, I'm sure," Marilyn said, nodding firmly. "I'll do it for you. Now, let's close up the hotel and tell everyone it won't be open for a few days."

Excitement and nerves surged through Jessica as she hugged her friend tightly. "You're such a good friend. Thank you so much!"

Marilyn smiled, taking a deep breath. "It's okay, darling. So, what are we waiting for? We need to be prepared—we should take our guns with us."

Jessica nodded and grabbed two firearms from the office drawer, her hands trembling slightly with anticipation.

"My name is Jessica, and this is my friend Marilyn. And you are?"

The man smiled as he untangled the jumper cables. "Jonathan McFarland. Pleased to meet you, Jessica and Marilyn." He glanced at the cars. "So, where are you both headed?"

Jessica and Marilyn exchanged uncertain looks, hesitant to reveal too much. "Well... we'd rather not say, if you don't mind," Jessica replied cautiously.

"Sure, that's fine," Jonathan said with a nod. He opened the front hood of his van, then Jessica's car, carefully connecting the cables. Once the setup was complete, he returned to his van to generate power. With a sudden roar, Jessica's car engine came to life.

"Wow! Thank you so much, Jonathan. You're a lifesaver!" Jessica exclaimed.

Jonathan smiled warmly. "My pleasure. I hope you both have a safe journey, wherever you're headed."

Marilyn, unable to contain herself, blurted out, "Actually... we're heading to Damascus!"

Jessica's eyes widened, and she shot an angry glance at her friend. *Why would she tell him?* she wondered, frustration rising.

"Why did you tell him we're going to Damascus?" she muttered under her breath.

Marilyn shrugged casually. "He helped us. The least we could do was be honest and give him the courtesy of knowing our destination."

Jonathan frowned, concern etched across his face. "Really... but that town has been abandoned for over seven years. Why would you go there?"

Marilyn answered firmly, "Jessica's new lover is traveling there, and she wants to make sure he stays safe."

Jonathan sighed. "Look, ladies, it's your choice where you go. Who am I to tell you otherwise? But legends say that strange things happen in Damascus—things no human has ever encountered before..."

Marilyn's brow furrowed, but she stood her ground. "I know the town has been abandoned for a long time, and strange things must have happened. But my friend is in love, and she wants to protect him. You know, things people do for love."

Jessica shifted uneasily. "Have you actually been to Damascus?"

Jonathan cleared his throat. "I was there many years ago. It was a lovely town... until that evening when I heard the news of many people killed. Since then, no one dared to go back. Anyway, let me grab my cables." He walked toward his van, retrieving the booster cables from the back.

Jessica and Marilyn whispered to each other. "Shall we let him come with us?" Marilyn asked cautiously.

"I'm not sure," Jessica said, frowning. "We only just asked him for help, and I'd rather not involve him. We don't want anyone getting hurt while we reach Damascus."

Marilyn turned to Jonathan. "Hey, Jonathan, would you fancy coming along with us to help my friend find her lover?"

Jonathan looked bewildered. "Look, ladies, I don't really want to go there. I'm worried about why you'd put yourselves in danger. But... I also understand why you feel you must."

"So... is that a yes?" Marilyn asked, smiling.

Jonathan hesitated, then nodded. "Okay, I'll follow you. Are you both armed?"

"We each have a gun," Jessica replied.

"Good," Jonathan said. "I'll come along—for your safety. I'm equipped, but I don't have a gun. I do have a baseball bat and a toolset, though."

Jessica laughed lightly. "Okay, that'll have to do. Just hold onto your bat, alright?"

Jonathan nodded and climbed into his van, starting the engine. Jessica and Marilyn slid into the Ford Mustang, and Jessica started the engine. With their new companion ready, the trio set off on their journey to Damascus.

12

THE DISCOVERY

It was 9:15 a.m. in Marion, Virginia, when Ebenezer, Christian, and Detective Marshall arrived.

"Here we are, guys," Detective Marshall said, surveying the quiet streets.

Ebenezer's eyes scanned the town. "Goodness! Look at the people here. They seem so relaxed, as if they have no idea what's happening just a few kilometres from Damascus."

Detective Marshall shrugged. "Why shouldn't they feel relaxed? Nothing has happened here. They're just getting on with their lives."

"If I knew what was going on nearby, I'd clear out of my home and head as far away as possible," Ebenezer replied, tension tightening his voice.

Detective Marshall glanced at the fuel gauge. "Okay, let me find a gas station and fill up the tank."

"I see one ahead!" shouted Ebenezer.

"Well spotted. Let's head there. We can grab a bite—burritos, if you're hungry."

"A burrito? It's 9:15 in the morning. I'd prefer pancakes with syrup or some eggs and bacon, thank you very much," Ebenezer said, shaking his head with a small smile.

"Whatever you fancy," Detective Marshall said with a chuckle.

As they drove toward the station, Christian's eyes widened. The gas station looked abandoned, rusty, and long unused.

"This is strange..." he murmured.

"What's strange about a gas station?" Ebenezer asked, raising an eyebrow.

"Well, look at it! It's old, rusted, and barely anyone is using it. From what I can see, there's no one inside either," Christian said, unease creeping into his voice.

Detective Marshall reached for his gun. "Okay, stay behind me. Let's investigate."

The three men climbed slowly out of the police car, approaching the gas station's front door. Detective Marshall led the way, turning the handle cautiously. A loud creak echoed as the door swung open.

"Hello? Is anybody here?" Ebenezer called, his voice tense.

The counter was empty. No one was in sight.

"This is odd. Why would anyone just leave a place like this?" Christian muttered, unease creeping into his tone.

"Let's check that door over there," Detective Marshall suggested, nodding toward a side entrance. Ebenezer followed, scanning the station as Christian moved beside him.

Detective Marshall raised his gun, sweeping left to right, eyes sharp for any sign of danger. He noticed another door on the right and rapped on it.

"Hello? Anybody here?" he called again.

A muffled voice answered from inside.

"Hold on a second..." Ebenezer frowned, puzzled.

"Why would anyone leave their business unattended like this?" Christian whispered.

"I don't know," Ebenezer admitted. "It's really strange."

The gas station owner slowly opened the door, revealing himself.

"Jesus Christ! Put that gun away before you give me a heart attack!" the gas station owner exclaimed.

Detective Marshall lowered his weapon, frowning. "What on earth are you doing, leaving your business unattended?"

"Sorry, Officer," the owner replied. "I was just taking care of something quickly. What can I do for you gentlemen?"

"Well, for starters, I wanted to fill up my car, but I wasn't comfortable doing it knowing no one was around," Detective Marshall explained, rolling his eyes.

"Apologies for that," the owner said.

"Next time, don't leave your gas station alone. Someone could steal from you. And why are you the only one here? Haven't you got any help?"

"No, it's just me. I own this station," he answered.

Ebenezer shook his head. "So much for breakfast, then."

Christian chimed in, trying to lighten the mood. "You could at least spruce up your gas station—it looks pretty outdated. Just my opinion. I'm sure you agree."

The owner sighed. "You're right. I know it needs work. Anyway, where are you headed?" He busied himself at the cash register.

"Damascus," Detective Marshall replied.

The owner stopped and studied the detective. "You gentlemen should stay clear of that town. It's a ghost town, and no one is supposed to enter."

"Yes, yes, we've heard that before," Detective Marshall replied firmly. "But we're going there for several reasons. First, my department sent officers there who never returned. Second, I'm a police officer, and I signed up to solve crimes. And third, if people keep ignoring Damascus and heeding warnings to stay away, it will remain isolated. It's my job to ensure every town is safe to visit; otherwise, nothing ever gets resolved. Is that clear?"

The gas station owner nodded slowly. "I may not agree with you, but that's your choice. And I trust you know what you're doing."

Ebenezer stepped forward. "By the way, what's your name, and how long have you lived in Marion?"

The owner glanced at him. "My name is Gary Swanson, and I've lived here all my life."

"Pleased to meet you, Gary. I'm Ebenezer, and this is my colleague, Christian. We're from the Virginia Daily. And this is Detective Colin Marshall." Ebenezer gestured toward the detective, who shot him a sarcastic look.

"I can introduce myself, too," Gary said, smiling faintly. "But thank you for the introduction, gentlemen."

"I hope you all know what you're about to face," Gary said solemnly. "I must tell you—I went there a few months back to see for myself. I noticed something... unusual, especially what I personally witnessed."

The three men leaned in, captivated. Ebenezer asked, "Really? Tell me more. What did you see?"

"Back in June, while I was working, I caught a news report about Damascus—why it's still isolated, and why no one goes there. It struck me as very strange. Something terrible must have happened for the residents to abandon their homes so suddenly. And to think this happened over seven years ago... Some people died mysteriously, others disappeared. I wondered if I could do something to help.

"One evening, I decided to close my gas station at eleven instead of midnight and drive toward Damascus late at night. When I arrived, the town was destroyed, with traces of blood everywhere. It was like stepping into a ghost town, filled with dead bodies—humans and animals alike. Cars and trucks were smashed and scattered. Then I saw something extraordinary... something no man or woman on earth has ever seen.

"A strange, demon-like figure appeared, clad in a gold-armored coat that looked like steel. Gold ran down to his ankles, and he had no boots. I quickly hid behind some old barrels outside a local bar in Damascus,

Detective Marshall glanced at Christian and Ebenezer. "Alright, continue, Gary. Tell us more about this... demonic thing."

Gary nodded, swallowing hard. "While I was hiding behind those barrels, I noticed his face. He had bright yellow eyes and horns on each side of his head, just above the ears. I thought... has Halloween come early for this thing? Then I saw a bright yellow light emanating from his hands. I was both amazed and terrified."

Detective Marshall narrowed his eyes. "Why didn't you warn your town or report this to the police?"

Gary fidgeted nervously. "I know I should have, but I feared no one would believe me. I thought they'd laugh, saying it was all in my imagination."

Detective Marshall's tone sharpened. "Exactly. You should have reported it as soon as you saw this creature—or whatever it is. Lives could have been saved, but now it may be too late!"

Gary's anger flared. "Detective, this being wasn't human. It was a walking, demon-like creature! Can you blame me for not alerting the police after witnessing it? I was shaken... disturbed... terrified."

Ebenezer nodded, understanding Gary's fear. "I can imagine how terrified you must have been. That kind of encounter would affect anyone emotionally."

Gary's anger flared. "Believe me, it did. As soon as he turned his head toward me, I ducked behind the barrel again and slowly made my way to my car. I drove off as fast as I could."

Detective Marshall pressed further. "So, you're telling me there's a demon-like creature lurking around the town—and it's been there for over seven years?"

Gary's face tightened. "I truly believe so, Detective Marshall. That's why I'm surprised you three want to go there at all."

Christian leaned forward. "Did this demon see you? Surely it must have noticed you leaving."

Gary shook his head. "I honestly don't know. I've never returned and have never encountered anything like that again."

Ebenezer's mind wandered back to his conversation with Grant at the Iron Man Inn bar in Blacksburg. "You know, I spoke with an old man named Grant. He also noticed something unusual in Damascus."

Gary added, "This demon seems to come out at night. From the way it moves and watches, it's clearly searching for someone."

Detective Marshall frowned. "So, you're saying it's looking for someone? How can you tell?"

Gary gestured with his hands. "It kept scanning the area, observing everything around it. I believe someone—or something—is still there."

Ebenezer nodded, a nervous edge to his movements. He wandered around the gas station while Detective Marshall and Christian continued to question Gary.

Christian's voice trembled with disbelief. "So, we're really going to Damascus knowing there's a strange demon out there—and we have no idea how to stop it? And no ammunition?"

Gary sighed. "There's no proof of how this demon came into the world, but if you search carefully around the town, you might find something that could help." Christian's worry deepened at the thought.

"Goodness gracious! I've seen strange things before on my first visit to Damascus. I even noticed a shadow lurking around... but I never imagined we'd be facing something like this."

Gary glanced at Christian, his expression serious. "I don't know why you men feel the need to be heroes, but that's your choice. I'd stay away from Damascus if I were you. Just take care of yourselves out there—that's all I can say."

Detective Marshall nodded. "Thank you for all the information. We'll be on our way... once I refuel my car."

"Stay safe," Gary said calmly.

Detective Marshall stepped outside, turning on the gas pump to fill his tank. Ebenezer and Christian followed and slowly climbed into the police car.

Ebenezer shook his head, disbelief written across his face. "I can't believe what we just heard. Gary has seen this demon and still lives here normally! If it were me, I would have left immediately. This creature isn't far from town, and more casualties seem inevitable."

Christian's tone hardened. "I agree. So many lives could have been saved already. Now it's our responsibility to make sure no more are lost. This demon has to be stopped, and we need to find a way to defeat it—or countless more will suffer."

Detective Marshall finished filling the tank and returned the pump to its stand. He slid into the driver's seat. "Let's move. We need to figure out how to stop this demon and put an end to this nightmare."

He handed the money to Gary, who was standing outside the driver-side window. "Keep the change and thank you for your cooperation. Now we know what we're up against."

"No problem, Detective Marshall. And remember what I said earlier... Please stay safe."

Detective Marshall turned the ignition, and the car roared to life, heading toward Saint Commerce Street in Marion. Soon, they veered onto Route 81, with Damascus just thirty-five minutes away.

Breaking the tense silence, Detective Marshall addressed Ebenezer and Christian. "Listen carefully. Our journey is about to take us into something we never imagined. There's something sinister out there, so I want you both fully armed. Is that clear?"

In unison, Ebenezer and Christian replied, "Yes, sir!"

13

Closer to the Ghost Town

Meanwhile, back in Radford, Jessica drove along Lee Highway with Marilyn, while Jonathan followed behind in his car.

"I'm worried, Jessica," Marilyn said, glancing at her friend.

"I'm worried too… and scared," Jessica admitted. "But I have to do this. This might be my last chance to see Christian alive. Who knows if we even make it out of this alive? All we can do is warn him and his friends—and somehow get them to leave with us."

Marilyn raised an eyebrow. "You really think you can persuade a police officer and two newspaper journalists to turn back? They're here to get the story… and the detective is just doing his job."

Jessica nodded, accepting that she couldn't stop the three men from pursuing the mystery. The only solution was to be there and help.

Jonathan muttered to himself as he followed them. "I still can't believe I'm heading to a ghost town. I must be crazy!"

Meanwhile, Grant, FBI Agent Julia, and her team sped along at 110 kilometres per hour as they neared Radford.

"Agent Miguel, do you copy? Over," Julia called into her walkie-talkie.

"Agent Julia, I hear you loud and clear. Over," Miguel responded.

"Good. We've reached a city called Radford," Julia continued. "We must pass through Dublin and Marion to reach Damascus as quickly as possible. Is that clear? Over to you."

Agent Miguel responded swiftly. "I'll alert the team to follow your instructions. Over!"

Agent Julia kept her eyes on the road as Grant gazed at the passing scenery.

"Ah, Radford! It's been a while since I was last here," Grant said.

"Oh really?" Julia replied. "This town is peaceful. I don't recall dealing with many dangerous cases here."

Agent Jonny picked up his walkie-talkie. "Agent Julia, do you copy?"

"Go ahead," she said.

"We've just arrived in Radford," Jonny reported. "We should slow down while driving through the town. There are people around."

Grant frowned at the suggestion.

"Please, don't slow down, Agent Julia," Julia muttered under her breath, rolling her eyes. Then, speaking into her radio, she continued, "Agent Jonny, do you copy?"

"Yes, go ahead," he replied.

"We need to drive through Radford as quickly and smoothly as possible. There are already visitors heading toward Damascus, and ensuring their safety is our top priority."

Jonny hesitated but followed orders. "Understood, but we must also consider the safety of the locals in Radford. We don't want any casualties. Over."

As they entered Radford, the locals noticed three vehicles speeding through town. One resident shouted angrily, waving his fists. "Learn to drive slowly, will you!"

Julia ignored him and continued through the town, keeping her team focused.

They merged onto Highway 11, heading toward Lee Highway as efficiently as possible.

"Goodness, I'm glad we're leaving Radford," Julia muttered. "Now we can focus on getting through the next town and on to Dublin."

Once the team passed Radford safely, Grant smiled. "Thank you, Agent Julia. That was impressive driving. We can get to Damascus faster now!"

Julia glanced at her road map. "We're still about an hour and a half away, but if we maintain this pace, we'll be there in under an hour."

The team, with Grant, continued their journey toward Dublin, another small Virginia town. Damascus was drawing closer.

14

Road to Ghost Town

At 9:54 a.m., Ebenezer, Christian, and Detective Marshall drove toward Damascus. Soon, a green road sign appeared on the right side of the road: **"Welcome to Damascus."**

"Look, we've finally arrived!" Detective Marshall exclaimed.

Ebenezer stared in horror. The town was completely isolated. No people, no animals, not a single vehicle in motion. Instead, the streets were littered with dead bodies, twisted metal, and wrecked cars.

"Look at this town! Dead bodies everywhere, wrecked vehicles... there's no one around. It really is like a ghost town!" Ebenezer said, his voice trembling.

Christian glanced at him, wondering if Ebenezer was beginning to grasp the grim reality.

"Now you believe me, Ebenezer?" Christian asked.

"This... this is beyond anything I could have imagined! A town completely deserted... and utterly silent!"

"Detective Marshall, do you mind if I take a few photos?"

"Go ahead," Detective Marshall replied. "I'm going to park, and then we can walk through the town."

The three men exited the car, surveying the surroundings. Their eyes fell on an unattended gas station, grimy and abandoned as if unused for decades. Ebenezer retrieved his camera and snapped shots from every angle.

"This is terrible! My first experience seeing a town like this…" he muttered, awe and disbelief mingling in his voice.

"Let's go inside the gas station and see if we can find any clues!" Detective Marshall urged.

Christian followed him, while Ebenezer remained momentarily distracted by his photos.

"Ebenezer, did you hear me? We're going inside the gas station," Marshall repeated.

"Sure, Detective. I'll be right there—just a few more photos," Ebenezer replied.

At that moment, two ravens appeared, circling high above the gas station.

"Will you look at that?" Ebenezer said, his voice tinged with unease.

"This looks just like the one we found back in Bisset Park!" Ebenezer said, his voice trembling. "He's turning purple—the body still looks fresh. God knows how long he's been lying here dead!"

"Seven years, to be precise," Christian muttered, rolling his eyes at Ebenezer's remark.

Detective Marshall knelt beside the corpse, examining it closely. "Look here, gentlemen," he said grimly. "This man has scratches all over his chest and arms. He must have fought something… these aren't human marks."

Christian ran his hands through his hair, shaken. "Oh, Lord. I've got a bad feeling about this, Detective. Maybe coming here was a mistake."

Ebenezer scowled. "A little late to say that now, don't you think?"

"Listen, Ebenezer," Christian shot back, frustration cracking through his voice. "I wanted you to believe me—and now you do. So what's the problem? Yes, I'm scared, but how do you expect me to react after seeing two corpses and a dead animal? You remember that don't you?"

"Enough!" Detective Marshall snapped, rising to his feet. "You two sound like school children squabbling over candy! Pull yourselves together. We're here now, and we're going to finish this. We'll find whatever demon is behind this and put an end to it—once and for all."

The sharpness in his tone silenced both men. Shame crept across their faces.

"I'm sorry, Christian," Ebenezer said quietly. "I shouldn't have raised my voice."

Christian exhaled and extended his hand. "Me too. I'm sorry."

Ebenezer took the handshake firmly.

Detective Marshall exhaled deeply, the weight of what they'd seen pressing on him. "All right," he said, steadying his voice. "We know this thing—whatever it is—kills in ways no human could. We've seen its work. It leaves bodies blue and purple. Humans, animals... it doesn't care. That much we know. Three times now, the evidence has been the same. So, we keep going. We will find more clues."

"I completely agree," Ebenezer said firmly. "We have to stop this demon—and figure out how to kill it."

The three men stepped out of the gas station and into the eerie stillness of the street. The silence was suffocating. Dead bodies littered the ground, sprawled across sidewalks and porches. The air smelled of decay and rust. Houses sagged under years of neglect; shattered glass crunched beneath their boots.

"Mother of God," Detective Marshall whispered. "Look at this place. Every home... gone. The windows are smashed, the roofs collapsed. It's like the whole town was wiped clean. That thing—whatever it is—must've gone door to door, killing everyone it found."

Ebenezer glanced at his watch. It was a few minutes past ten. The morning light did little to soften the horror before them. They had found one body inside the gas station and dozens more strewn across the streets of Damascus—the ghost town that lived up to its name.

"Guys, we need to keep looking for clues," Ebenezer said. "From what Grant told me, this demon only shows itself at night. That gives us time—enough—to piece this mystery together before it appears."

"Detective Marshall!" Christian called out suddenly, pointing ahead. "Look—over there! A church!"

Detective Marshall followed his gaze. A small, weather-beaten church stood at the end of the street, its white paint flaking away, the steeple leaning slightly to one side. The detective's expression hardened. He drew his revolver from his belt and nodded to the others.

"All right, gentlemen," he said quietly. "Guns out. Let's see what we find inside that church."

The three men stepped into the church—and froze.

Hundreds of bodies lay scattered across the pews, the aisles, and around the altar. The air was thick with the stench of decay. Instinctively, they raised their hands to their mouths and noses, trying to block the unbearable smell.

"Holy Christ!" Christian staggered outside and vomited on the steps.

Ebenezer stood rooted in place, eyes wide with horror. Detective Marshall, however, showed no visible sign of fear; his expression was grim but steady.

"I've seen things like this before in my line of work," Detective Marshall said quietly. "If you need a moment, take it."

Christian wiped his mouth and forced himself back inside. Ebenezer kept his hand pressed over his face, fighting the urge to gag.

"What in God's name have we walked into?" Ebenezer whispered.

Detective Marshall moved deeper into the church, stepping carefully over the corpses, his boots echoing on the wooden floor. "This is beyond sick," he muttered. "But we have to document it—every inch of it."

Ebenezer's stomach churned. Part of him wanted to run out, to breathe clean air again, yet he couldn't abandon the detective. Christian swallowed hard, still shaken from his reaction.

"Pull yourself together," he told himself. "Marshall can't do this alone."

"Look at this!" the detective suddenly called out. "After seven years of isolation, this—this is what we find. These bodies aren't decomposed. They look almost fresh, as if whatever killed them happened only recently."

He crouched beside one of the victims, studying the skin stretched tight over bone. "You could still identify them through DNA or a hospital post-mortem. Which means this thing—this demon—didn't just torture them." He paused, his voice lowering. "It drained them. It's as if everybody here has been completely...

sucked dry."

Christian crouched beside one of the many corpses and carefully nudged it onto its back. His breath caught when he saw the glint of metal. "Detective! Come take a look at this! It's a police badge—it says *Damascus Town Police Department!*"

Detective Marshall hurried over, pulling a pair of rubber gloves from his pocket. He knelt to inspect the body. "Good eye, Christian. Let's see if we can identify him."

He brushed away dust from the officer's shirt, revealing a nameplate. "Axel Jones," he read aloud, his voice tightening.

Ebenezer stepped closer, placing a hand on the detective's shoulder. "You knew him, didn't you?"

Marshall nodded slowly. "Yes. His wife came to me time and time again, asking where he'd gone. I never had an answer for her." His gaze fell to the floor. "Now I do."

"I'm sorry," Ebenezer murmured.

Marshall exhaled heavily. "Thank you. If anything, this makes me more determined to find the thing responsible—the demon, creature, whatever it is. I owe him that much."

Ebenezer scratched the back of his head; his face twisted in disgust. "Christian, when you came here before, where exactly did you go?"

"Mostly around the hotel area and a few nearby houses," Christian replied. "I didn't explore much—I just wanted a few notes for the article about what Damascus looked like. You know, the one I mentioned back in Blacksburg."

"A-ha, I see," Ebenezer said thoughtfully.

Detective Marshall straightened, looking down at the fallen officer. He raised his hand in a solemn salute. For a moment, the church fell silent—until a faint movement flickered in the shadows.

Something—someone—was there.

A shape drifted along the far wall, sliding closer. Then the heavy church door began to creak open on its own.

Detective Marshall spun around. "Who's there?" he called out, his voice sharp.

Christian and Ebenezer turned too, inching toward the doorway, unaware that the dark shape was gliding closer to Marshall from behind.

A chill wind swept through the church, brushing against the detective's back. He stiffened. "What was that?"

Christian peered outside, frowning. "There's no one here... that's impossible." He looked back toward the door, voice trembling. "It just opened by itself."

Ebenezer glanced toward the church entrance, scanning the area outside. "There's no one here. I'm going to shut the door."

He pulled the heavy doors closed with a thud, then started walking toward the far end of the church.

Detective Marshall drew his revolver from his belt and moved cautiously around the pews, eyes darting from shadow to shadow. "Who's there?" he barked, his voice echoing through the silent hall.

Ebenezer turned toward him, frowning. "What do you mean, Detective? There's no one here—the door opened by itself!"

"I don't know," Detective Marshall said, his tone tense. "But I felt something."

Christian's expression grew serious. "What exactly did you see—or feel?"

Detective Marshall paused, scanning the rafters. "It was like a gust of wind... blowing straight at me. And that's odd, considering we're inside a sealed church."

Christian's face paled. "That must be the same shadow I saw when I was here last time. The demon knows we're here."

Ebenezer's hands began to tremble, his voice unsteady. "Guys... let's get out of here."

Detective Marshall gave a firm nod, keeping his gun raised as he backed toward the door. "Agreed. We'll keep searching for answers—and find this creature. One way or another, we end this."

The three men stepped out of the church, leaving behind the lifeless bodies of the townspeople and the fallen police officer.

"Let's check out that saloon, Detective. We might find some clues there," Christian said.

Ebenezer glanced up at the sky, squinting against the sun. For a moment, he closed his eyes, then looked around the desolate town. How could one demon cause so much ruin?

They made their way toward the old saloon. The building looked weathered and half-rotted, its wooden boards gray with age, the windows clouded by decades of dust. Ebenezer pushed the door open, and a rusty hinge shrieked in protest. A rat darted out from the shadows, scurrying past his boots.

"Jesus! That scared the life out of me!" Ebenezer jumped back, heart pounding, then laughed shakily at himself.

Detective Marshall and Christian exchanged wary glances before following him inside.

"My God," Christian muttered, covering his nose. "This place smells like a brothel left to rot."

He moved toward the bar and froze. "Hey—look at this. I found a gun!"

Marshall joined him, eyes narrowing. "A magnum. Looks like it's been sitting here for years—rusted, worn down."

Ebenezer frowned. "Maybe someone tried to defend themselves."

"Could be," Detective Marshall said, scanning the room for signs of struggle. He crouched behind the counter and tugged open the drawer beneath the cash register. Inside lay several dusty cartridges.

"Well, gentlemen," he said, holding them up, "I found the bullets. Let's keep searching—there might be more clues."

Ebenezer circled the room, his boots creaking on the warped floorboards, until something caught his eye. A wooden trapdoor lay half-hidden behind a broken stool.

"Guys, over here!" he called. "There is a cellar door. Let's see what's down there."

Detective Marshall gave a tight nod. "Good work, Ebenezer."

As Ebenezer grasped the iron handle and pulled, the hinges groaned in protest. A cold, stale draft rose from the darkness below.

"Okay, Detective, I've opened it. Do you have your torch?"

Detective Marshall grabbed his flashlight from his belt and switched it on.

Christian leaned over beside Ebenezer, peering into the darkness below. The beam of light revealed a narrow staircase draped in thick cobwebs.

"Looks like no one's been down here for a long time," Detective Marshall muttered.

A foul stench rose from the depths. Ebenezer gagged. "What is that awful smell?"

The three men covered their noses as the air grew thick and rotten, like spoiled fish and damp earth.

"I think I'm going to throw up," Ebenezer groaned.

Carefully, they descended the creaking steps. The light flickered across the cellar floor—where two bodies lay motionless.

"My, oh my," Detective Marshall whispered. "This is starting to make sense now. Two more bodies—and they're still fresh. You'd think they'd have decomposed by now, especially if this happened years ago."

Ebenezer and Christian froze, their faces pale with horror.

"This demon has wiped out nearly the entire town of Damascus," Christian said quietly.

Detective Marshall nodded grimly. "And that's exactly why we're going to stop it—whatever it takes."

Both men agreed, though unease settled heavy in their chests. With so many lives lost in such gruesome ways, how could they end something so inhuman?

They began to search the cellar. The air was cold and damp, the silence broken only by their footsteps.

"Wait—look!" Christian said, pointing to the ground. "I found a key. And it looks... strange."

Detective Marshall brought his torch closer. "Let me see that."

Christian handed it over. Detective Marshall turned the key in his hand, studying its surface.

"It's old—hand-forged. And look here," he said, tracing the engravings with his thumb. "There are six different symbols carved into it."

The men exchanged uneasy glances as the beam of light glinted off the key's metallic edge—its markings faint but deliberate, as if part of something ancient and dark.

"I wonder what it means," Ebenezer murmured, glancing over his shoulder.

"Let me have a closer look," said Christian.

He stepped forward, examining the six symbols carved into the wall. The etchings revealed a strange, non-human figure clutching a key. Beneath it, the outline of a chest shimmered faintly in the lantern light.

"From what I can tell," Christian said slowly, "it looks like some kind of creature is opening a chest. Inside are two books. The first has a glow—some kind of energy swirling around it—and the second shows an alien-looking figure reading a dark, shadowed book. Then there is a spear held by a demon-like creature. After that, the same figure is placing an amulet around its neck. And finally..." He paused, tracing the last symbol with his finger. "The demon stands holding a spear in its left hand, the amulet glowing around its neck, its body surrounded by light."

Ebenezer frowned. "So, what you're saying is... this demon is searching for the key?"

"That's what it looks like," Christian replied. "If that's true, we need to find this chest before it does."

Detective Marshall nodded grimly. "All right. Let's keep looking—see if we can find anything else down here. Maybe that chest—or something connected to it."

The three men spread out, their flashlights cutting narrow beams through the dusty cellar air. The faint smell of rot mixed with damp earth. Then Marshall froze.

"I just found another body," he called out, voice low but urgent. "It's another officer—Stanley."

Christian hurried over, kneeling beside the corpse. His breath caught when he saw the man's skin—pale, unblemished, untouched by decay.

"Detective," he said softly, "we've seen this before. Just like the body in Bisset Park. And I know I keep repeating myself..."

Detective Marshall exhaled, tightening his grip on his flashlight. "Let's keep searching for more clues. None of this makes sense—and this mystery is far from over."

It was now 11:06 a.m. in Damascus. The three men continued their search through the dark cellar, eyes sharp, hearts uneasy, the weight of the unseen pressing closer with every step.

15

THE JOURNEY IS NEAR

Meanwhile, in the small town of **Chilhowie**, thirty-eight kilometers from Damascus, Jessica felt the fatigue of two hours behind the wheel. Her eyelids grew heavy.

Marilyn glanced over, worried. "Hey, Jessica, open your eyes!"

Jessica turned her head, her voice weak. "Can I pull over and let you drive, please?"

"Sure. But we'll be in Damascus in less than half an hour. I'll wake you when we get there, okay?" said Marilyn.

"Thank you, darling. You're such a good friend," Jessica murmured with a tired smile.

Jessica eased the car onto the shoulder and shifted it into park. She stepped out slowly, stretching as Marilyn climbed from the passenger side. They were circling the back of the car when headlights washed over them. A vehicle stopped behind theirs.

Jonathan stepped out. "Hey, ladies, is everything okay?"

Jessica frowned, still sluggish, and opened the passenger door. "I'm just tired. Marilyn's taking over for the next thirty minutes."

"Oh—okay, sure," Jonathan said.

Marilyn walked up to him, touching his left shoulder with a playful smile. She leaned closer and whispered, "You are so handsome. When we get to Damascus, I want to find a quiet place—just you and me."

Jonathan blinked, surprised but clearly flattered. "Really? You think I'm handsome? And why this sudden interest?"

"Enough talking, Mr. Hunk," Marilyn teased. "Just take the offer. I want a little fun—and who knows, this might be our only chance once we reach Damascus."

Jonathan hesitated, a flicker of concern in his eyes.

"Don't worry," she said lightly, brushing his arm. "We'll be fine. We'll come back alive. Now, let's get to Damascus—and then," she added with a grin, "we can have that fun."

Jonathan climbed back into his vehicle, while Marilyn slowly strutted toward Jessica's car, hips swaying deliberately. She opened the driver's door and slid in, starting the engine.

Jessica eyed her, half amused, half curious. "What was that all about, Marilyn?"

Marilyn grinned. "Just made him feel good, that's all I'm saying," she replied with a wink.

Jessica rolled her eyes and smiled. "Why are you smiling at me like that?"

"I know why," Marilyn teased. "Anyway, let's drive, girl!"

Jonathan's van rumbled to life ahead of them. Marilyn waited until he pulled onto the road before following.

"Why did you let him go first?" Jessica asked.

"Well, Jess, he's a man. I figured he should go ahead—protect us," Marilyn said with a laugh.

They both giggled as the road stretched before them, the Virginia countryside fading into mist and uncertainty. Their journey toward Damascus continued—one that could end in light... or descend into something far darker.

Back in **Dublin**, twenty kilometers from Radford, the FBI convoy pressed on toward Damascus. Inside one of the cars, Agent Julia stifled a yawn as her eyes burned from exhaustion.

"Oh my God, I'm so tired," she muttered. "But I have to keep going."

Grant glanced at her from the passenger seat. "We could stop for a short break—but not too long. We need to reach Damascus before Ebenezer and Christian do something they will regret."

Julia eased into the left lane and slowed down. "Can you grab my water bottle from the back seat?"

Grant unbuckled, reached behind, and handed her the bottle. "Here you go, madam."

"Thank you very much," she said with a tired smile.

Behind them, Agent Denzel noticed Julia's car slowing. "Agent Julia, do you copy?" he said into the radio.

Julia grabbed her walkie-talkie. "I'm fine, Agent Denzel. Just stopping for a drink, thirsty as hell."

Agents Miguel and Conrad stepped out of their car, stretching stiff limbs after the long drive.

"Goodness, my shoulders are killing me," groaned Miguel.

Conrad bent his knees and stretched his back. "Yeah, same here. This road feels endless."

"Me too. But we all know we must keep going and get to Damascus as soon as possible. This case is big, and we want to solve it," said Agent Conrad.

Agents Jonny and Mark were lounging in their cars nearby, gazing at their FBI teammates as they stretched their stiff arms and legs.

"I haven't been worried in all my years as an agent," Jonny admitted, rubbing the back of his neck. "But in this case... it's starting to freak me out. Don't you think, Mark?"

Mark nodded slowly. "It's worrying, yeah—but we're fully armed and ready to finish what we started."

Jonny exhaled. "What if this mysterious thing can't be defeated?"

Mark turned toward him, his tone steady. "We've got a strong team, Jonny. We just need to stay positive."

Jonny managed a small smile. "You are right. Let's focus on the job we were sent to do."

The two agents exchanged a firm nod, confidence settling back over them as the FBI team prepared to move out.

Agent Julia climbed into her car, straightened her jacket, and started the engine. "Okay, team," she said into the walkie-talkie. "Let's get back on the road to Damascus."

"Let's do this. Over," replied Agent Denzel.

"We're both ready, over," echoed Agents Miguel and Conrad.

"Ready here too, Agent Julia. Over," came the response from Jonny and Mark.

Engines roared to life as the FBI convoy rolled forward once more, Grant driving in the lead vehicle. The highway stretched ahead—Damascus only one hundred and thirty-five kilometers away.

Meanwhile, back in **Blacksburg**, Jacob Dalton left town, determined to track down his colleagues. He had already pieced things together—especially after realizing Grant was missing from the hotel.

As Jacob drove, he glanced up at a weathered road sign: *Christiansburg – Radford.*

He hesitated, scratching his head. Should he take Route 81 toward Christiansburg and follow the highway to Radford?

After a moment's thought, he made his decision. Jacob gripped the wheel and steered toward Christiansburg, the engine growling as he accelerated into the night.

16

The Secret Room

It was forty-three minutes past eleven in Damascus. The clouds moved swiftly, covering the sun as a chill wind swept through the trees, scattering brittle leaves across the ground. Ravens circled low over the deserted ghost town, their cries echoing through the silence.

In the cellar below, Ebenezer and Christian continued their search, their torch beams cutting through the dust and shadows as they looked for more clues—or perhaps more bodies.

Detective Marshall scanned the far wall and spotted something unusual. "Look, guys! I found a door!" he shouted. "Let's see what's behind it."

Ebenezer and Christian turned immediately, their torches flashing toward the old, weathered door. The wood was cracked, the handle rusted with age.

"First, let's see if it opens without a key," said Ebenezer.

Christian gripped the corroded doorknob and twisted. It wouldn't budge. "It won't open, Detective! There must be a key somewhere."

Ebenezer rubbed his chin thoughtfully. "Hmm... when I go to the bar back in Blacksburg, the owner keeps a stash of spare keys in a tin inside a safe. Maybe this bar has something similar."

Detective Marshall raised an eyebrow. "How do you know that?"

Ebenezer chuckled. "I spend too much time at the bar after work. The owner told me once. I assume that's where they keep the keys—but hey, I could be wrong."

Christian smirked. "So, you really do spend a lot of time there?"

"Yes," Ebenezer admitted with a grin.

"You must really enjoy your job," Christian teased, laughing lightly.

"Alright, gentlemen," said Detective Marshall, stepping closer to inspect the keyhole. "Let's get back upstairs and see if we can find the key. But first, take a good look at this lock so we know what we're searching for."

The three men exchanged glances, then headed toward the narrow stairs leading up to the bar, their footsteps echoing softly against the damp stone walls.

As they climbed the narrow stairs, a loud creak echoed beneath their feet.

"These stairs give me the creeps," said Ebenezer, glancing uneasily at the worn wood beneath him.

"It's only stairs, for goodness' sake," Christian muttered, rolling his eyes.

Detective Marshall pushed open the cellar door first and turned back with a mocking grin. "Need a hand?" he asked, laughing at his own sarcasm.

"Erm, no thanks—and that's not funny," Ebenezer replied, brushing dust from his jacket.

The three men stepped back into the dim bar, scanning the room for anything that might lead them to the missing key. Bottles sat crooked on dusty shelves, and cobwebs clung to the rafters above.

Ebenezer's eyes caught on a narrow door near the restrooms. "Look over there! I see another door. It leads to an office—there could be a safe inside."

"Alright, let's check it out," said Detective Marshall.

Christian grasped the handle and twisted. "It's not even locked," he said, surprised.

They pushed the door open and stepped cautiously inside. A leather armchair sat turned away from them beside an old wooden desk. The room smelled of decay and dust, and the faded wallpaper was streaked with something dark blood. Papers and broken frames littered the floor.

"Look—there's someone sitting in that chair," Christian whispered.

Detective Marshall and Ebenezer exchanged a tense glance.

"Hello? Can you hear me?" Detective Marshall called, stepping forward.

Christian moved closer and slowly turned the armchair toward them. His breath caught in his throat. "Oh my God…"

Ebenezer turned away, pressing a hand to his mouth, while Detective Marshall froze, his face pale.

"Mother of God," Detective Marshall muttered. "Would you look at this?"

The man in the chair was clearly dead, his expression frozen in terror—yet his skin still looked disturbingly fresh.

"Guys… this man's dead. But his body—it looks just like the others," said Detective Marshall.

He pulled on his rubber gloves and bent to examine the corpse. "Gentlemen, start searching the room for a key or any clue that might lead us to that safe."

Christian and Ebenezer exchanged uneasy looks, still shaken, but obeyed.

As Christian moved toward a large, framed portrait on the wall, something about it caught his attention. The man in the painting looked exactly like the body in the chair. He reached out and placed his hand against the frame.

The wall trembled.

Christian stumbled back, eyes wide, as the painting shifted slightly—then the wall itself began to move, creaking open like a hidden door.

Detective Marshall and Ebenezer stared at the shifting wall in pure amazement.

"Oh, look, guys!" said Ebenezer, his voice trembling with excitement. "I think we just found a secret room!"

"How did you do that?" asked Detective Marshall, stepping closer.

"I just looked at the painting and touched it gently," Christian replied, still wide-eyed.

"Well then," said Detective Marshall, his tone both cautious and eager, "let's see what we can find."

The three men stepped carefully through the narrow passage. Their flashlights flickered over shelves stacked with dusty bottles, boxes of jewelry, and bricks of gold gleaming faintly under layers of grime. In the center of the room stood an old steel safe.

"Oh my God," Ebenezer whispered. "Look at this place—it's full of gold, jewelry, and more alcohol than a distillery!"

Christian grinned, unable to hide his greed. "This is amazing! I'm claiming this!"

Detective Marshall didn't react. His attention was fixed entirely on the safe. "Gentlemen," he said quietly, "it looks like we've found what we came for."

Christian smirked. "You mean *I* found the safe."

Detective Marshall allowed himself a small smile. "Alright, you win."

Christian wandered toward the pile of gold and jewelry, while Ebenezer's eyes lingered on the stacked bottles. Detective Marshall crouched in front of the safe, brushing away the dust from its face.

"Look here," he said. "There's something engraved on the metal."

The others leaned in. Faint letters shimmered in the beam of Marshall's flashlight. He read aloud:

"The angel looks down at you. You have nothing to fear about your life. The universe is on your side and will continue to help you reach your final path."

The three men stood in silence, the air thick with unease. The riddle seemed to hum through the room, as though the words themselves were alive.

Detective Marshall studied the engraved words carefully, scratching his head as he tried to make sense of them. "Take a look at this," he said. "Tell me—what do you think this riddle means?"

Christian and Ebenezer stepped closer, reading the riddle over his shoulder.

"Hmmm... it mentions angels," Ebenezer said thoughtfully. "I'm thinking we need to find an angel sculpture."

"How the hell do you know that?" asked Detective Marshall, glancing at him skeptically.

"I've done some work studying angels in my spare time," Ebenezer replied.

Christian smirked. "Didn't think you would be the type. You must have a lot of free time."

Ebenezer shrugged. "I spend a lot of time alone. Gives me enough time to research."

Detective Marshall straightened. "Then what are we waiting for? Let's find that angel sculpture."

"I wonder if it's here in this room or somewhere else," Ebenezer said.

The three men stepped out of the secret passage and back into the office, scanning every corner.

"I don't see any angel sculptures in here," said Detective Marshall.

"It could be hidden somewhere else," Ebenezer replied. "Remember, it's a riddle. Whoever wrote it wouldn't make it easy for us."

"Let's check the bar," said Christian. "Maybe there's an angel sculpture there."

Hopeful, the three men made their way back toward the bar.

"Where would it be?" Detective Marshall muttered, frustration edging his voice.

Ebenezer's gaze drifted toward the bar counter—and then he spotted it. A small cupboard door hung slightly open. He hurried over, crouched down, and opened the side door fully. Inside, shelves lined with dust greeted him.

"Anything?" Christian called out.

Ebenezer peered inside. Resting in the darkness was a wooden case of whiskey—an old bottle of **Dalmore 40-Year-Old**, its label yellowed and the glass coated in decades of dust.

Ebenezer opened the case. Beneath the velvet lining sat a small white clay sculpture, no larger than a golf tee. He lifted it carefully, studying its delicate shape.

"Guys!" he called out, excitement sparking in his voice. "I found the little sculpture!"

Christian and Detective Marshall hurried over to the bar.

"Well done, Ebenezer," said Detective Marshall, his tone approving. "You've been very helpful in solving this mystery."

Christian smiled and clapped a hand on Ebenezer's shoulder. "Nice work, buddy."

"Thanks," Ebenezer replied, grinning. "But let's not stop here. Check the whiskey case again—there might be another riddle. Whoever left these clues clearly wanted to hide things in unexpected places. We need to stay sharp if we're going to solve this and open that safe. I'm betting that's where the key to the cellar door is."

"Yeah," said Detective Marshall, nodding. "It's strange. Whoever set this up didn't make it easy for anyone to find."

Ebenezer crouched and examined the bottom of the Dalmore whiskey case. Faint words were carved into the wood. His heart quickened. "I found another riddle!"

Christian and Detective Marshall leaned closer as Ebenezer read aloud:

"The book of love is not always what it seems; look hard enough, and you will find the missing key."

Christian frowned. "The book of love? What's that supposed to mean?"

Detective Marshall rubbed his chin thoughtfully. "Could be a clue about a real book. 'The Book of Love'—sounds like poetry. Maybe we need to find a shelf of books somewhere in this place."

Ebenezer nodded. "You might be right. We haven't searched every room yet. Let's check for a bookshelf—maybe that's where the next clue is waiting."

"Right, let's find that book!" said Christian.

Detective Marshall walked away from the bar beside Ebenezer and Christian as they moved along the left side of the room.

"Here—let's check this way. We haven't been through here yet," said Detective Marshall, gesturing toward a narrow door.

The three men approached it, a wave of unease settling over them. Detective Marshall gripped the doorknob with his left hand, raised his pistol, and slowly turned it.

Without warning, a skeletal figure lunged from the darkness behind the door.

"Arrrrghhh!" Christian shouted, stumbling backward.

Ebenezer bolted, while Detective Marshall tripped and hit the floor hard. "Ahh—my back! That pain is killing me," he groaned, struggling to stand.

Christian, still pale and speechless, helped him up.

"Thanks, Christian," the detective muttered, catching his breath. "Appreciate it."

Ebenezer crouched behind the bar, trembling. "I'm over here!" he called out. "Did you see that? That was a real skeleton!"

"Yeah, I noticed," Christian said grimly.

Detective Marshall stepped closer to the figure, squinting at it. "This is odd," he murmured. "There's still fresh plasma on the bones. It looks too new—like whatever killed this man happened recently. But this body's been here at least seven years."

Christian cautiously moved past the skeleton and glanced through the doorway beyond. "Come on, Detective. We can't stop now. Let's find that clue."

Ebenezer followed him, though his hands shook. Detective Marshall lingered a moment longer, examining the skull. A jagged crack ran across the top.

"The skull's split clean through," he said. "Almost like it was sliced open."

Christian and Ebenezer exchanged uneasy glances and stepped closer.

"Yeah," said Christian quietly. "Looks like someone—or something—did this on purpose."

Ebenezer turned his attention to a small wooden drawer beside the wall. He opened it and froze. "There's a note in here."

Christian joined him, leaning over to read the yellowed paper aloud.

"Those who find the key will discover *The Book of Secrets.*"

Detective Marshall scratched his head. "The Book of Secrets," he repeated. "Now what on earth could *that* mean?"

Ebenezer furrowed his brow, thinking hard. "*The Book of Secrets?* Hmmm... let me think about this for a moment."

He began pacing the length of the room, eyes scanning the walls as though the answer might reveal itself. After a minute, his expression changed—he seemed to have an idea.

"Guys, listen," he said, turning toward the others. "We need to find the key first. That's what the note said. Maybe the key will lead us to *The Book of Secrets.*"

Detective Marshall nodded firmly. "Agreed. If we find that key, we'll find the book."

The three men moved deeper into the corridor, stepping cautiously into an area none of them had explored before. Ahead, a narrow flight of stairs descended into darkness.

The air grew colder. The walls—painted a dull, oppressive black—seemed to swallow what little light there was. Detective Marshall reached for his torch.

"Hold on. I can barely see a thing," he muttered, feeling along the wall for a switch. He flipped it, but nothing happened. "The lights are out. I'll grab my torch."

He fumbled with it, but when he pressed the button, it gave only a weak flicker before dying. "Great," he grumbled. "Now the torch won't work either."

Christian sighed, peering into the pitch-black hall ahead. "Ah, just our luck. Guess we're going in blind."

Ebenezer chuckled nervously. "I *knew* I should've packed my matches."

"It is what it is," said Detective Marshall, his tone steady but uneasy. "Stay close and keep moving."

They advanced cautiously through the darkness, the sound of their footsteps echoing off the cold concrete. After several tense moments, a faint metallic glint appeared ahead.

As they drew closer, the outline of a heavy iron door appeared from the shadows—its surface marked with a strange symbol: a sickle, a hammer, and three nails.

Christian squinted into the darkness, his breath quickening. "Guys, I can't see clearly—but I think I see a door."

Ebenezer stepped forward cautiously and ran his hand along the surface. "This door is made of steel," he said, voice low with curiosity. "It feels like it's guarding something important."

Detective Marshall frowned. "How do you figure that?"

"Think about it," Ebenezer replied. "Every other door we've opened was made of wood. But this one—this one's solid steel. And look at the hinges—it's sealed tight. Whatever's behind it must matter."

Detective Marshall gave him a wry smile. "Now that's why you're the journalist and I'm the detective. We look at things differently."

Christian crouched near the handle, studying the keyhole's odd shape. "I think I know what kind of key it needs. Let's find the rest of them and see if they all connect somehow."

Detective Marshall nodded. "Good thinking."

Together, the three men turned from the heavy door and started down the dark corridor once more. Their footsteps echoed off the cold stone walls as they pressed forward—hoping, somewhere ahead, there was a way out.

17

THEIR FIRST EXPERIENCE

It was thirteen minutes past midnight in the small, remote village of Widener Valley—about nine kilometers outside Damascus. Jessica, Marilyn, and Jonathan were on the final leg of their journey.

"We're not far from Damascus, Jessica!" Marilyn said.

Jessica stirred awake at the sound of her friend's voice, stretching her arms with a long yawn. "Goodness, I needed that rest."

Marilyn smiled. "No problem, sugar. Anything for you, my dear friend."

Up front, Jonathan gripped the wheel, eyes fixed on the road sign that read: *Damascus 9 km.* He muttered under his breath, "Can't believe I'm doing this... but what the hell."

As the van rolled through the valley, Jonathan noticed clusters of old, detached houses scattered across the open fields—silent, weather-worn, and alone. Ahead, a farmhouse appeared, a scarecrow standing a few yards from the porch.

"Would you look at that," Jonathan said. "That's creepy."

Jessica leaned closer to the window. "It's beautiful in a strange way," she said.

Marilyn nodded. "It really is. I love the scenery."

Jonathan's gaze flicked back to the road. When he glanced upward, two ravens cut across the moonlit sky. "Ravens flying in pairs," he murmured. "Now that's a sign."

The birds kept flying until one suddenly turned—diving toward the van.

Jonathan suddenly noticed the ravens diving toward his van. Startled, he jerked the wheel and lost control.

"God Almighty!" he shouted.

Jessica and Marilyn gasped as they saw the van swerving wildly from left to right.

"What's wrong with Jonathan?" Marilyn cried.

Jessica's eyes widened as she stared through the windshield. "Marilyn—look! That bird's coming straight for us!"

Marilyn reacted instinctively, pulling the steering wheel toward the right shoulder of the road. The raven swooped past—just inches from hitting the car.

Jessica glanced in the side mirror, heart pounding, to see if the bird would circle back.

"That was terrifying," she breathed.

Marilyn accelerated, still shaken. "My heart's racing... what on earth was that about?"

"I don't know," Jessica said, catching her breath, "but ravens don't normally attack people."

The three continued toward Damascus, silent and uneasy after their strange encounter. They had no idea the ravens had been warning them—not to enter the town ahead.

"We're only a few kilometers away," Marilyn murmured, taking a deep breath as she steadied the wheel.

From the passenger seat, Jessica squinted at something ahead. Something unusual was waiting in the distance.

A view of Damascus came into sight—flocks of ravens circling above the ghost town.

"Look! Do you see what I see?" Marilyn whispered, staring ahead in shock.

"Mother of God... would you look at that. That's Damascus right there."

Jonathan gripped the steering wheel tighter as the outline of the deserted town grew clearer. His stomach turned. He glanced at a rusted road sign on the right:**Welcome to Damascus — on the Virginia Creeper Trail.**

"Oh, boy," he muttered to himself. "I must be out of my mind driving toward this place."

Marilyn followed close behind in her car as Jonathan slowed and pulled into the right lane. The view ahead was grim—streets empty, windows dark, no sign of life.

He stepped out of his van, staring up at the gray sky, wondering how fate had led him here.Marilyn parked beside him, and she and Jessica climbed out, their eyes fixed on the lifeless town.

"Look at this place," Jessica whispered. "It's so isolated... so quiet. It's frightening even to look at—and my Christian is somewhere out there."

"Don't worry," Marilyn said gently. "We'll find him—and the others too."

Jonathan opened the back of his van and pulled out a baseball bat. He tucked a few tools into his jeans pocket. "All right, ladies. I've got my protection—just in case."

Marilyn smiled faintly and stepped closer, lowering her voice. "Remember what I told you earlier—we'll find a safe spot for ourselves... maybe even have a little fun."

Jonathan couldn't help but grin, a flicker of excitement cutting through his fear.

Jessica rolled her eyes. "Okay, you two—enough. Let's move."

The trio started toward the ghost town—searching for Ebenezer, Christian, Detective Marshall... and whatever else waited for them inside.

18

THE LETTER

I t was thirty-six minutes past twelve in Damascus. Jessica, Marilyn, and Jonathan moved cautiously toward the heart of the ghost town, their footsteps echoing in the dead silence.

They looked around, taking in the desolation. Houses were half-collapsed, cars rusted where they had died decades ago, and not a single living soul stirred in the streets.

Jessica's eyes caught something on the right side of the road—a large, decaying building with a faded sign swinging in the wind. "The McAbees Inn," she read aloud. "There's a hotel over there. Let's check inside—maybe Christian and his friends took shelter."

Marilyn nodded, scanning the area nervously. "We need to search every place we can. They could be anywhere right now."

Jonathan led the way toward the hotel entrance. He gripped the handle and pushed—A long, drawn-out creak echoed through the air as the door gave way.

"After you two," Jonathan said quietly.

They stepped inside, the musty scent of rot and mildew clinging to the air.

"Goodness gracious," Jessica whispered. "Look at this place!"

Marilyn drifted toward an old reception desk, running her fingers along the thick layer of dust. "You can tell this hotel hasn't been open in years—at least seven, maybe more."

Jonathan's eyes wandered to the bar on the right. Behind it, he noticed a door slightly ajar. "Ladies, over here," he called.

Jessica and Marilyn joined him as he turned the handle, but it refused to budge. Jonathan frowned, twisting harder.

"Huh. It won't open," he muttered.

"Why don't you use your tools to unlock it?" Marilyn suggested.

Jonathan pulled a screwdriver from his pocket and crouched beside the door. With quick, steady movements, he began removing the screws from the handle.

Behind him, Jessica clung to Marilyn, her voice trembling. "I just hope Christian's out there—and that he's safe."

Marilyn wrapped her arms tightly around Jessica, her tone gentle but firm. "We'll find him. I promise. He'll be back in your arms soon."

A faint click echoed as Jonathan loosened the final screw. The handle came free in his hand. "Ladies first," he said, forcing a smile to ease the tension.

Jessica and Marilyn stepped cautiously into the dim room. Faded wallpaper peeled from the walls, and dust hung thick in the air. Jessica gasped softly.

"Take a look at this," Marilyn whispered, pointing toward a wall lined with framed portraits. "It looks like a family photo."

Curious, Jonathan stepped back into the hallway, glancing through a cracked window to check the hotel sign. "The McAbees Inn," he murmured. He returned to the room and said, "Looks like this place belonged to the McAbees family—the name matches the sign outside."

Jessica studied one of the photographs. "It's a man, a woman... and a little child," she said quietly.

The two women continued examining the portraits, their eyes tracing the faces as if searching for meaning—or warning.

"Let's not waste too much time," Jessica said impatiently. "We still have to find Christian."

Jonathan moved toward the old desk in the corner. Its drawers were half open;

papers yellowed with age. He tugged one drawer wider and froze.

Inside lay a folded letter, sealed and brittle with time.

"Look what I found," Jonathan said, holding it up for Marilyn to see.

"Here—it's a letter. Looks like it was written by the Maccabees," said Marilyn.

She picked up the yellowed paper, her hands trembling slightly, and began to read aloud.

"Whoever reads this letter, please read it carefully.My name is Ryan Maccabee, owner of the Maccabees Inn. I'm writing this to warn whoever finds it—my daughter, Lucy, is in great danger. My wife, Helen, and I were forced to leave Damascus because a demon haunts this town.

Lucy wears an amulet around her neck—a powerful charm that can make her invisible to the demon, but only during the day. At night, its power fades.

To destroy this demon, you must find the gold spear hidden in a cottage along Creeper Trail. The place is called *Brunswick Cottage*. That's where Lucy is hiding now, cared for by an elderly couple.

Please protect her. Do not let the demon take the amulet—it seeks its power. If the demon gets it, it will grow stronger and consume more souls.

—Ryan and Helen Maccabee."

Marilyn lowered the letter slowly, her expression tightening.

"So, there really is a demon in this town?" Jessica whispered, her voice shaking.

Marilyn nodded slowly. "That's right—and that's why this town has been cut off for the past seven years."

Jessica frowned. "So, this letter was written seven years ago? That would make the girl a teenager by now."

"Now it all makes sense," Jonathan said quietly. "That's why this place turned into a ghost town."

Jessica glanced at the paper again. "The letter says Lucy is staying in a cottage with an elderly couple so the demon can't find her. They're keeping her hidden."

Jonathan ran a hand through his hair. "Still, it sounds like the father abandoned his only daughter. What kind of man would do that?"

"There must be a reason," Marilyn replied. "Ryan did it to protect her. The amulet she carries is what the demon wants. If he'd taken her with him, the demon would've followed—and put everyone else in danger."

Jonathan hesitated. "So, you're saying he left her behind to keep the demon from spreading beyond this town?"

"Yes," Marilyn said firmly. "And according to the letter, the amulet keeps Lucy invisible during the day. But once night falls, the demon can see her again."

Jonathan frowned. "Then how has the demon failed to find her for seven years?"

"I find that strange too," Marilyn admitted, glancing uneasily around the room.

Jonathan straightened. "Then we should find this cottage—and Lucy, and the couple who are protecting her."

Jessica shook her head. "You two go. I'll keep looking for Christian."

Marilyn grabbed her arm. "No, Jessica. We should stay together. We might find him on the way."

"It's all right," Jessica said softly. "I'll be fine. I have my gun for protection. You two focus on Lucy."

Marilyn's voice wavered. "Are you sure? I don't want anything happening to you."

Jessica managed a small smile. "I can take care of myself. I came here to find Christian—it feels like fate."

Marilyn hesitated, then nodded. "All right. But leave us a sign, so we'll know where you've been."

Jessica asked, "What kind of sign?"

Marilyn thought for a moment. "How about we leave a one-cent coin on the ground?"

Jessica smiled faintly. "That sounds like a good idea."

"Okay," Marilyn said, her voice softening. "Take care of yourself—and don't forget to leave the coin so we'll know where you've been."

Jessica nodded. "I will."

With that, she turned and walked away, her footsteps echoing faintly down the empty street. Marilyn and Jonathan watched her go, uneasy but determined, before continuing their own journey in the opposite direction.

19

DEATH IS ONLY THE BEGINNING

It's one minute past one in the small Virginia town of Lodi, about thirteen and a half kilometers from Damascus. Agent Julia, Grant, and the rest of the FBI team drive steadily through the quiet highway, their convoy cutting through the fog as they near their destination.

"We're almost there, Grant," said Agent Julia, her eyes fixed on the dark stretch of road ahead.

"I'm glad we're getting closer," Grant replied. "Once we reach Damascus, we need to find Ebenezer and the two men he traveled with—and get them out as soon as possible."

"You have my word," Julia said firmly. "But we'll need to question Ebenezer and his colleagues before extraction. There's too much we don't know yet."

"Sure," Grant said, glancing out the window. "Just let me handle most of the talking. I know this town better than anyone."

Julia nodded and picked up her walkie-talkie. "Agent Miguel, Agent Conrad, Agent Mark, and Agent Jonny—do you copy? Over."

Static crackled before two voices came through almost in unison. "We read you, Agent Julia. Over."

Julia leaned closer to the mic. "We're nearing Damascus. Stay alert and keep your weapons ready. If anything, suspicious happens, do not hesitate to act. Everyone should be equipped with bulletproof vests and helmets. Is that clear?"

The four agents responded in perfect sync. "Yes, ma'am."

Julia lowered the radio, her expression hardening as the convoy rolled forward into the mist, toward whatever waited for them in Damascus.

Agent Julia clipped her walkie-talkie to her belt and kept driving, creeping closer and closer to Damascus. Thick clouds began to roll in, turning the scenery into a dark, miserable day. Rain started to fall—first lightly, then in sheets. Julia switched on the headlights and windshield wipers as water streaked across the glass.

"Of all times for it to rain, it had to be now," she muttered.

Grant shook his head, watching the rain hammer down before bowing his head. "We have to keep moving, no matter the weather."

A distant thunderclap rolled across the sky. Agent Denzel stared out the window, squinting through the downpour. "Good thing we packed our raincoats, Agent Julia!"

They were now barely five kilometers from Damascus when two ravens appeared again, perched high on a barren tree. Their dark feathers glistened under the rain as they watched the approaching convoy. One of the ravens suddenly took flight, swooping low toward Julia's car.

Grant caught sight of it first. "Watch out, Agent!"

Julia reacted instantly, jerking the wheel as the raven slammed against the windshield. The tires skidded on the slick road. "Hold on, Grant—Denzel, brace yourselves!"

The car swerved wildly, veering off the road and crashing through the rotted frame of an abandoned house. The impact echoed like a cannon blast. Metal screamed. Glass shattered.

Behind them, the other two vehicles collided. Agent Jonny's car slammed against a tree, while Agent Miguel's vehicle rolled several times before coming to rest upside down. Smoke drifted from all three wrecks, curling into the stormy air.

Julia groaned, gripping her shoulder, pain radiating down her arm. She turned toward Grant—his head slumped forward, blood trickling from his temple.

"Grant, can you hear me?" she shouted. "Grant, wake up!" She looked at Denzel. "Help him—now!"

Agent Denzel slapped Grant's face lightly. "Grant! Can you hear me?"

Julia reached over, checking his pulse and airway. "Get him out of the car and into the recovery position!"

"Yes, ma'am!" Denzel replied. He carefully dragged Grant from the wreckage and laid him on the wet ground, checking his breathing and circulation as thunder rumbled overhead.

Agent Julia knelt beside Grant, tears streaming down her face. "Please, don't die on me!" she cried, her voice breaking.

Agent Denzel started chest compressions, counting aloud to keep focus. "One, two, three, four, five, six, seven, eight, nine, ten—"

Moments later, Grant coughed weakly, gasping for air. Julia let out a shaky breath of relief and cupped the back of his head, meeting his eyes.

"Oh, thank God you're alive. I thought I'd lost you," she whispered.

Grant blinked, confused, glancing around at the wreckage. "What... what happened?"

"We were attacked by a raven," Julia said, still trembling. "It came right at us. We swerved off the road and crashed into a house."

Grant's voice grew urgent. "What about the others?"

Julia and Denzel exchanged a glance, then sprinted toward the other vehicles. "Let's get them out of the cars, Denzel!" Julia shouted.

But it was too late. The four agents lay motionless. Julia's breath caught as she realized the truth. She fell to her knees, tears mixing with the rain. "No... no, no, no!" she cried, her voice echoing through the storm.

Denzel stared down at their fallen colleagues, the weight of it crushing him. "Oh my God..." he murmured, before collapsing to the ground. He slammed his fists against the mud, grief shaking his body. "No! No! No!" His voice broke as the reality set in—his friends were gone.

Grant pushed himself upright, wincing in pain. When he saw the scene, his expression softened with sorrow. "I'm sorry for your loss, Agents Julia and Denzel," he said quietly.

Julia turned to him, overcome. Grant reached out, wiping away her tears. "They were brave men," he said. "You should be proud of them. They did their duty."

Agent Julia wept, her voice breaking. "It's all my fault... They would still be alive if I had not panicked on the road!"

Grant shook his head firmly. "No, Julia. It was not your fault—it was an accident. These things happen. Do not carry that blame."

Agent Denzel placed a hand on Julia's shoulder. "Grant's right. You are a strong leader and a good agent. I am proud to serve beside you. They were my colleagues too—and my friends. We will make sure they get the burial they deserve."

Agent Julia straightened, wiping her tears before raising her hand in a trembling salute toward the fallen agents. Nearby, Denzel moved toward the wrecked house, searching for a digging spade.

"Agent Julia, I need your help getting the bodies out from both cars," Grant called. His voice was steady, though his face was pale.

Julia hesitated, drawing in a shaky breath before nodding. "I'll help you. I owe them that much."

Together, they dragged the four bodies from the wreckage, placing them in a respectful line. The weight of their loss pressed heavy on the morning air.

"My sides are killing me," Grant muttered as they reached the last car.

Julia steadied herself against the doorframe, her leg throbbing from the crash. "I'll take Miguel's legs—you get his shoulders."

Grant nodded, and they worked together, lifting Agent Miguel's limp body from the car and laying him beside the others.

"Now for Agent Jonny," Julia said softly, her voice catching as tears threatened again.

"Stay strong, Agent Julia," Grant urged gently. "You are FBI—you have seen death before. You can handle this."

Julia swallowed hard and nodded, forcing herself to keep going. They moved to Agent Jonny's car next, pulling him free with slow, reverent care.

When they approached Agent Mark's car, a sudden flutter of black wings made Julia freeze. A raven sat on Mark's body, its beak tearing at the flesh of his cheek. Agent Conrad's body looked helpless.

Grant recoiled in horror and yanked open the car door—but the gruesome sight was too much. His vision blurred, and he collapsed to the ground.

"Grant!" Julia rushed to him, slapping his face gently. "Grant, wake up—snap out of it!"

The raven turned its head toward her, its dark eyes glinting before it blinked once and flew off into the gray sky.

Moments later, Grant groaned and stirred. "What happened?"

Julia exhaled in relief. "You dropped like a sack of potatoes the second you opened that door."

Grant rubbed his temples, trying to steady his breathing. "I remember now... I swear I saw that raven eating Agent Mark's flesh."

"This is all so strange," Agent Julia murmured. "A raven wouldn't eat human flesh... would it?"

Grant slowly got to his feet, still pale from shock. Julia handed him a bottle of water. "Here—take this. You need to hydrate."

Grant nodded and took a few slow sips, his hands trembling slightly. "I think you two should inform the family of your deceased agents."

Meanwhile, Agent Denzel's voice broke the silence, and agreed with Grant. "We need to inform their families and let them know they are dead!" Said Agent Julia. Agent Denzel agreed and responded calmly. "You are right. I will inform the family." Agent Denzel phoned the family of each deceased agent and let them know the sad news. Agent Denzel broke the news to the family of the deceased agents. Unfortunately, the members of the family were deeply upset and sad hearing the death of the news. The members of family knew the risks that the agents were up against and agreed with Agent Denzel that the agents could have a proper burial, as the family members are from Baltimore, Maryland, but I did give them a choice to contact Radford Hospital to send the paramedics by taking the bodies back to the hospital or, let the FBI deal with it instead, The families of the deceased agents agreed to get help from the FBI. So, Agent Denzel contacted the FBI and took the bodies home in a helicopter, as it's much quicker and safer, and the families can decide what to do, as they knew that there was no time to send the body back to their families. "Okay so I spoke to all four members of the agent's families, and you can imagine their reaction, so I asked them that there is no way for us to return their bodies, so I asked them to go to the hospital and the FBI will airlift the deceased to the hospital." Said Agent Denzel.

"Okay, Denzel, Let's cover their bodies so the family can agree in such a short and emotional time." she replied quietly.

Grant turned toward him. "Can you help me move the bodies of Agent Mark and Agent Conrad? I'll take their legs."

"Of course," Denzel said, stepping in to help. Together they lifted the bodies and laid them side by side on the damp ground. Soon after the bodies of the deceased agents were covered in a blanket, in which Agent Julia had in her bonnet. Denzel began covering the bodies, the sound of sadness striking through everyone echoing through the quiet day.

Julia watched, her face drained of colour. Grant put a steadying arm around her shoulders. The air was heavy with grief and the smell of wet soil.

When Denzel finished covering the bodies, he exhaled deeply. "Okay, Grant—let's cover the rest of the agents. We'll cover him safe enough, so the FBI can carefully take them."

Grant nodded, moving toward Miguel's body. He gripped the man's legs while Denzel lifted his shoulders. They lowered him carefully into the back seat of Agent Julia's car, even though the car was not in such condition to go on. Denzel saluted, then began to walk away from the car.

"Rest easy, Agent Miguel," he whispered.

They moved next to Agent Jonny. Working in a quiet rhythm, Denzel covered the body with a blanket while Grant looked on.

"Okay we are done," Denzel said hoarsely.

Despite exhaustion, he found a burst of strength and started to breathe normally. Sweat streaked his forehead, but his determination didn't falter. "I'm dedicating this case to my colleagues. I'll solve it—for them."

Julia managed a faint smile. "I'm very proud of you, Agent Denzel."

Grant joined him again, and together they covered Agent Conrad and Agent Mark. When the last of the agents were covered, Denzel stood back and saluted.

"Thank you, Grant," he said quietly.

"May you four rest in peace," Julia whispered, bowing her head. Soon after, The FBI helicopter arrived and took the bodies back to Radford Hospital.

A long silence followed. Then Julia straightened and looked toward the distant road. "We've got no car left," she said. "We'll have to walk the rest of the way—five kilometers to Damascus."

Grant gave a weary nod. "We don't have another choice, ma'am. Let's go."

And so, Agent Julia, Agent Denzel, and Grant began their slow walk toward Damascus—each step heavy with loss, their mission now burdened by the memory of four fallen men.

20

THE KEY TO SUCCESS

It was twenty-four minutes past one in Damascus. Ebenezer, Christian, and Detective Marshall had been searching for every inch of the bar for the *Book of Love* and the *Book of Secrets*. Every cupboard was open, every drawer emptied, every shadow checked—yet there wasn't a single bookshelf in sight.

Ebenezer refused to give up. "We've been searching this whole bar for the two books and still no luck," he said, frustration creeping into his voice.

Christian sighed. "What else can we do? We've looked everywhere—it's been over an hour!"

Detective Marshall leaned against the counter, thinking through the riddles again. "Maybe the books aren't in this bar at all."

Ebenezer frowned. "What makes you say that?"

"Well," Detective Marshall replied, "we've turned this place upside down. No bookshelves, no storage, not even a single drawer with paper inside. Whoever wrote that riddle may be trying to trick us."

The three men exchanged tired looks. They had wasted precious time searching for nothing.

"I have a suggestion," Ebenezer said suddenly. "Is there a library in this town?"

Christian's eyes widened. "Of course, there is—and that's brilliant, Ebenezer!"

Detective Marshall groaned, running a hand over his face. "Why didn't I think of that? It makes perfect sense. Whoever wrote the riddle wanted people like us to work for the answer."

Christian laughed, shaking his head. "Goodness! It's all just a big game to them."

Ebenezer turned toward the door, determination replacing his fatigue. "We've no time to waste. We're heading to the library."

"I know where it is," Christian said. "Follow me."

Detective Marshall and Ebenezer exchanged a glance, then followed him outside.

Rain poured down over Damascus, slicking the cobblestone streets as the three men trudged through the ghost-town silence. The night air was heavy, filled with the scent of wet earth and decay. Ebenezer brushed the rain from his face, his exhaustion deepening after more than an hour chasing riddles through the dark.

"I'm exhausted," Ebenezer admitted, rubbing the back of his neck. "But I'll be fine. No sense feeling sorry for myself."

Detective Marshall checked his gun, spinning the cylinder to make sure he still had bullets.

"Goodness," Ebenezer muttered, glancing around the deserted street. "Not a single sign of life."

Christian shook his head, his expression wistful. "This used to be such a beautiful town. I never imagined it would look like this in my lifetime."

They walked a few more yards until a broken liquor store sign caught their eye.

"I could use a free bottle of whiskey right about now—to drown our sorrows," Christian said with a half-smile.

Detective Marshall chuckled. "I think not. Try focusing, will you?"

Christian laughed softly. "Relax, Detective. I was only joking. Anyway, the library isn't far—it should be two blocks ahead on the right."

The road was littered with twisted wrecks of cars and trucks. As they passed, Ebenezer peered through the cracked windshield of a pickup and froze.

"Detective, look! There's a dead man inside this truck. Open the door!"

Detective Marshall approached cautiously, gun drawn. He opened the door with care. Inside sat a man, motionless—his skin pale blue, almost waxen. No blood, no wounds, just stillness.

Detective Marshall sighed. "Nothing new. Another corpse... same as the one back in Bisset Park."

Ebenezer didn't flinch. "Any clues?"

Detective Marshall shifted the body slightly and opened the glove box. Inside lay a small box of handgun bullets. "I'll take these," he muttered, pocketing them.

Christian rolled his eyes. "That's it? Just bullets? Figures. I'm sure you're thrilled to find more toys for your gun."

Detective Marshall smirked and tapped Christian's shoulder. "What can I say? I'm a detective. Protecting the law is my life."

The three men left the truck behind and continued down the rain-slicked street.

"There it is," Christian said, pointing ahead. "Damascus Library."

Ebenezer stared at the crumbling building. Bullet holes riddled the stone walls, blood stained the pavement, and the main entrance was barricaded with overturned cars.

"Great," Ebenezer said. "Now how do we get in?"

Detective Marshall thought quickly. "Let's see if there's a rear entrance. That might be our way inside."

Christian gave a sly smile. "I know how to get in. Follow me."

Detective Marshall and Ebenezer followed Christian into a narrow alley beside the library. Ahead of them stood two massive waste disposal containers, reeking faintly of decay.

"Watch and learn," Christian said with a grin. He climbed onto one of the containers, balanced himself, and pried open a small window above. With surprising ease, he slipped inside the dark library.

Marshall shook his head. "He's lucky I didn't arrest him for breaking and entering."

From inside, Christian's voice echoed softly. "Come on, you two! It's clear."

Detective Marshall and Ebenezer exchanged a look—half amusement, half reluctance—before shrugging and climbing onto the bins one after the other. They hoisted themselves through the window and dropped into the dim library interior.

Outside, Jessica passed the blocked front entrance, scanning the empty street for any sign of the men. The rain had stopped, leaving the air heavy and still. She glanced at the wrecked cars near the building, her heart pounding.

"Where could they have gone?" she murmured to herself.

Her attention shifted to a nearby post office. Faded letters across the front read **"Damascus Postal Services."** She pushed the door open a few inches—and froze.

Inside lay several lifeless bodies sprawled across the floor, their skin pale and waxy. The stench of death hit her instantly. She clamped both hands over her mouth, suppressing a scream. "Oh God…"

Jessica stumbled backward, shut the door quickly, and hurried away down the deserted street.

Inside the library, the men spread out under the faint beam of a flashlight. Dust motes drifted in the still air. Ebenezer scanned the *Love* section, hoping to find something—anything—that could lead them to the key to the cellar or the steel door mentioned in the riddle.

The shelves stretched endlessly before them, neatly arranged in alphabetical order. The silence pressed around them as they began to search.

"Guys, the bookshelves are in alphabetical order, but the books are all over the place. We'll have to look carefully," said Ebenezer.

Christian scanned the shelves and pulled out a dusty volume. "A chemistry book? Hmm, I wonder what this one's about."

Detective Marshall rolled his eyes and snatched it from his hands. "We don't have time to fool around, Christian. Focus on the book we came for. Three of us searching gives us better odds."

Christian smirked. "Alright, alright—don't get your knickers in a twist. I'll keep looking for this mysterious book of love."

Ebenezer moved methodically through the shelves, stopping at the *L* section. He slid books from right to left, frustration creeping in. "It's not here. Maybe it's somewhere else."

Christian frowned. "What makes you think that?"

"I just have a feeling. Whoever set this riddle probably wants us to look somewhere obvious—like an office."

Detective Marshall glanced around and pointed. "There's a door at the far end. Maybe it's in there."

The three men crossed the room. Marshall twisted the rusty handle, forcing it open after a moment's struggle. Inside stood a lone desk—otherwise, the room was empty.

"Great. An empty desk," Christian muttered.

Ebenezer knelt and peered underneath. His eyes widened. "Wait—there's something here." He tugged at an object taped to the underside of the desk. "It's a book!"

Christian and Marshall hurried over as Ebenezer pried it free, peeling away old duct tape. He brushed off the dust and opened it. "*The Book of Love!* Jackpot."

He flipped through the pages until he reached the center, where the paper had been neatly carved into the shape of a key. "Yes! The key to the safe!"

"Excellent work," said Detective Marshall, allowing himself a rare smile.

Christian threw an arm around Ebenezer. "Smart boy," he said, grinning.

Ebenezer held up the book, flipping through the pages carefully. "Thanks, guys, but I'm sure there must be another riddle somewhere."

As he turned the pages, he found a small slip of paper tucked inside. "Hey... another riddle!"

"What does it say?" asked Detective Marshall.

Ebenezer read aloud: "'Well done for finding the key. Those who find the key will find The Book of the Dead. Find The Book of Secrets, and you shall wield the power to destroy the demon.'"

"Who wrote this riddle?" Christian asked, furrowing his brow.

"Good question..." Ebenezer murmured, studying the slip.

Detective Marshall took a closer look at the book, flipping to the last page. A photograph caught his eye: the same man they had found dead at the bar office. "This is the guy we found dead, sitting at that table back at the bar!"

"So, someone clearly wants to guide whoever finds the key, and we're the ones piecing the puzzles together," said Ebenezer, his voice tense with realization.

"Who is this man? And what exactly is his job? Aside from being a bar owner..." Marshall paused, shaking his head.

Ebenezer explained, "By reading this book—which now has some pages torn out—it's clear he was also an alchemist. He brewed potions in his spare time. This is his published work, which means someone else must have been here before us... leaving clues to help anyone clever enough to solve the riddles."

Christian's eyes widened. "So the demon killed the man back at the bar, and someone else has been leaving these riddles?"

"Exactly. That means we must go back to the bar and open the door in the cellar," Detective Marshall said firmly, determination in his voice.

"Yes, we need to go back and open the safe," Ebenezer said, his voice tense with determination. "Inside that safe, I believe there's a chest. We should find The Book of Secrets, the key to the steel door... and I'm guessing some potions behind the cellar door as well."

"Okay, so what are we waiting for? Back to the bar!" Christian shouted, urgency in his voice.

The three men made their way to the window they had first used to climb into the library.

Meanwhile, Jessica wandered the deserted streets, fear making her voice tremble. "Christian! Christian! Where are you?" she called, her voice rising in panic. She listened intently for a reply, but the streets remained silent.

Detective Marshall glanced up at the window, frowning. "Christian, Ebenezer! We can't leave through the window—it's too high!"

Ebenezer turned and walked back toward the library's interior, determination set in his expression.

"Where are you going, Ebenezer?" Christian asked.

"I need to find a ladder so we can climb out safely," Ebenezer replied. Detective Marshall nodded in agreement, following him.

The three men now had to figure out a way out of the library, the tension of the ghost town pressing in around them.

21

It Was Fate

It was 1:58 p.m. in Lodi, Virginia. Grant, Agent Julia, and Agent Denzel walked slowly through the deserted streets.

"We've been walking for over forty minutes. How far is Damascus on foot, Grant?" Agent Denzel asked.

Grant glanced ahead, calculating. "I'd say we're about eleven kilometers from Damascus, so we've still got quite a walk ahead of us."

"Over an hour more? Seriously?" Agent Julia groaned.

Grant sighed. "At this pace, we're moving slower than we should, considering everything we just went through."

"Let's keep going," Agent Julia urged.

The three continued through Lodi, scanning their surroundings. An abandoned building caught Grant's eye.

"Look at that building," he said, pointing.

Agent Denzel and Julia followed his gaze.

"You know this place?" Julia asked.

"Of course," Grant replied. "This was once a school—Liberty Hall School."

He approached the crumbling structure and tried the main entrance. "I just want to see what it looks like inside," he explained.

Agent Denzel glanced around the empty streets. "Even this town is completely abandoned. Damn it."

Grant stepped slowly inside, eyes scanning left and right, until he froze for a moment.

"Are you okay?" Julia asked.

Grant nodded. "I need a moment."

"Why? There's nothing special here—we should keep moving," she said, puzzled.

Grant's gaze fell to the ground a few feet away. A key lay there, gleaming faintly.

"Agent Julia, look," he said.

Julia stepped closer, and Grant held up the long, golden key. He examined it from every angle, noticing an inscription etched onto it. "My eyesight isn't great... can you read the words?" he asked.

Agent Julia read the inscription carefully.

"'Those who unlock the key will unlock the power to destroy true evil, R. Maccabee.' Who is R. Maccabee?" she asked.

Grant smirked. "There's only one way to find out. Let's get to Damascus—quick! Agent Denzel, see if you can find an abandoned car. We need to move."

Agent Denzel stepped deeper into the empty town, scanning the deserted streets. "Not a single soul around. This town is dead!"

Grant nodded. "Seems the residents moved away long ago. Lodi is only a few kilometers from Damascus; maybe that's why."

Julia kept her eyes peeled for a vehicle. Moments later, Grant spotted a Ford Mustang abandoned near a gas station. "Look! That car might work."

Both Agents Julia and Denzel hurried toward it. Denzel opened the driver's side door and found the keys still in the ignition. "Jackpot!"

Agent Julia raised an eyebrow. "What's with the excitement?"

"The keys are still here," Agent Denzel grinned. "I found them first, so I claim to drive this beauty to Damascus."

Agent Julia rolled her eyes. "Fine, you win. Everyone, get in!"

Agent Denzel checked the interior. "Grant, I'll adjust the front seat for a bit more room in the back. Don't want you cramped."

Grant nodded. "As long as we reach Damascus safely, I'm good."

They climbed in, Agent Denzel fired up the engine, practically vibrating with excitement. "Look at this baby! A Ford Mustang! We'll be in Damascus in no time!"

Julia waved a hand. "Okay, enough showing off. Let's move."

Agent Denzel shifted into drive, and the Mustang roared down the empty streets. Damascus lay over thirteen kilometers ahead.

Meanwhile, a few kilometers away, Jacob had been driving for several hours, trying to catch up with Grant. The heat inside the car was oppressive, so he rolled down the window to let in fresh air. He took a few deep breaths, steadying himself.

The sunlight glinted off the dashboard. Jacob opened the glove compartment and retrieved his sunglasses. "That oughta do it," he muttered.

As he drove, he noticed that the town of Lodi was only five kilometers away. He pulled over to the side of the road, grabbed a bottle of water, and drank quickly to rehydrate. Tossing the empty bottle gently onto the passenger seat, he resumed driving, eyes fixed on the road ahead.

22

FINALLY REUNITED

Meanwhile, back in Damascus, Marilyn and Jonathan wandered through the quiet streets, taking in the empty town.

"I want you now," Marilyn said, her tone playful and flirtatious.

Jonathan hesitated, looking nervous. "Are you sure about this?"

"Is there a problem with how I look?" she asked, raising an eyebrow.

"No, not at all. I am just... not sure why we are doing this in the middle of a ghost town."

She winked. "Well, handsome, I want to live life to the fullest. And right now, I'm craving you."

Jonathan smiled and leaned in, kissing her. The kiss deepened, becoming more passionate with each moment.

"Wait," Marilyn murmured, pulling back slightly. "Let's find a suitable place so I can see what you're made of."

Holding his hand, she scanned the town for a place to be alone. A weathered hotel stood about a hundred yards ahead. "Look at that hotel! Let's go inside," she said.

Jonathan squinted at the sign: *The Virginia Hotel, Bar, and Restaurant.* Marilyn pushed the door open, revealing a reception area thick with cobwebs.

"Oh, my goodness, Jonathan! Look at this place!"

Jonathan shook his head. "Not surprising. This town's been abandoned for over seven years."

"Let's check the rooms upstairs; maybe they're not as untidy," Marilyn suggested.

"All right. Let's see what we find."

She dashed up the stairs, only to slip near the top. "Oh god, I slipped!" she laughed, while Jonathan quickly steadied her with a helping hand.

"Thank you, handsome. Now, let's find a room and get comfortable," she said with a mischievous grin.

Jonathan tried the first door handle he saw—it was unlocked.

"Ladies first," he said with a playful grin.

Marilyn stepped inside. The room was dusty, the bed untouched for years. She pressed her hand against the mattress.

"It looks fine to me," she said.

Jonathan approached her, and they shared a warm, lingering kiss. Slowly, they embraced, their connection growing more intimate as they held each other close. Clothes were loosened, hands intertwined, and their whispered words and soft laughter filled the quiet room.

Marilyn smiled, guiding Jonathan toward the bed. The old mattress creaked slightly under their weight, but it was enough. They lay together, holding each other, warmth spreading as they reveled in the closeness and trust they shared.

After a while, they rested side by side, wrapped in the faded duvet, sharing quiet words and gentle touches.

"Goodness, this duvet is ancient!" Jonathan laughed softly.

Marilyn chuckled, resting her head on his shoulder. "It doesn't matter. We're together, and that's what counts."

Marilyn sighed, leaning back. "We should rest for a moment."

"No," Jonathan replied, glancing around. "We need to see if Jessica is okay out there."

"She'll be fine," Marilyn insisted. "The town is practically dead. There isn't anyone around."

"No, Jonathan. She's my friend. I need to check on her," Marilyn said firmly.

Jonathan nodded. "All right. Let's get dressed and move quickly."

They dressed briskly, their urgency mirrored in each movement. As Marilyn straightened her jacket, something on the floor caught her eye.

"Look, Jonathan! I found a note!" she exclaimed, picking up the yellowed paper.

Jonathan adjusted his clothing, curious. "What does it say?"

Marilyn read aloud: "'Whoever finds this letter needs to go to Creeper Trail, where you will find a cottage called Brunswick Cottage. A young girl is living there with an elderly couple. Kind regards, anonymous.'"

Jonathan frowned. "It doesn't say who wrote it... or why. That's strange."

Marilyn folded the note, determination in her eyes. "So, Creeper Trail it is. Let's find Jessica and head toward Brunswick Cottage immediately."

Together, they left the hotel room, careful not to disturb anything else in the abandoned building.

23

LOVE HAS FOUND ITS WAY

Meanwhile, about fifteen hundred yards from the hotel where Jonathan and Marilyn were staying, Jessica shouted across the town.

"Christian! Christian! Where are you?"

Her voice echoed through the empty streets. Luckily, Detective Marshall, Ebenezer, and Christian were close enough to hear it. They all looked up simultaneously.

"Did someone just call my name?" Christian asked.

"It sounds like it," Ebenezer replied.

"Hello? Who's there?" Detective Marshall called.

Jessica froze for a moment, surprised to get a response. "It's Jessica! Christian, it's me!"

Christian's expression shifted, a mix of relief and concern. "Jessica! What are you doing in Damascus? It's dangerous here!"

"I know, Christian, but I had to find you," Jessica said as she ran toward the echoes. "I came with Marilyn and Jonathan just to be with you."

Detective Marshall interjected firmly, "Jessica, meet us near Damascus Town Hall. You'll see a bookshop on the left-hand side of the road. Go there."

Jessica pushed on, her pace urgent, while Christian ran toward her, determined.

"Jessica, don't worry—I'll find you!" he shouted.

Through the empty streets, they spotted each other from a distance. Both were breathless but kept moving. After running another five hundred yards, they slowed to a walk, finally closing the gap.

Christian pulled Jessica into a tight embrace. "Oh, Jessica... why did you come all the way here? It's dangerous!"

Jessica rested her head against his chest, relief washing over her. "I couldn't stay away. I had to see you, Christian."

They stood together for a moment, the silence of the ghost town surrounding them, hearts pounding but safe in each other's arms.

Jessica's voice trembled as she spoke, "I know, but I missed you... I was scared I might not see you again."

Christian's eyes widened. "You really came all the way to Damascus just to be with me?"

"That's right, honey," she said, gripping his hand. "I couldn't let you go with your friends without seeing you. My feelings for you are too strong, so here I am."

From a distance, Ebenezer and Detective Marshall were running toward them.

"Listen, Jessica," Christian said, "we've discovered a lot in this town—dead bodies, riddles... I'll tell you everything once the detective and Ebenezer catch up."

"Sure, my love," Jessica said, kissing him gently. Christian wrapped his arms around her as they watched the two men approach.

Suddenly, a shadow flickered across the street ahead of them, moving faster than expected.

"Look, Detective! Did you see that?" Ebenezer called out.

Detective Marshall, breathing heavily from the run, barely registered it. But Christian and Jessica saw the shadow slinking toward them.

Jessica's eyes widened in terror. "Did you see that? What... what is it?" She clutched Christian tightly.

Christian stroked her hair and pulled her close. "This is what I saw the first time I visited this town. That shadow... it appears whenever there's human presence."

"How do you know that?" Jessica stammered, panic in her voice.

"I just... feel it," Christian replied.

Moments later, the shadow moved closer, gliding toward them. Jessica's body shook uncontrollably.

"Oh my god! There it is again!" she whispered.

Ebenezer and Detective Marshall finally reached them, stopping to catch their breath. The four stood together, tense, watching the shadow's movements across the deserted town.

"Oh, boy! I've never run this much in my life! But... we made it," Detective Marshall said, catching his breath.

Ebenezer turned to Jessica. "What are you doing here, Jessica? It's not safe!"

Jessica smiled, her eyes on Christian. "I had to make sure my love was safe. I wanted to be by his side."

Christian kissed her softly. "Now that you're here with me, I will always protect you."

Detective Marshall rolled his eyes and glanced at Ebenezer, then back at Christian. "Okay, now that you have Jessica with you, both of you will have to come with Ebenezer and me."

Christian nodded. "Sure. But I need to tell you—we just saw that shadow lurking nearby. I think it knows we're here."

Ebenezer tapped his foot impatiently. "All right, everyone. Let's head back to the bar, then down to the cellar to claim the Book of Secrets."

Jessica looked puzzled. "The Book of Secrets? What is that?"

Ebenezer chuckled softly. "When we arrived in Damascus, we started gathering clues and solving riddles. We've finally found the missing piece to the puzzle. I believe the creature that has been terrorizing this town for seven years is about to face its reckoning."

Detective Marshall nodded in agreement. "Exactly. We have the keys to the safe, the code to what's inside, and the key to the steel door. This might be our chance to defeat this creature for the last time."

Jessica still looked confused, shrugging slightly. "Christian, I need to alert the others that I found you and your friends."

"You didn't come alone? Who are the others with you?" Christian asked.

Jessica nodded. "While I was worried about you, I asked my colleague at the hotel to help find you, and we invited this kind gentleman to come along as well."

Christian frowned slightly. "Okay... did you tell them where to find you?"

"I left a one-cent coin on the ground, so they'd know where I'd be," Jessica explained.

Detective Marshall stepped in. "All right, here's what I suggest: leave a sign near the coin. That way, they'll know where the coin is and where you're headed."

Jessica's eyes lit up. "Great idea, Detective!" She picked up a stone from the pavement and carefully carved the words: *Meet us at the saloon bar.*

"There we go!" she said, satisfied.

Christian reached out his hand to her. "It's time to go."

Ebenezer's impatience was evident as he quickened his pace. "Let's head back to the saloon and unlock the cellar door."

24

WE ARE NOT ALONE

It was twenty-seven minutes past two in the afternoon when Grant, Agent Julia, and Agent Denzel approached Damascus. Grant squinted into the distance, spotting the ghostly town. "Look, we're almost there!"

Agent Julia rubbed her eyes, taking in the view. "Oh God... it already looks like a ghost town, and we haven't even set foot there yet!"

Agent Denzel scanned the road for a safe spot to park. "Agent Julia, I'm pulling over next to that old rusty car." He parked and cut the engine.

"Sure. But look at this place... so much destruction—bodies, twisted metal everywhere," Agent Julia said, her voice tight with concern. "Agent Denzel, let's arm ourselves and move cautiously."

Denzel drew his gun, sweeping from left to right. "What on earth could have caused this?"

Grant shook his head. "Now that... is something you're about to see. Something I've never encountered before. Consider yourselves warned."

As the trio entered Damascus, Grant spotted two figures walking about six hundred and fifty yards ahead. "I think I see two people up ahead," he said, rubbing his eyes to focus.

Agent Julia's gaze sharpened. She recognized Marilyn and Jonathan. "Hey! You two, hands where I can see them!"

She and Agent Denzel sprinted toward the pair. Jonathan turned, spotting the approaching agents in uniform. "Oh my God... who are they?" he exclaimed.

Marilyn glanced at Jonathan. "It looks like we're not alone. From what I can see, it seems they're from the FBI."

"How do you know it's the FBI from that far away? And what should we do?" Jonathan asked.

Marilyn smiled, a hint of sarcasm in her expression. "Let's just keep our hands up and do as they say. It's not like they're going to shoot us."

The agents were now just three yards away. Agent Julia and Agent Denzel raised their guns, keeping their eyes fixed on Jonathan and Marilyn. Agent Julia cleared her throat before speaking.

"My name is FBI Agent Julia, and this is my colleague, Agent Denzel. What brings you both to Damascus? You are aware this town has been deserted for over seven years... Any particular reason for your visit?"

Marilyn kept her hands raised. "We're here to find three people who are currently in Damascus. We came with a friend, and we're looking for her as well."

From behind, Grant appeared, slightly out of breath from running. "God, I'm not quite as fit as you two, so I apologize if I'm a bit slow."

Agent Julia smirked, assessing him. Grant approached Jonathan and Marilyn for the first time. "And who exactly are you two? What brings you to Damascus? Are you looking for anyone, or are you just lost?"

Marilyn spoke steadily. "Let me introduce ourselves. I'm Marilyn, and this is Jonathan. We're looking for my friend, as well as three other people."

Grant's eyes narrowed slightly. "Three people? Are their names Ebenezer and Christian, by any chance? And who is the third person?"

Marilyn acknowledged Grant's question. "That's right! We're here to find Ebenezer and Christian, as well as the police officer."

Grant's brow furrowed in confusion. "Police officer?"

Marilyn continued, her tone measured. "My friend Jessica is out there on her own, looking for Christian and his friends. Jonathan and I went our separate ways to cover more ground."

Grant scratched his head. "And who is Jessica?"

"She's my colleague from the Radford Hotel," Marilyn explained.

Agent Denzel gave Jonathan a skeptical once-over, his expression disapproving. "And you are...?"

Jonathan smirked, unbothered. "That's a charming look you just gave me, Mr. FBI."

Denzel's eyes narrowed. *That man cannot be trusted. There's something off about him.*

Agent Julia's attention shifted, her brow creased. She wondered why a police officer had come along with Ebenezer and Christian.

"Anyway," she said sharply, "what are you two doing here? What business brings you to Damascus?"

Marilyn spoke confidently. "We came to find Jessica's new love. I agreed to accompany her, and we met Jonathan briefly. We asked him to join us, and he agreed."

Agent Julia cut through the conversation with impatience. "Enough of this talking nonsense!"

Grant looked at her in surprise. "Alright, everyone, we are all here for several reasons. First, I came with these two FBI agents—four of whom are dead, may God rest their souls—but I came to this ghost town to ensure Ebenezer and his journalist friend Christian leave safely before anything mysterious—or dangerous—happens."

Marilyn looked confused. "If you don't mind me asking, why are you all here if you're warning others about this ghost town?"

Grant stepped forward. "Well, ma'am, we are the FBI. Our goal is to find out what has been happening in this town—what strange activities have been occurring for the past seven years. Fortunately, we came across this wonderful old-timer who knows a lot about the area. With his help, we might finally solve a case that has been lingering for far too long."

"Oh, thanks for calling me an old-timer, by the way, Julia!" Grant said, his tone a mix of anger and irritation.

"You know what I mean, Grant," Agent Julia replied smoothly. "Anyway, enough explanation from my side. How long have you both been here?"

Marilyn shrugged. "Not too long—maybe an hour or so."

"Okay. Did you find anything—or anyone—while you were here?" Agent Denzel asked sharply.

"We did, as a matter of fact," Jonathan said, a sly smile crossing his face, "but we aren't telling you."

"Excuse me? What did you just say?" Denzel barked.

"You heard me, FBI. We are not telling you anything," Jonathan replied coolly.

Agent Denzel's hand moved to his holster. "Listen here, cowboy. You think you are safe with that attitude? I think not. You'd better tell us what you found while exploring this town."

Grant stepped between them, his expression firm. "Agent Denzel, enough! Let us handle this civilly and work together. I came here to remove Ebenezer and Christian from this town, but apparently, they never listened."

Jonathan finally relented. "Okay, fine. We did find something. Marilyn and I discovered a letter in the hotel—the one we had just exited when you found us."

Grant squinted at the building in the distance. "The Virginia Hotel Bar and Restaurant..."

Agent Julia and Agent Denzel at once focused on the hotel. "So you found a letter? May we see it?" Julia asked.

Jonathan glanced at Marilyn, then carefully handed the letter to Agent Julia. "Here you go."

Julia read the letter quickly. Grant's eyes narrowed as he recalled the key he had found back at Liberty Hall School. "I believe this key will come in handy. Agent Julia, Agent Denzel, let us find Ebenezer and Christian while Jonathan and Marilyn head to Brunswick Cottage to find the girl. It's best we avoid disturbing the cottage for now—especially since we have two armed FBI agents with us. We do not want to alarm the elderly couple or the girl."

Marilyn protested, "But Jessica is expecting Jonathan and me to find her!"

"Do not worry. I will explain everything to Jessica when we reach her," Grant reassured her.

"One last thing," Marilyn added. "Keep an eye out for a coin on the ground. Jessica will leave a clue about where she might be going."

"Thank you. I will keep that in mind while we search for any sign she has left," Grant replied.

"Once we find them, we will meet you two at Brunswick Cottage. And whatever you do, do not leave—just stay at the cottage," he instructed.

"No problem. We'd better split up," Jonathan said. Grant and the two FBI agents moved off to search for Ebenezer and his friends.

Jonathan leaned toward Marilyn. "This place is creepy... and so was that FBI agent."

Marilyn rolled her eyes. "Stop it, Jonathan! Let's just be grateful we were not shot—and that the law is on our side."

Jonathan smirked and nodded. "But we don't even know where this cottage is."

"We'll find it, even if it takes an hour," Marilyn said. Hand in hand, they set off through the ghost town, making their way along Creeper Trail toward Brunswick Cottage.

25

It Is All Starting to Make Sense

I t was fifty-one minutes past two in Damascus. The weather was beginning to clear, as thick clouds drifted away and the sun pierced through the deserted town, casting long shadows over the scattered dead bodies. Rusted cars and abandoned trucks lay haphazardly in the streets.

Ebenezer, Christian, Jessica, and Detective Marshall walked cautiously back toward the saloon bar, now in possession of the keys to the cellar door, the safe, and the steel door.

About four hundred and fifty yards away, Grant and the FBI team moved in the opposite direction. The likelihood of the two groups crossing paths was minimal.

Detective Marshall broke the silence. "I don't know about you three, but I'm starving—and parched!"

Ebenezer and Christian exchanged a glance, nodding in agreement.

"Same here," Jessica added.

"The problem is there's nothing edible here. The food's rotten, especially since the town's been abandoned for over seven years," Detective Marshall said grimly.

A few yards farther down the street, a white Dodge Ram van rolled into

Damascus. Behind the wheel sat Ryan Maccabee, a fifty-four-year-old man with piercing blue eyes, brown shoulder-length hair, and a clean-shaven face. He wore a blue checked shirt, blue jeans, brown boots, and black gloves, exuding an air of quiet menace as he surveyed the ghost town.

Ryan squinted at the dusty road ahead and slowed the van. In the distance, four figures were crossing toward the old saloon. "Helen, they're here," he murmured. "I'll keep the engine low, so they won't hear us."

Helen Maccabee, his wife, leaned forward from the passenger seat. At forty-four, she still carried that sharp, steady grace he'd fallen for—blue eyes alert, long blond hair tucked beneath a denim jacket. She wore a red V-neck shirt, tight blue jeans, and white sneakers, casual but ready for anything.

"Good," she said quietly. "If they've found the keys, our daughter will finally be safe."

Ryan clipped the walkie-talkie back into his pocket. "Okay. I'll meet you at the van."

"No problem, honey." Helen exhaled slowly, her gaze fixed on the saloon. "I just hope they open the right doors this time—maybe then the pieces will start to fit together."

Inside the saloon, Ebenezer stepped through first, followed by Christian, Detective Marshall, and Jessica. The air was thick with dust and something sour, like spilled whiskey and decay.

"All right," Ebenezer said, scanning the room. "We're back where it started. Let's use those keys and see what these doors are hiding."

Christian hesitated, glancing toward the far wall. "I'm starving, man. There's gotta be a kitchen somewhere. I'm gonna take a quick look."

Ebenezer frowned. "Are you serious? This place has been abandoned for decades. There's no food here. Stick with us—we're heading to the cellar."

Christian shrugged. "Won't be long. Jess, wanna come with me?"

Jessica hesitated, then nodded. "Sure, baby. Let's go."

Detective Marshall gave them a wary look. "Don't wander too far. We need to stay together."

Ebenezer and Marshall exchanged a glance, then descended the creaking cellar stairs. The light dimmed behind them.

Outside, Ryan climbed out of the van, waving briefly to Helen before opening the back doors. Inside, a cardboard box held ham sandwiches wrapped in wax paper. He grabbed a few, along with a bottle of water, and took a long drink.

"Helen," he called softly, "I'm going to take them some food and water. They've been out there for hours—they must be starving."

"Fine," she said, adjusting her jacket. "But take your gun. You'll scare them half to death if you just appear out of nowhere."

Ryan chuckled. "That is why I married you, Helen. Fourteen years and still the voice of reason."

"It's just common sense," she replied with a faint smile.

Ryan tucked his pistol into his jeans pocket, then packed four sandwiches and four bottles of water into his backpack.

"Okay, I'll head out now," Ryan said, checking the walkie-talkie on his belt. "Keep an eye out for anything unusual. I'll radio if there's trouble. I love you."

"I love you too, Ryan."

Ryan started down the dusty road toward the ghost town. The air was still—too still—and the silence pressed against his ears. Then a sharp rustle broke the calm. The branches of a nearby tree shivered, swaying slightly to the left.

He stopped in his tracks. "Hmm," he muttered, narrowing his eyes. "There's no wind strong enough to move that tree. Something's in there."

Before he could step closer, two ravens exploded out of the branches, their wings beating wildly. Startled, Ryan yanked his gun from his pocket just as the birds dove at him, screeching.

Two quick gunshots shattered the silence. The birds dropped, limp and dark against the dirt. Ryan lowered the weapon, chest heaving. "Well," he said under his breath, "that was strange."

Back inside the saloon, Detective Marshall and Ebenezer froze mid-step as the echo of gunfire reached them.

"Did you hear that?" Marshall whispered.

Ebenezer nodded grimly. "Yeah. Sounded like shots—outside."

Across the room, Christian and Jessica, who had just stepped into the kitchen, heard it too. Jessica grabbed Christian's arm. "Christian, I'm scared."

He moved toward the window, pulling her gently with him. Through the dusty glass, they saw a man standing in the street—gun in hand, backpack slung over his shoulder—staring down at two dead ravens.

"Jessica," Christian said quietly, "let's move. We need to tell the others."

"Yes," she whispered. "There's a man out there with a gun."

Christian's brow furrowed. "Those birds... They look familiar. I swear I've seen them before—since we left Blacksburg. They've been following us all the way to Damascus."

Jessica turned to him, uneasy. "Then maybe he isn't the only one watching us."

"Really? How would you know?" Jessica asked, uneasy. "There are plenty of ravens around."

"I just have a feeling," Christian replied. "I've seen those same two more than once. They've been following us."

Meanwhile, nearly fourteen hundred yards from the saloon, Marilyn and Jonathan heard the echo of gunfire roll through the ghost town as they made their way toward Creeper Trail.

"Did you hear that?" Marilyn asked, stopping in her tracks.

"It sounded like a gunshot," Jonathan replied, scanning the empty street.

"Should we go back and see what happened?"

"I think we should keep moving," Jonathan said. "Let's get to Brunswick Cottage. Maybe it was the FBI."

"Maybe," she said quietly, glancing over her shoulder as they continued down the trail.

Back in Damascus, about nine hundred yards from the saloon, Grant and the FBI agents also heard the shots.

"Guys, that definitely sounded like gunfire!" Grant shouted.

"Yeah, it did," said Agent Julia, her eyes narrowing. "Let's move in and check it out."

"Listen, you two," Grant grumbled. "I'm an old man. I can't sprint like you can. Let's take it slow."

"Fine," Agent Denzel said, exchanging a look with Julia. "But we'll find whoever pulled that trigger."

The three continued on, walking cautiously as they ventured deeper into the abandoned streets.

Back at the saloon, Ebenezer and Detective Marshall climbed up from the cellar, leaving the door ajar as they searched for Christian and Jessica. Outside, Ryan Maccabee scanned the area nervously. Spotting a narrow alley beside the saloon, he ducked into the shadows to stay unseen.

Moments later, Ebenezer spotted Christian and Jessica approaching.

"Did you two hear the gunshots earlier?" Ebenezer asked.

"Yes, we did," Christian said. "We even saw who fired—he shot two ravens."

Detective Marshall frowned. "Why would anyone shoot ravens?"

Ebenezer's expression darkened. "Detective, remember when I told you how those birds were following us on the way here? Those weren't just ordinary ravens."

Jessica interrupted the two men. "Enough, guys! As Christian said earlier, we saw who shot the ravens—and we are not alone in this town. There's a man wandering around out there, and I think we'd better keep a close eye on him."

Detective Marshall sighed deeply. "All right, you know what we have to do. Let's find this man and approach him calmly."

"Did you just say *calmly*?" Christian asked, raising an eyebrow.

"That's right," said the detective. "And that's exactly what we'll do."

"Okay, you're the detective—the law," Christian replied.

Jessica crossed her arms. "So, what are we waiting for? Let's go out there and find him."

Ebenezer stepped forward. "What about the keys to the doors? That's why we came back to the saloon bar in the first place."

"Let's leave that for now," said Detective Marshall. "Finding this man is more important. We need to know why he's here all alone—and why he shot those birds."

The four of them slowly stepped out of the bar, scanning their surroundings for any sign of danger.

A few moments later, Grant and the FBI agents spotted movement in the distance. Four figures were walking along the dusty street.

"Look, Julia, Denzel—it's Ebenezer and Christian! I just know it's them!" Grant exclaimed.

Agent Julia squinted toward the group. "And who are the other two with them?"

"I don't know," said Grant, "but let's find out." He cupped his hands and shouted, "Ebenezer! Ebenezer!"

Ebenezer turned, his face flashing with shock and disbelief. "Grant? What on earth are you doing here?"

Before anyone could respond, Detective Marshall instinctively reached for his gun. Agent Julia caught the motion and reacted instantly, drawing her weapon.

"Stop right there! Don't even think about it!" she barked. Her voice was steady, but her stance was tense and ready.

Detective Marshall froze, then slowly dropped his gun and raised his hands.

He looked at Agent Julia, narrowing his eyes. "So, we meet again—under very unusual circumstances."

Agent Julia smirked faintly. "Well, well. It's Detective Marshall. I haven't seen you since that story you told about your missing officers."

"That's right," Detective Marshall replied. "And I never guessed the FBI would get involved. Then again, your organization always seems to get in the way."

"Enough talking," Agent Julia ordered. "And I suggest your friends, Ebenezer and Christian, put their hands up as well. You two—empty your pockets and drop everything, including any weapons you might have!"

Ebenezer and Christian exchanged uneasy glances but did as they were told. Coins, keys, and small items clattered to the ground.

"And you too, young lady," Julia added sharply.

Jessica hesitated, then emptied her pockets and slowly set her gun on the ground.

Grant stepped forward, voice firm but controlled. "Agent Julia, Agent Denzel—there's no need for this. They're all innocent."

Julia didn't lower her weapon. "Grant, I don't know that yet," she said evenly. "I'm going to ask them a few questions about their visit to this isolated town."

Detective Marshall, still holding his hands in the air, replied, "We could ask the same thing—why are *you* three here?"

Ebenezer looked toward Grant and spoke before anyone else could. "We came here to investigate, to find answers. Detective Marshall joined us to uncover what really happened in Damascus."

Then, turning to Agent Julia, he frowned. "Wait—Agent Julia, haven't we met before?"

Julia blinked, taken aback. Her expression tightened, her voice suddenly uncertain. "Erm... I don't think we have."

"Yes, we have," Ebenezer insisted. "I walked past you at the Iron Man Inn yesterday. You were talking to Grant at the bar as I was leaving."

Grant stepped in quickly, his tone conciliatory. "That's right, Agent Julia. Look, there's no reason for hostility. Why can't we just work together? We're all here for the same reason. I warned Ebenezer not to come to this ghost town, but—"

"Look," Christian interrupted, his voice rising. "We brought Detective Marshall with us for a reason—to help us uncover why so many of his fellow officers disappeared. And now we know. There's something out here... something not human. A demon-like creature that's slaughtered the people who once lived in this town. That's what we're dealing with!"

Agent Denzel glanced around the desolate street, his expression hard. "Take a look around you—what do you see? I see bodies scattered all over this town... and twisted metal everywhere. Agent Julia, we should work with them."

Ebenezer felt a flicker of relief, while Agent Julia's shoulders sagged with reluctant agreement. "Okay, Agent Denzel. Fair enough." She motioned for everyone to lower their weapons. "So—did any of you find anything useful while you've been here?"

Ebenezer nodded, steady but cautious. "Yes. We've found quite a bit while searching. If you look where I dropped those keys on the ground, you'll see what I mean. We might've just uncovered a clue—maybe even the key to defeating this demon."

Detective Marshall turned toward Agent Julia. "He's right. Ebenezer might be onto something."

Jessica, still uneasy, added, "What about that man who shot the ravens earlier?"

"What man?" Agent Denzel asked, frowning.

"We saw someone wandering around," Jessica explained. "While Christian and I were in the saloon's kitchen looking for food. The place right there on your left."

Agent Julia's brows drew together. "So, there's another person out here?" She paused, scanning the silent street. "Alright, then we need a plan. If you all agree, let's be honest and come to a real conclusion about our next step."

Ebenezer bent to retrieve the keys, then held them up so the faint sunlight glinted off the metal. "Let me go with Detective Marshall, Christian, and Jessica back into the saloon. We'll unlock every door and start piecing this puzzle together."

From the other side, Grant raised a small key between his fingers. "Look, everyone—I found one, too. Back in Lodi. I'm certain this will come in handy."

Ebenezer studied it closely. The brass surface bore a faint engraving: *Those who unlock the key will unlock the power to destroy true evil.* Beneath it, the initials: **R. Maccabee.**

"This key's longer than the others," Ebenezer murmured. "I'd bet it opens something big—maybe a chest... or whatever Maccabee left behind."

The group exchanged uneasy looks as the wind swept through the silent town, the sound of rusted metal creaking in the distance.

Suddenly, a figure stepped out from behind the saloon and into view. Ryan Maccabee.

"That's right," he said calmly. "And I'm the one who placed that key on the ground at Liberty Hall School."

At once, both FBI agents and Detective Marshall drew their guns, training them on him.

"Who are you? Hands where I can see them!" Detective Marshall barked.

Agent Julia's voice cut in sharply. "Identify yourself—and keep those hands up!"

Ryan slowly set a canvas bag on the ground. "Easy. I just have sandwiches and water in there. For all four of you."

Agent Denzel advanced a few steps. "What's in the bag? Pass it over—carefully."

Ryan nudged the bag forward with his boot until Denzel picked it up. Ebenezer, Christian, Grant, and Jessica watched tensely.

Christian squinted. "That's the guy we saw earlier—the one who shot the ravens!"

Jessica nodded. "That's him!"

Grant and Agent Julia exchanged a quick glance, then walked toward the two lifeless birds lying in the dust.

"Could these be the same ravens that attacked us on the road?" Julia asked quietly. "The ones that made us lose four agents before we even reached Damascus?"

Ryan's tone darkened. "Those ravens were following you. They're controlled by the Demon Sorcerer."

Jessica's voice trembled. "Demon Sorcerer?"

"Correct," Ryan said. "That's why I left the clues—hoping someone brave enough would follow them. What you're all about to face is something far worse than you imagine—something truly evil, the kind no man has ever seen."

Ebenezer stared hard at him. "Are you R. Maccabee?"

"Yes," Ryan replied, straightening. "Ryan Maccabee. And I'm relieved to finally meet all of you."

Agent Julia kept her gun raised. "Why are you relieved, Mr. Maccabee?"

"Let me make this simple," Ryan said. "I've been waiting for people with the courage to uncover what happened here. For seven long years, this town has been cursed—and at last, you came."

Grant frowned. "Ryan, this is my second time in Damascus. I was here after it was destroyed. Why didn't you ever approach me then?"

Christian interjected, "Yeah—why wait until now?"

Detective Marshall holstered his weapon but kept his guard up. "I've been investigating this place myself. I figured someone must still be keeping watch, even though we were warned not to come here."

Jessica spoke up. "Ryan, when we stopped at that gas station, a man described a demonic-looking creature. Do you know what it is—or what it can do?"

Ryan nodded slowly. "Good question, all of you. Let me tell you the story of Damascus."

Agent Julia eased her stance. "We've got time. Go ahead."

Detective Marshall lowered his weapon completely, realizing Ryan wasn't a threat.

Ryan drew a breath. "Where do I start? Over seven years ago—on March 11th, 1957—my wife, Helen, who was eight months pregnant, and I moved here to Damascus to start a new life. We bought a small hotel, just a few miles from where we're standing now. We left Pittsburgh behind, hoping for peace and a fresh start."

Ebenezer and Detective Marshall exchanged a knowing glance, then looked toward Christian—as if they could already sense where Ryan's story was heading.

"So, you went back to your hotel," Ebenezer said, "and I presume you gave the bag of nails to your builders?"

Ryan nodded slowly. "He was a good friend of mine from the day I settled in Damascus. His name was Max. He was not just a builder—he was also an alchemist and an archaeologist. One afternoon, after finishing some financial paperwork in his office, he told me he was bored. He decided to visit the local library. There, he started asking questions about Ancient Egypt and borrowed several books on the subject.

A few days later, he came to see me. He said he wanted to talk privately. That's when he told me he planned to travel to Egypt. His passion for archaeology had never faded, and he wanted to continue his research where it all began."

Agent Julia leaned forward. "So, your friend Max just decided to go to Egypt—just like that?"

"Correct," Ryan said. "And I was thrilled for him. Two days later, he asked if I could drive him to Washington Dulles Airport. Of course, I agreed. I told my wife I'd be back later that day."

Christian frowned. "And how did your wife feel about you driving all the way to Washington?"

Ryan gave a faint smile. "Helen wasn't thrilled at first. She questioned why I had to go so far, but I reassured her I'd return soon."

"Okay," Christian said, gesturing for him to continue.

Ryan nodded. "We reached the airport, checked in his suitcase, and sat down for coffee. We talked for nearly two hours about his plans—what he hoped to discover. When I asked what exactly he wanted to explore, Max said he was searching for something unusual in the Giza region."

Detective Marshall rubbed his chin. "So, your friend believed there was something hidden in Giza? He must have researched it thoroughly."

"Correct, Detective," Ryan replied. "He'd been studying for months. That's why he was so determined to go—he wanted to see it for himself."

"Interesting," Ebenezer murmured.

Ryan continued, his tone darkening. "He mentioned reading about a buried chest hidden deep beneath one of the pyramids of Giza. According to the book, the chest contained four items: *The Book of Secrets*, an amulet, a golden metal bar that unfolds into a spear, and—most dangerously of all—*the Book of the Undead*."

Detective Marshall leaned forward, visibly intrigued as Ryan continued his story. "Please, go on, Ryan. What happened next?"

Ryan drew in a deep breath before speaking. "Once Max uncovered the treasures buried beneath the pyramid, he found an Egyptian hieroglyph carved onto both the chest and the books I mentioned earlier. The image showed a demonic figure—tall, gaunt, holding a spear in its right hand, and wearing an amulet around its neck. When Max studied the next hieroglyph, it became clear that the two artifacts somehow enhanced the demon's power."

He paused, his voice lowering. "Max took the chest and noticed another set of hieroglyphs engraved on its base—ten symbols this time. The carvings seemed to depict the demon absorbing or draining the souls of human beings."

Detective Marshall's expression tightened. "Are you certain that's what the symbols meant?"

Ryan nodded solemnly. "Max cross-referenced the markings using a hieroglyphic book he'd borrowed from the Damascus library. After translating, he discovered the words *'Sparda the Soul Collector'* inscribed along the bottom of the chest."

At that moment, Agent Julia stepped forward, interrupting. "Hold on—are you saying this demon, Sparda, actually collects human souls?"

"Yes," Ryan replied firmly. "That's exactly what I'm saying."

Ebenezer exchanged a grave look with Christian and Detective Marshall. "That explains everything we've witnessed throughout our time in Damascus," he said quietly.

Grant frowned. "Explain how?"

"Yeah, please enlighten us," Jessica added, folding her arms.

"It all makes sense now," Ebenezer said, his tone measured. "This creature—the one depicted in those hieroglyphs—feeds on human souls. That's why everybody we've seen has turned pale blue, even the animals."

Christian nodded in agreement. "He's right. On our way here, we saw a dead animal, then a man in Bisset Park—both with that same bluish hue. And now, looking at the bodies scattered around this town, the cuts and bruises make it clear they were attacked. The demon must have taken their souls afterward."

"That's right, Christian," Ryan said gravely. "But let me tell you something else about this demon. Not only is it powerful—its strength grows even greater once it claims both the amulet and the spear."

"Please, continue the story," Agent Julia urged.

"Sure," Ryan replied, pausing briefly before continuing. "Back in the Giza region of Egypt, Max took the chest—along with the amulet, spear, and the two books—back to his hotel. That's when something strange happened. The chest began trembling violently, and suddenly the sound of a sandstorm filled the air outside. When Max looked out the window, he saw a massive wall of sand rolling toward the nearby town of Al Duqqi, just outside Cairo. Then he realized something far worse was happening. The storm began to take shape—forming into Sparda, made entirely of swirling sand. The creature looked straight into Max's eyes, glanced at the chest, and then turned away."

"My goodness," Ebenezer murmured. "I bet Max was terrified."

"Terrified is an understatement," Ryan said. "He started acting strangely afterward. He began reading *The Book of Secrets* and *The Book of the Dead*, and as he went through them, he realized something shocking—this chest did not originate on Earth. It came from another universe. In other words, Sparda did not arrive here by accident. It came to conquer."

Detective Marshall and Agent Julia exchanged bewildered glances. Both spoke at once, voices overlapping. "Tell us more!"

Detective Marshall gestured politely. "Ladies first."

"Thank you, Detective," Agent Julia said with a faint smile before turning back to Ryan. "How did your friend Max discover that Sparda came from another galaxy?"

Ryan cleared his throat. "Here's how he found out. In *The Book of Secrets*, it describes everything about Sparda—its powers, its weaknesses, even its origins. One section, written in ancient hieroglyphs, revealed that Sparda was always drawn to Egypt. The pyramids and ancient symbols resonated with it somehow. But that wasn't all Max uncovered. He learned that Sparda had ruled over nine other planets across different galaxies—and every one of those planets had one thing in common: pyramids. His goal was always the same—to dominate every world where pyramids existed."

Ebenezer's expression hardened. "So, what you're saying is that this chest somehow fell from another galaxy... and just happened to land in the sand dunes of Egypt?"

"Let me finish the story, Ebenezer," Ryan said calmly. "*The Book of Secrets* also mentioned that Sparda isn't acting alone. It has an alliance—beings or forces that helped send the chest to Earth. They ensured it landed in the Sahara Desert, hoping that someone in Egypt would find it and open it. But the chest could only be opened if the words were spoken aloud. Luckily, Max never read the hieroglyphs while he was there. He placed all the objects—the amulet, the spear, and both books—back into the chest and decided to leave the hotel immediately."

"I'm getting a little confused, Ryan," Ebenezer admitted. "You said this demon ruled nine planets across nine galaxies—so does that mean the demon can read or write Egyptian?"

"Excellent question, Ebenezer," Ryan replied. "Sparda communicates both telepathically and vocally. When it ruled those nine worlds, each planet had its own ancient symbol or script. Earth happened to be one of them—its language recorded as ancient Egyptian hieroglyphs. That's why those same symbols appear in *The Book of Secrets*."

Ebenezer nodded slowly. "I see. So now it all makes sense. Sparda came to Earth to claim its tenth world—ours. It wants to rule over ten planets, consuming every soul it finds. And the only way it can fully reawaken is if someone opens the chest and reads from *The Book of Secrets*, allowing it to walk this Earth again."

Ryan nodded grimly. "That's right. Fortunately, Max was smart enough not to read from the book. Instead, he decided to take the chest back to the United States."

"I have a question," Agent Julia interjected. "How did Max manage to pass through security at Cairo Airport with something like that?"

"Simple," Ryan said, a faint smile forming on his face. "First, the chest wasn't made on this planet—it could not be x-rayed. Second, the spear only reveals its sharp point when the activation words are read in hieroglyphs, which can only be found in the book. To ordinary eyes, it looked harmless. And finally, since the chest didn't contain any illegal substances, security didn't bother inspecting it. They cleared it as safe for boarding."

Agent Julia looked horrified by what she had just heard. "Let me get this straight," she said slowly. "You're telling me the chest can't be seen on an x-ray—and even if someone searched it, they wouldn't question what's inside?"

Ryan nodded. "That's absolutely correct, Agent Julia. As I mentioned earlier, this chest isn't from our world, so it posed no recognized threat to the United States—or to anyone—at the time."

"Please, continue the story," Grant urged.

Ryan took a breath. "Anyway, Max called me the moment he landed at Dulles Airport. I picked it up right away. He was thrilled rambling about what he'd found in Egypt and how extraordinary it was. I told him to save the details until we met in person. Later, I mentioned to my wife, Helen, that I was driving to pick Max up and bring him back to Damascus. She wanted to come along—and so did our daughter, Lucy. I didn't see any harm in it, so I agreed. We all went together to meet him."

"That's sweet of you—to bring your wife and daughter," Jessica said warmly.

Christian rolled his eyes at her.

Jessica frowned. "What was that look for?"

Christian smiled, leaning in to kiss her lightly on the lips. "I just know how much you love a little romance," he teased.

Ryan chuckled. "Well, if you two want some romance, you're welcome to stay at my hotel. Kidding, of course."

Christian laughed. "Thanks for the offer, but we'll pass."

Agent Julia tapped her pen impatiently. "Can we get back to the story, please?"

"Of course," Ryan said, straightening in his seat. "So, my wife, my daughter, and I made the drive to the airport. Smooth trip—no traffic at all. We waited at arrivals, watching the board. His flight had landed earlier than scheduled, and about twenty-five minutes later, we saw him. Max walked toward us looking... off. His face was pale, tense—like thunderclouds were sitting behind his eyes. I asked him if he was feeling all right, but his answer... Well, it was strange. Very strange."

"So, what did he say?" asked Agent Julia.

Ryan took a breath before answering. "He said, *'Let's talk somewhere private—where no one else can hear us.'* So, my wife, my daughter, Max, and I went to the parking lot outside the airport. We loaded his luggage into the trunk and started our five-hour drive back to Damascus."

Detective Marshall leaned forward. "I presume you all had plenty to talk about during those five hours, Ryan?"

"Yes, we did," Ryan replied. "At first, I asked if he was feeling all right—how his trip went. But he looked shaken… lost, almost. Then he said, *'I want to tell you something I discovered in Egypt, but you have to believe me—and promise you won't tell anyone.'* My wife and I exchanged a glance, wondering what could've possibly happened. We promised to keep his secret safe."

Ebenezer looked intrigued, though concern flickered across his face. "What did Max tell you and your wife in the car?"

Ryan's tone grew more serious. "He told us about what he'd found in the pyramids at Giza—the same story I've shared with you. The chest was in his luggage. When I heard that, I'll admit, it frightened me. About half a kilometre later, I pulled the car over to the side of the road because I needed to see the chest with my own eyes. My wife wasn't happy about it—Lucy was with us, and she wanted to keep driving—but I told her to stay calm. I had to know what Max had brought back."

Detective Marshall suddenly raised a hand. "Sorry to interrupt, but there's a woman walking toward us."

Ryan turned to look and immediately recognized her. "That's my wife!" he said quickly. "I told her I'd radio if I needed anything—she must've wondered why I was taking so long."

Agent Julia and Agent Denzel exchanged a glance as the others looked on.

"Helen, my sweetheart!" Ryan called out.

Helen's voice carried across the lot, sharp with worry. "Why didn't you radio me? I thought something terrible had happened!"

"Sorry, my love," Ryan replied, stepping forward. "I met some people while I was here."

Helen's eyes darted to the others. "Who are these people—and why are there two FBI agents and a police officer with you?"

Agent Julia folded her arms. "We can hear you, just for your information."

Helen glared at her. "I don't care if you can hear me or not, *FBI.*"

Ryan sighed and rolled his eyes before turning to his companions. "Excuse me a moment while I talk to my wife," he said, walking toward Helen.

Christian and Jessica exchanged a glance, both smiling.

"That's love right there," Jessica said softly.

"But Ryan's wife seems upset with him for not radioing her," Christian replied.

Jessica chuckled. "I actually find it sweet—how they used walkie-talkies just to stay in touch."

Ryan gestured toward the woman approaching them. "Ladies and gentlemen, this is my wife, Helen Maccabee."

Everyone turned their attention toward her as Ebenezer stepped forward.

"My name is Ebenezer O'Rourke," he said warmly. "Let me introduce everyone. This is my colleague Christian, his girlfriend Jessica, and Detective Marshall."

The three greeted her in unison. "Hello, Helen!"

Helen smiled faintly. "It's a pleasure to meet you all—though under rather unusual circumstances and in such an unusual place."

Detective Marshall nodded. "You're right about that. It's not exactly the prettiest location."

Ebenezer continued the introductions. "And these are Grant Hennessy, FBI Agent Julia, and Agent Denzel."

Helen's expression shifted the moment she heard the titles. Her tone hardened. "I don't see why the FBI needs to be here. Shouldn't you be chasing down drug cartels or something?"

Agent Julia raised an eyebrow. "And what exactly is that supposed to mean?"

Helen met her gaze coldly. "It means your lives are about to be in danger. This isn't a simple case—it's a matter of death without life."

Agent Denzel straightened. "We're fully aware of the situation we're facing but thank you for your concern."

Before tension could rise further, Ryan stepped between them. "Alright, that's enough. No more arguing. Now that you've all met my wife, I'll finish the story about Max."

Detective Marshall nodded. "Please do, Ryan."

Ryan drew in a long breath; his eyes briefly fixed on the ground before lifting to meet the group. "Now that Helen's here, she can help me fill in some details."

Helen placed a reassuring hand on his shoulder. "Of course, honey."

Ryan continued. "So, I pulled over on the side of the road, parked the car, and got out. Helen followed, holding our daughter. I went to the trunk and opened it—and there it was."

He paused, his voice lowering. "A chest. Old, strange, and unsettling. I'd never seen anything like it in my life."

Ebenezer scratched his head, nervously waiting for Ryan to continue.

"I picked up the chest," Ryan said, his voice low. "I looked at Max and my wife, amazed by what I'd just seen. Max told me not to open it until we got back to Damascus, and I agreed. But Helen looked shocked—almost frightened. She got back in the car and refused to look at it again."

Helen nodded. "That's right. I told Ryan and Max to get back in the car and keep driving. I didn't want to stay there any longer. We agreed we'd take a closer look at the chest once we were safely back in Damascus."

Ebenezer leaned forward. "And what did you talk about during the drive back?"

Ryan and Helen exchanged a glance before Ryan spoke again. "Well, I kept my eyes on the road, but my mind was spinning. I couldn't stop thinking about that chest. I kept asking myself what I'd gotten into by volunteering to pick Max up from the airport. He'd brought something back from Egypt that didn't feel... earthly. Max noticed how quiet we were, and he tried to make small talk, but the mood in the car was uneasy."

Christian looked at Ebenezer and Jessica, his nerves showing as Ryan went on.

"What did Max say next?" Christian asked.

Ryan drew a breath. "He started acting strangely—but not scared. Excited. Like he'd found something that could make him rich. Then he told Helen and me that we mustn't tell a soul about what he discovered. He said that once we returned to Damascus, we'd uncover the truth about the chest—and about something called *The Book of Secrets*, *The Book of the Dead*, an amulet, and a spear."

Detective Marshall began pacing, hands on his hips. "And how did you both react?"

"We promised Max again that we wouldn't tell anyone," Ryan said. "We agreed to look into everything once we got home. By then, our daughter had woken up from her nap—tired and cranky after all the traveling between Damascus and Dulles. She started fussing, so I decided to pull over at a service station to give her a break."

Ebenezer nodded. "I assume you didn't want to leave that chest unattended in the car?"

"Correct," Ryan replied. "Max carried the luggage inside with us. We found a small American diner next to the gas station and went in for a bite to eat."

Helen looked at her husband, hesitating—as if she wanted to add something more to the story.

"Can I say something, please?" Helen asked.

"Sure, you can," Ryan replied with a smile.

Helen gestured toward the saloon. "Everyone, follow me inside Max's Saloon Bar. Let's make ourselves comfortable so we can finish the story properly."

The group followed her inside. The air smelled faintly of aged whiskey and wood polish. Helen clapped her hands lightly. "Ryan, darling, why don't you give everyone some of those sandwiches I made? I'm sure they're hungry."

Ryan nodded. "Of course, my love. I forgot to mention—we brought sandwiches."

Detective Marshall and Agent Julia exchanged a polite grin and accepted theirs.

"Thank you, Ryan," said Agent Julia.

Soon everyone had a sandwich in hand. They ate quickly, almost hungrily, as if they hadn't eaten all day. Helen watched in surprise.

"Goodness gracious! You poor souls must've been starving. But I'm glad you trusted a stranger's food," she said with a laugh.

Jessica smiled. "Thank you, Helen. It's delicious."

"You're very welcome," Helen said warmly. "Now, let me continue the story and give Ryan a little break. I'm sure he'll appreciate that."

Ryan chuckled. "Thank you, dear."

Once everyone had finished eating, Helen motioned toward the back. "Alright, everyone. Follow me to the basement—the same place where Ebenezer, Christian, and Detective Marshall went earlier."

She pulled a small flashlight from her handbag. "Luckily, I've got a torch so we can see where we're going," she said, leading the way down the creaking stairs.

Ebenezer exchanged a knowing glance with Christian and Detective Marshall. They all understood what lay beyond that door—the one that could reveal *The Book of Secrets*.

Detective Marshall spoke up. "So, Helen, would you like to continue the story from there?"

Helen nodded. "Yes. We all sat together at that diner, and Max asked Ryan to dig deeper into what he'd found in Egypt. Ryan's reaction said it all—he agreed to help Max with the research."

Ryan exhaled slowly. "Helen wasn't happy about it. She felt we were meddling with forces we didn't understand—something that should've stayed buried. But I told her everything would be fine."

Helen gave a faint smile. "Eventually, I agreed with both Ryan and Max. We decided to explore the chest further—but I made one thing clear: our daughter was to stay away from it. I didn't want her anywhere near that danger."

She paused, her expression tightening. "We chose to store the items in different parts of the bar, keeping them apart so no one could easily piece the puzzle together. Then we created a riddle—a trail of clues that only the determined could follow."

Her voice lowered, almost a whisper. "That way, if anyone ever tried to find *it* again, they'd have to earn it... and risk everything to uncover the truth."

"So, you got it all figured out!" Detective Marshall said. "Ebenezer, Christian, and I had to solve the riddle to find the keys.”

“Yes, that’s right!” Helen replied. “We left the diner, got back into the car, and drove straight to Damascus. We arrived late at night.”

“What happened when you got there?” Ebenezer asked.

Helen took a deep breath. “Ryan, Max, Lucy, and I went inside Max’s Saloon Bar. We grabbed the chest from the trunk and placed it carefully on the bar table. Then... it started shaking! You can imagine our reaction—it wasn’t pretty.”

“Really? It was shaking?” Ebenezer asked, wide-eyed.

“Yes, and while it shook, we heard noises... like some non-human being speaking in a strange language,” Helen said, shivering at the memory.

“Max took the chest to the basement,” Helen continued. “Ryan followed him, though I’m sure he was wondering why. I stayed behind in the bar with Lucy, as Ryan instructed. Then... Max looked possessed. His expression was sinister, his eyes wide, and he laughed in a hysterical, unnatural way.”

“What do you mean, ‘possessed’?” Agent Julia asked.

“Well... his face changed. He looked like he was controlled by something else. Completely different, almost inhuman,” Helen explained.

“Goodness! So, you’re saying the voice of a demonic creature-controlled Max?” Detective Marshall asked.

“That’s right,” Helen said. “Max and Ryan went down into the basement in complete darkness. I followed Lucy. What we saw next... I’ll never forget. Max opened the chest and began speaking in that strange language. Seconds later, a beam of yellow light shot from the chest, and what appeared was something we never thought we’d see in our lifetime.”

“Let me guess—the demon emerged from the chest?” Grant asked.

“Yes, Grant! The demon had finally awakened on this planet,” Helen said.

Ryan shook his head, still haunted by the memory. “Let me finish the story, Helen.”

Everyone turned their attention to him.

“As Helen mentioned, the demon had been awakened. I paused for a moment, watching in disbelief. Then the demon spoke... in English. It said, ‘My name is

Sparda. I am the demon sorcerer, and I am here on this earth to claim as many souls as possible.' Suddenly, Max fainted. I grabbed the chest as quickly as I could and told my wife and daughter to run for their lives."

"What about Max? Did you leave him behind?" Ebenezer asked, alarmed.

"Unfortunately, I couldn't take Max with me," Ryan said, his voice heavy. "The demon looked at me, my wife, and my daughter, laughed loudly, and warned us that we couldn't hide for long."

"So, what did you do after escaping the basement?" Christian asked.

"I had to get out of there, even though I felt guilty leaving Max behind. We all got into the car and drove toward Creeper Trail," Ryan replied.

Detective Marshall interjected. "Ryan, when Ebenezer, Christian, and I first visited this bar, we found Max in his office... lying dead. He looked fresh. So, the demon must have taken his soul."

"Correct, Detective," Ryan said, nodding. "But before leaving Max in the basement, we saw him... and he wasn't the same."

"Tell us more. Why was he different?" Agent Julia asked.

"He didn't look like himself," Ryan explained. "He was pale, disturbed, and clearly possessed. We left immediately and drove toward Creeper Trail. It wasn't far—maybe three minutes through Damascus—when we noticed a cottage in an area called Wright Branch, next to Laurel Creek River. I told my wife we needed somewhere to hide, to protect her and Lucy. Soon after, I realized we had to hide the chest so the demon couldn't get the items, including the two books. I took the amulet and placed it around my daughter's neck."

"What did you do with the books and the spear? And why put the amulet on your daughter?" Ebenezer asked.

"I don't know why it came to me, but I felt the demon would try to claim the amulet," Ryan said.

"And the spear and books?" Detective Marshall pressed.

"They were in the chest," Ryan said. "We knocked on the door of the cottage, called Brunswick Cottage, and an elderly couple answered."

"I'm still trying to understand why you would put your daughter in danger, giving her the demon's amulet," Grant said, concerned.

Ryan sighed and replied calmly, "To be honest, Grant, it was the right decision. The demon wouldn't be powerful without the amulet."

"So, you're saying the demon needs the amulet to regain strength?" Christian asked.

"Yes! I knew this by examining the amulet before placing it on Lucy's neck. The edges of the amulet have hieroglyphic symbols indicating the demon would become extremely powerful if it had the amulet—and the spear—together."

"Well, that makes sense now," Christian said.

"Ryan, tell us about the elderly couple at Brunswick Cottage. Did they let your family in?" Agent Julia asked.

"Yes," Ryan replied. "They asked who we were, and I told them we are the Maccabees and that we needed their help. The elderly man introduced himself as Ron Brunswick, and his partner as Janet Brunswick."

"They were a lovely, sweet couple," Helen added. "They welcomed us into their beautiful cottage and offered tea and biscuits, but we politely declined. We needed to explain why we had come—they could see we were in serious danger."

"Exactly," Ryan said. "I carefully explained to Ron that we were in grave danger. Our friend Max had brought something back from Egypt that could change the world. Ron and Janet exchanged a look and, sensing the urgency, asked us to sit on their sofa and tell them everything."

"I'm sure the Brunswicks were frightened when you told them about a demon somewhere in Damascus," Detective Marshall commented.

"They didn't seem alarmed," Ryan said. "They listened calmly as we explained. I told them about the chest and showed them the items inside: the two books—*The Book of Secrets* and *The Book of the Dead*—and the spear. Ron immediately grabbed his reading glasses and studied the inscriptions. To our surprise, he could read ancient Egyptian hieroglyphs! That was an incredible stroke of luck. I asked him to explain what it all meant and what the demon wanted."

"After studying the books, he told us that the amulet on Lucy's neck is the key for the demon to keep its power while on this planet. The spear is the ultimate weapon capable of destroying everything—even the planet itself. But now, with Lucy wearing the amulet, the demon can only appear at night, taking souls during the day only as shadows. Once the clock strikes nine, it transforms into a demon, but it is significantly weaker without the amulet and spear."

"That all makes perfect sense now," Ebenezer said. "Christian, Detective Marshall, and I have seen a shadow lurking—not just in Damascus, but even outside the town."

"Correct, Ebenezer," Ryan said. "This demon can move as a shadow during the day, and when the clock strikes nine, it appears—but not fully rejuvenated. It needs the amulet and the spear to reach its full power and destroy mankind."

"Did Ron tell you anything else?" Jessica asked.

Ryan nodded. "He said it's best for him and his wife to look after our daughter while we escape Damascus. At first, I wasn't sure about that. He also mentioned something specific about the amulet."

"What did he say?" Grant pressed.

Ryan continued, "As long as Lucy wears the amulet around her neck, the demon cannot track her. The amulet renders her invisible to it. Our reaction? A huge sigh of relief. We trusted Ron and Janet completely to protect Lucy while we briefly left Damascus."

Helen quickly added, "It was a heartbreaking decision to leave our daughter behind, but we promised to keep an eye on her whenever it's safe."

"She was emotional, as you'd expect from a seven-year-old," Ryan said. "We reassured her: don't worry, we love you, and it's our duty to keep you safe."

"Then Ron said we should give him the spear and keep it in their safe while he read *The Book of the Dead*," Helen continued. "The hieroglyphs explained that the spear must be placed against the demon's heart and the word 'Djed'—which means 'Pillar' in Egyptian—is spoken before striking or throwing it. My husband and I exchanged a glance, wondering if it was wise, but we agreed. I handed the spear to Ron, and he placed it in his safe. Then he gave me the key to the safe, instructing me to keep it secure."

Grant reached into his pocket and held up the key he had found at Liberty Hall School in Lodi, Virginia. "And this is the key for the spear."

Ryan smiled. "Exactly, Grant. That key opens the Brunswick Cottage safe. Keep it safe—we will need it to destroy the demon."

Ebenezer leaned forward. "What did you do after you left Brunswick Cottage?"

"Guys and girls," Ryan began, "my wife and I left the cottage, knowing that the two elderly people looking after our daughter would keep her safe. We headed toward the car and drove back to Damascus. I couldn't stop thinking about leaving Max with the demon. About five minutes out of the cottage, my wife and I saw a beam of yellow light piercing the night sky. I assumed Max was still with the demon and immediately accelerated, feeling extreme concern. I kept asking myself why we had left a possessed-looking Max behind, but my wife comforted me, saying it wasn't my fault. Her words made me feel much better. It was incredibly reassuring."

Helen smiled at Ryan. "It's my pleasure, honey."

Ryan returned her smile. "Thank you, sweetheart. When we returned to Max's bar and parked along the side, we saw the demon walking alongside Max. We were completely speechless. There it was—Sparda himself. From what we could see, it had horns, yellow glowing eyes, gold-plated armour, and lizard-like feet. But something seemed... off."

"What do you mean?" Agent Denzel asked.

"Well," Ryan explained, "the demon looked half powerless, as if it were missing something—like it hadn't fully regenerated, just as Ron had warned in the cottage. It appeared as a figure that was half shadow, half demon. Then, suddenly, it completely turned into a shadow."

Christian and Grant exchanged knowing glances.

"This is exactly what I noticed in Damascus," Christian said. "There was some sort of shadow lurking around the town."

"Same here," Grant added. "I felt it too when I visited Damascus."

Ryan continued, "After seeing the demon transform into a shadow, we realized

Max had now been possessed. My wife and I ducked our heads down inside the car, hoping neither the demon nor Max would see us."

Ebenezer leaned forward. "What happened next?"

"I opened my car window," Ryan said. "Max was clearly talking to the demon—even in its shadow form—but he wasn't acting normally. His eyes were wide, his body stiff. He kept repeating, 'I need the chest, I need the spear, and I need the amulet.'"

"So Max was possessed by the demon," Jessica said, her voice tense. "What did you both do after that?"

Ryan continued, "Max walked into the middle of town, where some residents were milling about—some confused, others approaching him normally. Then, suddenly, his behavior changed—he became aggressive. He spotted a man he knew and punched him squarely in the face. And then... all hell broke loose. He kept striking the defenseless man repeatedly, over a dozen times, until the man lay motionless on the ground. Blood flowed from his head, nose, eyes, and mouth. It was... horrifying.

"Several residents rushed to intervene, grabbing Max by the shoulders and trying to pull him away. But then... the demon claimed the souls of those who held him, and chaos erupted."

"Did the man die?" Detective Marshall asked, his voice tense.

Ryan nodded grimly. "Yes. The blows were lethal. Concussion, brain trauma, a cracked skull—it was inevitable. But strangely, the demon didn't take his soul. It seems this demon only collects the souls of those who are still alive."

Ebenezer shook his head, unsettled. "Goodness... so the demon essentially turned Max into a controlled, aggressive human being."

"Exactly," Ryan confirmed. "Moments later, the Damascus police arrived and found a man lying in a pool of blood."

Agents Julia and Denzel exchanged uneasy glances, silently acknowledging the story's shocking intensity.

"What did you and your wife do after witnessing such brutal violence?" Denzel asked.

Ryan replied, "After seeing all that, my wife and I stayed in the car until Max, and the demon were far from the bar. I told her, 'Let's quickly place the key in the cellar.' We hoped someone would eventually find it. Then my wife reminded me that we needed to carve a message on the other key—the one that opens the chest containing the demon's spear—which Grant currently holds."

Ebenezer rubbed his chin, thinking. "So, it was you who wrote the riddles on the safe so we could find the key?"

Ryan nodded. "Yes. May I continue the story, Ebenezer?"

"Please, go ahead," Ebenezer replied.

Ryan cleared his throat and drew a deep breath. "My wife and I went into Max's bar and opened the door to his office, looking around for anything that could help us save him. Then my wife had an idea. She said we should write a riddle on the safe—something that would guide anyone who came after us, maybe the police or the FBI—so they'd have to solve each clue in order to destroy the demon.

"She looked around and spotted a painting on the wall. She grabbed her black marker pen, turned to me, and asked, *'What should I write on the painting?'*

"I told her it wasn't a good idea. But as she touched the painting, the wall began to move. It trembled... and opened! Behind it was a hidden room—filled with jewelry, bottles of alcohol, and a safe. My wife and I just stared at each other in disbelief. We decided to step inside and see what else was there. Then she told me to go back into the bar to look for something that could serve as the riddle while she stayed behind to think.

"So, I went out front and looked around. That's when I noticed a case of Dalmore whiskey. I opened it and found a bottle inside. There was a small angel sculpture nearby, and I thought—*that* could be perfect for the riddle. I wrote the words: *'The book of love is not always what it seems. Look hard enough and you will find the missing key.'* Then I placed the angel sculpture inside the case, set the whiskey bottle carefully on top of it, and closed it back up.

"Later, I returned to Max's office and told my wife what I'd done. She was impressed."

Detective Marshall frowned. "This seems so odd. Why would anyone write riddles in a time of crisis?"

Helen turned toward him. "Because, a detective, whoever solves this case needs to be someone who can think in riddles—and believe in themselves. It may sound strange, but we had to come up with something. I told my husband to find Max's stash of keys so we could hide *The Book of Secrets* somewhere safe."

Ebenezer shook his head and laughed. "Well, I must say—we solved those riddles pretty well!"

Helen smiled warmly. "You did. I'm grateful it was a group like you—men brave and clever enough to save my daughter... and maybe the whole human race."

Ryan continued his story. "I found the key to the safe, went upstairs, and called out to my wife. I told her to open it so we could place *The Book of Secrets* inside. When we did, we also found a stash of keys. Max must have wanted to keep the entire set locked away."

Detective Marshall interrupted. "So, what you're saying is, there were two sets of safe keys—and you placed one of them in the whiskey case with the angel sculpture?"

"That's correct, Detective," Ryan said. "We placed *The Book of Secrets* inside the safe but took the stash of keys with us. We needed them to hide *The Book of the Dead* along with the chest in another room."

Agent Julia frowned. "So, you were working on riddles while that demon was still on the loose—and your friend was possessed?"

Ryan nodded grimly. "We had no choice. We had to think logically about what could be done in the meantime. After securing *The Book of Secrets* inside the safe, we looked through the stash of keys and thought about how to build more riddles to protect what was left. I came up with another plan and wrote a new riddle on a sheet of paper. We asked ourselves how we could close the secret passageway—and that's when my wife touched the painting again. Instantly, it moved back into place. The wall sealed itself, just like before."

He paused for a breath, his expression darkening. "We stepped out of Max's office and looked toward the far end of the bar. Suddenly, we saw a man coming toward us—his eyes glazed, his movements unnatural. He was possessed. We panicked. I grabbed a beer glass and smashed it against his head. He dropped like a sack of potatoes."

"That explains the skeleton we found on the other side of the room," Detective Marshall murmured.

"But I'm not finished yet, Detective," Ryan continued. "That man wasn't dead. He woke up moments later and started whispering— 'Sparda... Sparda... Sparda.' My wife and I hid in the next room; the one stacked with barrels of beer. I looked through a crack in the door and saw Max... and the demon. It appeared as a dark, shifting shadow. It was draining the flesh from that poor man's body—pulling it off him like smoke."

Grant wiped the sweat from his forehead with his handkerchief, his voice trembling. "My God... the demon sucked the flesh right off him?"

Ryan nodded slowly. "That's right, Grant. And believe me—it wasn't a sight you'd ever want to see."

Ebenezer exhaled sharply, shaking his head. "I'm just amazed at how quickly you both managed to think through all of this, especially with that creature haunting the town."

"I know, right? But it wasn't easy—we had to keep going, no matter how hard it got," said Ryan.

"So, you were both hiding behind the barrels. Did you notice any other strange activity going on?" asked Christian.

Ryan exhaled slowly, his expression darkening. "While my wife and I were hiding, we looked through the window and saw the residents of Damascus running through the streets—terrified, panicking, completely lost. What we witnessed next was something I never thought I'd see in my lifetime. People started turning blue and purple as the demon, still a shifting shadow, drew the souls straight out of them. Others tried to escape town—cars speeding in every direction—but the creature tore through everything. It twisted metal, flipped cars like toys... there was blood everywhere."

Jessica covered her mouth, trembling. "Oh God... I need to sit down. Someone please, water..."

"Here, Jessica, I have a bottle," said Helen, handing it to her.

Christian leaned forward, concerned in his voice. "Are you feeling all right, love?"

Jessica nodded weakly. "I'll be fine, handsome. I just... needed to process all this."

Ryan stepped closer, sympathy softening his tone. "I know how disturbing this sounds but imagine what it was like for my wife and me—seeing it unfolds right before our eyes."

Jessica took a sip of water, managing a faint smile. "Thank you, Helen."

"My pleasure," Helen replied gently.

Ryan hesitated. "Would you like me to continue?"

Jessica steadied herself. "Don't worry about me. Please—go on. We need to hear what happened, especially now that we're all here."

Ryan nodded. "Very well. After watching the chaos—people dying, the demon attacking, and Max completely under its control—we ran down the alley where that poor man had been killed. There, we spotted a steel door. My wife looked through the bunch of keys and found one with a shape that matched the keyhole. Together, we tried it—and the door opened."

Detective Marshall leaned forward. "What was inside?"

"It was a room filled with strange potions—bottles, jars, tools, everything an alchemist might use," Ryan said.

"Interesting," murmured Detective Marshall.

Ryan continued, "Yeah, it was fascinating but also unsettling. Hard to believe Max would be involved in something like that. I told my wife we should leave *The Book of the Dead* there. The room seemed secure, especially with that heavy steel door."

Ebenezer looked genuinely impressed with Ryan. "That's a smart idea, I must say."

"Thanks," Ryan replied, "but we had to keep it somewhere secure—to make sure whoever found it would have the time and patience to read *The Book of the Dead* and understand what to do to defeat the demon."

Helen smiled, running her fingers gently through his hair. "My husband is a smart man. That's why I married him."

Grant leaned forward. "So, what happened after you left the room with the steel door?"

"I made sure the door was sealed tightly so no one could get inside without the key," Ryan said. "But as soon as my wife and I walked away, we heard noises coming from the other direction. I told her I'd heard something, so we kept quiet—and then the sound came again."

Helen nodded. "I heard it too. We ran the other way, but we didn't realize there was nowhere to go. I asked Ryan, *'What do we do now?'* Then he looked down and spotted a trapdoor leading to a basement. We opened it quickly and saw stairs heading down into the dark."

Christian exhaled. "You two were pretty lucky, I must say."

"We were," Ryan admitted.

Detective Marshall asked, "Did you find out who it was making those noises?"

Helen answered, "We did. The trapdoor had a small hole, so Ryan went back up the stairs and peeked through it—and it was Max."

Agent Julia leaned in. "Did he find both of you hiding in the basement?"

"Luckily, he didn't," Helen said. "But then we heard the demon—Sparda—talking to Max. It didn't sound pleased at all. Max was apologizing to it, almost in a trance, his eyes wide and lifeless. Then they both walked away together. My husband and I crept farther down into the basement, which was full of beer barrels, cupboards, and shelves of alcohol. That... that was the last time I ever saw Max."

Ebenezer's expression softened. "Ryan, we found Max later in his office—dead."

Ryan's shoulders sank. "I couldn't save him. I feel terrible for not helping."

Helen placed a comforting hand on his shoulder. "Don't blame yourself. There was nothing you could have done, not with the demon controlling him."

She took a slow breath before continuing. "We followed the far end of the basement and found another flight of stairs leading to a second trapdoor. We climbed up, but it was sealed shut."

Ryan nodded. "Good thing I still had the key ring. I tried every key I could until finally one fit. The trapdoor opened, leading us behind the saloon bar. I told Helen we needed to hide the next key somewhere safe—in the library. Even though she was terrified, she came up with a riddle to hide it."

Helen gave a faint, nostalgic smile. "Believe me, I was scared out of my mind, but I had to think fast. We ran toward the library, passing cars speeding in the opposite direction and people running for their lives. We were the only ones running toward danger—but we knew we had to. We had to protect our daughter from that demon. We hoped that one day, someone would return to this town and solve the mystery, since we wouldn't have the time to destroy the demon ourselves using *The Book of the Dead*."

Ebenezer leaned back, awe in his voice. "I'm truly amazed you managed to think so clearly under those circumstances."

Ryan gave a weary nod. "We had no choice, Ebenezer. We just had to."

Christian smiled, relieved and proud that he, Ebenezer, and Detective Marshall had managed to find all the keys by solving the riddles. "Good job, everyone! We actually solved them all, didn't we, Ryan?"

"Yes, it's great, Christian," Ryan replied, "but the job isn't quite done yet."

Agent Julia leaned forward, breaking into their moment. "Sorry to interrupt, but please—go on, Ryan. What happened when you reached the library?"

Ryan cleared his throat. "It's fine, Agent Julia. My wife and I reached the library, and as you can imagine, it was completely deserted. We decided to check the poetry section and look for *The Book of Love*. After searching the shelves, I found it and showed it to Helen. She took the book from my hands and told me to look for an office—somewhere with a desk—so I could find scissors or maybe a knife."

"That's right," Helen said. "My husband found a knife in the kitchen at the back of the library. I took it and carefully carved one of the pages of *The Book of Love* into the shape of a key."

Ebenezer's eyes widened. "That's right! And that's the key I found later!"

Helen smiled proudly. "You've done well, Ebenezer. I even wrote a note inside the book that said, *'Well done for finding the key. Those who find it will also find The Book of the Dead, uncover The Book of Secrets, and use their power to destroy the demon.'*"

Detective Marshall nodded in admiration. "You two did remarkably well, considering how chaotic things were in town."

Ryan sighed. "We were only thinking about our daughter, Lucy. That was all that mattered. We just wanted to keep her safe."

Helen kissed Ryan gently on the cheek. "That's my husband—the proud father. Anyway, to cut a long story short, we placed *The Book of Love* underneath the library desk and sealed it with duct tape so it would stay secure, even for seven years if needed."

"Wonderful work," said Ebenezer with a smile.

Ryan continued, "After leaving the library, we saw people collapsing on the streets. Police sirens echoed in the distance, and from afar, we could see the shadow of Sparda moving across the town—still taking the souls of everyone it touched."

Jessica shuddered. "You must have been terrified, seeing all that."

"Believe me, Jessica," Helen said, "I think Ryan was more traumatized than I was. I had to tell him to pull himself together. We knew we had to leave town immediately and get rid of the key that belonged to Brunswick's safe. We needed to take it as far away as possible."

She took a deep breath before finishing. "We placed the key inside Liberty School Hall after circling back through the saloon bar, careful not to be seen by the demon. Then we got in the car and drove as fast as we could."

Grant frowned. "I still don't understand why you simply left the key somewhere safe—and why it ended up in Liberty School Hall."

Ryan nodded slowly. "I understand your confusion, Grant. But it was either that, or some lunatic could've taken the key and threatened the Brunswick family—and our daughter."

Detective Marshall crossed his arms. "And what if we were the lunatics, Ryan?"

Ryan gave a faint, weary smile. "Anyone willing to risk their lives the way you have wouldn't do something like that. And besides, we were always keeping watch—just in case someone tried to retrieve the key."

Grant's eyebrows rose. "So, you're saying you've been following us this whole time?"

"Not exactly," Ryan replied calmly. "But yes, we stayed in Lodi for a while. It's not far from Damascus. And... I saw what happened there—the horrific deaths. Four FBI agents lost their lives, and I'm truly sorry about that. We also saw the ravens attack your car."

Agent Julia slammed her hand on the table, her voice sharp with anger. "So, you just waited in Lodi for someone to show up and find the key? You were hoping it would be discovered by anyone who came along? That sounds insane to me! Don't you think so, Denzel?"

Agent Denzel raised a hand, his tone even and calm. "Easy, Julia. We may have lost four agents on the road to Damascus, but the point is—Grant found the key. And it led us here, to this town. Maybe it wasn't a coincidence at all. Maybe it was fate. Grant found that key in Liberty School Hall—hidden just enough to be discovered when the time was right. I'd say it was meant to happen."

Detective Marshall leaned forward. "So, you're saying you and your wife have been staying in Lodi for seven years? Is that right?"

Ryan sighed. "We've stayed in several places over the years—but yes, we spent a few of those years in Lodi."

Jessica took a deep breath, her voice trembling slightly but steadying as she spoke. "Everyone, calm down. We've done what we could, and we can still solve this mystery. I may be scared out of my mind, but we've come too far to stop now. I say we search for *The Book of Secrets* and *The Book of the Dead*—and retrieve the chest too."

"I have a plan, guys!" Ebenezer said suddenly, eyes lighting up.

Agent Julia gave a short, skeptical laugh. "Oh really? And what kind of plan could *you* possibly come up with?"

Ebenezer smirked. "Well, I've done more research and solved more of this case than you ever have."

"Alright, that's enough," Christian interrupted, raising both hands. "Now, now, now—let's all calm down. We need to work as a team here. No arguments. We're in this together. Ebenezer, the floor's yours."

Ebenezer cleared his throat, lifting his head with quiet confidence. "Thank you, Christian. The idea is quite straightforward. As Jessica said earlier, we need to retrieve the chest as well as the books. My plan is simple—we'll split up."

He pointed around the group as he continued. "Grant, Agent Julia, and Agent Denzel—you three head to the Brunswicks' cottage. Let them know you have the key to their safe and retrieve the Spear. Is that clear?"

Agent Julia exchanged a glance with Denzel, almost agreeing before Grant gave her a small nod of encouragement.

"Alright, Ebenezer," she said at last. "We'll go to the Brunswicks' and pay them a visit."

"Excellent," Ebenezer replied with a brief smile. "And thank you for agreeing."

He turned to the others. "Christian, Detective Marshall, and I will retrieve the items in the saloon bar. We'll meet you three later at the Brunswicks' cottage."

"Good idea," Detective Marshall said.

Ryan and Helen exchanged uncertain looks.

"What about us, Ebenezer?" Helen asked.

"You two will work together," Ebenezer instructed. "Set up a booby trap—something that can distract or slow the demon when it appears tonight. Use whatever you can find. And Jessica," he added, turning toward her, "I need you to stay with the Maccabees."

Jessica nodded, then leaned forward to kiss Christian softly on the lips. "Jonathan and Marilyn should still be somewhere in town—you have to find them too."

Agent Julia spoke up. "Agent Denzel and I passed your friends earlier, walking along the main street. I'm sure they'll be fine."

Jessica exhaled in relief. "Thank goodness. I hope you run into them again."

Ryan nodded firmly. "I think I know what to do, Helen. Let's go back to the hotel and grab some gas cylinders, a flamethrower, and a few weapons."

"Great initiative, Maccabees," Ebenezer said. "We'll make sure your daughter stays safe."

Helen's eyes softened. "Please make sure Lucy is protected. And tell her we love her very much—and that we'll see her soon."

"Good luck, everyone," Ryan said.

They split up, each group heading off to carry out their task.

It was six minutes past four in Damascus. The afternoon sun blazed over the ghost town, heat shimmering off the broken pavement—thirty-four degrees and cloudless.

Jonathan and Marilyn walked slowly along the dusty road, exhausted and parched.

"We've been walking for over an hour," Jonathan muttered. "I think it's time we drive to Brunswick Cottage."

Marilyn glanced over both shoulders and spotted a weathered signpost by the roadside. The white letters were barely legible, but the message was clear:

"No cars or heavy vehicles allowed beyond this point. Please use a mountain bike. Thank you. – Virginia Creeper Trail."

"Look, Jonathan," she said, pointing. "There's the sign to Creeper Trail."

Jonathan squinted at it and groaned. "So now we can't drive the rest of the way?"

Marilyn sighed, frustration clear on her face. "Oh, great. So, we have to find two mountain bikes just to get to Brunswick Cottage."

"Looks like it," Jonathan replied. "We'd better look around—maybe someone left some bikes behind."

They turned back the way they came, unaware they were walking in the wrong direction.

"I'd say we check the houses," Marilyn suggested. "Someone around here must have left something behind."

As they wandered down the quiet street, the faint sound of an engine broke the stillness. A car was heading straight toward them. Behind the wheel, Agent Julia squinted through the windshield.

"Agent Denzel—look! It's them!" she called out.

"Oh, those two," Denzel muttered. "They still haven't made it to Brunswick Cottage. Unbelievable."

Grant, seated in the back, lifted his head and frowned. "I thought they'd already arrived."

Julia hit the brakes and pulled over beside them. "Hey, you two! You look a little lost, aren't you?"

Marilyn's relief was instant. "Oh, thank goodness—you found us!"

Grant and Agent Denzel stepped out of the car, exchanging puzzled looks.

"Why aren't you at the cottage yet?" Julia asked.

Jonathan crossed his arms, his tone sharp and defensive. "Because we're lost. Does that answer your question?"

Julia's patience snapped. "Listen here, hillbilly! I ought to handcuff you and toss you in the back seat—but unfortunately, we need your help with this case."

Marilyn quickly stepped between them. "Stop it, you two! Look, we really are lost. We saw a sign saying, "only bikes can go up Creeper Trail."

Denzel chuckled, shaking his head. "You're heading the wrong way. That route will take you straight to Abingdon—about fifty-five kilometers from here."

Grant nodded in agreement. "Yeah, I know the trail well. Abingdon's where I live, and Creeper Trail actually leads up toward Whitetop Station. Trust me—you don't want to go that way."

Marilyn exchanged a sheepish look with Jonathan. "So... we've been walking the wrong way all this time?"

Grant gave a sympathetic smile. "Afraid so. But don't worry—we'll get you turned around."

"Thank goodness you told us! If it weren't for you, Agent Julia, we'd have driven all the way there and ended up completely lost," said Marilyn.

Jonathan looked embarrassed. "I'm really sorry for my behavior earlier, Agent Julia."

Julia smiled, the tension easing from her face. "Apology accepted. Now, you two better hop in. We'll head to Brunswick Cottage together—but fair warning, it might get a little cramped in the back seat with three of you." She laughed softly.

Marilyn's eyes brightened. "Oh—Agent Julia, is Jessica safe?"

"Yep," Julia replied calmly. "She's fine. We left her with the Maccabees—a kind couple we met, along with the others."

Marilyn froze, then touched Jonathan's shoulder. "Wait... did you say the Maccabees?"

Julia nodded. "That's right. Why?"

"You actually met them? Spoke with them?"

Another nod from Julia. "Erm, yes."

Marilyn broke into a relieved smile. "That's wonderful! When we meet the Brunswicks, we can tell them their parents are here. Their daughter will be so happy to know that."

"Yes," Julia agreed, her tone softening. "But remember, we'll need to remove our FBI jackets and go in unarmed—just as Grant mentioned earlier. We don't want to startle anyone."

Grant gestured toward the road ahead. "All right then. Let's get moving. Take the next turn as if you're heading toward Laurel Creek—you'll reach Adkins Street from there."

Agent Julia started the engine, and the group climbed back into the car. As they pulled away, the last traces of tension faded. The path to Brunswick Cottage awaited them—finally, things were starting to make sense.

26

Their First Discovery

Meanwhile, back in the saloon bar, Ebenezer entered Max's room with Christian and Detective Marshall, ready to unlock the safe. They all knew **The Book of Secrets** was hidden inside.

"Okay, gentlemen," Ebenezer said, steadying his breath. "I'm going to touch the painting in this portrait—once I do, the secret passage will open, and we'll retrieve *The Book of Secrets* behind it."

Christian and Detective Marshall exchanged uneasy glances as Ebenezer placed the key—won by solving a riddle—into the lock. The safe clicked open.

Ebenezer lifted the book out carefully, his eyes wide. "Wow. Would you look at that?"

Christian stepped closer, inspecting the heavy volume. "Look at the color—it's coated in gold, and there's a symbol on the front... It looks like a demon."

Detective Marshall traced a finger across the cover. "That could be **Demon Sparda**, gentlemen."

Ebenezer nodded grimly. "Then we waste no time."

They turned from the open passageway. "Christian, close it up behind us," Ebenezer said. "Touch the portrait again so the wall seals."

"Sure thing." Christian pressed his hand to the painting; the hidden door rumbled, and the stone walls slid shut with a deep echo.

"Good. Now let's open the steel door and retrieve *The Book of the Dead*—and the chest," Ebenezer said.

The three men left Max's room, the lifeless figure of Max still seated in his chair. Ebenezer paused, looking back.

"We'll destroy Demon Sparda for you, Max," he said softly. "And we'll save Damascus—and the world. Rest in peace."

Christian and Detective Marshall exchanged a look of shared determination.

"We'll finish this together and restore the town," said Detective Marshall, nodding firmly.

"Correct, Detective," Christian replied, his voice rising with conviction. "We'll end the demon's reign together—and together we'll be victorious!"

"Let's move," Ebenezer said. They stepped into the dim corridor leading toward the steel door.

"I'm opening it now!" Ebenezer called over his shoulder.

Christian and Detective Marshall stood ready, their faces taut with anxiety and anticipation, as the heavy hinges groaned and the darkness beyond the door stirred.

Ebenezer struggled to pull open the steel door—it was far heavier than expected. "Can you both give me a hand here?" he grunted.

Christian and Detective Marshall rushed over, gripping the handle beside him. "Almost there, guys! One more pull—yes, finally!" Christian gasped as the door creaked open with a metallic groan.

A wave of stale air drifted out. In the left-hand corner of the dim room lay three dead rats. A single table sat in the center, cloaked in darkness. There was no electricity.

"Let's stick close—it's pitch-black in here," Detective Marshall murmured.

He squinted into the gloom, rubbing his eyes to adjust. "I can just make out a table ahead of us."

Ebenezer and Christian kept hold of each other's arms while the detective reached forward, his fingers brushing across the table's surface. Dust and cobwebs clung to his hands.

"All right," he said, coughing lightly. "I'm going to feel around. If The Book of the Dead is here, I should be able to tell by its size."

Moments later, his hand landed on something solid and thick. "Gentlemen—I've got something. Let's move toward the doorway where it's a bit lighter."

"Is it heavy?" Ebenezer asked.

"It is—and filthy," Detective Marshall replied, suppressing another cough.

Just then, a faint sound echoed from beyond the steel door.

Christian stiffened. "I just felt a draught..."

Detective Marshall handed the book to him carefully. "Hold on to this, Christian. I'll check outside."

A gust swept through again, colder this time. The detective tensed. "There's something out there," he said quietly.

Christian's eyes darted toward the corridor. "It's the same feeling we had back in the church... and when we met Jessica in town," he whispered.

Detective Marshall drew his revolver—though he knew no mortal weapon could harm what they were dealing with. "Follow me," he ordered. "We'll head to the cellar. That's the only door we haven't opened yet."

Christian followed close behind, clutching The Book of the Dead. Ebenezer stayed right at his shoulder, his breath shallow as the darkness seemed to close in around them.

"Let's move fast," Ebenezer urged. "The quicker we get to the cellar, the better."

They made their way through the corridor, the floorboards groaning beneath their boots. At last, they reached the cellar door. Ebenezer fumbled in his pocket and held up a key.

"I've got it," he said, forcing a nervous smile. "Let's see what secrets this door's been keeping."

Detective Marshall and Christian scanned the bar carefully, making sure no one was around. Once the coast was clear, the three men slipped through the cellar door, Christian closing it quietly behind them to keep intruders out.

"This book is so heavy," Christian muttered, clutching it to his chest. "I wonder what's written inside."

"We'll find out soon enough," said Detective Marshall, stepping carefully down the narrow stairs. "Once we meet the Maccabees at their hotel, we'll study it properly."

Ebenezer reached the bottom first and approached another door. He pulled out the final key and fit it into the lock. The door creaked open, revealing a room shrouded in darkness.

Inside, a faint outline of a table stood in the center, surrounded by twelve bottles of strange liquid, a few unlit candles, and a small box of matchsticks.

"It's pitch dark in here, but I think I see candles," Ebenezer said, pointing toward the table.

Detective Marshall stepped forward and brushed his hand across the dusty surface until he felt a small cardboard box. He picked it up and smiled. "Gentlemen, we've got matchsticks."

Christian exhaled in relief. "Finally! Now we can actually see where we are."

Ebenezer examined the bottles. "None of these seem related to destroying the demon," he said quietly. "Looks like they were just part of Max's old experiments."

Detective Marshall struck a match. The flame flickered to life, casting long shadows across the room. "There," he said. "Let's light the rest of these candles and get a better look."

Within moments, the room glowed with a soft orange light. Ebenezer leaned closer to read the handwritten labels. "This green one is called *Health Potion*, and the red one says *Healing Potion*."

Detective Marshall inspected two more bottles. "Here's a purple one—*Potion for the Soul*—and this pink one says *Rage Potion*." He frowned. "Strange names for harmless-looking liquids."

Christian glanced at the remaining bottles. "Guys, look at these eight—they're sealed with metal caps marked *Secret Potion*. They have to mean something. We should take them. They might be useful later."

Ebenezer nodded in agreement. "Good idea. Let's divide them up. Six each."

Detective Marshall handed a candle to Christian. "Take this so we can see our way back upstairs."

"Got it," Christian replied.

The three men carefully ascended the narrow steps. Ebenezer pushed the cellar door open just enough to peek through before stepping out, balancing six glass bottles in his arms as the flickering candlelight followed behind them.

Ebenezer glanced around the cellar one last time before pulling open the creaking door. "It's time to meet the Maccabees and tell them we found both books," he called over his shoulder.

The men hurried toward the front of the saloon. Outside, the weather had turned wild—the wind howled through the dusty streets, lifting grit into the air. Detective Marshall lowered his head against the force of it. "Stick together, everyone!" he shouted.

Ebenezer and Christian exchanged a quick look, both squinting as the dust stung their eyes. "There's dirt blowing right into my face!" Ebenezer yelled. "Same here!" Christian replied, shielding his eyes with his arm.

Moments later, the wind died as suddenly as it had risen. The sky darkened, gray clouds swallowing what remained of the blue. Then a long shadow began to stretch toward them across the ground.

Christian's breath caught. "Guys—the shadow's back! And... it's Sparda!"

All three turned to watch the shape twist and rise, coiling into a demon-like figure surrounded by thick black smoke. Its yellow eyes burned through the gloom, its expression pure fury.

"What do we do?" Christian asked, his voice trembling.

"Stand your ground," Detective Marshall said firmly. "Let's see how it reacts when we show no fear."

The demon's laughter rolled through the air like thunder. "Ha ha ha ha ha! I am Sparda—the sorcerer of the universe."

Ebenezer blinked, startled. "He speaks English?"

"You fool," Sparda hissed. "You have no chance of survival. I see you hold the *Book of Secrets* and the *Book of the Dead*. But you mortals will never grasp their power. Hand them over, and I shall return to the Land of the Pyramids to rule this world. First, I need the amulet and the spear—then I will be whole again."

Christian turned toward Ebenezer. "He's been searching for them for seven years!"

Sparda's eyes glowed brighter as he listened. "I will find what I seek. Once I do, the human race will end."

Detective Marshall drew his revolver and leveled it at the creature. "You'll go back to where you belong!"

The demon laughed again, the sound echoing across the silent street. "Ha ha ha ha! Nothing will stand in my way. When I reclaim the amulet and the spear, I will destroy you all. At the stroke of nine this evening, my power will return—and I will take the books from your hands. Until then... I'll be watching you."

With a final roar of laughter, Sparda dissolved into shadow and vanished into the sky.

For a long moment, none of them spoke. Then Ebenezer looked upward, his voice barely above a whisper. "Guys... I'm speechless."

Christian nodded, his breath still unsteady. "This is the first time we've faced Sparda—and we're lucky to be alive."

Detective Marshall lowered his gun and glanced between the two men. "That demon didn't even attack us. Why do you think that is?"

Ebenezer adjusted his coat and exhaled. "There's only one way to find out. Let's meet up with Ryan and the others—and quickly."

The wind died completely, the gray clouds parting as the light began to break through once more. The eerie silence that followed only deepened the unease in the air.

"Let's move, gentlemen," said Detective Marshall, his tone brisk but wary. "You heard what that thing said—it'll regain its strength soon. Once it's reenergized, it'll have the power to destroy us. We need to use the time we have—wisely."

Meanwhile, after a long drive, Jacob arrived in Damascus.

He stepped out of the vehicle and surveyed the desolate streets, his pulse quickening as his eyes fell on the devastation around him—bodies strewn across the road, twisted metal glinting in the dim light, dark streaks of dried blood marking the ground.

Two vans and a pair of cars stood parked nearby—miraculously intact amid the ruin.

"They must be here," Jacob muttered, scanning the shadows. "I'd better find cover before anyone sees me."

He slipped into the nearest abandoned house, moving carefully over broken floorboards and scattered debris. The place smelled of dust and decay.

"Look at this place," he whispered. "It's disgusting."

He crossed to the window, brushing away the grime on the glass to get a clearer view of the deserted town.

"I'm sure Christian and Ebenezer will come through here eventually," he murmured. "I'll make myself known when the time is right."

Pulling a rickety chair toward the window, Jacob sat down and fixed his eyes on the empty streets outside watching... waiting.

27

Lucy

Back at Creeper Trail, fourteen minutes past four in the afternoon, Agent Julia, Agent Denzel, Grant, Jonathan, and Marilyn arrived at the Brunswick Cottage near Laurel Creek.

Agent Julia slowed the car, taking in the sight of the cottage. She looked amazed at its charm—the roof layered with hay, the exterior crafted from oak, and a sturdy wooden front door.

"Look at this—there's a wooden sign. It says, 'The Brunswick's,'" she said.

Grant stepped out of the car, his eyes scanning the property. "Now that we've found the cottage, I suggest only the three of us approach. Marilyn and Jonathan should stay in the car until we signal them. We don't want to startle the old couple with all five of us at once."

Agent Julia nodded and removed her FBI jacket, as Denzel did the same.

"Okay, Denzel. Make sure your gun is out of sight," she instructed.

Denzel unloaded the bullets from his gun and tucked them into his pocket. Jonathan, frowning, whispered to Marilyn, "Why are they so important? What gives them the right to tell us what to do?"

Marilyn shrugged. "Let's just cooperate and wait for their signal."

Jonathan rolled his eyes but silently agreed.

Grant stepped closer to the front door and knocked three times.

Inside the cottage, Ron glanced at Janet, startled.

"Janet, did you hear that?"

"Yes. It sounds like someone knocking."

"Hand me the rifle, please." Janet went to the wall and retrieved the rifle from its mount near the head of a stuffed bear.

Lucy emerged from her room, where she had been staying for the past seven years, watching quietly.

Ron slowly opened the front door; rifle raised toward the approaching agents and Grant.

"Who are you three, and what are you doing on my property?" he demanded.

The three raised their hands.

"Easy with the rifle, old man. My name is Agent Julia. This is Agent Denzel, and we are with the FBI. This is Grant, and we know who you are."

Ron's eyes widened. "What do you mean? How do you know me?"

"Does the name Ryan and Helen Maccabee ring a bell?" Agent Julia asked.

Ron slowly lowered his rifle, his expression a mix of surprise and suspicion. "How do you know them?"

"Well, Ron, we—I and the two men—came all the way from Blacksburg to Damascus to find out what has been happening in this ghost town."

Ron glanced behind Agent Julia to see if anyone else was around. He noticed two people sitting in the car. "And who are they?"

Agent Denzel looked at Agent Julia, then back at Jonathan and Marilyn. "These two came along with us. Originally, they were supposed to be standing here looking for your cottage, but they couldn't locate where you live," he explained.

"Okay. I suppose you three should come in as well, along with the two in the car," Ron said, nodding toward the entrance.

Grant signaled to Jonathan and Marilyn to get out of the car and join them.

Jonathan turned to Grant, then looked at Marilyn. "Grant wants us to come in. Let's go." They climbed out of the car and walked toward the cottage.

Janet Brunswick greeted them warmly as they entered, a calm smile on her face. "Greetings, everyone, and welcome to our home. Please, take a seat and make yourselves comfortable."

Agent Julia smiled and settled onto the sofa. "Thank you."

Agent Denzel sat beside her, while Grant, Jonathan, and Marilyn took the opposite sofa.

"Would you like some tea and biscuits?" Janet asked.

Agent Julia looked slightly puzzled. "No, thank you. But may I ask a quick question?"

"Of course," Ron replied.

"How did you manage to survive for seven years? And where did you get all the food?" Agent Julia asked.

Ron stepped forward, closing the front door behind him. "That is a very good question. I will explain everything later, I promise."

"Sure thing," Agent Julia nodded.

Ron turned to Jonathan and Marilyn. "What are your names, and what brings you here?"

"My name is Jonathan McFarland," Jonathan replied.

"I'm Marilyn Keywood," said Marilyn.

"Very pleased to meet you," Ron said, nodding to both of them.

Jonathan smiled in acknowledgment. "I'm pleased to meet you and your wife," he added.

Janet interjected gently, "So, I take it you are all here because of Lucy, the daughter of Ryan and Helen Maccabee?"

Agent Julia nodded. "Yes, that's right. But we also came here for another reason..."

"We have been told by the Maccabees that you have the spear hidden somewhere safe, as well as an amulet placed around Lucy's neck," Agent Julia asked.

"That's correct," Janet replied.

Lucy quietly listened from behind her bedroom door, absorbing every word.

Marilyn rose from the sofa, retrieving a note from her pocket. She walked over to Janet and said, "Here, Janet, I thought you should read this note Jonathan, and I found it in one of the rooms at Maccabees Hotel."

Janet opened her reading glasses case on the table and placed them on her nose. Taking the note from Marilyn, she read aloud:

"'Whoever finds this letter needs to go to Creeper Trail, where you will find a cottage called Brunswick Cottage. You will find a young girl living with an elderly couple. Kind regards, Anonymous.'"

Suddenly, Lucy emerged from her room. "That's right, and that note was written by my dad!"

Agent Julia, Agent Denzel, Grant, Marilyn, and Jonathan stared at her in complete shock.

"Lucy!" Grant exclaimed.

"Yes. I'm the daughter of the Maccabees, and I am much wiser now than I was seven years ago," she said, smiling.

"Well, I'm sure you have a lot to say to our guests!" Ron said.

"Absolutely. I have a lot to explain," Lucy replied.

Grant glanced at the amulet around Lucy's neck—it belonged to Sparda.

"I'm very happy to see people like yourselves who want to help me, but I must also warn you," Lucy said cautiously.

"We understand, Lucy. We have capable people ready to help you—especially your parents. They've been waiting over seven years to find trustworthy people who can resolve this once and for all," Agent Julia reassured her.

"No, you don't understand! This demon has been searching for me for seven years. Luckily, it never found me because I'm wearing the amulet. It cannot see me—I remain invisible to the demon," Lucy explained.

"How did you manage to live daily life knowing this demon has been around for seven years?" Marilyn asked.

Lucy responded, "Well, since the demon cannot see me, Ron devised a plan. He asked me to come to his basement, and I was gobsmacked by what I discovered at the end of it."

Ron interrupted, "Yes. In order to survive with food and water, I had to act quickly. While Ryan and Helen asked me to look after their daughter, and knowing something strange had happened around Damascus, I had to devise a plan. I phoned Jack, my friend who owns a shop nearby, and told him to start securing his shop to protect himself. I will explain everything in detail, but first, everyone follows me to the basement. I'll show you what Lucy is talking about."

Agent Julia and Denzel exchanged glances, curiosity and apprehension evident on their faces.

"I'll stay here in the kitchen while you all go to the basement," Janet said.

Ron led the group to the back of the cottage and opened the basement door, which led into the garden. In the centre, a small patch of grass, plants, an apple tree, and flowers grew. Ron lifted a turf of grass to reveal a hidden trapdoor.

Grant's eyes widened. "Wow, this is unusual! Where does it lead?"

Ron smiled. "Good question. I'll show you."

Using a key, Ron unlocked the trapdoor. Agent Julia leaned toward Agent Denzel and whispered, "This is going to be interesting."

"There's only one way to find out—once we see it with our own eyes," Denzel replied.

"Watch your step; this trapdoor can be slippery," Ron cautioned.

As they descended, the space beneath the trapdoor revealed a tunnel-like cave. Mud, roots, and small worms littered the floor. Lucy pulled a tiny torch from her pocket, illuminating the secret passageway.

"Everyone, we are under the ground now. This tunnel is at least eight hundred meters long," Ron explained.

"This is where Ron and I go every few days. We'll show you where it leads," Lucy added.

Grant asked, "Did you dig all this yourself?"

Ron nodded. "Yes. I've been working on it for seven years to ensure the demon could never see me or my wife."

Agent Julia and Denzel turned on their torches to examine their surroundings. "This is remarkable," Julia said, clearly impressed.

Lucy continued, "This tunnel was the only way Ron and Janet could move unseen to fetch food."

Grant rubbed his head and smiled. "So, all that time you lived with the Brunswicks, they went back and forth through this tunnel to feed you and themselves?"

Lucy nodded. "That's right! At the end of this secret passageway, we will reach a small shop where Ron's friend Jack will meet us and pass the food underneath his store."

Jonathan and Marilyn exchanged amazed looks. "This is a very well-organized plan," Jonathan said.

"Absolutely!" Lucy agreed. "And thankfully, the demon hasn't noticed anything so far."

"So, this friend of yours... how does he feel knowing there's a demon lurking around town?" Jonathan asked.

Lucy responded calmly, "As far as I know, the demon has never come near the Brunswick cottage."

"You are very lucky, then," Agent Julia commented.

Lucy continued, "So far, we have continued to use this passageway to collect food and other necessities without incident."

Ron added, "Okay, everyone, we're about halfway there. When we reach the end, I'll knock on Jack's trapdoor so we can meet him."

"We'll grab something to eat while we're there," Lucy said.

"That's not a bad idea. I'm feeling hungry—I haven't eaten properly since arriving in Damascus," Marilyn admitted.

28

A HELPING HAND

As Ron, Lucy, and the others walked through the passageway, a small light glimmered ahead.

"Can you all see that light?" Lucy asked.

Agent Julia looked straight ahead and nodded. "I see it."

"That's where our friend Jack is!" Lucy said.

"Good! I feel like I've adapted to a subterranean lifestyle, just like a mole," Marilyn laughed. Jonathan chuckled at her comment.

"Funny," he said.

"We're almost there," Ron noted. Lucy moved closer to the end of the passageway.

"Finally. We've reached the end. It's a long walk, but it's safer this way to get to Jack's," Lucy explained.

Ron knocked three times on the trapdoor. "Jack, it's Ron. Are you there?"

Jack heard the noise and called back, "Hey, Ron! I'm coming!"

Grant turned to Agent Julia and Agent Denzel, awed by what they had just witnessed.

"This is incredible, Ron! I'm very impressed with your clever work," Grant said.

"Oh, it's nothing. I had to think fast to protect Lucy, my wife, and myself," Ron replied modestly.

Agent Julia nodded approvingly. "This is very well orchestrated and executed! Excellent planning."

"Thank you, Agent," Ron said. Jack opened the trapdoor, not realizing that Ron was bringing not just Lucy, but five others with him.

"Thank you, Jack," Ron said. Lucy climbed out of the trapdoor and into Jack's shop, followed by Agent Julia, Marilyn, Agent Denzel, and Jonathan.

"Wow! You have a very secure shop!" Agent Denzel observed. The shop was fortified with metal bars, leaving no way for anyone to trespass from outside.

Jack Talbot, a sixty-four-year-old man with long grey hair, piercing blue eyes, and a long grey beard, stood at 168 cm tall with a medium build. He had lived in Creeper Trail all his life. "So... who are all these people, if you don't mind me asking?" he said, glancing at Ron.

Ron looked at the group. "Introduce yourselves, ladies and gentlemen."

Agent Julia stepped forward first. "My name is Agent Julia Hague. I'm with the FBI."

Agent Denzel followed. "I'm Agent Denzel Price. I also work for the FBI."

"Nice to meet you both. I feel much safer now knowing we have two FBI agents here," Jack said, visibly relieved.

Agent Julia smiled. "Of course. At a critical time like this, it's our duty to keep everyone safe."

Jack then turned to Marilyn. "And who is this young lady?"

"This is Marilyn Keywood. I'm from outside this town—Radford, to be precise," Marilyn replied.

Jack smiled. "I know the place, though I haven't been there in years."

Marilyn grinned. "It's an honor to meet you. I really admire what you've done here; it looks incredibly secure."

"Thank you, Marilyn. It's been this way ever since the demon appeared in Damascus," Jack said.

"I can imagine," Marilyn replied. Jack then looked at Jonathan.

"And who might you be?"

Jonathan cleared his throat. "My name is Jonathan McFarland. I'm also from Radford."

"So both of you are from out of town?" Jack asked.

"Yes," they responded in unison. Jack turned to Grant.

"And last but not least... I'm guessing you're around my age," Jack said with a laugh.

Grant chuckled. "Actually, I'm seventy-two."

Jack cleared his throat and shifted the conversation. "Now that I know your names, let me properly introduce myself. I'm Jack Talbot, sixty-four years old, and I've lived in Creeper Trail my entire life. This is my small grocery shop, and for over seven years, I've been helping the Brunswicks free of charge."

Agent Julia asked, "How do you sustain your business?"

"Good question, Agent Julia. I only have a handful of customers from the nearby cottages," Jack replied.

"And how do they cope knowing the demon is only a few kilometers away?" Agent Julia asked.

Lucy interrupted. "This amulet around my neck protects the entire area for up to three kilometers."

"How do you know that?" Grant asked.

Lucy explained, "I can sense a force field of energy from this amulet. It absorbs fear from anyone nearby. I believe the demon draws its strength from fear, so I've asked the nearby residents to continue living their lives normally. The amulet protects anyone within its circumference."

Grant's eyes widened. "Are you saying... that this amulet not only makes you invisible but also protects others around you?"

"That's right, Grant. That's why the demon values the amulet—it channels enough energy to empower itself while shielding those nearby," Lucy replied.

Agent Julia and Denzel exchanged glances, then turned their attention back to Lucy. "So as long as we stay close to you, the demon cannot attack us unless we move more than three kilometers away?" Julia asked.

"Exactly," Lucy said. "It all makes sense. The demon needs the amulet to access its full power, especially in dangerous circumstances."

Ron spoke next. "Lucy, kindly remove the amulet and show it to everyone."

Lucy carefully removed the amulet and handed it to Ron. "Thank you, Lucy. On the other side of the amulet is a symbol representing the demon. Surrounding it is a circle-shaped force field. Another symbol indicates that it protects others nearby. In short, as long as Lucy wears the amulet, those around her are safe."

Ron passed the amulet around, allowing everyone to examine it. Grant studied it closely, followed by the others. Agent Julia and Denzel were visibly stunned by the revelation.

"So that's why the residents of Creeper Trail can live normal lives," Jack said. "And why can I continue running my shop safely, as long as Lucy isn't more than three kilometers away."

Lucy smiled. "I'll share more information soon, but first, let's have something to eat."

"That also explains why Ron has been tirelessly digging the tunnel," Julia added. "He knew it was safe as long as Lucy wore the amulet."

Everyone agreed, moving around the shop.

Jack invited them, "Please, help yourselves—fresh fruits, vegetables, and chilled foods are all available."

Grant frowned, trying to understand how the food was delivered safely to Jack's shop. "Can I ask you a quick question?" he said.

"Sure," Jack replied.

"You said Lucy's amulet protects a three-kilometre radius, but who actually delivers the stock to your shop?" Grant asked.

Lucy answered before Jack could respond. "Let me explain, Grant. Janet, Ron, Jack, and I travel to a medium-sized wholesale store near Terry's Drive, about 2.2 kilometres away, to pick up our weekly stock. We've done this for the past seven years. And as I mentioned earlier, the amulet protects everyone within a three-kilometre radius, so the residents remain safe as long as I wear it."

Marilyn smiled and hugged Lucy. "You're all incredible! You work together to keep the Creeper Trail community safe."

"Thank you, Marilyn. We do our best to stay one step ahead of the demon," Lucy said.

Grant approached the chiller and grabbed a cheese sandwich. "I'll take a sandwich, if you don't mind, Jack."

"Of course! Help yourself to a drink as well," Jack said.

Grant smiled and took a bottle of water. Meanwhile, Jonathan's eyes kept darting toward Lucy's amulet, arousing Marilyn's curiosity.

"Everything okay, Jonathan?" she asked.

Jonathan hesitated. "Yeah... yeah, I'm fine. Thanks."

Marilyn frowned at his response and continued browsing for food. Agent Denzel noticed Jonathan's odd behavior. Leaning toward Julia, he whispered, "Julia, something's not right about Jonathan. My instincts are warning me he's up to no good."

Julia shook her head slightly. "Don't overthink it, Denzel. Let's focus on the matter at hand."

Denzel nodded but remained uneasy.

Ron clapped his hands. "Okay, everyone, let's leave Jack in peace. Grab your food, and let's head back to my cottage."

Jack smiled warmly. "It's been a pleasure meeting all of you. Please stay safe. God bless."

Everyone took their food and waved goodbye. "Goodbye, Jack, and thank you again," Ron called.

"Anytime, my friend," Ron said as he opened the trapdoor. "Ladies first."

"Well, thank you very much! You're such a gentleman," Marilyn replied. She, Lucy, and Agent Julia descended the tunnel slowly, followed by the men. Julia switched on her torch so everyone could see the path ahead.

Grant leaned toward Ron, holding a key. "Ron, I found the key to your safe—the one where the spear has been for the past seven years."

Ron's face lit up, a mix of delight and confusion. "You found it! That's wonderful! But why would Ryan leave it in Liberty School Hall? That's the mystery I want to solve."

Grant shrugged. "I don't know. While the two FBI agents and I were in Lodi, I went into the abandoned school hall and spotted it on the ground. A long key, just waiting for me."

"Well, I'm glad it's in the right hands," Ron said. "So, what do we do when we get back to my cottage?"

"I'll open the safe and show everyone the spear," he continued.

"Wonderful," said Grant. Meanwhile, Jonathan listened to the conversation, a grin spreading across his face, hinting at a devious plan.

Agent Denzel noticed Jonathan's expression. "Jonathan? Are you okay?"

"I'm fine. Why do you ask?" Jonathan replied smoothly.

"Just checking," Denzel said.

Marilyn glanced at Jonathan. "Come here, Jonathan. Hold my hand."

Jonathan complied, taking her hands gently. Denzel's expression hardened, and he whispered to Julia, "Trust me, Julia. I can spot a bad apple, and he's definitely the bad apple here."

Julia whispered back, "Are you really convinced he's up to no good?"

"I've encountered many people in my line of work, Julia. He's in that category I don't trust. Let's see how it plays out today," Denzel said.

"I'll keep that in mind," Julia replied.

Lucy and Ron focused on the passageway ahead. "We're almost there," Ron said.

Grant exhaled, feeling a mix of relief and gratitude. "That's great. I don't know how you two have managed this back-and-forth for the past seven years, but I trust you had your reasons."

Agent Denzel stepped closer to Jonathan, his voice low and sharp. "You're lucky I don't use my fist—there's a teenager present. But believe me, if I have a reason, I won't hesitate!"

Grant quickly intervened, placing a calming hand on Agent Denzel's shoulder. "Okay, guys, let's just calm down."

Jonathan's frown faded into a smug smile, and he walked away. Grant raised an eyebrow. "Now... what was that all about?"

"There's something off about him," Agent Denzel replied quietly. "I have a feeling he's up to no good."

"Maybe it's just your imagination," Grant said with a sigh. "Let's go inside and have some tea."

"Sure... but I'll be watching him like a hawk," Agent Denzel muttered.

Grant draped an arm over Agent Denzel as they followed the group into the basement leading to the cottage. Ron gestured for everyone to sit.

"Relax, everyone, and take a seat. My wife will serve the best tea and homemade biscuits—you'll enjoy them!"

As they settled, Grant and the two agents exchanged glances, their impatience barely contained.

"When can we see the spear?" Julia asked.

Ron smiled. "Soon, Julia. First, let's enjoy some tea together, and then we'll all have a look."

"Alright," Julia said, trying to hide her eagerness.

Jonathan's gaze lingered on Lucy's amulet. "Isn't it uncomfortable to wear while you sleep?"

Lucy shrugged. "It can be, but I have no choice. I must keep it on to protect everyone around me—and to stay invisible to the demon."

Jonathan nodded thoughtfully. "I see."

Lucy looked at him, slightly surprised, as if questioning his curiosity about the amulet. Janet entered, carrying a tray of tea and biscuits, and placed it carefully on the coffee table.

"Here we go! Tea and biscuits. Now, don't all fight over them at once!" Janet said with a smile.

Everyone took a cup of tea and a biscuit. "Thank you, Janet, that's very sweet of you," Marilyn said.

"You're welcome, dear," Janet replied.

Grant and the two agents carried their tea as they approached Ron. "Okay, now that we have tea, we'd like to see the spear," Julia said.

Ron chuckled. "You really are impatient, aren't you, Julia?"

"Sorry for being impatient, but I have that FBI mindset—I like to see things quickly," Agent Julia said.

Ron sighed. "Very well. Grant, if you'll hand me the key to the safe, I'll show you the spear."

Grant fished the key from his jeans pocket and passed it to Ron. "Here."

"Thank you. Okay—here we go," Ron said.

Marilyn pushed herself up from the sofa and moved closer so she could get a better look. Ron opened the safe and withdrew the spear. Agent Julia's breath caught at the sight of it. "Would you look at that? It's immaculate... and pure gold."

Everyone clustered around to admire the spear—everyone except Lucy and Jonathan.

"Come on, Jonathan—have a look!" Marilyn called.

"No thanks. I can see it from here," he said, staying seated beside Lucy.

Agent Denzel frowned. "Why not?" he asked.

"Because I don't want to," Jonathan replied. He scooted closer to Lucy and sat very near her. Lucy visibly tensed.

Then, suddenly, Jonathan produced a screwdriver from his pocket. He thrust a hand around Lucy's throat and held the screwdriver blade to the side of her neck.

"Hey, everybody!" Jonathan shouted, his voice sharp. Heads snapped toward him, stunned. He addressed Marilyn, his voice low and dangerous. "Give me the gun, Marilyn, or I'll shove this screwdriver through her neck! You don't want that to happen, do you?"

"Don't do anything foolish!" Agent Denzel warned.

Jonathan laughed, hard and ugly. "You heard me, Marilyn. Give me the gun." Shaking, Marilyn handed her weapon over.

"Help me!" Lucy whimpered.

"Jonathan—what are you doing? Don't—" Marilyn sobbed.

Jonathan stepped back slightly, brandishing the screwdriver. "Everyone don't move! Denzel! Julia! Drop your guns now so I know you aren't going to shoot!"

Julia's voice was steady but icy. "Okay, one at a time. You know there are three of us who are armed—and you're on your own here."

"Shut up and do as I say!" Jonathan snapped. He jabbed the screwdriver a little closer to Lucy's skin. He spat, "And you—old man!" His glare landed on Ron.

Ron looked at him with disgust. He kept his hands where they could be seen but made no move to comply.

"What's gotten into you? Just... don't hurt the girl, please," Agent Denzel said, his voice tense.

"Hand me the spear, and she won't get hurt," Jonathan replied. He glanced at Ron, then nodded toward him.

"Give him the spear," Ron said reluctantly.

After a pause, Ron surrendered. "Okay... take the spear—but you're making a very wrong decision."

Jonathan rolled his eyes. "Carefully now." He picked up the spear from the floor.

"Now, Julia," he said, turning toward Agent Julia, "I'm taking your car. Hand me the keys."

With a resigned sigh, Julia tossed the keys to him.

"And I'm taking Lucy with me," Jonathan added, a wicked grin curling his lips. "Somewhere you won't find her."

"Please! Help me! Someone help!" Lucy screamed, panic rising in her voice.

Jonathan shoved open the door, gun raised and marched out of the cottage. He flung Lucy into the trunk of Agent Julia's car, slammed it shut, and circled to the driver's side. Sliding in, he started the engine and sped away.

Agent Julia and Agent Denzel ran to the open doorway, watching helplessly as Jonathan disappeared down the road with Lucy in the trunk.

"So... Jonathan has the spear and Lucy," Agent Julia said, her voice tight with anger and worry. She turned to Denzel, who gave her a hard glare.

29

Abduction

It was eight minutes past five in the evening on Creeper Trail. Marilyn stood frozen, feeling both shocked and betrayed by what she had just witnessed. She had never imagined Jonathan capable of something so cruel—abducting a fourteen-year-old girl who hadn't seen her parents in more than seven years. And now, he had taken the spear as well.

Agent Julia was fighting to stay calm, forcing herself to think clearly. After a few tense moments, a plan began to form. She turned to Ron, desperation flickering in her eyes.

"Ron, we need to move—fast. Can I borrow your car? Denzel, Grant, Marilyn, and I will track Jonathan down."

Ron trembled, still shaken by what he had seen. "Ah, yes, of course you can. But please—find him. He can't keep that spear. The demon will use Jonathan as its slave, twisting him—and anyone near him—to its will."

Grant frowned, trying to make sense of it. "What do you mean by 'twisting him'?"

Ron took a deep breath. "When the clock strikes nine, Sparda will be able to see Lucy—because she wears the amulet. But if Jonathan removes it from her neck and uses it for himself, the demon will see them both. The amulet's protection won't work under Jonathan's corrupted heart."

"So, you're saying the amulet only works if it's worn by someone pure of heart?" Grant asked.

"That's exactly what I believe," Ron replied. "You need to go—now. Retrieve the amulet before things turn truly sinister."

Janet stepped forward quickly, her voice trembling. "My husband's right. Lucy's had that amulet for so long because she's pure and good. The demon feeds on fear—it will destroy everything in its path. Look at what's already happened in Damascus! Lives have been lost... souls taken. You must get both the amulet and the spear back before Jonathan falls completely under its control."

Ron grabbed his car keys and handed them to Julia. "Here—take these. Hurry!"

Julia nodded firmly and took the keys. "Everyone, into the car," she ordered. They rushed outside to Ron's Ford Cortina. "Buckle up. This is going to be a bumpy ride!"

Agent Denzel climbed into the front passenger seat, while Grant and Marilyn settled in the back. Julia started the ignition, giving a final wave to Ron and Janet. The couple waved back, worry etched across their faces.

"Good luck," Ron called after them. "You're all going to need it."

Julia pressed the accelerator, and the car shot forward into the fading light, the tires crunching gravel as they raced down the trail toward Damascus.

Meanwhile, only a few yards from the town limits, Jonathan spotted Detective Marshall, Ebenezer, and Christian walking toward the Maccabees Hotel. He ducked his head low, gripping the steering wheel tightly so they wouldn't see him.

From the trunk, Lucy pounded desperately, her feet striking the metal.

Detective Marshall spotted Agent Julia's car barreling toward them, then saw it wobble—one of the tires had blown. "Goddammit!" Jonathan cursed as he brought the car to a shuddering stop. Detective Marshall hurried over, unaware that Lucy was trapped in the trunk.

Jonathan forced a nervous smile as the detective approached. "Everything all right? Why are you driving Agent Julia's car?" Marshall demanded.

Jonathan's smile vanished. He pulled a gun and aimed it at the detective. "Empty your pockets and hand over your weapon—slowly," he snapped.

Detective Marshall's face went hard, bewildered. A scream ripped from the trunk. "Help! Help!" Lucy shouted.

"Looks like you've got someone in your trunk," Detective Marshall said grimly.

"And so, what if I have?" Jonathan replied with sarcasm. "Put your hands up, or I'll shoot."

Marshall set his gun on the ground and lifted his hands. "All right—here's the gun. Don't do anything stupid." Ebenezer and Christian watched helplessly as the detective complied.

Jonathan hopped out, picked up the gun from the ground, and barked, "Start walking away from me while I open the trunk."

Christian and Ebenezer turned to see Ryan and Helen appearing from the Maccabees' hotel. They froze when they saw Detective Marshall approaching. Jonathan yanked the trunk open and hauled Lucy out. Helen screamed.

"Lucy—oh my God! What have you done with my daughter?" she cried.

"Hey, that's our daughter—leave her alone!" Ryan shouted.

Jonathan smirked, training the gun on Ryan. "I'll hold her until I get that amulet off her neck. Don't do anything you'll regret. One move and I'll shoot."

Jessica rushed out and took in the scene. "Jonathan, what are you doing?" she demanded.

Jonathan laughed, voice cold. "Don't even think about moving. I'll take the amulet from Lucy and deal with the demon myself."

Ebenezer stepped forward, incredulous. "What are you thinking? You don't stand a chance fighting that demon alone."

Jonathan laughed hysterically. "I have the spear, and when the clock strikes nine, I'll defeat it myself!"

From a distance, Agent Julia, Agent Denzel, Marilyn, and Grant spotted Jonathan and the others. Julia slowed the car and turned onto a narrow side road, out of sight. "All right, Denzel," she whispered. "We'll move in closer. When I give the signal, you shoot—understood?"

Agent Denzel nodded. "Crystal clear. It'll be my pleasure."

Grant stayed behind in the car as the agents crept closer. "Let me signal Ryan—get his attention," he said, ducking low.

Ryan looked up and caught sight of Agent Julia motioning to him with raised hands. He immediately understood her signal and began forming a plan.

Jonathan gripped Lucy's arm tightly. "Give me the amulet," he demanded.

Lucy hesitated, then unclasped the necklace from around her neck—the first time in over seven years—and handed it to him with trembling fingers. As soon as the amulet left her skin, a low whispering sound filled the air. Jonathan's face lit up with awe. He slipped the amulet over his neck.

Instantly, the sky darkened. The temperature seemed to drop. Everyone stared upward in horror.

"No! What have you done?" Ryan shouted.

Agent Denzel raised his weapon, eyes flicking between the dark sky and Jonathan.

Jonathan smirked. "Would you believe it?" He tightened his hold on Lucy. "Now, everyone—drop your weapons, or she dies."

Ryan lowered his head, pretending to give up. "All right," he said heavily. "Everyone, put down your weapons. But please let me have my daughter in exchange. You can take everything else."

Helen turned to him, bewildered. "Ryan, what are you doing?"

Ryan whispered to her, "Trust me—I've got a plan."

Meanwhile, Agent Julia whispered to Agent Denzel, "Aim for his legs. Wait for my count."

Jonathan sneered. "You heard him! Drop the weapons!" Everyone exchanged tense looks, unaware that FBI agents were lying in wait. Julia raised her hand slightly toward Agent Denzel.

"On my count," she murmured. "One... two... three—now!"

Agent Denzel fired from two hundred yards. Both shots hit cleanly—one in each leg. Jonathan let out a piercing scream, collapsing to the ground. "Aargh!"

The dark sky instantly began to clear, returning to a calm blue.

Lucy broke free and ran toward her parents. Helen dropped to her knees, tears streaming down her face as she embraced her daughter for the first time in seven years, holding her close as if she might vanish again.

Agent Denzel exchanged a sharp glance with Agent Julia as Marilyn stormed toward Jonathan, fury blazing in her eyes. Without a word, she struck him across the face.

"I can't believe you kidnapped Lucy!" she shouted. "I don't even know who you are anymore."

Ryan rushed forward and wrapped his daughter in his arms. "Our precious Lucy," said Helen, her voice trembling.

"My princess! You've grown from a little girl into a young woman," Ryan added, his smile breaking through his tears.

"Oh, Dad—it's so good to see you and Mom again!" Lucy said, holding them tightly.

"We're just grateful you were safe with Ron and Janet," Ryan replied.

"They've been wonderful," Lucy said warmly. "They took great care of me—but I'm so glad to finally be home."

Jonathan groaned on the ground, clutching both legs as blood seeped through the torn denim of his jeans. Agent Denzel stepped closer, a hard grin forming on his face.

"I knew you were trouble," he said coldly. "My instincts were right about you all along."

Jonathan grimaced through the pain. "Go to hell, you pig!" he spat, sending a glob of blood toward Denzel's face.

Agent Denzel wiped it away, then drove a fist into Jonathan's cheek, forcing his head down to the dirt.

"I'll fetch that spear from your car," Agent Denzel said. "Did you really think you could run from us? You're even dumber than you look."

Despite the pain, Jonathan began to laugh—a dry, unsettling sound. "You don't get it. I have the amulet now. I can't take it off, even if I wanted to."

Agent Denzel crouched down, eyes narrowing. "Take it off. Now."

Jonathan tugged at the chain around his neck, panic rising in his voice. "I... I can't. It's stuck!"

Ryan stepped forward, realization dawning in his eyes. "Oh my God—it's starting to make sense. The amulet only releases from someone with a pure soul."

Agent Denzel frowned. "A pure soul? What are you talking about?"

Ryan met his gaze steadily. "If the soul is tainted, the amulet binds itself. It won't let go until the darkness inside fully awakens. And from the looks of it, Jonathan—" he paused, voice dropping "—that happens when the demon rises at nine o'clock tonight."

Jonathan's expression collapsed into terror. "What have I done?"

Ryan exhaled grimly. "Looks like you're in deep trouble, son."

"What am I going to do?" Jonathan asked, panic flickering in his voice.

Ebenezer stepped toward Ryan, his expression grave. "It's all starting to make sense now—and I need to ask you something, Ryan."

Ryan nodded. "Go ahead, Ebenezer."

"Well," Ebenezer began, "Detective Marshall, Christian, and I encountered the demon—Sparda—a few moments ago. What I noticed was that it only attacks when its target feels fear. None of us showed any fear, and it didn't even try to take our souls."

Marilyn, Jessica, and the FBI agents exchanged stunned looks.

"You've actually seen the demon?" Agent Denzel asked in disbelief.

"Yes," Ebenezer replied, "but only in shadow form. After nine this evening, it'll take on its true shape—and with it, real power."

Ryan rubbed his head, piecing the facts together. "That's right. The demon feeds on fear. It can steal a person's soul only when they're terrified. Just look around this town—people screaming, running for their lives. That fear gives the demon strength to consume them."

Agent Denzel broke in. "So, are you saying the amulet can't be removed because this man"—he gestured toward Jonathan— "isn't afraid?"

Ryan nodded firmly. "Exactly. When Lucy wore the amulet all those years, she lived in constant fear, but it also shielded her from evil. It's a kind of defence mechanism. Her suffering—her fear—gave the amulet its power. That's what kept her alive."

At that moment, Ron arrived, having overheard the conversation. "You're absolutely right, Ryan," he said. "The amulet granted Lucy protection within a three-kilometer radius and even made her invisible to the demon. But now that *this lowlife* is wearing it, the demon will be drawn to him—and it's going to enjoy every second of it."

Agent Julia turned sharply toward him. "Ron? Where the hell did you come from? I thought we left you back at the cottage!"

Ron smirked. "I followed on my motorbike. I needed to see this for myself. Didn't think Jonathan would get caught so fast—but I guess I was wrong."

Ebenezer folded his arms. "Then what do we do with him now?"

Ron's tone hardened. "Now that the amulet's bound to him, the demon will see Jonathan as its servant. The only way to break the bond and reclaim the amulet is to destroy the demon. You have to pierce its heart with the spear—and while doing so, speak the word *'Djed'* while locking eyes with it."

Without hesitation, Agent Denzel walked over to the car and retrieved the spear.

"Well done, my most trusted partner," Agent Julia said, a rare smile breaking through her usual composure.

Agent Denzel returned the smile. "Thanks, Julia. So... what do we do with him now?"

Detective Marshall spoke up. "Let's take him to your hotel, Ryan. That way we can keep him under close watch."

Julia frowned slightly. "Are we sure that's wise? Keeping him as a hostage might be dangerous—especially now that we know the demon intends to use Jonathan."

Ryan hesitated; his eyes fixed on Jonathan and the cursed amulet glinting at his throat. "You're right," he said at last. "But we don't have much time. We'll need to come up with a plan—and fast."

30

Is there a Plan B?

Now that Jonathan wore the amulet, the original plan to confront Demon Sparda had to be revised—Jonathan's impulsive betrayal had blown it apart. Helen and Marilyn moved toward him and used pliers to pull the bullets from his legs.

"Argh!" Jonathan screamed, more from shock than pain.

"I'm not surprised—you had bullets in both legs," Helen said. "This could all have been avoided if you hadn't tried to kidnap my daughter."

Marilyn nodded, disgust clear on her face. "Why would you do that? We could have all worked together. Instead, you chose to play hero and almost got Lucy killed."

Jonathan bowed his head, shame washing over him. "I'm sorry. I don't know what I was thinking."

"It's too late for apologies," Marilyn said. Ryan and Lucy pressed cloth to the wounds to staunch the bleeding.

"You're lucky I didn't clout you," Ryan said, voice low. "You tried to take my daughter. You'll face the consequences. I don't know if we can save you once Sparda regains power at nine, but we'll try—because we're not monsters."

Jonathan sank to his knees at Ryan's feet, sobbing. "Please, Ryan—don't let the demon kill me!"

Ryan exhaled, worn. "We'll see."

Ebenezer glanced at his watch. "It's twenty-eight minutes past five. We'd better start preparing."

A hush fell—then the air shifted. The clouds darkened and rain began to fall. Demon Sparda materialized, a shadowed thing that poured mockery into the wind.

"You fool," Sparda boomed. "At last—the amulet is in mortal hands. After seven years of searching, it rests on a fool I can use to pluck your souls and resurrect the dead. Time ticks: soon I will be renewed. I will take that amulet and you will all suffer."

"You'll suffer first," Ebenezer shot back.

Sparda laughed—long, cruel, full of hunger. "Ha! Talk all you like, mortal. You show me no fear; impressive. I can read your souls. I could take the one who betrayed you and use it against you. Perhaps I will wait a little longer... then I will feed on him and crush you all. Ha ha ha ha!"

The demon vanished into the clouds, leaving the air thick with tension.

Grant, still inside the car, had seen the creature for the first time in his life. His hands trembled slightly on the steering wheel—not from fear, but from disbelief.

Ryan looked around at everyone, his voice cutting through the silence. "None of you looked scared... well, except you, Jonathan."

Christian's brow furrowed as he replayed Sparda's words in his mind. "Did anyone catch what he said? He could've taken Jonathan's soul and used it to raise the dead—but he didn't."

"Exactly," Ryan replied. "That's not good news for you, Jonathan, but we'll do what we can to protect you. Still, if the demon takes full control of you—like it did with Max—it'll be over. I don't want to scare you, but that's the truth."

Grant stepped out of the car, his boots splashing into the wet dirt. "Mother of God," he muttered. "I've just seen the demon with my own eyes. I warned everyone not to come to the ghost town of Damascus... but now that I've seen it, I'm more determined than ever to finish this."

Agent Julia exchanged a quick glance with Agent Denzel. "Absolutely," she said, her voice firm. "We need to find a safe place, gather as much ammunition as we can, and get ready. I've got a feeling Sparda's power will raise an entire army of the undead."

Ryan nodded. "Alright, everyone. Split up—search every house, every store, and grab whatever ammo you can find. We'll regroup at Max's saloon. We can use the bar as cover and the roof as a vantage point to shoot anything that moves. Once we're ready, Ron will read from the book—he's the only one who can interpret the ancient Egyptian text—and we'll use the spear to end this."

Detective Marshall smirked. "You make it sound easy."

"Then let's make sure it is," Ryan said, raising his voice. "Stick to Plan B, work together, and don't lose faith. Can I get a hallelujah?"

"Hallelujah!" everyone shouted in unison.

Jonathan stayed quiet. The others' energy didn't reach him. Deep down, he knew the demon's next return could be his end. With the amulet around his neck and corruption already stirring inside him, he could feel Sparda's darkness creeping closer.

Meanwhile, a few hundred yards away, Jacob noticed the sky had darkened unnaturally fast. He stepped outside, rain dripping from the porch roof. "That storm... it's not right," he whispered.

He moved cautiously toward another abandoned house and slipped inside. The air smelled of dust and rot. "Where is everyone?" he murmured, creeping through the hallway. "I'll find them. I won't give up."

Jacob's flashlight flickered as he spotted a staircase leading up to the bedrooms. Slowly, he began to climb, every creak of the steps echoing through the silence.

"I should go upstairs," Jacob muttered to himself. "From there, I might get a better view of the town... maybe even spot Ebenezer, Christian, or Grant."

The house was eerily quiet. Three-bedroom doors lined the upper hallway, their paint chipped and peeling. Jacob hesitated, then opened the first door on the left.

The stench hit him immediately.

A woman's corpse lay sprawled across the bed—her skin tinted blue, her expression frozen in agony. Though the body hadn't yet decayed completely, the air was thick with the sour scent of death. Jacob gagged, then turned and vomited into the corner of the room. His stomach heaved until there was nothing left.

Coughing and trembling, he stumbled downstairs toward the kitchen, praying the water still ran. He turned the cold tap—nothing. Just a dry groan of rusted pipes.

Frustrated, he looked around and spotted an old refrigerator. He opened it, half-expecting more horror. The interior was dead and powerless. Inside, rotten food oozed across the shelves, but a few sealed bottles of water sat untouched in the corner.

He grabbed one, twisted off the cap, and took a small sip to rinse his mouth before spitting it out. The cool water calmed his throat and nerves.

Feeling steadier, Jacob made his way back upstairs. He avoided the first room and pushed open the second door.

This time, there was no corpse—just dust, silence, and the faint scent of old fabric. Relief washed over him.

"Thank goodness," he whispered.

He walked to the window, brushing aside a torn curtain. Outside, the ghost town stretched beneath a bruised sky. Jacob peered through the drizzle, searching the streets for any sign of movement—any hint that he wasn't completely alone.

But the only thing that moved was the fog.

31

THE BOOK THAT HAS ALL THE SECRETS

It was forty-eight minutes past five in the evening in Damascus. The air inside the saloon bar felt heavy with tension.

"Everyone, come inside," Christian said. "Ebenezer's got the two books. Let's take a look at them."

Ryan exchanged a knowing glance with Ron, aware of his rare skill. "There's something I should've mentioned earlier," Ryan began, his voice weary. "Ron can read Ancient Egyptian. He's going to translate the books for us."

Ebenezer, Christian, Ron, and Detective Marshall already knew, but the others looked up in surprise.

Ron rose from his chair and addressed the group. "All right, everyone, please take a seat. I'll read the important sections and explain what we need to do to defeat Sparda."

Jessica and Marilyn glanced at each other—fear and curiosity flickering across their faces—as they stared at the ancient volumes resting on the table.

Jonathan sat apart, withdrawn.

Agent Denzel settled behind the others, both legs bandaged. "Sit over here, you traitor!" someone shouted from the back.

Jonathan's face fell. The betrayal still stung. Marilyn felt a tear slip down her cheek. She had trusted him—believed in him—and now that trust was broken beyond repair.

Agent Julia and Detective Marshall sat side by side, with Ryan, Helen, and Lucy Maccabee opposite them. Ebenezer and Christian remained in the corner, whispering quietly, while Grant poured himself a glass of whiskey behind the bar.

Ron gestured to Jessica and Marilyn. "Ladies, would you please sit next to Agent Julia?"

"Sure, Ron," Jessica replied softly.

Ron waited until everyone settled. "I know this has been a horrific experience for all of you," he said, his tone firm yet calm. "But we have to cooperate with Ryan. It's the only way forward."

Detective Marshall nodded. "You have our word. We'll cooperate."

Agent Julia added, "Agreed. But no one goes off alone. We stay together and watch each other's backs."

Ebenezer raised his hand. "Count us in. We'll cooperate too."

"Me too!" Christian chimed in.

Jessica clutched Christian's arm, her voice trembling. "Christian, will you protect me? No matter what?"

"Of course, I'll look after you," Christian said gently.

Grant leaned against the counter, holding up a bottle. "Does anyone care for a glass of whiskey?"

Detective Marshall rolled his eyes. "No, thank you, Grant."

Helen slipped an arm around Lucy's shoulders. "How are you feeling?"

Lucy's voice trembled. "I'm worried. I don't have the amulet anymore, and we all know Sparda can hurt us if we show fear."

Ryan spoke calmly, trying to steady the group. "Stay calm, Lucy. If we stick to the plan and watch out for one another, we can defeat Sparda together."

Ron cleared his throat, drawing their attention. "All right. I'm going to read from the book and translate it for everyone."

He opened **The Book of Secrets**; the pages lined with intricate Egyptian hieroglyphs. "Amazing," he whispered. "This isn't just an old text — it feels like something not of this world."

Ryan nodded. "Luckily, you can actually read and write Ancient Egyptian."

Ron slipped on his reading glasses and began to study the symbols. "This is fascinating," he murmured. "Here it says, *'Those who hold the amulet will feel both good and evil.'*"

Ebenezer leaned forward. "That clearly means Lucy represents the good—and Jonathan the bad."

"Exactly," Ron replied. "The amulet reacts differently depending on who holds it. With Lucy, it responded positively. But with Jonathan..." Ron hesitated, glancing toward him. "It's possible he's already opened Pandora's box. And Sparda will relish that."

Jonathan overheard and scowled. "Thanks for reminding me."

Ron met his eyes. "It's true. You've made things far worse than you realize."

Agent Denzel rose from his chair, limping toward Jonathan. "I sensed the evil in you from the start. You're lucky you're still here. If it were up to me, you'd be locked in a cell right now."

"Enough, Agent Denzel," Detective Marshall barked.

Agent Denzel glared but backed away, returning to his seat. The tension in the room thickened as everyone waited for what came next.

Ryan bent over **The Book of Secrets**, pointing to a series of strange markings. "Ron, what does this symbol mean?"

Ron adjusted his glasses and studied the page. "Let's see... this one resembles a wooden staff shaped like the letter U. Next to it is a rug pattern with three rectangular symbols—one in the center and two at each end. Then comes a falcon, an oval-shaped rope, another bird, a resting lion, a reversed number nine, an owl, a hairbrush, and... something that looks like a slug."

Ebenezer pointed at the page and asked Ron, "What does this symbol mean?"

Ron smiled wryly. "Good question — I was about to translate it.""Sorry. Fire away," Ebenezer said.

Ron studied the hieroglyphs a moment, then read aloud. "This line says, 'Sparda will scent fear in everyone.'"

Detective Marshall nodded. "Not surprising. Christian, Ebenezer and I already found that out the hard way."

"Very well," Ron said, closing the book gently.

Ryan leaned forward, the urgency in his voice sharp. "We all know what Sparda is after and what it's capable of. We need to set up a shelter and gather as much ammunition as we can."

Grant rubbed his chin. "There's a gun shop a few yards from here. I say we go and take what we need."

Agent Julia was already on her feet. "Then what are we waiting for? Let's move."

Ryan raised his hand. "Wait — strategy. Ebenezer, Christian, and Detective Marshall should go to the gun store. Agent Denzel, Agent Julia, and Grant, you and I will fortify the saloon: front entrance, back entrance, and cellar. Block the doors and hold them."

Detective Marshall agreed at once. "Absolutely. That's our best shot."

As everyone stood and prepared to move, Jonathan sat apart, eyes hollow. He watched them readying themselves and knew he could not be part of the plan.

32

PLANNING TO STAY ALIVE

It was 6:06 p.m. in the gloomy town of Damascus. Ebenezer walked out of the saloon with Christian and Detective Marshall. Ryan, his wife Helen, and their daughter Lucy remained inside, huddled together, while Grant, Marilyn, Jessica, Agent Julia, and Agent Denzel talked quietly. Ron sat near the bar, studying *The Book of Secrets* to pull whatever information he could about Sparda. Christian realized he still had the potions with him.

"Guys," he said, "should I leave the potions with Ron?"

Detective Marshall answered, "Yes. Travel light. We'll need all the room we can spare for ammunition."

Ebenezer headed for the detective's car. "I'll wait in the car with you," he told Detective Marshall.

Christian smiled. "I won't be long." He went back inside and handed the potions to Ron. "Can you look after these?"

"Of course," Ron said.

Jessica slipped up behind Christian and kissed him. "Look after yourself out there, my love."

Christian met her eyes. "I won't be long. I'll grab as much ammunition as I can so we're safe."

Jessica smiled and hugged him. "That's why I love you. I know you'll come back—for me and for everyone."

"I love you too," he said.

Ryan approached Christian with a stern, practical look. "Get the best guns you can. If there's anything heavy—shotguns, a high-powered rifle—bring it. We need to be ready."

Christian nodded. "We'll make sure."

"Good," Ryan said. "My wife and I will go to the van. We'll take nails and a hammer and board up the doors. The undead aren't getting into this bar on our watch."

"Good idea," Christian agreed. "Okay—I better head to the gun store and load up. See you soon."

Ryan gave him a thumbs up. "See you soon."

Christian finally left the bar and climbed into the car, where he joined Ebenezer and Detective Marshall for their trip to the gun store.

Meanwhile, inside the saloon, Agent Julia prepared herself alongside Agent Denzel to assist Ryan. "So, what would you like us to do?" she asked.

Ryan turned to them. "Can the two of you drive to Creeper Trail and gather some wood? There should be plenty lying around."

Agent Julia shook her head. "How about we just look around here and dismantle some of the old furniture instead?"

Ryan considered it and nodded. "That's fine. You can start with this wooden table."

Agent Julia and Agent Denzel exchanged glances, then called out to Jessica and Marilyn. "Marilyn, can you check if there's a saw anywhere in the bar?"

"I think I know where to look," Marilyn said. "Let me check the cellar."

"I'll come with you," Jessica offered quickly.

The two women walked side by side toward the cellar door. Grant, standing behind the bar, spotted a torch resting beside the beer fridge. He grabbed it and called after them. "Hey, ladies—take this. It's bound to get dark down there."

Jessica turned back and smiled. "Thanks, Grant." She took the torch from him, then followed Marilyn down the creaking cellar steps.

At a nearby table, Ron continued reading *The Book of Secrets*, scanning every line for clues. Grant approached, a half-empty bottle of Dalmore whiskey dangling from his hand. "How's the reading going?" he asked.

Ron didn't look up. "There's a symbol here mentioning an amulet. It says, *'Sun sets, the moon rises, look around you—there might be some strange surprises.'*"

Grant scratched his head. "What do you think that means?"

Ron shrugged. "I'm not sure, but my guess is that the sun will set soon—and when night comes, something's going to happen."

Grant gave a short laugh, though it lacked conviction. "We'll just have to wait and see."

Down in the cellar, Jessica and Marilyn searched carefully among the shadows. "Let's split up," Jessica said softly. "Check over there—I'll look on this side."

Marilyn moved slowly, her flashlight trembling in her hand. She was quiet for a long moment, lost in thought. Jessica glanced over and noticed tears welling in her friend's eyes. "I know why you're crying," Jessica said gently. "It's Jonathan, isn't it?"

Marilyn nodded and wiped her tears away. "I'm so stupid! Why am I crying over a guy who tried to kidnap Lucy?"

Jessica placed a reassuring hand on her friend's shoulder. "Maybe you thought he was a nice guy—that's why."

"Don't worry about me, Jessica. I'll be fine. Let's find a saw so the guys can cut the wood and block the saloon's entrances."

Jessica hugged her tightly. "I'm here for you, always. You know that, right?"

Marilyn smiled, feeling the warmth and care. "Thank you. You're such a great friend."

"You too, Marilyn. You're a great friend as well," Jessica said.

As they continued down the cellar, a large chest came into view at the far end. Jessica aimed her torch at it and called out. "Look! A chest! Let's see what's inside."

Marilyn nodded and approached. "Goodness! It's so rusty!"

Jessica shone the torch inside, revealing a toolbox. "We hit the jackpot! A toolbox! Quickly, open it!" she said excitedly.

Marilyn lifted the lid. Inside were all the tools they needed—including a saw. "Yes! There's a saw! Let's take it and alert the others," she said.

As Marilyn grabbed the toolbox, a swarm of cockroaches scuttled out of the chest. Both girls screamed. "Argh! Quick, let's get out of here!" Jessica yelled.

They ran side by side, toolbox in hand. Grant, hearing the commotion, called out from above. "Guys! I heard screaming—it's coming from the cellar!"

Agent Denzel dashed down to meet them. He found Jessica and Marilyn emerging, panting but carrying the toolbox. "What happened?" he asked.

Jessica caught her breath and spoke slowly. "It's okay. We just found some cockroaches inside the chest."

"That's right," Marilyn added, "and a toolbox with all the tools we need."

Ryan, Helen, and Lucy Maccabee hurried over. "I see you found something useful in the cellar," Ryan said, smiling.

Marilyn opened the toolbox to show him. "This is perfect! Everything we need is here," she said.

Helen grinned at the girls. "Well done!"

"Thank you, Helen," Jessica said.

Agent Denzel turned to Marilyn. "Is there a saw inside the toolbox?"

Marilyn nodded and handed it over. "Here you go, Agent Denzel."

"Thank you. Now I can start cutting some wood to barricade the saloon," he said.

"Well done, girls!" Ryan exclaimed. "I'll get my nails and hammer from the van, and we can start as soon as Ebenezer and his friends return from the gun store."

Agent Julia scanned the saloon with her hands on her hips, then approached Ron, glancing at *The Book of Secrets*. "So, Ron... what are our chances of surviving this?"

Ron's eyes flashed with anger as he looked toward Jonathan before turning back to Agent Julia. "To be honest, Agent Julia, our chances would be good if Jonathan hadn't removed the amulet from Lucy's neck. Now, survival is minimal.”

Agent Julia’s brow furrowed, but she spoke calmly. “So... what do we do? Is it even possible to kill Sparda?”

Ron took a deep breath. “With Jonathan wearing the amulet, Sparda has already glimpsed his soul. Eventually, Jonathan will fall under his control. To fight Sparda, we must work together—and eliminate the living dead as we go.”

Agent Julia paced anxiously, wringing her hands. Ron stepped closer and gently took her hand. “We will do this. We have a strong team, and together, we can face the demon. It won’t be easy, but we’ll survive if we plan carefully.”

Agent Julia smiled and hugged him, pressing a quick kiss to his cheek. “You’re a good man.”

Ron’s cheeks flushed. “Don’t make me feel shy,” he murmured, smiling.

She grinned. “Anyway, I think we better start barricading the saloon.”

“Absolutely. Let’s check on the others,” Ron agreed.

Jonathan cleared his throat. “Hey, can I have some water? A man needs his fluids.”

Ron chuckled. “Of course.” He walked to the bar. “Helen? Can you pass me a bottle of water?”

Helen stepped out of the saloon, asking Ryan to bring her a few more. “Darling, could you please bring six bottles of water?”

“Of course, my love,” Ryan replied, grabbing the bottles.

Ryan grabbed his hammer, a box of nails, and six bottles of water, each wrapped in plastic with a handle in the middle. “Well, Helen, looks like we have everything. Now we just wait for the others to bring the weapons,” he said.

“I hope they won’t take too long,” Helen replied.

“We have time. It’s only sixteen past six in the evening. We’ve got under three hours before Sparda rises—though not fully rejuvenated yet,” Ryan said.

“That’s true, my love,” Helen agreed.

“Okay, let’s get to work and keep an eye out for Ebenezer and his friends so we can let them in when they return,” Ryan instructed.

He closed the back door of his van and walked back into the saloon with Helen, carrying the tools they would need. Helen removed the plastic cover from the bottles and handed one to Ron. "Here's the water."

Ron took the bottle and tossed it toward Jonathan. "Here's the water you asked for."

Jonathan caught it with both hands and quickly opened it. "Thank you," he said.

Ron's voice was sharp. "Thank you for what? For creating a problem that could have been avoided if you weren't so reckless?"

Jonathan looked downcast and worried.

"Exactly. Got nothing to say? That's what I thought," Ron snapped.

Agent Denzel intervened. "There's no point wasting your energy on this one. He's done."

Ron frowned. "Soon, he'll be under Sparda's control."

"It's a shame we have to keep him with us," Agent Denzel muttered.

"I know," Ron said, "but he has the amulet. We need to retrieve it once we complete our mission. In the meantime, we should keep him restrained so he can't escape."

"I'll take care of that," Agent Denzel said, moving toward Jonathan. He handcuffed him and guided him to a seating area in the bar. "Here—take a seat. I'll keep an eye on you."

Jonathan sank into the chair, wincing in pain from the gunshot wounds in both legs.

"Okay, Marilyn and Jessica, can you help Agent Julia and me break some tables? We need a pile of planks to barricade the bar," Ron instructed.

They both nodded and began helping. And so the work started—preparing for what could be a long, harrowing few hours ahead.

33

ARMED WITH CONFIDENCE

Ebenezer, Christian, and Detective Marshall arrived at the gun store. Detective Marshall stepped out of the car, his eyes scanning the storefront. "Here we are. Let's grab as many guns and as much ammunition as we can."

Christian and Ebenezer exchanged nervous glances, aware that the next few hours could be fatal—or heroic, if they managed to defeat Sparda. Ebenezer walked slowly toward the store, Christian following closely behind.

"Let's do this. No turning back."

Christian left the car door open so they could load the weapons quickly. Detective Marshall suggested, "Do me a favor, Christian. Can you open the trunk too?"

Christian smiled. "Sure thing, Detective! Why didn't I think of that?"

"You have to think fast, especially in times like this," Marshall replied.

Christian nodded, opened the trunk, and then followed Ebenezer into the store.

Ebenezer froze for a moment, astonished at the sight before him. "Oh, my goodness! That's... a lot of dead bodies."

"Forget about the bodies!" Marshall shouted as he grabbed guns and ammunition. "Take as much as you can so we can get back to the saloon and help the others."

"Right, Detective," Ebenezer replied, shaking off his shock.

Christian's eyes fell on a glass cabinet containing a Pulse rifle. "Oh, I'm taking this!"

Detective Marshall gestured toward it. "Then take it—now!"

Scanning the store, Christian noticed a fire extinguisher near the fire exit. Using it, he smashed the glass to retrieve the Pulse rifle.

"Will you look at this? I've never used one before, and now I'm about to—for the right reasons," he muttered.

Ebenezer rolled his eyes. "I guess that's one way to look at it."

A few seconds later, a shadowy figure materialized in the store. Detective Marshall spotted it immediately.

"Look, guys! It's Sparda!" he shouted. Both Ebenezer and Christian turned sharply to see what he was pointing at.

"It's Sparda!" Ebenezer yelled, his voice steady despite the danger.

Sparda laughed, his voice echoing through the gun store. "I see you pathetic humans who think you can stop me with mortal weapons! In less than two hours, your feeble lives will be mine. I shall claim my spear and amulet, and the human race will never be the same again! Ha ha ha ha ha!"

Ebenezer squared his shoulders, unflinching. "You don't scare us, demon! We will end your pitiful existence and destroy you!"

For a brief moment, Sparda laughed, but then his expression darkened. "Oh, the weak human speaks! I am touched by your courage, but you puny mortals stand no chance. Once I raise the dead, you will witness the true power of the demon sorcerer Sparda! Ha ha ha ha ha!"

Detective Marshall's voice rang with determination. "We will stop you! And you will return to where you belong—straight back to hell!"

Sparda laughed again. "The sands of time are against you, but until then, I will see you all very soon. This is your last chance to live—enjoy it, for soon you will be dead!"

Ebenezer smirked. "We shall see about that."

In an instant, Sparda vanished as suddenly as he had appeared.

"That was quite the entrance," Christian muttered, eyes wide.

Detective Marshall shook off the shock quickly. "I know. Let's grab all the guns and load them into my car. Time is not on our side."

"You heard him!" Ebenezer added urgency in his voice. "The dead bodies across this town will soon rise as the undead. We'd better hurry back, build barricades around the saloon bar, and prepare for war—because that's exactly what's coming, whether we like it or not."

Ebenezer swiftly grabbed a shotgun, a smart gun, and four Magnum pistols, while Christian lifted the Pulse rifle and placed it carefully in the trunk. Then he dashed back into the store, collecting the remaining weapons and loading them into the car with precision.

"Well done, guys! It looks like we've gathered a solid collection of weapons and all the ammunition," said Detective Marshall.

Ebenezer's eyes fell on a first aid kit tucked next to the cabinet. "I'm taking this with me—just in case," he said, grabbing it.

"Sure, toss it in the trunk," Detective Marshall replied.

The three men surveyed the pile of weapons already crammed into the back seat and trunk. "Looks like we have enough firepower to last us a while," Marshall advised. "My suggestion: when you get the perfect shot, aim for the head—every time."

Ebenezer hesitated. "But Detective, there are still more weapons inside the store!"

"I know," Detective Marshall nodded, "but if we have time, we'll have Agent Julia and Agent Denzel collect the rest."

"Not a bad plan," Ebenezer said approvingly.

The three men opened the car doors. Ebenezer and Christian struggled to wedge themselves into the back seat, maneuvering around the heaps of guns and ammunition.

Christian grumbled, "This is going to be a very uncomfortable ride back to the saloon bar."

Ebenezer nodded in agreement. "Yeah, and I'm not liking it so far."

Detective Marshall started the engine and pulled away. "Buckle up, gentlemen. I'll drive fast so we don't waste a single second."

34

A Team Effort

The sky darkened over Damascus as the sun sank lower, and the wind picked up, tugging at the thickening clouds. Ryan watched Agent Denzel sawing through the tables. "How's it going over there?" he called.

"Not bad, Ryan," Agent Denzel replied. "I'll keep cutting as much wood as I can from these tables—used to be a place where people could actually socialize over a drink or two."

"I know," Ryan said with a sigh. "It's sad we have to dismantle everything, but on the bright side, it's safer. We definitely don't want the undead getting inside."

Agent Julia, Marilyn, and Jessica handed the cut planks to Ryan and Helen.

"Here we go, Ryan and Helen!" one of them called.

Ryan and Helen took the wood and began nailing the planks across the saloon bar's entrance. A loud pounding echoed as Ryan hammered from the top while Helen worked from the bottom.

Lucy frowned at Jonathan. "If it weren't for you, none of this would be happening."

Jonathan groaned. "Will you please stop reminding me?"

Agent Denzel stopped sawing, stepped toward Jonathan, and struck him with a sharp punch to the left side.

"Shut up, you narrow-minded idiot!" he barked.

Jonathan spat blood onto the floor, staring downcast.

Lucy walked away and clutched her mother. "I'm scared, Mom."

Helen hugged her tightly. "I know, sweetheart. We need to stay strong together. That's what the Maccabees have done for the past seven years. We'll focus, stay united, and defeat Sparda together."

Lucy smiled, holding her mother tightly. "I love you, Mom."

"I love you too," Helen said. "Now go on, make yourself useful. Maybe you can help your dad."

Lucy nodded and ran to help Ryan by passing nails.

"Here we go, Dad!" she said.

Ryan kissed her left cheek. "Thanks, sweetheart."

Meanwhile, Grant paced, worrying how long Ebenezer and the others would take to arrive. "What's taking them so long?"

Agent Julia looked at him calmly. "They should be here soon."

Grant exhaled and continued pacing. Ron approached, placing a hand on his shoulder. "Don't worry, Grant. They'll arrive soon."

"I'm sure they will," Grant said, "but I'm worried about the time."

"Why don't you help Ryan and take your mind off it?" Ron suggested.

"Sure. What should I do?"

Ryan nailed the final plank across the saloon bar's front door and called out, "Grant, can you take the planks from Agent Julia and Denzel and make sure all the windows are blocked off?"

"No problem. I'll start with the window closer to the entrance."

"Excellent!" Ryan replied.

Grant approached the FBI agents and grabbed four planks of wood from them.

"Thank you, Grant!" said Agent Julia.

Grant smiled and then asked Ryan if he had a spare hammer.

"I'm not sure," Ryan admitted. "I can check my van, though."

"Don't worry, I'll take a look," Grant said.

"Sure! Feel free to check in the van," Ryan said. "I suggest you use the back entrance and work your way to the front of the saloon bar."

"Got it!" Grant replied.

Ron decided to go with him. "I'll come along."

The two made their way to the back of the saloon bar—the only door not yet barricaded. Grant opened it with Ron following close behind.

"I hope this isn't a mistake, coming all the way to Damascus," Grant muttered.

Ron looked concerned. "Why do you say that?"

"I just have a feeling it's going to go horribly wrong," Grant admitted.

"Think positive," Ron said. "We're here to save this town—and maybe even the planet."

"You're right. I'm just worried because the plan had to change due to Jonathan's mistake, that's all," Grant said.

"I know. It's unfortunate, but we'll handle it. Somehow, I believe we'll finish the job," Ron replied.

"I like your confidence," Grant said.

"Of course," Ron said firmly. "In these horrid circumstances, we must not only save ourselves, but humanity too!"

As they reached Ryan's van, Grant said, "Okay, let me open the back door and see if I can find another hammer."

Ron watched as Grant flung the van doors open. A few moments later, Detective Marshall, Ebenezer, and Christian arrived from the gun store.

Ron waved at them. "Hey, guys! So glad to see you—especially you, Grant! You were worried about them."

Grant frowned. "You didn't have to tell them that," he muttered.

Ron tapped Grant's shoulder. "Ah, it's okay! I meant no harm."

Grant laughed. "I know. Anyway, let me grab a hammer, and I'll catch up with you and the others shortly."

"Okay. I want to see how many weapons they brought back," Ron said.

"Sure! Go ahead," Grant replied.

Ron walked toward Detective Marshall, Ebenezer, and Christian. "Hey, guys! How was the journey?"

Detective Marshall stepped out of the car with Ebenezer and Christian. "Hello, Ron. The journey went well, but I have something else to tell you all—though we'll wait until we get inside the saloon bar. I'll fill you in there."

Ron's curiosity piqued. "Let me guess—you met Sparda?"

Ebenezer nodded. "Yes, we did. But first, go get everyone so they can help us unload the weapons and ammunition from the car."

Christian opened the trunk and gestured to Ron. "Here! Feast your eyes on this!"

Ron's eyes widened. A grin spread across his face. "Fantastic! Looks like you brought enough weapons for all of us!"

Detective Marshall added, "Not only do we have plenty of weapons, but we also have enough ammunition to deal with the undead."

Ebenezer pointed out, "And there are still more guns and ammo left in the store."

Ron paused, thinking. "So, what are you saying?"

"That we need to make another trip to the gun store—quickly," Ebenezer replied.

"Ah, okay. I'll gather everyone to help bring the weapons inside the bar," Ron said.

Meanwhile, Grant had found a hammer in Ryan's van. Ron noticed him and said, "Great! I want to go inside through the back door. Detective Marshall and his friends have something to tell us, but first, we need everyone to help carry the weapons inside." Grant smiled, pleased.

The five men hurried toward the back of the bar. Inside, Agent Julia, Agent Denzel, and Ryan were busy placing wood over every door and window. Detective Marshall entered first, calling out, "Hey, everyone, stop for a moment. We're back from the gun store, and I need each of you to help bring the weapons and ammunition inside."

Ryan smiled. "Well done, Detective! Of course, we'll be glad to help."

Agent Julia and Agent Denzel immediately paused their work and walked to the back door to see the weapons. Marilyn followed the agents, and Jessica ran to hug Christian.

"Oh, Christian, my love! I'm so happy to see you," she exclaimed.

Christian kissed Jessica. "Me too, beautiful. Come on, quickly! We need to show you all something."

Jessica grasped Christian's hand, and together they stepped out the back door. Ryan stared in astonishment at the sheer number of weapons in the car and trunk.

"Wow! This is incredible! Just what we need!"

Helen and Lucy's eyes widened in shock. "I've never seen so many weapons in my life," Helen whispered.

Lucy clutched her mother's arm, fear written on her face. "Mom, I want to go inside."

"Okay, my love," Helen said gently. They entered the saloon bar together.

Detective Marshall approached Ryan. "I need to talk to you inside."

"Sure. What's it about?" Ryan asked.

"Everyone, please come inside," the detective commanded, ignoring Ryan's question and pointing toward the bar. Ebenezer and Christian exchanged knowing glances, understanding exactly what he wanted to discuss.

Agent Julia and Agent Denzel, each carrying six guns in their arms, looked puzzled. Jessica and Marilyn lugged boxes of ammunition from the trunk, while Ron and Grant took some guns as well. Soon, the car was empty, and all the weapons were inside the saloon bar.

Detective Marshall instructed, "Place the weapons and ammunition on the floor. Everyone, just leave them there."

Carefully, everyone set the weapons down and turned their attention to the detective.

Clearing his throat, Ryan asked, "So, Detective, what is it you wanted to discuss with me and the others?"

Detective Marshall's expression darkened. "While we were at the gun store, we encountered Sparda. This demon mentioned the dead rising. I suggest we continue barricading the saloon bar immediately."

Ryan surveyed the room. "The team has done a remarkable job so far. We've secured the front entrance and the windows, but there's still much to do."

Ebenezer stepped forward. "What else needs doing? I'm more than happy to help if it keeps us alive."

"That's good to hear," Ryan said. "We need to cover the upstairs windows and start securing the back entrance. The only escape route will be the basement, where you three solved the riddles. Keep it secure, and we can reinforce the basement door with chains. Meanwhile, start barricading upstairs as quickly as possible. Check every room—any door or window you see, cover it with planks."

Agent Julia interrupted the conversation between the two men. "Looking at the number of weapons we have, it's a huge stockpile, but in my experience, we still need more."

Detective Marshall nodded in agreement. "Agent Julia, why don't you and Agent Denzel quickly head back to the gun store and collect the remaining weapons and ammunition? There's still a lot left there."

Agent Julia glanced at Agent Denzel. "What do you think?"

"Let's go and gather the weapons without delay," Agent Denzel said firmly.

Ryan chimed in. "Please hurry—time is against us."

Agent Julia smiled. "We'll head to the gun store immediately and bring back as much as we can."

Thinking quickly, Ryan tossed the van keys toward Agent Denzel. "Here, take my van keys. That way, you'll have enough space to collect as many weapons as possible."

Agent Denzel caught the keys. "Thank you. Let's go, Agent Julia."

"We'll be back soon," Julia added. Without hesitation, the two agents headed toward the back of the saloon bar, the only door that had not yet been barricaded.

35

FIGHTING THE TIME FOR SURVIVAL

The time was approaching eight o'clock in the evening—an hour until the demon would rise, rejuvenated but not fully. Back in the house, Jacob peered out, scanning for any sign of movement. From a distance, he noticed Agent Julia and Agent Denzel opening the van doors.

"Hmmm... I wonder who they are," Jacob murmured to himself. Luckily, he had brought binoculars. He clipped them from his trousers and carefully observed the agents. They were armed with guns and moved with the precision of a trained organization. "I wonder who they work for. This is interesting," he whispered.

Jacob quietly descended the stairs, wanting a closer look. The two FBI agents were preparing for a short journey to the gun store.

"Are you ready for this, Agent Denzel?" Agent Julia asked.

Agent Denzel nodded. "I'm ready, but I really hope we make it through the night, knowing what we're up against." Julia placed a reassuring hand on his left shoulder.

"We'll get through this—I know we will," she said firmly.

Denzel shook his head. "I never imagined I'd be dealing with the undead... and now a demon too. I never thought I'd say this in my lifetime."

Julia smiled wryly. "Neither did I. Looks like we're in the same boat."

"I've worked with you for years, Agent Julia, but I never expected to face a case like this—unusual, dangerous... and involving both a demon and the undead."

"It's strange, yes. But we signed up for this job because we care about the safety of others," she replied.

Agent Denzel smiled. Julia returned the smile.

"Let's stay positive and collect as many weapons as we can, ensuring we're all equipped and protected," Julia said.

"Absolutely! Let's do what we have to do and get back to the saloon bar before nine o'clock," Agent Denzel agreed.

"That's the spirit, Agent Denzel! We have each other's backs and will continue to protect everyone," Julia said firmly.

Denzel started the engine and drove off, knowing there was no time to waste.

Meanwhile, back in the saloon bar, Ebenezer held a Magnum and noticed it was unloaded. "Detective Marshall, can I ask you a question?"

"Of course, Ebenezer," Detective Marshall replied.

"I've never used one of these guns before. Could you tell me which bullets I should use?" Ebenezer asked nervously.

Detective Marshall glanced at the floor, where boxes of ammunition were scattered everywhere.

"I can help with that," he said. "What you're holding is a Mexican Magnum—a very powerful handgun. We need to find the appropriate Magnum bullets for it." A few seconds later, he located a box. "Here you go, Ebenezer. Take as many as you need. And remember one thing... this gun is perfect for aiming at the undead's head."

Ebenezer carefully collected the bullets. "I'll keep that in mind, Detective," he replied.

Meanwhile, Christian and Jessica worked together, making sure all the windows were securely covered.

"Here we go, my love. The kitchen window is now blocked. The undead won't get in… unless they bring a chainsaw," Christian joked lightly.

Jessica clutched his hand. "You'll protect me, won't you?"

"Of course," Christian reassured her. "Stay by my side at all costs, and we'll be fine. Here—take this handgun and the ammunition. You've got over a hundred bullets. I suggest you reload six at a time, as the gun only holds six rounds."

Jessica buried her face on his shoulder, tears spilling. "I'm so scared! What if they break into the saloon bar?"

Christian rubbed her hand gently. "Don't worry. We made sure every window and door is reinforced. We even left small gaps so we can shoot the undead as they approach."

Ryan interrupted, raising his voice. "Jessica, we'll be fine. Everyone, I think we should also use the roof. Shooting from above will give us a better angle once the undead numbers thin out."

Grant scratched his head. "But what if Sparda attacks us?"

Ron didn't answer Grant directly. Instead, he said, "According to *The Book of Secrets*, the demon only attacks once the undead have been defeated. That's when we'll see a reaction."

Ebenezer paced nervously, thinking about what could have happened if Lucy still wore the amulet. "Ron, what if Lucy had the amulet instead of Jonathan?"

"Good question," Ron said. "If Lucy still had the amulet, the demon wouldn't be able to raise the dead. Sparda would only target the amulet at night, since he can only see Lucy within a five-kilometre radius during darkness—not during the day."

Jonathan looked down, feeling guilty. "Maybe I should leave. The demon could control me and use me against all of you."

Marilyn cried hysterically at his words. Jessica tried to comfort her. "Don't worry. Jonathan will face the consequences for what he did to Lucy, but we need him here because of the amulet."

Ron reassured him. "Even if Sparda controls you, Jonathan, you won't faze us. You're handcuffed and unarmed."

Ron flipped through the book, finding more information about the amulet. "Everyone! There's a passage about a bad soul and an amulet. It says: 'Those who kill the undead will unlock the amulet and restore life.'"

Ebenezer's eyes widened. "So, to remove the amulet from Jonathan, we must kill every undead?"

"Exactly," Ron confirmed. "Sparda will lose some of his power. The book also says the previous human who wore the amulet must wear it again to restore the souls of the undead, freeing them."

Suddenly, all eyes turned to Lucy.

"What are you all looking at me for?" she asked.

Helen kissed her on the forehead. "Lucy, my sweetheart, it looks like you'll have to wear the amulet. You have a clean and beautiful soul."

Lucy felt a mix of apprehension and duty. "Okay, that's fine. But we must make sure the undead are killed once they rise."

"That's right, my sweet girl," Helen replied softly.

Christian turned to Ron with a question. "So, what will happen to Jonathan once we kill the undead? What does the book say?"

Ron carefully flipped through *The Book of Secrets*. "Let me see... Hmmm, interesting. Here it is: 'Once the bad soul wearing the amulet sees the undead all killed, the amulet will burn the bad soul, leaving only ashes.'"

"Oh dear," Christian muttered. "That means Jonathan will turn to ashes after we kill the undead."

Jonathan's face paled. Fear overtook him, and he began to cry like a child. "Oh, my goodness! What have I done?"

Detective Marshall's expression hardened. "Jonathan, if you hadn't acted so foolishly, you might have survived. But you chose to abduct Lucy, thinking you were a hero. That was a terrible idea. I have no sympathy for you."

Jonathan sobbed, voice trembling. "I... I'm sorry, everyone. I have no choice but to sacrifice myself for you all."

Grant softened slightly, placing a hand on Jonathan's shoulder. "Young man, you made a reckless choice, but we must do the right thing: kill the undead and restore their souls. That way, Sparda cannot claim them."

Marilyn, overcome with emotion, slipped away to the restrooms and locked the door. Jessica approached, pleading gently.

"Marilyn, are you okay? Could you open the door?"

"Leave me alone!" Marilyn snapped. "I don't want to talk to anyone!"

Grant pulled Jessica close. "Give her some space. She's in shock over Jonathan. She'll come around."

Jessica nodded, appreciating Grant's support. Christian added softly, "Thank you, Grant. Jessica, what's done is done. Marilyn trusted Jonathan and feels heartbroken. She'll come out eventually—we all have work to do."

Jessica kissed Christian on the lips. "You're right, my handsome man."

Christian half-smiled, feeling sympathy for her.

Ryan cleared his throat to regain everyone's attention. "Okay, everyone. Thanks to Ron, we understand the situation. Let's inspect the saloon bar and ensure everything is secured. The back isn't fully barricaded yet; we'll wait for the FBI agents to arrive and seal it."

Ebenezer grabbed three wooden planks that had been part of a table. "I'll go to the back with Christian and watch for the FBI agents. Once they arrive, we'll secure the door immediately."

Ryan nodded, smiling. "Thank you, Ebenezer. It's now 8:15 p.m. Agent Julia and Agent Denzel should be here soon."

Ebenezer and Christian walked toward the back, scanning for the approaching agents.

Soon enough, Agent Julia and Denzel appeared. "Goodness! We have enough weapons now! Let me alert the others so someone can open the back door," she called out. Agent Denzel honked the van horn.

Ebenezer and Christian looked outside.

"Look! They've returned! Let's help them bring more weapons inside," Ebenezer said.

Christian opened the door and stepped toward the back of the van. "How was it, guys? Did you manage to clear out the store?"

Agent Julia nodded. "We cleared the gun store. That's a relief. Now let's get everything inside!"

Ebenezer stepped forward to help with the weapons and ammunition. "Alright, let's move quickly. Nine o'clock is getting closer than we think."

He grabbed five guns while Christian carried two bags of ammunition. Agent Julia and Agent Denzel took the remaining weapons and ammunition, making their way into the back of the saloon bar.

Ebenezer retrieved three sturdy planks of wood. "Okay, that's everything. I'm going to secure the back door with these planks. Once we're done, we'll be protected inside and out."

Christian took the hammer and nails, holding a plank in place. "Alright, Ebenezer, I'm going to start hammering now—watch your fingers."

"No worries," Ebenezer replied.

Together, Christian and Ebenezer worked efficiently, making sure the back door was firmly sealed, each plank driven securely into place.

36

GETTING READY TO FACE THE UNDEAD

Back in Brunswick Cottage, Janet was ready to leave. She took her keys and stepped slowly out of the cottage, sensing that something significant would happen at nine o'clock—but she had no idea the undead would rise. She drew a deep, steadying breath, aware this could be her only chance of survival. Alone, she felt vulnerable; her odds were far better if she were with her husband and the others at the saloon bar.

She glanced around the cottage one last time, ensuring she hadn't forgotten anything. With a deep sigh, she unlocked the front door. "Okay... here I go," she whispered to herself.

Closing the door behind her, she locked it and climbed onto her bicycle, pedaling into the darkening evening. The sun dipped slowly below the horizon, casting an eerie glow over the isolated ghost town. The wind whipped her hair as night fell, and a black shadow appeared behind her. Janet pedaled on, unaware that Sparda was following her.

Glancing over her shoulders, she felt momentarily reassured. Then thunder rolled across the sky, and rain began to pour. Droplets soaked her body, and she slowed, seeking shelter.

"Oh, my goodness! It's pouring! I need to find cover," she muttered.

Spotting an old cottage nearby, she dismounted. "I better go in," she murmured, approaching the door and knocking, hoping someone would answer. Silence. She tried the handle—it was unlocked. "Well, at least I'll stay dry," she said, stepping inside.

The moment she entered, her expression changed. The smell of decay hit her immediately. Corpses littered the floor. Janet screamed, pressing both hands over her mouth in shock. "Oh my God! Oh my God!"

Suddenly, Sparda's shadow emerged. "So, you have been hiding my amulet and my spear? In under an hour, I will raise the undead and destroy you and your pathetic mortals. Run to your friends all you want, but when the undead surround you, your lives will end! I will take your souls. I can smell your fear—and I will use it against you!" Sparda's laughter echoed, both dramatic and hysterical.

Janet bolted from the cottage, scrambling onto her bicycle and pedaling away as Sparda's laughter chased her. "Ha ha ha ha! You can run, but you puny mortals cannot hide!"

Breathing heavily, Janet pedaled steadily through the rain. "Oh goodness! I just saw the demon for the first time!" she exclaimed, pushing faster. "I have to warn the others."

As she rode toward Damascus, the rain ceased and the clouds began to break apart. Janet looked up at the sky, surprised by the sudden change. "I better cycle through Orchard Hill Road—that'll get me to the others faster," she decided.

Finally reaching Orchard Hill Road, she gazed over Laurel Creek. Sadness washed over her as she observed her town: abandoned cars, scattered bikes, and corpses lying across the road. "This is going to be catastrophic once the dead rise," she whispered.

Janet navigated carefully to the end of Orchard Hill Road, cycling for another five minutes until she neared the saloon bar, where Ebenezer and the others were working to barricade the building.

Meanwhile, back in Damascus, Ebenezer and Christian had finished securing the back door of the saloon bar. Together, they ensured it was firmly sealed.

"Thank goodness we blocked the back door. Hopefully, the undead won't get through," said Ebenezer.

"I'm sure they won't—unless they have the strength of an ox," Christian replied, raising an eyebrow.

Ron approached the back door to check on Ebenezer. "Have you secured it fully?"

"Yes, it's all locked and reinforced," Ebenezer confirmed.

Ron's thoughts drifted to his wife. "I hope Janet will be okay on her own. I told her to secure our cottage, so she doesn't have to get involved in what we're about to do."

"Shouldn't you make sure she's safe? It seems risky to leave her alone," Ebenezer questioned.

"She'll be fine," Ron assured him. "Besides, we have that secret hideout. She'll stay quiet there, and the undead won't find her."

Christian frowned. "I don't know, Ron... I think she'd be safer with us."

"Don't worry. She'll be safe," Ron insisted.

Moments later, Janet arrived at the saloon bar, her bicycle resting at the side of the road. She knocked urgently on the door. "Can somebody open the door, please?"

Ryan heard the loud banging. "Is that Janet?"

Detective Marshall dashed toward the door. "Quick, open the windows!"

"It's too late!" Ryan shouted. "We need to tell her to climb onto the roof!"

"Where's the ladder?" Detective Marshall demanded.

Ryan gestured helplessly. "I don't know, but we have to look!"

Detective Marshall grabbed Ryan by the neck. "Well, hurry up! This demon will be fully rejuvenated in under forty minutes, along with the undead!"

"Okay—can you not squeeze my neck?" Ryan gasped. "We'll find it—relax!"

Agent Julia shook her head, clearly irritated. "Detective Marshall, that was completely unnecessary."

"I'm sorry," Detective Marshall said, loosening his grip. "But there's a woman out there begging us to open the door!"

Agent Denzel didn't wait for further argument. "Standing around complaining won't bring the ladder. Let's all search the rooms!"

Jessica and Marilyn rushed upstairs to help. Grant headed to the kitchen, checking cupboards where cleaning supplies were stored. Ron, Ebenezer, and Christian walked toward the bar, puzzled by the commotion. Helen and Lucy looked toward the front door, then at Ron.

"Why is everyone searching the rooms? And why are you two just standing there? You look like you've seen a ghost," Ron asked.

From outside, Janet shouted: "Guys! Let me in!"

Recognizing her voice, Ron sprinted toward the door. "That's my wife! Open the door quickly!"

Helen explained, "Everyone's looking for a ladder so she can climb to the top of the saloon bar."

"Oh, I see!" Ron said. "Don't worry, Janet. We'll get you inside. Wait while we find a ladder, then you'll have to climb to the roof. Understand?"

"Yes, thank goodness you're okay. I'll wait—but hurry!" Janet replied.

"We'll find the ladder," Ron assured her.

Moments later, Grant opened the cleaning cupboard and found an extended metal ladder. "I found it! Quickly! Let's take it upstairs to the roof."

Christian and Ebenezer worked together to ensure the back door remained fully sealed, ready for whatever was coming next.

Agent Julia exhaled with relief. "Well done finding the ladder!"

They carefully scrambled with the heavy ladder. Grant led the way, holding it steadily as they moved toward the stairs. Glancing up, he noticed an attic door in the ceiling. A round screw with a hole marked the latch.

"We need a stick with a hook to pull this attic door open," Grant said. "We'll have to search each room—it's a team effort."

Agent Julia nodded in agreement, while Agent Denzel and Ron looked visibly panicked.

"Hurry! Hurry! We need that hook! My wife is out there!" Ron shouted.

Agent Denzel hurried into the room where Max lay slumped in his office chair—dead. Covering his nose, he grimaced. "What a horrible smell..."

Christian followed, leading him toward a hidden passage behind a painting. Inside, they found a safe, stacks of gold bricks, and bottles of whiskey.

"Check inside this secret passage," Christian instructed Agent Denzel.

Agent Denzel's eyes widened as Christian pressed the painting, revealing the hidden space.

"Wow... what's behind here?" Agent Denzel asked in awe.

"You'll see once you step inside," Christian replied. Agent Denzel shielded his eyes from the glare of the gold. "Would you look at this!"

Behind the safe, Agent Denzel spotted a stick with a hook. "Look, Christian! I found it!"

"Excellent!" Christian said, grabbing the stick. "Let's take it to the attic—quickly!"

They dashed upstairs with Ron and Grant waiting. "Here we go, guys!" Christian called.

Ron took the stick from Christian and pulled at the attic door, which finally swung open after a few moments.

"Well done, Ron!" Grant said.

"Place the ladder close to the attic window so Janet can climb up safely," Ron instructed.

Ron climbed the ladder himself, directing Grant and Denzel to help lift and position it.

"Keep pushing the ladder toward me," Denzel called. Grant and Ron held the bottom steady while Agent Denzel pulled the top into the attic.

"Well done, everyone! It's inside. I'll open the window now!" Agent Denzel shouted.

"Great! Now get my wife inside," Ron said urgently.

Agent Denzel carefully positioned the ladder at the window. "Janet, up here!" he called.

Looking up, Janet saw the ladder and breathed a sigh of relief. "Oh, Agent

Denzel, thank you!"

"Climb quickly, Janet. I'll hold the top, so it doesn't slip!"

"Okay!" she shouted, beginning her ascent.

"Don't look down. Keep your eyes on me—I'll be right behind you," Agent Denzel reassured her.

Janet stared nervously at the ladder stretching from the roof to the ground. Taking a deep breath, she started climbing, whispering, "Oh God... I'm going to try not to look down."

Ron stepped behind Agent Denzel. "Can you give me some space while I look through the window? I need to see my wife."

"Sure," Agent Denzel replied, "but can you also hold onto the ladder, so it doesn't slip?"

"Of course," Ron said, gripping the ladder tightly. He looked down, his heart pounding, as Janet slowly climbed upward. "Hey, my love, stay calm. You can do this. Just don't look down—keep your eyes on me. When you get close, I'll hold your hand."

Janet's voice trembled. "Oh, my goodness! I won't look down. Please don't let me fall!"

"Don't worry. You'll be fine—just keep going."

She continued up the ladder, nerves and fear mixing in every step.

"Denzel, hold the ladder steady while I reach my wife," Ron called.

"I've got it," Denzel said. "I'm here to help."

Janet neared the window where Ron waited.

"Grab my hand, and I'll pull you in," he said.

Her fingers found his, and he carefully lifted her into the attic. They stumbled inside, and the ladder slipped from the saloon bar, clattering loudly to the ground.

"Oh, thank goodness you're safe!" Ron exclaimed, holding Janet tightly. She gasped for air, as if she had just survived a panic attack. "You're safe now, my love," he whispered, hugging her.

Agent Denzel glanced out the window, contemplating whether the undead would attempt to climb the ladder once Sparda rose at nine. "Do you think they'd be clever enough to climb up?"

Ron shook his head. "I'm sure they won't, but let's secure the window just in case."

Janet stood, brushing herself off. The attic was dusty, stacked with crates that once held beer bottles, and a cobweb-covered cupboard sat in the corner.

"Look at this attic! You can tell it's been untouched for over seven years," Janet said.

Ron studied her. "Anyway... why did you come all the way here? I told you to stay in the cottage and hide in the secret tunnel until we could deal with the demon."

"I couldn't stay alone," Janet admitted. "Knowing the demon is about to rise—it was unbearable."

Ron wrapped his arms around her, comforting her. "I suppose you're right. You're better off with us—even if I didn't want you to face what's coming."

Janet's mind flashed back to the encounter with Sparda. "On my way here, I saw him. He warned that the undead will rise, surround the saloon bar, and kill every one of us. Then... our souls will be taken!"

Ron's eyes widened. "Is that what Sparda said? We need to warn the others immediately."

Agent Denzel turned to the attic windows. "Ron, help me move this cupboard to cover the window. Then we must secure the attic door and lock it completely."

"Right," Ron said, pushing the dusty old cupboard alongside Denzel.

"Excellent work," Ron said once the window was secured. "Now let's leave and warn the others about what Janet told us."

Meanwhile, Ebenezer, Christian, and Agent Julia looked up at the attic door.

"Hey, are you all okay up there?" Ebenezer called.

Agent Denzel peered down. "Ebenezer, can you step back while I jump?"

"Sure thing!" Ebenezer replied.

Agent Denzel leapt down, landing safely on the floor. "Okay, Ron and Janet, you can jump one at a time. I'll catch you."

Ron looked down, his heart racing, and jumped. Denzel extended his arms, steadying him as he landed.

"Got you!" Agent Denzel said. "Now, Ron, let's make sure your wife can jump safely." Both Ron and Denzel held out their arms. Janet took a deep breath and jumped from the attic. They caught her without incident.

"Thank goodness you both caught me!" Janet said, catching her breath.

"You're welcome," Agent Denzel replied. "Now we need to secure the attic door. Let's close it and find something to cover it—just in case the undead try to get out."

Ryan ascended the stairs with Helen, who looked relieved. "Oh, thank God you're all right," Helen said.

Janet forced a nervous smile. "Me too. But we must be prepared. I came face to face with Sparda while cycling here. He said, 'The undead will rise and surround us, and our souls will be taken.'"

Ryan's eyes widened. "Oh my God... so that means Max could rise too, and he's inside the saloon bar."

"Let's handcuff Max to the chair so he won't be able to move his hands," Agent Julia said.

Ebenezer glanced around. "So... what are we waiting for? Let's do it now!"

Agent Julia ran to Max and swiftly handcuffed him. "Done!" she announced.

"So, what's next?" Ebenezer asked.

Agent Denzel scanned the bar. "As I told Ron and Janet, we must ensure the attic is fully covered. We need to find another cupboard and place it near the attic door."

Ryan turned to Detective Marshall and Ebenezer. "We need to look around quickly and find a cupboard to block the attic. That should stop the undead from coming out. If they're clever enough to use a ladder and break through the window... we won't take any chances. Let's think ahead and stay safe."

37

THE AWAKENING

It was almost nine o'clock in Damascus. The sky was dark, and thick clouds pressed across the horizon. The moon cast an eerie glow over the town. Detective Marshall peered through the planks covering the window. Lucy clutched her mother's hand tightly, while Ryan loaded bullets into his Magnum and carefully attached the silencer.

Agent Julia and Agent Denzel exchanged a glance, their eyes fixed on Jonathan, knowing he would be the key to controlling Sparda's power. Ebenezer and Christian hugged each other, while Jessica and Marilyn trembled with fear—but also steeled themselves for what was coming. Upstairs, Grant, Ron, and Janet readied their machine guns, preparing to fire from above.

Ebenezer drew a deep breath, the weight of the moment pressing on him. "Ladies and gentlemen, can I have your attention, please? We are here for one reason—to save mankind and destroy Sparda. If we fail, at least we tried. If we succeed, we will be remembered as heroes. Are we ready?"

All eyes in the saloon turned to him. Nods and murmurs of agreement followed.

"Can you hear me up there, Grant, Ron, Janet?" Ebenezer called.

Ron shouted back, "Yes! We hear you, and we're ready!"

"Good! In about four minutes, the demon sorcerer Sparda will rise—and he won't come alone. The undead will rise with him. Our mission is to eliminate every single one of them. Can I get a Hallelujah?"

"Hallelujah!" the group shouted in unison.

"Excellent. Make sure your weapons are fully loaded and ready," Ebenezer instructed. Everyone checked their guns, aiming through the gaps in the boarded windows.

Grant grabbed a bottle of whiskey and drained it in one gulp. Ron rolled his eyes but then followed suit.

"Let's save humanity," Ron said with determination.

Grant smiled, while Janet carefully opened a window, aiming her gun downward. "I never thought I'd say this, but here I am, holding a gun to kill the undead."

Ron looked at her and sighed. "I know, my love. But we have to stay strong and do what must be done."

Ebenezer glanced at Christian and Detective Marshall, his voice softening. "You two... these past two days have been surreal. I'm proud to have you by my side, and I can't thank you enough."

Detective Marshall shook his head. "Ebenezer, no time for emotions. We will win this. But I will feel justice has prevailed when Sparda is defeated."

Christian nodded. "Same here. I never imagined holding a gun, but here I am—doing it for the right reasons."

Ryan interrupted, his voice tense. "Gentlemen... I can feel a tremor. Do you feel it too?"

Everyone exchanged worried glances, then aimed their guns through the window boards, ready for what was coming.

The ground shook violently. Slowly, the residents of Damascus began to rise, their eyes snapping open—the undead had awakened.

"Oh my God! It's happening!" Ebenezer shouted.

Moments later, Jonathan's body began to turn a chilling shade of blue.

"I'm going to die! I'm going to die!" Marilyn cried, tears streaming down her face as she raised her gun toward him. Jonathan pleaded, trembling. "Please... don't shoot me!"

Marilyn's tears dripped down her chin as she raised the gun. After steadying her hands, she pulled the trigger. The bullet struck Jonathan squarely in the forehead. A deafening bang echoed through the saloon bar. Jonathan's body crumpled, blood spilling as his head fell forward.

Marilyn sobbed. Jessica quickly moved to her side, offering support. "Don't cry, Marilyn—you did the right thing. He was going to turn anyway."

Marilyn shook her head, grief-stricken. "I thought... we had something, but I guess we didn't."

Jessica hugged her gently. "Focus, Marilyn. We need every hand on deck. Look at them—they're rising in numbers."

A yellow beam of light cut through the saloon. Sparda had arrived. Everyone turned, eyes wide.

"Look! It's Sparda!" Ryan shouted.

Sparda's body shimmered, partially rejuvenated, though the spear and amulet were missing. His voice cut through the chaos. "You pathetic humans are surrounded by thousands of the undead. Soon, I will command them to break into this wretched shelter and claim what is mine!" His laughter rang like metal on stone, maniacal and chilling.

Ryan barked orders. "Everyone! Shoot to kill! NOW!"

Ebenezer and Christian aimed carefully for the undead's foreheads. Detective Marshall and Ryan fired their rifles, while Jessica and Marilyn followed suit. Agent Julia and Agent Denzel exchanged a brief nod, then opened fire with shotguns. A shell connected with one undead, decapitating it instantly.

"Hold steady! Keep shooting!" Ebenezer shouted.

Sparda observed a smirk of confidence on his face. From above, Ron fired down on the undead, some dropping lifelessly as bullets found their marks.

Suddenly, Janet heard a commotion from Max's office—screams, the words *"Sparda, my lord."*

"I'm going after Max; I think I can hear him," Janet called to Ron and Grant.

"Be careful! Shoot him in the head," Ron warned.

Janet sprinted toward Max's room and froze. The chair where he had been handcuffed was empty. "Oh no you don't!" she yelled, firing three precise shots into Max's forehead. He collapsed, dead as a doornail.

A faint blue light escaped his body, then faded to grey. Janet scratched her head in confusion.

Sparda's eyes narrowed as he watched his undead army fall in increasing numbers. He roared, "I will show you true power!" The fallen undead bodies glowed blue as their souls escaped, then turned grey.

"Did you see that?" Grant exclaimed.

Ron nodded. "The souls are leaving the undead. Keep firing, Grant!"

Grant continued shooting, picking off one undead after another.

"There are too many of them! Will we have enough ammunition?" Grant shouted.

"We will!" Ron reassured him. "Start throwing grenades but aim far!"

Grant grabbed six grenades, carefully releasing the safety lever on one, then hurled it deep into the mass of undead. Moments later, a massive explosion shook the ground. At least thirty undead were obliterated. Sparda's confident smirk faltered.

"We're winning! Keep it up!" Ryan yelled.

Detective Marshall noticed a terrifying development: one undead had picked up the ladder Janet had used to climb to the attic. "Guys! They can grab objects just like us!"

Christian aimed his pulse rifle at the undead holding the ladder. "Not on my watch!" He fired a precise shot, sending the undead crashing to the ground.

"Have some of that!" Christian shouted, a grim smile on his face. The helpless undead, dressed in a police uniform, collapsed, dead on the floor.

Detective Marshall's face fell. "That looked like a Damascus police officer... may he rest in peace." Blue light drifted from the fallen body, ghostly and faint.

Sparda screamed, his voice echoing through the dark night. "I will destroy you all! Rise! Rise!"

Jessica's eyes darted toward the shadowed ceiling. "Oh no... this doesn't look good!" A swarm of bats descended toward the saloon, flying straight for the chimney and into the bar. Jessica and Marilyn screamed as the creatures swarmed.

Ryan hesitated, grabbing the flamethrower from the table. Marilyn panicked, thrashing wildly as the bats tore at her skin.

"Hurry, Ryan! Burn the bats!" Helen shouted. Lucy screamed and dove behind the bar, terror etched on her face.

Ryan aimed the flamethrower at the swarm—but in the chaos, flames engulfed Marilyn along with the bats. She screamed as fire consumed her. Jessica lunged forward, pushing Ryan to the floor in panic, then ran to the kitchen and grabbed a fire extinguisher.

"Oh my God, no... Marilyn! No!" she cried, dousing the flames. Marilyn collapsed, unconscious, her body severely burned, almost eighty percent scorched. Jessica held her, tears streaming.

Lucy's voice trembled. "Oh Marilyn... Please don't die!"

Marilyn looked at Jessica weakly. "Jessica... my dear friend... look after everyone... promise me... you will destroy this evil demon."

Jessica shook her head, sobbing. "I promise, we will kill this demon. Please... don't leave me like this!"

Marilyn's voice faded as her heart slowed. Her pulse disappeared from her neck and wrists. Jessica's sobs intensified and Marilyn was gone. Lucy stepped forward and embraced her.

"I'm so sorry for your loss," Lucy whispered.

Jessica's hands trembled as she turned to Helen. "Give me a gun. I'll take Sparda down."

Helen tossed her a rifle. Jessica caught it, aiming through the window at Sparda. Bullets fired, but the demon merely laughed, unphased.

"You fool! Your weapons won't harm me, pathetic mortals! Your friend is dead, and her soul is mine!" Sparda cackled as he absorbed Marilyn's spirit.

"No!" Jessica screamed, rage and grief mixing.

Sparda's laughter continued, sinister and unrelenting. "Soon, I will consume all your souls, once my army of the undead annihilates you all."

Ebenezer and Christian continued firing at the undead, but it was clear the battle could last forever. Over ten thousand undead surrounded the saloon bar.

Ryan clenched his fists, uneasy. "There must be another way…"

Agent Julia, exhausted, signaled Agent Denzel to continue shooting.

"We're fighting a losing battle! There are too many of them!" Denzel shouted.

Detective Marshall fired five shots in quick succession, eyes scanning the encroaching horde. "We need a bright idea—fast! Sparda's winning, and he won't stop while the amulet, spear, and books are with us!"

Jessica moved toward Jonathan, who lay unresponsive, and carefully removed the amulet from his neck. "I'm taking this amulet with us," she said, determined in her eyes.

Ron's voice cut through the chaos. "Everyone, head to the basement! Take as many weapons and as much ammunition as you can. I'll carry the books, potions, and the spear myself."

Everyone nodded and moved quickly toward the cellar. The gunfire had ceased, and Sparda's attention sharpened. The undead pressed closer, encircling the saloon bar, relentless and hungry.

"You're losing, just as I predicted! Now hand over what belongs to me!" Sparda snarled, a sinister laugh echoing through the night.

Ebenezer opened the cellar door, motioning for the others to follow. "Inside! I'll make sure the door is sealed behind us if any of the undead get in."

Christian bolted down the steps first, panic etched on his face, followed by Jessica, Grant, Detective Marshall, and Agent Julia. Soon after, Agent Denzel, Ryan, Helen, Lucy, and Janet joined them, moving swiftly toward the basement. Ron carefully carried the books, potions, and spear behind them.

Meanwhile, a few hundred yards away, Jacob finally spotted Sparda from a distance, along with the undead swarming every corner of the town. He sprinted to an abandoned house nearby, climbing a metal staircase to the roof. A sturdy metal door blocked the way. Jacob yanked it open, then slammed it shut behind him to prevent the undead from following.

"Oh my God! I need to hide... I can't believe what I'm seeing. This... this is why Damascus has been abandoned for seven years!" Jacob whispered, heart racing.

He crouched low on the roof, keeping out of Sparda's line of sight. A door leading into the house caught his attention. He opened it cautiously, stepping inside and feeling a slight sense of relief.

"I need to find a safe hiding place... fast," he muttered to himself. Moments later, he spotted a cellar door. Without hesitation, he ran to it, threw it open, and descended quickly into the basement. He slammed the door behind him, trembling with terror.

38

Is there any hope?

The clock read nineteen past nine in the evening in Damascus. The town was overrun with the undead, and Sparda's laughter echoed through the streets as Ebenezer and the others huddled in the cellar. Lucy knelt on the cold floor, hands clasped in prayer.

"Oh, please... let there be a miracle. Please, let this all end," she whispered.

Ryan and Helen held their daughter tightly, faces drawn with worry. Christian and Jessica clung to each other, seeking comfort in the moment. Detective Marshall surveyed the group, his expression heavy with defeat.

"Looks like it's the end of the road for all of us," he muttered. "But I must say, you're a brave bunch."

Ryan stepped forward. "Detective Marshall, don't give up! I know we're outnumbered, but if we work together, we can survive this."

Detective Marshall's eyes flashed with anger as he closed the distance between them. "I'm sick and tired of you thinking there's another way! Look around! We're hiding in a cellar with those things out there! Thousands of them, and only a handful of us! Can't you see it? We've lost!"

Agent Julia turned to Ron. "What does the book say about being trapped? Is there any solution?"

Agent Denzel echoed, "Yeah, does it offer anything?"

Ron's gaze fell to the floor, disappointment etched across his face. "The book doesn't mention our current situation. All we can do is pray and hope for a miracle."

The group lowered their heads, resignation weighing heavy. Outside, Sparda's voice reverberated through the cellar walls.

"You mortals are finished! Once the undead breach your fragile little shelter, I will claim your souls, twist your fear against you, and take what is mine! Hand over the spear, the amulet, and my books!"

Ebenezer squared his shoulders, refusing to bow. "Hang in there, everyone. Remember, we have our weapons. Even if the undead come in, they won't find us easily."

Grant frowned. "How do you know? They're dead—they must smell our flesh, right?"

Christian's eyes hardened. "If they find us, we'll give it everything we've got."

Jessica trembled, clutching Christian's shoulder. "You said you'd protect me! Looks like you were wrong!"

Christian tightened his hold. "I kept my promise. I'll see it through, no matter what."

Ryan and Helen hugged Lucy even closer, knowing this might be their last embrace as a family. Ron and Janet clung to each other, exchanging a brief kiss on the cheek.

A sudden roar pierced the night—a heavy truck barreled into Damascus, crushing undead beneath its wheels. Gary Swanson was at the wheel, driving with reckless speed.

"Woohoo! Look at that! They're dropping like bowling pins!" Gary shouted to himself, exhilarated.

Sparda's eyes narrowed, rage flashing across its face. "Another mortal thinks he can save his friends. I'll show this puny mortal the true power of Sparda!"

With a wave of its hand, the ground trembled violently, shaking Damascus as though an earthquake had struck the town.

Gary gripped the steering wheel, eyes fixed on Sparda. He floored the accelerator, aiming the truck straight at the demon.

"Tonight isn't your lucky night! I'm going to run you over!" he shouted.

The earth trembled violently beneath them, and the undead turned their attention toward Gary. Slowly, they began to drift away from the saloon bar. Sparda roared, commanding its army.

"Annihilate this human once and for all!"

Undeterred, Gary drove at full speed, navigating the shaking ground and treacherous conditions. His plan worked: the truck struck the undead one by one, squashing them beneath its wheels. Blood splattered across the hood as Gary pushed forward, exhilarated.

"Well, well, well... looks like your army is losing, you demon freak!" he yelled.

Sparda's eyes narrowed, fury replacing its earlier confidence as its army fell before him.

Back in the cellar, Ebenezer sensed a shift. He sprinted to the door and unlocked it.

"Look, everyone! The undead aren't surrounding the saloon bar anymore! And if I'm right... I think I hear a truck honking!"

Agent Julia and Agent Denzel grabbed their guns and ran to the window. Their eyes widened as they witnessed the heavy truck plowing through the undead.

"Oh my! Who's doing that?" Julia gasped.

Agent Denzel didn't hesitate. "I don't care who it is... it's working!"

Detective Marshall turned to Ebenezer and Christian, determination blazing in his eyes. "Gentlemen, we've come this far. It's time we go out there, take down the undead army, and finish Sparda once and for all!"

Ebenezer nodded. "Agreed. But first, we reload, grab three different weapons each, and take some grenades—we need to wipe out as many as possible."

Ryan glanced at Helen and Lucy. "My precious family, stay here where it's safe. I'll handle the undead outside."

Tears welled in their eyes. "Look after yourself... and finish the job. We trust you," Helen whispered.

Grant joined the group, loading his shotgun. "You two have been with me every step. We will finish this together."

Agent Julia stepped forward, voice firm yet emotional. "Grant's right. This is for our team—Agent Conrad, Agent Mark, Agent Jonny, and Agent Miguel. We fight for them too!"

Denzel wiped a tear. "Let's do this, Agent Julia."

Ron and Janet stayed behind with Jessica, Helen, and Lucy. "We'll hold the fort here," Ron said firmly.

Ebenezer gathered the team. "Everyone let's move! Ron, once we defeat the undead, we'll need you to read from the book so we can end Sparda. Will you help?"

"Of course! I have *The Book of the Dead*. And don't forget the spear. When I say 'djed, djed, djed' three times, throw it into the demon's heart."

Ebenezer adjusted the plan. "Ryan, give me your walkie-talkie. Helen, hand yours to Ron. When he signals, I'll throw the spear into Sparda's heart."

Ryan and Helen obeyed, handing over the devices.

"Okay, everyone! Let's do this!" Ebenezer shouted.

Six brave men and one resolute woman charged from the saloon bar, fighting for survival—and for the future of their world.

39

THE LAST BATTLE

Darkness enveloped Damascus. Only the headlights of Gary's truck cut through the night. The earth trembled violently as Sparda unleashed its power, trying to stop him from annihilating the massive army of undead.

Lucy clutched the amulet tightly but couldn't bring herself to put it around her neck. A bright yellow light radiated from it, illuminating the cellar in a surreal glow.

"Mum, look! The amulet is shining! What does that mean?" Lucy asked.

Helen shook her head, anxiety in her voice. "I don't know, my dear. Any ideas, Ron? What does the book say?"

Ron flipped through *The Book of Secrets*, struggling to maintain focus as the saloon bar trembled beneath them.

"I... I can't fully concentrate with the Earth shaking like this, but I'll try to figure it out," he muttered.

Outside, Sparda's attention was entirely on the saloon bar, intent on reclaiming the amulet and restoring its full power. Agent Denzel and Agent Julia aimed at clusters of the undead, but the sheer numbers were overwhelming.

"There are too many of them, Agent Julia!" Agent Denzel shouted.

Julia's eyes narrowed. "I know, but we can't give up! Aim for their heads!"

Agent Denzel felt a spark of hope. "Agreed!"

Together, they downed at least twenty of the undead but still faced an uphill battle. Grant quickly stepped in, yelling for them to take cover.

"Duck!" he shouted, hurling a grenade into the mass of undead.

The explosion sent dozens to the ground. Both agents Julia and Denzel dove for cover, covering their ears. Julia's face broke into a relieved smile.

"Well done, Grant! Thanks!"

"No problem! Let's keep it up!" he replied, reloading.

The trio resumed shooting, systematically reducing the horde. Yet Sparda remained unimpressed.

"You mortals think you are winning? I will show you my true power!" Sparda bellowed. Its voice shifted into a strange dialect as a beam of blue light tore through the sky.

From the light appeared a massive, Minotaur-like creature. It wielded a colossal axe, its two horns towering above each ear. Silver-plated armor gleamed across its body, green eyes glowed, a gold ring pierced its nose, and a blue aura radiated outward. Its hands ended in sharp claws, and talon-like nails protruded from its feet.

"Humans! Meet my creation!" Sparda laughed hysterically, mocking the FBI agents and Grant.

Ebenezer, Christian, and Detective Marshall rushed toward Grant and the agents. Meanwhile, Ryan darted into a nearby abandoned house alone, outnumbered by at least fifty undead men and women.

Ebenezer's gaze searched frantically. "Where's Ryan?"

"He must be somewhere... fighting," Detective Marshall replied.

The Minotaur-like creature's gaze fixed on Ebenezer and the others, radiating fury. Gary, still in his truck, assessed the beast.

"Oh, I better do something! I've got it! I'm going to run this creature down!" he shouted to himself, determination blazing. Foot pressing down hard on the accelerator, he roared, "I'm coming to save you guys!"

The truck sped through Damascus at over sixty kilometers per hour, crushing a vast number of undead beneath its wheels. Blood splattered across the windshield as Gary pressed on, eyes fixed on the Minotaur-like creature looming ahead.

"You're dead now, freak!" he shouted, adrenaline and determination overriding any fear.

Inside the saloon, Ebenezer and the others watched in alarm.

"No, don't drive towards the creature!" Ebenezer yelled.

But it was too late. The Minotaur-like creature unleashed its power, lifting the truck into the air as though it were magnetically drawn toward it. Gary's expression shifted from determination to concern as the vehicle hovered ten meters above the ground.

Sparda's laughter echoed through the town.

"Now watch my creation destroy this puny mortal—and soon, I will claim his soul!"

Ebenezer, Christian, and Detective Marshall reloaded their weapons, aiming at the towering creature. Bullets struck its armor, but it remained unfazed.

"You think your pathetic Earth weapons can defeat my creation? Think again!" Sparda bellowed.

With a surge of supernatural force, the Minotaur crushed the truck. A massive explosion rocked the street as the vehicle smashed to the ground. Gary was gone.

Shock rippled through Ebenezer and Christian, while Detective Marshall and Grant continued firing at the advancing undead. Agent Julia and Agent Denzel did the same, keeping as many down as possible.

Suddenly, an idea struck Ebenezer.

"Christian! I think the potions might be able to destroy that creature!"

"They're in the saloon bar," Christian confirmed.

"In that case, we need to get them. But we're heavily outnumbered—Sparda, the undead, and now that monstrous creation... survival doesn't look promising."

Detective Marshall noticed Christian moving away. "Where is he going?"

"I have a plan," Ebenezer said. "First, we need to find a hiding spot. Then I'll explain Christian's next move."

Agent Julia, Denzel, and Grant followed his advice, hoping to find temporary safety. Detective Marshall scanned the area and spotted a dilapidated pharmacy with a ladder leading to the roof.

"Quickly! That ladder is our best choice. Climb up, keep firing from the roof, and wait for Christian," he shouted.

"Brilliant idea!" Agent Julia exclaimed. In unison, they sprinted toward the pharmacy and began the climb.

Meanwhile, Ryan hid inside a nearby house, grateful for his temporary safety. He crept upstairs into a bedroom, wrinkling his nose at a foul stench.

"What is that smell?" he muttered to himself.

Peering through the window, he saw the chaos below: the undead, Sparda, and the Minotaur-like creature.

"This doesn't look good... but I can't shoot, or they'll find me," he whispered.

Outside the saloon bar, Christian reached the barricaded doors and banged urgently.

"Jessica! Someone! Grab the potions—hurry!"

Jessica, Helen, and Lucy heard his calls.

"It's Christian! Hurry! Let's see what he needs!" Lucy exclaimed, moving quickly toward the front.

Jessica sprinted to the front window and saw Christian standing outside.

"Christian, did you forget something?" she shouted.

"Jessica, my love, can you pass me the potions, please?" he called back.

Ron overheard and rushed to the table where he had placed *The Book of Secrets* and *The Book of the Dead*. The six potions sat there. He quickly grabbed them and handed them to Jessica.

"Here you go. Pass them to Christian. They'll come in handy," Ron said.

Jessica removed the barricades from the door and handed the potions to Christian. Through the window, she glimpsed Sparda in the distance.

"Here, my love. Please be safe... come back to me and the others," she cried.

Christian gently wiped away her tears, holding her hand tightly. "I love you, Jessica."

"I love you too! Now go, my love. Kill this vile demon and that creature," she urged.

Christian nodded and ran as the undead army surged toward the saloon.

"I must go, my love! Keep shooting, all of you!" he called.

Jessica loaded her gun alongside Helen and Ron. Ebenezer spotted Christian sprinting toward the pharmacy building and climbing the ladder. Agent Julia fired from the roof above.

"Die, die!" she shouted.

"Hurry, Christian!" Ebenezer yelled.

The undead noticed Christian climbing and moved swiftly toward him.

Finally, he reached the top. "Oh, that was close! I've got the potions."

"Well done, Christian. Now these potions will be put to good use," Ebenezer said. "I'll need to grab the creature's attention before you throw them."

Grant quickly formulated a plan. "I've got it! I'll whistle to lure it toward us."

Agent Julia hesitated. "Are you sure this is a good idea?"

"Trust me! Christian, when it comes near, throw the potions and hope for the best," Grant instructed.

Agent Denzel nodded. "We have to try. I'm with you."

Grant whistled loudly, and the Minotaur creature lumbered toward them. Sparda's voice rang out, commanding the monster.

"Destroy them all! Once they're gone, I'll take their souls, retrieve my spear, and reclaim my amulet!"

The Minotaur screamed, its massive hands raised toward the dark sky. Ebenezer and the others watched, uneasy.

"This doesn't look good," Ebenezer muttered.

Christian held the potions tightly. "Let's see if Max's creation does anything..."

Detective Marshall yelled, "What are you waiting for? Throw it at the creature!"

Christian picked up the blue potion and hurled it toward the Minotaur. A glass-shattering sound rang out as it hit the creature. Sparda's eyes widened in anticipation, expecting disaster—but the reaction was unexpected.

The Minotaur grew even larger.

"Oh no! It's made the creature even bigger! What do we do now?" Ebenezer exclaimed.

"Run! That's what we should do!" Detective Marshall shouted.

The three men sprinted away from the monstrous creature, followed closely by the FBI agents.

"Let's run for it, Agent Denzel!" Agent Julia called.

"I'm right behind you!" he responded, and together they fled.

Sparda laughed hysterically.

"You fool! You think you can run from my creation? I think not! Now, kill them all!"

The Minotaur let out a deafening roar and charged toward the five of them. Detective Marshall and Grant ran toward an abandoned house, while Ebenezer and Christian sprinted toward the church. Detective Marshall looked confused.

"What are you guys doing?" he shouted.

"I think it's better to split up," Ebenezer replied. "That way, we can distract this hideous creature."

Christian threw open the church doors and dashed inside. Their first visit to the church had been unsettling—but this time, it was far worse. The dead inside was fully animated as the undead.

"Oh great! Now we have to shoot them all!" Ebenezer exclaimed.

Christian and Ebenezer fired at the undead inside the church, trying to hold them back. Meanwhile, Detective Marshall hid in the old house.

Outside, the Minotaur's reaction to the blue potion intensified—it grew even larger. A deep, echoing roar reverberated through the town.

"Oh my God! This thing is about to burst my eardrums!" Agent Julia yelled.

Both FBI agents covered their ears as they ran for their lives. Suddenly, the Minotaur inhaled deeply for several seconds, then exhaled a massive ball of fire aimed directly at Agent Denzel.

Agent Julia sensed danger just in time. The fiery blast hit Agent Denzel, engulfing him. He fell to the ground, screaming as flames consumed him.

"No! Agent Denzel!" Agent Julia screamed in shock.

Sparda laughed triumphantly. "Now I will take your soul!"

A beam of blue light rose from Agent Denzel's charred body, entering Sparda's glowing yellow eyes.

"Now that I have your friend's soul, I will be even more powerful!" Sparda declared.

Agent Julia, devastated, screamed, "You will pay for this, Sparda!"

"The brave human speaks! How touching! But soon, you will be dead, and I will take your soul too!" Sparda sneered. "Now, destroy her!" he commanded the Minotaur.

Meanwhile, Christian and Ebenezer ran toward the back of the church, heading to the house where Ryan was hiding. Agent Julia fired relentlessly, taking out undead around her before aiming at the Minotaur. Sparda's laughter echoed over the chaos.

"Your puny weapons are useless! Nothing can kill my creation. Say your last prayers!" he bellowed.

Agent Julia sank to her knees, exhausted and helpless. Christian saw her in distress and quickly rummaged through the bag, grabbing the black potion. He didn't know its effects—but he decided to take the chance.

"Here, creep! Take this!" Christian shouted, hurling the black potion. The glass shattered against the Minotaur's body.

The creature screamed in agony. Sparda's face contorted with concern. The black potion was working.

Suddenly, the Minotaur collapsed, melting into the ground and leaving a dark, viscous pool behind.

"No!" Sparda screamed. "This cannot be! My creation has never been defeated!"

Christian laughed. "Well, never say never!"

Furious, Sparda raised his hands and commanded the undead.

"Kill them both! Ebenezer and Christian must die!"

The army of undead surged toward Ebenezer and Christian. Without hesitation, Ebenezer grabbed Agent Julia's hand.

"Take my hand, Agent Julia!" he urged.

Wiping away her tears, Agent Julia clasped his hand tightly. Together, the three dashed toward the abandoned house where Ryan and Detective Marshall were hiding.

"Let's get to the house," Ebenezer said, "and figure out how to alert the others in the saloon. We need Ron to read from the book while we secure the spear."

Christian nodded, but his mind lingered on the Minotaur. He still couldn't believe what had just happened.

"I can't believe it... I actually killed a non-human creature for the first time!" he muttered, both shocked and exhilarated.

"I'm extremely glad you did," Ebenezer replied, "but our fight isn't over. There's still work to be done."

The three pressed on, sprinting a few more yards before slipping inside the old house. From their vantage point, they could catch their breath and begin devising a plan to finally confront Sparda.

40

IT'S MAKE OR BREAK

It was ten o'clock in Damascus. Agent Denzel had tragically fallen to the Minotaur, and Gary Swanson, despite his bravery, had become the second life lost in such a short span. Agent Julia had almost given up hope, but Ebenezer's hand offered her a lifeline, a reason to continue fighting for survival.

Ebenezer, Christian, and Agent Julia huddled inside the old, deserted house where Ryan, Grant, and Detective Marshall were also hiding. Ebenezer scanned the room, searching for a way to alert Ryan and Detective Marshall that they were safe.

"Detective Marshall! Grant! Ryan! We're inside now!" he shouted.

Ryan heard the call and sprinted toward the group as fast as he could, relief washing over him.

"Oh, thank goodness you're all alive! But... where is Agent Denzel?" Agent Julia's voice trembled as she stared at the floor, tears streaming down her face.

"He didn't make it... it's my fault!" Ebenezer said gently. "We never leave anyone behind, and now... he's gone."

Detective Marshall and Grant entered the room, noticing Agent Julia's grief.

"What happened? Why are you crying? Where is Agent Denzel?" Detective Marshall asked.

"He didn't make it," Ryan replied quietly.

Detective Marshall wrapped his arms around Agent Julia, offering comfort. "I'm so sorry for your loss."

"I... I failed him. It's all my fault," Agent Julia whispered, shaking with sorrow.

"It's not your fault," Detective Marshall assured her. "You stayed by his side. You never gave up on him."

Ebenezer stepped closer, gently wiping her tears. "You're a remarkable agent. You did everything you could. Agent Denzel would be proud of you."

Agent Julia leaned on Ebenezer's shoulder, her voice soft. "He always wanted to be better than me. That was his drive. I'm just sad he never got the chance... he loved a challenge, and this... this was his moment."

Detective Marshall smiled faintly, reflecting on the past tension between them. "I know we never saw eye to eye over the years, especially with your role as an FBI agent. But after everything we've faced... I realize we can truly work together. I want to apologize for how I treated you in the past."

Agent Julia smiled, placing a hand on his shoulder and gently kissing his cheek. "Thank you, Detective. And I apologize too, for any friction between our teams. I accept your apology."

Detective Marshall returned her smile, shaking her hand. "Thank you, Agent Julia."

Grant spoke softly, regret in his voice. "He was a great man. Always wanted to do good."

"He sure did," Agent Julia agreed.

Ryan hugged her firmly. "Don't worry. We'll fight to the end, and we'll come out on top."

Suddenly, Ebenezer's eyes widened as he peered out the window. A massive army of undead surrounded the house.

"Quickly! Block every door and window—don't let them in!" he shouted.

Christian spoke urgently, "We need to get back to the saloon bar. We have the spear, but we'll need Ron's help to read from the book. Hopefully, one of us can strike Sparda's heart with it!"

"Agreed," Ebenezer said. The group quickly began moving old furniture and cupboards to barricade every window and door of the old, creepy house, keeping the approaching undead at bay.

Outside, Sparda strode slowly toward the truck where Gary Swanson lay helpless. A beam of blue light emerged from Gary's body and entered Sparda, who looked up at the dark sky and laughed after claiming the soul.

Sparda's gaze then shifted toward the saloon bar, just five hundred yards away, where Ron, Janet, Jessica, Helen, and Lucy were hiding. Ryan peered through the window, alarmed.

"Guys! It looks like Sparda is heading for my wife and the others inside the saloon bar!"

"We need to stop him," Ebenezer said. "If he gets the amulet, he'll grow even more powerful!"

Agent Julia glanced out the window before turning to Christian. "Christian! You're coming with me. You have the potions—maybe you can use them on the undead while we get to the saloon before Sparda."

Christian hesitated, his brow furrowed. "I just hope I choose the right potion. I don't want a repeat of what happened with the Minotaur."

Agent Julia grabbed his arm, urgency in her grip. "We don't have time! Let's move!"

Ryan scanned the house, searching for a safe escape route. "Follow me!" he called, leading them to the back of the house.

They reached an old, rusty door near the kitchen. Ryan pushed it open. "Looks like a garage."

Inside, an old white Ford Pinto gleamed under the dim light. Ryan's eyes widened. "Wow! A car! Quick, let's find the keys!"

Christian searched for a light switch, but Agent Julia quickly spotted a set of keys on a nearby table. A car key dangled among them.

"No need to search any further! I found the keys!" she said, smiling. Ryan and Christian exchanged relieved looks. "What are we waiting for? Let's get in the car, Christian!"

Christian hesitated for a moment, then slid into the car as Agent Julia opened the door for him. "Here we go!" she said.

Ryan approached the garage door carefully. "I'll open it slowly—don't want the undead noticing us."

"I'll deal with them if they try to stop us," Agent Julia said, turning the ignition and revving the engine.

"Good luck! We're all counting on you to reach the saloon before Sparda!" Ryan shouted.

Agent Julia slammed the accelerator, and the car shot out of the garage. A group of undead heard the engine and rushed to block the exit, but Ryan raised his gun and fired, taking them down one by one.

Agent Julia slammed the accelerator, running over several of the undead. Christian panicked. "Kill them all, Agent Julia!"

She screamed triumphantly as the car mowed down at least seven of the creatures. "Take that!"

Christian grinned and offered her a high-five. "Nice one!" Agent Julia pressed on, hope rising—they had to reach the saloon bar before Sparda.

High above, Sparda glared down at the ground, fuming. His eyes caught sight of a car moving swiftly toward the saloon. "Those puny mortals think they can stop me. My power will show them!"

A green light suddenly appeared in their path. Christian pointed. "Agent Julia! Sparda's clearly trying to block us from reaching the saloon!"

Agent Julia thought quickly. "Christian, throw a potion at him—maybe we can slow him down!"

Christian hesitated, analyzing his options. His intuition nudged him toward the orange potion. "Okay... the orange one," he said.

"Now throw it!" Agent Julia urged.

Christian hurled the potion, but his aim was off. Sparda laughed hysterically as the vial shattered on the ground.

"You humans are truly pathetic!" he sneered.

Christian groaned, disappointed. "I missed..."

"Don't worry! Let me handle this," Agent Julia shouted, revving the engine and speeding up.

The orange smoke began swirling around the undead. "Agent Julia! Look! It's working—they're dropping like flies!" Christian exclaimed.

Agent Julia laughed with relief. "Woohoo! Well done! The potion is taking them out!"

Christian chuckled, "Guess I got lucky this time."

Sparda's anger boiled as he watched the undead fall helplessly. "You may run, but you cannot hide from me!"

The orange smoke spiraled into the sky, then struck Sparda directly. He staggered. "What... What is this? What's happening to me?" he roared, before collapsing to the ground.

Agent Julia and Christian exchanged relieved glances. "Looks like the orange potion works! Let's alert Ron and the others!" she shouted.

Christian nodded and called toward the saloon bar. "Jessica! Ron! Open the back door!"

Ron heard him instantly and turned to Helen. "Helen! Quick! Open the back door! Christian's outside!"

Helen dashed to the back door. Meanwhile, the orange smoke seeped into the car, and Agent Julia and Christian instinctively covered their mouths. The remaining undead collapsed one by one.

"Hurry, you two! Get inside!" Helen shouted as the door swung open.

Agent Julia pulled the car into the saloon yard and slammed it into park. She and Christian jumped out. Ron reached for her hand as she ran inside the bar, while Jessica rushed to Christian, hugging him tightly.

"Oh, my love! Are you okay?" she asked.

Christian nodded. "I think so. That orange potion—it's poisonous to them."

Ron gestured at the fallen undead. "It's poisonous! Look at them—they're not handling it well at all."

Helen looked puzzled. "Why are you two back here? Where are Ryan and the others?"

Christian coughed harshly, the orange smoke choking him slightly. "We came here to warn you all—Sparda is after every one of you. And it won't stop until it gets the amulet, as you can all imagine!"

Ron scratched his head, anxiety written across his face. He turned toward the book, steadying himself. He was ready to read from *The Book of the Dead*, knowing that what he was about to do could decide the fate of everyone in the saloon.

41

ONE LAST HOPE FOR SURVIVAL

It was nearly twenty minutes to eleven in the evening in Damascus. The sky was dark, with fires burning in a few houses. Gary Swanson's truck lay abandoned, his body consumed by flames. The town was littered with the undead, most of them lying still thanks to Christian's quick thinking. Sparda sprawled on the ground, weakened by the orange potion's poisonous smoke.

Inside the creepy old house, Ebenezer, Detective Marshall, Ryan, and Grant regrouped. Agent Julia and Christian had safely made it into the saloon bar. Damascus had become a bloodbath, its streets filled with dead bodies, while the undead that remained were mostly incapacitated—shot, burnt, or crushed. The orange smoke had dispersed into the night sky, revealing the devastation of the town once more.

Meanwhile, Sparda's yellow eyes snapped open. Rising from the ground, he staggered slightly, still weakened but resolute. He fixed his gaze on the saloon bar, moving deliberately, a low growl vibrating through the earth. The sound shattered windows across the town.

"I will not give up what is mine! I will claim my spear and my amulet!"

Christian and Jessica pressed themselves against the saloon's windows, watching as several of the undead began to rise again—and Sparda advanced toward the bar.

"Sparda is coming! What do we do now? Ron! Think of something!"

Ron had already begun reading from *The Book of Secrets* before quickly turning to *The Book of the Dead*. "Christian, you have the spear, Lucy has the amulet. I'm reading a passage from *The Book of Secrets*. It will ensure the demon's death. Listen carefully: 'A long pillar will enter from heaven.' Repeat it three times, then throw the spear into Sparda's heart. *The Book of the Dead* will unleash the power to draw Sparda back inside the book."

Christian squared his shoulders. "Let's do this!"

Back at the old house, Ebenezer, Detective Marshall, Grant, and Ryan prepared to move. Guns loaded, they assessed the streets. Most of the undead were still down, though a few began to stir as the poison potion's effect waned.

"Christian and the others need our help," Ebenezer said, eyes narrowing. "Especially now that Sparda is back on his feet. He's heading straight for the saloon!"

Ryan checked his firearm, confirming it was fully loaded. Detective Marshall and Grant did the same, readying themselves for the final confrontation.

Ryan's voice was firm. "The fate of the world is in our hands, and we will put an end to this nightmare."

Grant braced himself, then kicked the front door open and charged outside, guns blazing. He screamed as he shot five of the undead. "Take that, you creep!"

Ryan and Ebenezer quickly followed.

"Let's run and shoot them! That way we can get closer to Sparda," Ebenezer shouted.

As they moved, Ryan fired at the advancing undead, while Ebenezer kept pace, shooting from cover to cover.

Inside the saloon bar, Agent Julia's head snapped toward the windows at the sound of gunfire. "Everyone! I think the guys are coming!"

Helen and Janet hurried to the window. "I hope they'll be okay out there! The undead are still swarming," Janet said nervously.

Sparda turned, his glowing yellow eyes spotting Ebenezer, Detective Marshall,

Ryan, and Grant advancing, weapons raised. A low, mocking laugh rumbled from him.

"You think you can surround me? You think you can destroy me? I will not allow it."

Ron motioned for everyone to remain calm while he read from the Book of Secrets in Egyptian. "I will end Sparda's pitiful life once and for all," he murmured. Then, opening *The Book of the Dead*, he recited the incantation:

"The evil will enter the gates of hell. The pillar will rise from the heavens above. Throw the spear into the heart and say the words: Pillar, pillar, pillar."

Christian bolted out the back of the saloon, spear in hand. Ron followed closely, clutching the books.

Jessica shouted after him, "Be careful, my love!"

Christian glanced back, giving her a reassuring smile.

"Save the world, guys!" Janet called.

Outside, Christian and Ron faced Sparda. Christian urged, "Ron, read from the book again. Let's end this and send the demon back to hell!"

Sparda's gaze was sharp, menacing. "So, you two have the books and the spear? You dare to destroy me? I will not allow it, puny mortals!"

Ron turned a page, taking slow, deep breaths as he continued reading in Egyptian. Sparda's expression shifted to surprise.

Ebenezer, Detective Marshall, Grant, and Ryan were only a few feet away, weapons ready, watching every move.

Meanwhile, Lucy stealthily emerged from the back of the saloon. Helen and Janet pressed against the window, witnessing the scene unfold. Lucy stood beside Ron.

"Ron! Please, read from the book!" she shouted.

"What are you doing outside? Stay inside where you're safe!" Ron warned.

Sparda's eyes locked on Lucy and the amulet around her neck. "Give me the amulet, child," he roared.

Lucy clutched it tightly. "I don't think so."

Ron resumed reading in Egyptian. The word *Djed* echoed three times. Sparda's eyes widened in worry. The wind began to whip violently through the ghost town of Damascus.

Ebenezer braced against a lamppost as the gale intensified. Detective Marshall, Grant, and Ryan sprinted toward a nearby isolated house for cover. Sparda tilted his head skyward, a rare look of defeat on his monstrous face.

Then, three massive pillars descended from the heavens, crackling with electricity. They looked as if they were from another plane entirely. Christian, Ron, Agent Julia, and Lucy watched in awe, unable to look away.

"Would you look at that! These pillars are... extra-terrestrial!" Christian shouted.

Sparda screamed, the pillars propelling toward him, crushing and battering him mercilessly.

Sparda was slammed to the ground as the pillars clamped down on every part of his massive body.

Ron shouted to Christian, giving clear commands. "Christian! Place the spear into the demon's heart!"

Christian nodded and sprinted toward Sparda. Before driving the spear into the demon's chest, he spoke firmly: "Go back to where you came from and release all the souls you've stolen from humans and animals! Set them free!"

Sparda laughed, a cruel, echoing sound. "Death is only the beginning," he sneered.

Christian's gaze hardened. With a final shout, he drove the spear straight into Sparda's heart. "Go to hell!"

A brilliant blue beam erupted from Sparda's mangled body, streaming upward as the souls of thousands of humans and animals escaped his form. Ebenezer, Ryan, Grant, and Detective Marshall dashed from the house, gazing in awe at the blue light rising toward the sky.

Agent Julia, Janet, Helen, and Jessica rushed out the back of the saloon bar. Ron and Lucy stood frozen, witnessing the release of the captured souls.

Opening *The Book of the Dead*, Ron watched as Sparda's body transformed into a yellow beam of light. The energy lifted off the shattered corpse and floated toward Ron, entering the book. He slammed the cover shut and shouted with uncontained joy, "Yes! We finally did it!"

Everyone rushed toward Ron—except Christian, who collapsed unconscious.

"Oh no! Christian! Somebody help him!" Jessica cried, running alongside Ebenezer.

Ebenezer knelt beside Christian, supporting his head. Jessica clutched his shoulders, tears streaming. "Christian, please say something!"

Moments later, Christian's eyes fluttered open, meeting Jessica's gaze. "Jessica... my love... I feel some discomfort in my heart," he whispered weakly.

Panicked, Jessica called out to Ron. "Ron! Please, tell me he's going to be okay!"

Ron's face was grave. "Let me see what the book says after the demon was destroyed." He flipped through *The Book of Secrets*, reading aloud:

"Those who place the spear into the demon will face consequences."

"What does that mean?" Jessica cried.

"It means Christian has sacrificed himself by driving the spear into the demon's heart," Ron explained.

Ebenezer sprang into action. "Take the potions out of Christian's bag! Surely one of them can bring him back!"

"Yes, of course. Let me see!"

Ebenezer carefully retrieved the potions. One bottle had "Resurrection" inscribed on the yellow vial.

Detective Marshall and Agent Julia exchanged a relieved glance and embraced briefly. Ebenezer gently pried Christian's mouth open and administered the potion.

"Let's see if this works," he murmured.

Jessica kissed Christian softly on the cheek, fearing it might be her last. Seconds later, his eyes blinked open—the potion had worked.

Christian looked around at the gathered group, relief washing over him. "Oh... I'm alive!"

"You're back!" Ebenezer exclaimed.

Jessica laughed through tears. "For a moment, I thought I'd lost you!"

Christian smiled. "For a moment, you thought you did!"

They kissed passionately, relief and love blending in that single embrace.

Ebenezer and Agent Julia wrapped their arms around each other, while Ryan, Helen, and Lucy shared a tight family hug. Grant, Ron, and Janet did the same.

Detective Marshall turned to Christian and Ebenezer, his voice full of pride. "I need to say this: I am very proud of you both. Finally, I can put this case to rest, knowing what happened here in Damascus. Losing my fellow officers and seeing the destruction was heartbreaking—but now, I can finally move on."

Ebenezer extended his hand to Detective Marshall with a warm smile. "You're welcome, Detective. It's been a pleasure working with you."

Christian finally rose from the ground, shaking Detective Marshall's hand. "I'm just happy most of us survived—and that we finally solved this unusual case."

Ron held open the chest, addressing Ebenezer and Lucy. "Ebenezer, can you hand me the spear? And Lucy, please take the amulet off your neck and place it inside the chest."

Both complied, giving the objects to Ron. He carefully placed them in the chest and closed it securely.

Grant tilted his head. "So... what now? What do we do with the chest and the books?"

Ron's expression was serious. "Ebenezer, I want you to safeguard the chest and the books. Whatever you do, do not open them—or *The Book of the Dead.*"

Agent Julia frowned. "And what would happen if we did?"

Ron's voice dropped. "The demon could rise again and threaten the world, especially if he regained the spear and amulet, according to *The Book of Secrets.*"

Agent Julia handed the chest to Ebenezer. "It will be safe in your hands," she said.

Ebenezer smiled and, almost impulsively, kissed her on the cheek. "Well, thank you!"

Agent Julia blushed. "I wasn't expecting that—but I'll accept it."

Ryan and Helen exchanged proud glances. "I just want to thank everyone for risking their lives. I'm thrilled to say we were the ones who saved humanity!"

The group applauded, celebrating their victory. Jessica gazed at the darkened sky, where thousands of human and animal souls floated free. "Look at that! The souls are finally free," she said, smiling.

Christian grinned at her. "I'm so glad our souls are in sync."

Ebenezer rolled his eyes but smiled. "Looks like you two need some alone time."

Christian laughed. "I love you, Ebenezer! You're my best friend! Come here for a manly hug."

Ebenezer walked over and hugged him firmly.

Detective Marshall cleared his throat. "Okay, everyone, it's time to leave this town. Let's go home."

Christian turned to Jessica. "My love, come with me to Blacksburg."

"Sure, my handsome man," she replied.

Agent Julia held Ebenezer's hand. "Want to ride with me?"

"Absolutely! I'd be delighted," Ebenezer said with a grin.

Meanwhile, Ron and Janet approached, addressing Ebenezer. "Seeing as this was your first time in Damascus and your first encounter with strange occurrences, we want to entrust the books and chest to you."

Ebenezer glanced at Christian, then Detective Marshall, before nodding. "Alright, I'll take the books and chest."

Agent Julia frowned as she started the car. "Maybe it's better if you don't take them."

Ebenezer chuckled. "It's fine. Consider it a special souvenir."

Julia smiled and finally agreed. "Okay... you can take it."

Ebenezer placed the books and the chest carefully in the backseat. Ron and Janet said their goodbyes.

"It was nice meeting you both," Ron said warmly.

"Likewise," Ebenezer replied. "Stay safe now."

Ron smiled. "Now we know for sure the town of Damascus will be demon-free, with no undead left roaming."

Ebenezer nodded and waved at them as Agent Julia drove off. Despite the carnage, the Maccabees chose to remain in Damascus, determined to honor the town, even if it was scattered with the dead.

Detective Marshall turned to Grant. "Grant, would you like to come back to Blacksburg with me?"

"Sure, why not?" Grant replied.

"Great! I guess I'll see you all in the future, then," said Detective Marshall, waving goodbye to everyone.

Jessica and Christian walked hand in hand, choosing to return with the Brunswicks.

"Can we stay with you and Janet tonight before we leave in the morning?" Christian asked.

Ron nodded. "Of course, you can stay over."

Jessica hugged Ron and Janet tightly, gratitude shining in her eyes. "Thank you so much!"

Everyone then set off on their separate journeys, heading in different directions.

Meanwhile, Jacob quietly sneaked out of the basement, hoping to meet his colleagues from the *Virginia Daily*. Closing the basement door behind him, he breathed in the fresh night air. The town lay before him, filled with twisted metal, wrecked homes, and scattered corpses. He felt a pang of defeat, having missed the chance to meet his colleagues.

"This is insane! I need to take some photos as evidence," Jacob muttered to himself. He snapped at least fifty photos of Damascus, hoping to have them developed once he returned to Blacksburg. Unsure what else to do, he walked toward his car and drove off, leaving the devastated town behind.

42

A New Adventure

A month after the mysterious battle in Damascus, Virginia, Ebenezer and Agent Julia were in Blacksburg together as a couple, preparing for a new adventure. Their destination: Galway, in the Republic of Ireland.

Ebenezer moved in and out of the apartment, carrying boxes.

"Oh, I cannot wait to get all these boxes into your car, Julia!" he said.

"It's almost done, my love," Agent Julia replied with a smile.

Ebenezer returned to the empty apartment and suddenly realized he had forgotten the chest and the two books. Talking to himself, he muttered, "Hmmm, I better take the chest and the books with me to Ireland."

He went to the bedroom, opened the built-in wardrobe, and paused. Should he take it or leave it? Carefully, he picked up the chest.

"I better take it," he decided. "At least I'll never open it or the books. If I leave them here, whoever moves in could unknowingly release hell all over again."

Outside, Agent Julia waited.

"Okay, have we got everything?" she asked.

Ebenezer stepped out, carrying the chest and books in both hands. Julia frowned.

"Let me guess, my love—you want to take the chest and books to Ireland, just in case someone else opens them? Am I right?"

"You're right, sweetheart. I can't just leave them here," Ebenezer admitted.

"Fair enough," Julia said with a smile.

Moments later, the real estate agent pulled up next to Agent Julia's car. Ebenezer carefully placed the chest and books in the trunk.

He glanced over his shoulder. "Oh, hello, Mr. Eric Johnson!"

Eric Johnson, a middle-aged Scottish American, smiled. "Good morning, Mister Ebenezer O'Rourke! Are you both ready for your new lives?"

"Absolutely! We're ready!" Ebenezer said enthusiastically.

"Good to hear. Do you have the keys to the apartment?" Eric asked.

Ebenezer handed them over. "Here are the keys."

Eric placed them in his pocket. "Thank you. Do you mind if I take a quick look inside? Just a routine check to ensure there's no damage."

"Sure, go ahead," Ebenezer replied.

Agent Julia rested her face on Ebenezer's shoulder and kissed him. "I feel so happy with you, my sweet man."

"Me too, my sweet girl," Ebenezer replied, putting his arm around her as they looked at the apartment one last time.

Eric walked out, impressed. "Well, Mr. O'Rourke, the apartment is spotless. No damage at all. You're all set to go!"

"Thank you so much!" Ebenezer said.

"Good luck on your new adventure," Eric added.

"Thank you. We'll enjoy it," Agent Julia said as Eric closed the door and locked it.

"Let's start our long drive to Boston, my love. We don't want to miss the ship," Ebenezer said.

"Let's go, my love," Julia replied, climbing into the car alongside him.

A few moments later, Christian and Jessica appeared, waving. Ebenezer asked Julia to pull over.

"Look, sweetheart, it's Christian and Jessica! Stop the car, please?"

"Of course!" Julia said, pulling over to the sidewalk.

They got out, greeting Christian and Jessica warmly.

"Hey, Christian! Boy, I haven't seen you in nearly a month!" Ebenezer said.

"I know! It's been a while!" Christian replied.

Jessica looked at Ebenezer. "What have you both been up to? Where are you off to?"

"We're leaving Blacksburg to start a new adventure—we're settling in Ireland," Agent Julia explained.

Christian frowned. "Oh, Ebenezer, why didn't you tell us?"

"Sorry for not letting you both know," Ebenezer replied. "I just wanted to start a fresh life with Julia. I hope you understand."

Christian looked a little upset. "Yes, I understand—but you could have at least told us! We would have been happy for you both."

"Thanks for understanding," Ebenezer said. "Anyway, what about you two? What have you been up to over the past month?"

Jessica smiled. "Well, we have some great news... I'm pregnant!"

Agent Julia beamed and hugged her. "Congratulations to both of you!"

"Thank you, Julia," Jessica replied.

"You can call me Julia," Agent Julia said.

"Oh, okay!" Jessica smiled.

Ebenezer shook Christian's hand firmly. "Well done, Christian! Soon you'll be a dad, and I know you'll be a great one."

"Thank you, Ebenezer," Christian said.

"So, do you know if it's a boy or a girl?" Julia asked.

"We'd rather not know until the child is born," Jessica replied.

"That sounds like a wise decision," Julia said approvingly.

Ebenezer changed the subject. "So, Christian, did you tell Virginia Daily about what happened in Damascus?"

Christian shook his head. "Don't worry, I won't tell anyone."

"Good," Ebenezer said. "I decided to take the chest and books with me to Ireland. I want to make sure no one knows what happened in Damascus—so it's our little secret."

"Of course, your secret is safe with us," Christian promised.

Jessica asked, "So, what will you do in Ireland? What are your plans?"

Julia smiled. "I've decided to leave the FBI, and my partner here will start his own business in Ireland."

"What sort of business, if you don't mind me asking?" Christian inquired.

"I'm going to open a bar in Ireland, alongside Julia," Ebenezer explained.

"Wow, that's exciting! I wish you both the best of luck!" Christian said.

Ebenezer smiled and patted Christian's shoulder. "Thank you. By the way, look after yourselves, and we'll stay in touch."

"I appreciate it," Christian replied.

"Okay, we better get going now—we need to drive to Boston and catch our ship to Ireland," Ebenezer said.

Christian warned, "Sure... and please, be careful with the chest and books. Make sure the chest stays closed."

"Don't worry," Julia assured him. "We'll keep them safe when we settle into our new home."

Jessica hugged both Julia and Ebenezer. "Well, I guess this is goodbye."

"Take care, and I look forward to meeting your child once it's born!" Ebenezer said warmly.

"Definitely, Ebenezer. We'll keep you updated," Christian replied.

Ebenezer and Julia got into the car, waving their final goodbyes.

"I'm glad we bumped into them, but I feel bad for keeping this a secret," Julia said.

"I know," Ebenezer replied. "But I feel better now, especially that they didn't react negatively."

"That's true. Anyway, let's enjoy the moment and our new lives together," Julia said.

Ebenezer held Julia's hand, gazing into her eyes, proud to have someone to share his life with.

Epilogue

As Ebenezer and Julia began their new life in Ireland, Christian resigned from his job as a journalist at Virginia Daily, wary of the knowledge he carried. He planned to start his own private journalist business.

Jessica lived with Christian at their apartment, while Detective Marshall quietly took time off from police duties without revealing the Damascus events. The Maccabees had relocated to Raleigh, South Carolina, opening a hotel, seeking a better life. Grant returned to Abingdon, Virginia, laying low from the press.

The Brunswicks continued living near Creeper Trail, while Damascus slowly returned to normal, thanks to the Abingdon Police Department. The demon Sparda's deadly rampage remained unreported, known only to a few survivors. Gary Swanson and Max O'Leary, the only witnesses, had tragically passed away a month prior.

Jacob and Sheriff Alan Montgomery were the only other people aware of the true events. Whether the world would ever know the full story of Damascus remained uncertain. Only time would tell.

About the Author

William C. O'Sullivan is a writer and a creative. He is the author of the children's book, The Birds and the Bee, Billy, the Fox, The Wise Eagle and his First Novel, The Day I wandered to the Ghost Town, A Mystery in Virginia. He is passionate about empowering people by sharing positive and inspiring content. His mission is to bring more joy to the world by teaching others to follow their dreams.

www.williamosullivan.co.uk
Instagram- @williamosullivanwriter
Tik-Tok- william_osullivan1
X.com- WillPositive1